"Have I broken a law, Detective?"

He half smiled. "Tell you what. You take my truck into Painter's Bluff."

"I'm staying at the hotel."

"Which one? There's Skye Painter's Mountain House, the Hollowback Inn and Annie's Barn on the edge of town."

For a moment Sasha forgot to be cold and laughed. "Let me guess—Annie ran a bordello?"

"Rumor has it Butch and Sundance were regulars."

"Spoken like a proud local." She tipped her head. "And yet your badge says Denver PD. Are you a man of mystery, Nick Law?"

His eyes caught hers and held. Sasha shivered. She had the ridiculous feeling that he was stripping away her clothing piece by piece. It felt exciting, but unnerving at the same time.

He pulled off his glove and caught her chin between his thumb and finger. "I have my moments."

HER MOUNTAIN PROTECTOR

JENNA RYAN

&

ALANA MATTHEWS

Previously published as *Cold Case Cowboy*
and *A Wanted Man*

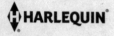 **HARLEQUIN®**

Recycling programs
for this product may
not exist in your area.

ISBN-13: 978-1-335-42479-2

Her Mountain Protector

Copyright © 2021 by Harlequin Books S.A.

Cold Case Cowboy
First published in 2007. This edition published in 2021.
Copyright © 2007 by Jacqueline Goff

A Wanted Man
First published in 2012. This edition published in 2021.
Copyright © 2012 by Alana Matthews

This edition published by arrangement with Harlequin Books S.A.

For questions and comments about the quality of this book,
please contact us at CustomerService@Harlequin.com.

Harlequin Enterprises ULC
22 Adelaide St. West, 40th Floor
Toronto, Ontario M5H 4E3, Canada
www.Harlequin.com

Printed in U.S.A.

CONTENTS

Jenna Ryan started making up stories before she could read or write. She tried out a number of different careers, including modeling, interior design and travel, but writing has always been her one true love. That and her longtime partner, Rod.

Jenna lives in a rural setting fifteen minutes from the city of Victoria, British Columbia. It's taken a lot of years, but she's finally slowed down and adopted a West Coast mindset. Stay active, stay healthy, keep it simple. Enjoy the ride, enjoy the read. But what she continues to enjoy most is writing stories she loves.

Books by Jenna Ryan

Harlequin Intrigue

Night of the Raven
Raven's Hollow
Stranger on Raven's Ridge
Raven's Cove
Dakota Marshal
Darkwood Manor
Shadow Protector
A Perfect Stranger
Kissing the Key Witness

Visit the Author Profile page
at Harlequin.com for more titles.

COLD CASE COWBOY

Jenna Ryan

For Kathy and for the mom we still miss so much.
I love you.

Prologue

He'd made a mistake, a big one. They'd catch him now for sure, lock him in a cell and throw away the key. His mother had warned him not to let his emotions get the better of him. Truthfully, she'd nagged him half to death on the subject, but he'd stopped listening to her a long time ago. Unless he counted the echo of her whiney voice that popped into his head at random moments and made him want to break things.

He'd broken something tonight. The blood on his hands was proof of that. Now, back in his hotel room, fear as dry as Colorado dust was setting in.

He opened and closed his mouth several times to loosen his jaw.

"Shut up!" he ordered, when his mother's voice threatened to intrude. "It's done, and there were no witnesses.

I'm here. I'm safe. I'll deal with the problem, talk to my idiot cousin and get out of this rat-hole town."

Unless he got caught first.

He balled his hotel room key in a bloody fist.

The woman at the front desk had been flirting with him for the past two days. He'd pitched himself as Anthony Rush, a loner from Telluride, Colorado, looking to buy a small ranch here in the northern part of the state. She'd swallowed the lie whole and popped open another button on her shirt. He'd smiled and winked at her.

She'd vouch for him. He was a nice man who only drank beer and didn't like to be disturbed after 10:00 p.m.

It would be fine.

He continued to flex his jaw as he turned on the radio. The announcer was droning on about some bigshot local landowner. He spun an Eagles' song while Anthony went into the bathroom to deal with the blood.

One thing Anthony Rush knew how to do was cover his tracks. Oh yes, Mother had taught him to be thorough in all things, large and small.

Cleanup accomplished, he switched off the lights and collapsed on his bed.

He must have slept, didn't know how with so many thoughts chattering in his mind, but it was full morning when his eyes opened and he sat up, fuzzy headed and blinking.

He groaned when he saw the blizzard outside. It was the second in two days. Then he heard the radio newscaster and froze.

The liquor store had been robbed last night. An hour later, someone had done a gas and dash at the filling station on Center Street. A 4x4 had hit a lamppost on Wilmot, and there was a big commotion brewing out near Painter's Bluff. The sheriff would be a very busy man today.

Anthony absorbed the details of the broadcast through a haze. His head swam. He pictured the blood on his hands and worked his jaw open and shut, open and shut.

Can't get caught, a voice in his head whispered. *Have to get away. No more time to wait.* Prisons were hell for people like him.

But first...

Fingers curled, teeth grinding, he bolted for the bathroom. And threw up everything in his stomach except the icy ball of fear.

Chapter 1

"Skye Painter is a hard-nosed perfectionist, Sasha. I've read about her. She'll expect you to do your best and more. Don't disappoint her, or me."

Inside her Land Rover on an icy Colorado back road, Sasha Myer set her cell phone on the dash and squinted through the windshield at the blowing snow. The prediction that Sasha's architectural skills would be a strong reflection on her mother's success as a parent became a buzz in her ears. Sasha had lost track of how many similar conversations they'd had, but it must be in the thousands by now. Barbara Leeds's life had not gone according to plan, so it was up to her children—Sasha and her half brother, Angus—to fill in the blanks.

"Skye is a direct descendant of the town's founder, George Painter," Barbara continued. "She has money, social standing and more business savvy than any of her late husbands. Do me proud and design a stunning resort for her."

Careful not to let her amusement show, Sasha asked, "What kind of social whirl do you think I'll find in Painter's Bluff?"

"Don't be smart, Alexandra. You're three days late arriving. It's not a promising start."

Sasha hated when her mother used her formal name. "I've been through this with Skye, Mother. She and I have worked out a number of details already, over the phone and through e-mail. I've explained why I'm late for the site inspection."

"You don't explain, you apologize. And you don't call her Skye."

"She told me to, and I did apologize. She's not upset."

"Of course she isn't. Why would she be?" Contrary as always, Barbara huffed out a breath. "Her son's an attorney with the Justice Department. Lucky woman. Mine's a college dropout who plays on his charm and is forever giving in to his itchy feet. Speaking of which, have you seen Angus lately?"

"Not since Christmas."

"He should be in school."

"He's twenty, Mother. And backpacking through Europe never hurt anyone."

"Stop making excuses for him."

"I'm not."

"Yes, you are. You do it all the time, for Angus and for yourself." She sighed. "You're twenty-nine, Sasha. You should be settled."

Sasha considered breaking the connection and blaming it on the weather, but that never worked. Barbara would simply call the hotel tonight and harangue her until—well, until she got tired of it, Sasha supposed. Unfortunately, her mother seemed to have an inexhaustible supply of energy for haranguing.

"You could have married that cosmetic surgeon in Philadelphia," Barbara stated. "You'd have been set for life."

"Well, one of us would have."

She imagined her mother's neck turning pink. "He only did one small lift for me."

"On the house," Sasha reminded her. "We weren't compatible, okay? You got your lift, I got out. Everyone's happy." Not entirely true, but Sasha really wanted this conversation over. "I enjoy living in Denver. I like being near Dad and Uncle Paul."

"You like being away from me."

Sorely tempted now to toss her phone out the window, Sasha made a face at it instead. "My new firm's doing well, Mother, and Denver's always felt like home to me."

"Yes, as I recall, I wasted seven years of my life there once."

"Eight, and to date it was your longest marriage."

"Also my longest and, I might add, least satisfying teaching assignment. Eight fruitless years spent trying to instruct teenagers on how to speak, read and write the English language, appreciate poetry and recognize literary genius. If nothing else, my private school students here in Boston know how to listen. It's an art you and Angus never quite mastered."

Wind swooped down to batter Sasha's SUV. "The weather's really bad here, Mother. I need to concentrate on the road."

"You need to concentrate on the job you've been hired to do."

"Does that mean you're going to hang up?"

"Sasha, Skye Painter—"

"Is an important woman, and you want me to impress her. Got it. I'll do my best." Determined to end the call, Sasha crinkled a food wrapper. "You' re breaking up. I'll talk to you later. Love to Hans."

"His name is Richard."

"I know. I liked Hans better."

A note of anger crept in. "My personal life—"

"Is none of my business. You're right. I'm sorry."

"Say that to Skye Painter, not me. And—"

"Breaking up, Mom. Bye."

Flipping her phone shut, Sasha switched off. She spent the next few seconds shuddering away the antlike prickles that invariably lingered after a conversation with her mother.

Not even by the most generous emotional gauge could her relationship with Barbara be considered good. Tolerable perhaps, regrettable definitely, but not pleasant, not warm and not remotely close to what Sasha had spent much of her life wishing for.

Didn't matter, she reminded herself. Her father, her uncle and her half brother, Angus, lived in Denver. She had partners and friends and a reputation that people in the western states were beginning to notice. It was enough.

With the prickles receding, she turned her mind to the job Skye Painter, president and CEO of the Painter Development Corporation, had commissioned her to do.

It was a straightforward and potentially lucrative task: design a resort for all seasons. Not solely for skiing, although people would be eager to shush down the formidable slopes of Hollowback Mountain, but for year-round outdoor activities. Keep it clean and simple, incorporate a strong Western flavor, bring the outside in and connect the entire complex to the land.

Skye had made it clear to Sasha from the outset that her architectural firm had not been at the top of her contact list. Beat, Streete and Myer had been recommended by an associate whose private retreat in Colorado Springs had, quote, "blown the boulders out from under him." To Sasha's mind, that said Skye Painter wanted a fresh perspective and a unique design for her project. Anything short of that, and she would be taking her business elsewhere.

Roads aside—and access was a problem that needed to be addressed—Sasha was looking forward to the challenge. She wouldn't allow a case of nerves to disrupt her. Failure wasn't an option. Her company was new and fragile for that reason. Plus, her partners were depending on her, and God knew her mother would never let her live it down. Heaven help anyone who disappointed Barbara Leeds.

Twilight approached early in mid-January. Snow clouds hung low and threatening over Hollowback Mountain. The ruts were so deep in places that Sasha had to slow her vehicle to a crawl to get over them.

"Really need a wider road," she decided, then bounced so hard she bit her tongue.

She spied headlights approaching, but it was difficult to judge the distance in near whiteout conditions. Refocusing, she blinked, did a disbelieving double take and hissed out a breath.

She had to be seeing things. There couldn't possibly be a huge pickup bearing down on her.

She swung the wheel to the right. The halogen lights

ahead danced like lanterns in a high wind. As she'd somehow known it would, the approaching vehicle lost traction and went into a full three-hundred-sixty-degree spin.

The back end of the truck whipped around to tag her front fender. It struck her again near the tire well, slowed briefly, then spun its wheels and fishtailed away. The best Sasha could do—and she'd been driving in the snow since her sixteenth birthday—was steer into the skid and pray the ravine beside her wasn't a sheer drop.

An eternity later, she felt something catch on the undercarriage, and her Land Rover jolted to a halt. If she hadn't been belted in, she would have been flung into the passenger seat. Peering out, she saw nothing, just emptiness, and realized that one good blast of wind would send her tumbling over the side of the cliff.

Need guardrails, she reflected through a jittery blur. Big heavy suckers to embrace the soon-to-be-widened road.

She took a precious moment to catch her breath and calm her racing heart. *Breathe in, breathe out,* she told herself. *Don't make any sudden moves.*

She pried her clenched fingers from the steering wheel, visualized the road, covered with snow but safe and solid beneath her feet. The Land Rover rocked as gusts of wind pummeled it. She used her shoulder and every ounce of strength to fight the door open. As she hit it, the vehicle pitched sideways and seesawed for a moment.

Sasha shot a look upward. "I'm not ready to die," she warned whoever might be listening.

With her arm braced against the door, she switched off the engine and pulled out the keys. Determined to escape, she gave a heave—or started to. Instead of resistant metal, she encountered only air, and toppled out of her seat into the snow.

A pair of gloved hands prevented her from landing facedown on the ice. Grateful despite her surprise, she looked up into a blurred face.

"Who…?" A blast of wind carried her question away. She pushed her hair back. "Thank you."

"Are you hurt?"

It was a man, and he had a nice voice, a very nice voice, even when raised.

"I don't think so." He helped her to her feet. "Someone in a gray pickup sideswiped me." She batted at the snow on her jeans. "I saw five guys crammed into the front seat."

"Sheriff'll pick them up. You sure you didn't hit your head?"

"Why?" She probed her temple. "Am I bleeding?"

"Hope not. I can rescue your vehicle, but I'm not so good with blood."

Love the voice, she thought again, and looked closer. From what she could see of his face, he had an incredible pair of hazel eyes.

Beside them, the Land Rover groaned and slid another few inches downward.

"Uh…" Although she wanted to make a grab for the door handle, Sasha regarded his SUV instead. "Now might be a really good time for that rescue."

"I'll get the cable. Can you turn my truck around?"

If she couldn't, her father, who'd been designing North American race cars for thirty years, would disown her.

Drawing up the hood of her coat, Sasha crunched through a frozen drift to the driver's-side door. Six more payments. That's all she had left on the four-wheel drive vehicle her mother had warned her not to buy. She glanced skyward for the second time. "If you have any compassion, you won't let her find out about this."

The stranger's truck was blissfully warm, the passenger seat strewn with papers, files, a laptop computer and various other electronic gadgets. A badge sat front and center on the dash. Under it she glimpsed a photo driver's license. Too curious to resist, Sasha regarded the badge. Denver PD. Now what would a Denver cop be doing in the northernmost part of the state. Then she extracted the license and the question slipped away.

"Wow." Stunned, she studied the man's picture. *Gorgeous, gorgeous, gorgeous* was all she could think, and, God, this probably wasn't even a good shot.

She scanned the personal info. Dominick Law. Thirty-six years old; six feet two inches tall; brown hair—too long, but also gorgeous; hazel eyes; one hundred and seventy pounds. That would make him tall and lean as well as stunning.

His features were positively arresting, on the narrow side and highlighted by a great mouth, a straight nose and the hint of a dimple in his right cheek.

"Okay, not good." As if singed, her fingers dropped both badge and license back on the dash. "You're on a business trip, Sasha. It's no time to mimic Mommy dearest."

As a distraction, she set the wipers in motion and watched Detective Gorgeous hook the cable to the winch and secure the other end to her rear bumper.

Blustery gusts buffeted the windshield and almost blotted out the sight of her tilted vehicle. She waited for

his signal, then maneuvered the truck around and revved
the engine. Officer Law kept it very well tuned.

All in all, it took them less than ten minutes to get her
Land Rover back on level ground. Well, relatively level.
The ruts were treacherous underfoot, and the driving
snow stung her eyes.

With her hood up, Sasha worked her way back to him.
"You're a lifesaver, Detective."

"Saw the badge, huh?" Crouching, he checked the
cable. "You're good to go now, Ms…"

"Myer. Sasha." She caught her hood before it blew
down. "Just Sasha."

"Nick."

"I'm really happy to meet you, Nick." Then she noticed a dent in the front end of her Rover and bent to inspect it. "That better be fixable." She went to her knees,
peered underneath. "Did you see any damage?"

"Other than the dent, no. Where are you headed?"

"Painter's Bluff."

His amazing eyes grew speculative. "You have blond
hair, don't you?"

"Courtesy of my Swedish grandmother. Why?"
Amusement kindled in her as she stood, a mood she
couldn't discern in the serious detective. "Are blondes
illegal in Painter's Bluff?"

"Apparently you never saw Skye Painter in her prime."

Sasha smiled. "You mean she's not in her prime now?
Could have fooled me. I'm going to be working for her,
on her resort." She gestured into the blizzard. "Up on
Hollowback Mountain."

"You're a contractor?"

"Architect. Beat, Streete and Myer. We're new but extremely innovative, or so our PR claims."

"Do you work out of Denver?"

The cop tone surprised her. "I do, yes. Is that a problem, Detective Law?"

His lips took on a slight curve. "Beautiful women are usually a problem—one way or another."

Unperturbed, she widened her smile. "Sounds like the voice of bad experience to me. Thanks again for your help. Now if you'll unhook us, we can both be on our way."

His stare seemed to penetrate her skin and made her want to step back. She held her ground and his gaze. "Have I broken a law, Detective?"

"It's Nick, and not that I know of."

"Then I can go."

"If your vehicle cooperates."

"I thought you said it wasn't damaged."

"That I can see. The proof will be in the drive."

"Unless we freeze to death first. Neither of us is dressed for this."

He half smiled. "Tell you what. You take my truck into Painter's Bluff, and I'll check out your Land Rover."

Because her teeth were going to chatter in a minute, and he was, after all, a cop, Sasha went with the suggestion. "I'm staying at the hotel."

"Which one?"

"There are two?"

"Three. Skye Painter's Mountain House, the Hollowback Inn and Annie's Barn on the edge of town."

For a moment, Sasha forgot to be cold, and laughed. "Let me guess, Annie ran a bordello, right?"

"Rumor has it Butch and Sundance were regulars."

"Spoken like a proud local." She tipped her head. "And

yet your badge says Denver PD. Are you a man of mystery, Nick Law?"

"I have my moments. You're at Mountain House, right?" At her nod, he walked her back to his truck and opened the door. "I'll go first. Once you're settled you'll need to see Sheriff Pyle about the guys who sideswiped you." His eyes caught hers and held.

Sasha shivered. She had the ridiculous feeling that he was stripping away her clothing piece by piece. It felt sexual, and yet it didn't, exciting in a kinky sort of way, but unnerving at the same time. And just plain weird all around.

Before she could comment, he'd pulled off his glove and caught her chin between his thumb and fingers. "Drive safely, Sasha Myer, and don't stop for anyone."

Then he was gone, and she was alone in a stranger's truck in the middle of a blizzard, with Bruce Springsteen pouring from the speakers.

Gorgeous and odd. What was she getting herself into up here?

"You're not Nick."

Barely five feet through the front door of Mountain House, Sasha found herself nose to nose with a blond man in his midthirties. He wore jeans, a pale blue shirt and a sheepskin vest. Sky-blue eyes traveled past her to the snowy street, then returned to give her a thorough head-to-toe assessment.

"I'd know that black 4x4 anywhere. Why are you driving it?"

In the warmth of the rustic lobby Sasha pushed back her hood and unzipped her coat. "Nick's got my Land Rover. Since I didn't pass him, I assumed he'd get here before me. Guess not." She offered the man a perfunctory smile. "Who are you?"

"Dana Hollander." He cast another frowning glance at the street. "I'm the mayor of Painter's Bluff. I also own the feed and seed on Center Street and fix computers on the side."

"Sounds like a full plate."

"More than full. The sheriff and I have been run off our feet today."

"Well, I hate to add to your burden, but five kids in a gray pickup are joyriding out on Hollowback Road."

"Kids? Oh, that'll be the Sickerbies."

"All five of them?"

"Six boys at last count, and every one a hell-raiser."

Sasha would have moved on to the reception desk, but the man's expression made her pause. "Look, I didn't run your friend off the road and steal his truck, if that's what you're thinking. The Sickerbies left me hanging, literally, and Nick helped me out. He wanted to make sure my vehicle wasn't damaged, so we swapped. He said he'd meet me here."

Dana gave a preoccupied nod. "Maybe he stopped by Sheriff Pyle's office first."

"Maybe."

Shedding her coat, Sasha let her gaze roam the lobby. For a small hotel, the place had charm, plus, if she wasn't mistaken, original wood walls and floorboards. The varnished oak was scarred, the river-rock hearth and chiseled mantel massive, and it wouldn't have surprised her to discover that the light fixtures were kerosene conversions.

She looked closer at the seating area. "Are those horsehair chairs next to the fireplace?"

"You have a good eye. They were made in Salt Lake City in 1883. Belonged to Skye Painter's great-grand-daddy. He kept them in his mountain cabin. Skye used them up at the lodge until a nephew tried to perform surgery on one of the arms. Seemed safer to bring them down here." A sudden smile appeared. "You're her architect, aren't you? Sasha Myer from Denver. Skye told us you'd be coming. You're a bit late."

"Three days," Sasha agreed. She started for the desk. "I'll call Ms. Painter after I check in."

Dana accompanied her across the plank floor. "You can call, but you won't be meeting up with her anytime soon. She left town late yesterday morning. Lucky woman," he added, in an eerie echo of Barbara's earlier sentiments.

"Lucky because she missed the blizzard?"

"That, too." Dana addressed the redheaded receptionist. "April, this is Skye's architect from Denver. Give her a good room and a hot dinner on the house."

"That's very kind of you, Mr. Hollander, but I don't want to take advantage."

"Dana, and you're not." He returned his gaze to the door. "Are you sure you didn't pass Nick coming in?"

"Very sure. I was watching, for both my SUV and your Sickerbies."

The lobby phone rang. Tucking the receiver into the crook of her neck, the redhead handed Sasha a key. "Room 27, second floor." She raised her voice. "Hang on, Dana. Sheriff Pyle's on the line. He's asking about Detective Law."

"Who isn't?"

Sasha debated as he took the handset, then gave his arm a tap. "Do you have Nick's cell phone number?"

"Hang on, Will." He covered the mouthpiece. "He didn't answer when I called, but go ahead. It's the Denver area code and NICK LAW."

Straightforward and simple, she acknowledged. Two qualities she admired.

Taking out her cell phone, she walked away from the desk.

A moment ago, a woman had been sitting in the brown horsehair chair. Now two men stood beside it. The one with dark hair combed away from his face and a short, tidy beard struck her as vaguely familiar. The other had his collar turned up and a stained cowboy hat pulled low on his forehead. His shoulders hunched as he shuffled his feet. He kept his hands in the pockets of his parka and used his elbows to gesture.

Head tilted, Sasha studied his companion. She felt certain she'd seen or met him somewhere. He had a bookish look about him. Maybe he was a friend of her mother's.

When he caught sight of her, his brows went up. He said something to the man in the hat and started toward her, his right hand outstretched.

"Sasha Myer, hello. I've been waiting for you."

Head cocked, she lowered her phone. "It's Max, isn't it?"

"Max Macallum. I'm flattered you remember me. Or did Skye tell you she hired my company to work on the access problem for her resort?"

"Skye and I haven't spoken about anything except design features and layout." Her eyes sparkled. "My memory of you involves our respective Christmas parties unfolding at the same time in the same restaurant. Your party ran out of vermouth before dinner, so you, being partial to martinis, snuck in and raided our bar."

"Then collided with you in my rush to escape unnoticed, and caused you to break a very expensive high heel. I hope you got it repaired."

"The bartender helped me out. Have you been in town long?"

"Three days."

"Waiting for me, huh?" She grinned. "I feel so guilty."

"You are a little late."

"It's been mentioned." She leaned her hip against a support beam. "I got tied up on a site in Minnesota, then it snowed and they closed the airport. Flights got canceled, fog rolled in. More delays. I called Skye five times. She didn't seem put out."

"She likes your work. It doesn't matter, anyway. She's not here. Left town yesterday, missed all the excitement."

It was the second cryptic remark she'd heard since her arrival. "How much excitement can there be in a town of only three thousand residents?"

Max spread his hands. "I'd have asked myself that same question until—"

Dana cut in. "Will Pyle hasn't seen Nick! Neither have his deputies."

"Look, I promise I didn't drive past him on my way in. Although…" Sasha gnawed on her lip "…my Land Rover is white, and so's the snow. And the road. And everything else." She considered for a moment, then shook her head. "I'd have seen him."

"Did you try his cell phone yet?"

"Dialing now."

To get better sound, she walked toward the door. She noticed the man in the stained cowboy hat had vanished.

Nick answered on the fifth ring. "Law."

"Myer." Pulling off her long wool scarf, she shook out her hair. "Where are you?"

"Do I detect a note of concern in that lovely voice?"

"Not unless you habitually confuse concern with irritation. There's a guy here named Dana whom I'm sure thinks I coldcocked you and stole your truck. The sheriff's already called the front desk looking for you. Some kind of excitement is brewing, and it seems as though Skye Painter and I are the only ones who missed it. So I repeat, Detective Law, where are you?"

"Just turn around."

His voice came into her other ear; however, a lifetime of similar ambushes kept her from jumping. Brows arched, she swung slowly on her heel to confront him.

"Welcome to Painter's Bluff, Detective. Why the delay?" She sniffed. "I don't smell any liquor, so you didn't stop for a beer. I didn't pass you, so my SUV must be fine. And you don't strike me as an addle-brained cop, so I can't believe you got your hotel wires crossed."

"Nick!" Dana hastened over. "You made it."

Nick unzipped his lined leather jacket. "I stopped by the clinic on my way in."

Concerned, Sasha gave him a once-over. He was even more gorgeous out of the snow. "Did you hurt yourself hooking up our vehicles?"

A frown appeared. "I wanted to see something. Someone, actually. She was about your age and height. Blond-haired, blue-eyed, of Swedish descent."

A slippery tendril wound its way through Sasha's stomach. "Was. Past tense. I take it she's dead."

For an answer, he curled his long fingers around the

nape of her neck. "Her name was Kristiana Felgard. Her body was discovered up at Painter's Rock early this morning. She was murdered."

Chapter 2

"I think we're dealing with a serial killer."

In the Mountain House bar, Nick went over the grisly details. "The case has gone cold twice since the first murder eight years ago," he said, "but back then the media dubbed the perpetrator the Snow Globe Killer because at each murder scene he left a snow globe with an angel inside."

Sasha felt trapped and edgy, but refused to let either feeling show. "Dana said the police found nothing at the scene of Kristiana Felgard's murder, so your theory already has a hole in it."

A big one, she hoped. Because ever since Nick had appeared tonight, her stomach had been tied in knots.

Nick slid her a sideways look. "There was an imprint in the snow to the right of the victim's head. That's where the killer always placed his mementos. The impression is consistent with the bases of previous snow globes."

She wanted to leave. More than that, she wanted Nick and Dana to stop looking at her as if she had a big red X on her chest.

She drew a deep, steadying breath, caught the smells of leather, whiskey and wood smoke from the bar's enormous stone fireplace.

The room felt like an old saloon, warmed with polished oak tables and a mirrored bar that spanned the entire back wall. Everything was gouged and timeworn and, given Skye Painter's reputation, no doubt authentic, down to the glasses currently being placed in front of them by a rather baffled-looking server in high-heeled cowboy boots.

Sasha waited until she'd left and the drinks had been rearranged. "The waitress is a blonde. Why aren't you terrifying her with your serial killer story?"

"Mandy's color comes from a bottle." Dana looked through the crowd to the entrance. "She's a lovely woman, a grandmother of three whose husband passed away last month, which is why Skye hired her. Believe me, Mandy Cullen's not our boy's type."

"No, according to Nick, your boy prefers women with Scandinavian ancestry."

Nick eyes remained steady on hers. It was unnerving how he did that.

"He does, Sasha. In every case I've investigated I've found a Swedish or Finnish connection. And you already told us you're Swedish."

If she hadn't been so freaked, she would have been tempted to laugh at the absurdity of the situation.

She'd come to Painter's Bluff to design a resort and

now she found herself the target of a serial killer. Or so the cop and mayor sharing the booth with her believed.

"My grandmother's only half-Swedish, Nick. Her father came from Finland. He built ships in Sweden, but he was born in Helsinki."

Nick's eyes didn't waver. "There you go then."

Her hackles rose. "No, there I don't go. You said it's been five years since this guy's murdered anyone."

"That we know of."

"But you would know, wouldn't you? You're a homicide cop."

"I *was* a homicide cop. I work cold cases now. They're my specialty. My partner and I have been working on this particular case for the past nine months. Six weeks ago, just after Thanksgiving, a woman was attacked in Aspen."

"Attacked," Sasha repeated. "Not killed?"

"She managed to get away, but she couldn't tell us much. It was getting dark and her attacker was wearing a wool mask when he grabbed her. She'd been skiing all day and took the lift up to one of the more difficult slopes, hoping to squeeze in another run before meeting her friends for dinner. He skied right into her, then dragged her into the trees. She was disoriented, but not as badly as he believed. When he started to tie her up, she fought him."

"And either pulled off his mask or scratched him. No description, so I'll go with scratched."

"Not bad, Detective Myer. Long story short, we were able to get his DNA from the blood and skin under her fingernails. We had a suspect in mind. Unfortunately, his DNA didn't match. The investigation continued through

Christmas, but for all intents and purposes, the case has gone cold again."

Sasha felt as though she'd been thrown into a patch of quicksand, one that was sucking her in deeper and deeper. She spread the fingers of both hands on the table. "Okay, say Dana was right to call and tell you about Kristiana Felgard's death. Here you are in Painter's Bluff, a police officer from Denver who specializes in cold cases. Why on earth would the killer still be in town? I wouldn't hang around, would you?"

"No, but then I'm not a killer."

"Nick, he'd have to be crazy— No, scratch that, obviously he is crazy. He'd have to be stupid to remain at the scene of a murder that he must surely know is bound to attract even more police attention than usual."

"Havoc," Nick replied simply. "Some serial killers thrive on it. They get a rush from the act, then relive it through the media attention."

"You said the murderer strangled Kristiana and left her naked inside a snow angel?" God, but that was a grisly image. "And he's murdered seven other women the same way over the past eight years?"

Nick nodded, rolling the base of his beer glass on the table. "Two of the victims were discovered in Boise, one in a town outside Minneapolis, another in Otter Lake, Utah."

"That's only four."

"It's the first of two clusters. He murdered those four women eight years ago, then appeared to stop. Three years later, three more women died. The first was visiting her sister in Lake Tahoe, the second was skiing in Wyoming, the third was killed on the rim of Yellowstone

Park. The woman in Aspen six weeks ago was extremely fortunate to escape."

There were times, Sasha reflected, when an imagination could be a curse. She envisioned eight clones, lying naked in snow angels, with the wind blowing their hair over their faces and their eyes wide open and staring. She could even picture the angel snow globes, like the one her uncle Paul displayed on his console table every Christmas.

Across the bar table, Dana drummed his fingers on the scarred wood. "I told Will Pyle to meet us here at seven o'clock. It's eight now. Where is he?"

Sasha didn't know or care. If there was one person she had no desire to meet it was the sheriff. She was having a difficult enough time dealing with the men beside her.

"Maybe the Sickerbies ran him off the road," she suggested.

"Or hit the liquor store again," Nick murmured.

Dana rubbed his temples. "Thanks for that, Nick. The Sickerbies into theft. God help us if that's true."

Sensing an opportunity to change the subject, Sasha asked, "Were you a local boy once, Nick?"

"In a way. I grew up in Outlaw Falls, about a hundred miles from here. Dana and I went to grade school together. His family moved away before we started high school, but we managed to stay in touch."

Dana continued to massage his temples. "We made a point of going fishing every summer at Sun Lake—that's near Outlaw Falls—but the fish got scarce and the licensing laws changed. Now we hike up Hollowback and do the camping thing. My five-year-old's already pestering me to take him along next summer. Fawn would love it. Fawn's my wife," he added. "We're celebrating our fourteenth—" His pager went off, and he unhooked it from his belt. "And even as we speak, she wants me." Taking a quick sip of beer, he slid from the booth. "My cell phone's dead. Gotta use a pay phone."

"My cell's charged," Sasha said, but Dana waved her off.

"I want to call Will, too. Besides, it's quieter in the lobby." He stabbed a finger at Nick. "Tell her about Kristiana Felgard's features."

"No, don't tell her," Sasha said when he was gone. "She has a pretty good idea already. Tell me about camping on Hollowback Mountain."

Nick shrugged. "Hundreds of urbanites do it every summer, which is probably why Skye Painter wants to build a resort."

Sasha smiled. "You don't like cities, do you, Nick?

"I don't mind them."

Humor nudged aside fear. "My, but you are an enigma."

The ghost of a smile appeared on his lips. "Not so much. I work in the city but grew up on a ranch. I like to hike up mountains in the summer, fish when I can. Doesn't seem overly enigmatic to me."

"I sense a strong desire for solitude."

The dimple in his cheek deepened. "Point taken. Rocks and trees don't ask questions."

"Or commit crimes." She regarded him in profile, noticed the length of his lashes and the way his hair curled over his shirt. "Are you married?"

The vague smile held. "Not anymore. You?"

"Almost. I did the runaway bride thing, except I was more civilized and left him in his living room rather than at the altar. Do you have a partner?" Amused by the way his eyes narrowed, she clarified, "I mean a police partner." Then she raised her brows. "Oh, that's right, you don't like questions, do you? But I'm not a rock or a tree. You and Dana want to pry into my background, I'm going to pry into yours. Fair's fair, Detective Law."

"I ask questions for a reason, Sasha."

"So do I."

"You don't want to talk about Kristiana Felgard. Why not?"

"For the same reason I don't walk behind horses. If you were me, would you want to spend your first evening in a strange town talking about a dead woman?"

"I would if her death might pertain to me."

"Guess that makes me totally perverse then. Or maybe I just find it a little spooky that a lunatic killer who couldn't possibly know I was coming to Painter's Bluff might want me dead."

She saw Nick's lips curve as he watched a group of rowdies at the bar. "Are you trying to goad me, Sasha?" he asked.

Her own smile blossomed. "Maybe a little. If I am, I come by the trait honestly. I also know a loner when I meet one. And I'm truly curious about why a person like you would want to separate himself from the rest of the world."

"News flash, loners don't all live in caves."

"Or even close to it in your case. Why Denver?"

"Why not?"

"Okay, let's go back further. Why a cop?"

He tipped his face to the ceiling. "You are perverse, aren't you? And persistent. There's no deep mystery. I'm a kid from Colorado who watched TV and fell in love with the idea of becoming a cop. The kid grew up, moved to Chicago, learned the difference between reality and fantasy and slowly made his way back to the mountains."

She watched the play of expressions in his eyes when he turned them toward her. They truly were amazing.

"That's a very succinct story, Nick, but it's not an answer. Why a cold case cop?"

"Why an architect?"

She regarded him for a moment, then sighed. "My mother wanted me to design clothes."

With the glass raised to his lips, he chuckled. "That wasn't succinct—it was downright confusing."

"Not if you knew my mother. And our relationship." She watched Mandy the waitress spill a shot glass of whiskey onto the bar, and relented. "Okay, give, why do you think the man who killed Kristiana Felgard will come after me?"

"I didn't say he would. I said he might."

"Subtle difference. Come on, Nick, I don't even live here. And not that I want any woman to be killed, but in a town of three thousand residents, there must be one or two blond females with Scandinavian backgrounds."

"The sheriff and his deputies are looking into that."

"So you're what? Here in an official capacity, or merely as an interested Denver cop?"

He reached for and captured her right hand. Stroking the back of her fingers with his thumb, he said, "Dana contacted me early this morning. I'm official." He regarded her through his lashes. "Stories about this serial killer were all over the newspapers eight and five years ago. How is it you never read any of them?"

Tiny threads of electricity raced up her arm. Sasha considered removing her hand from his, but for the moment the sensation fascinated more than it unnerved her.

"Eight years ago, I lived in Atlanta, and Philadelphia after that. The East Coast has murders of its own, serial and otherwise. I moved back to Denver three years ago when two of my Atlanta associates decided to make a lifestyle change and thought I might like to do the same."

"So you've lived in Denver before." When his thumb grazed her knuckles and made her shiver, she knew she really should pull away. That she didn't both surprised and intrigued her.

"I was born in Denver. I lived there until my parents divorced and my mother took me to New York. She remarried, divorced again. We moved to Miami. By then I had a brother. Another marriage, another divorce, on to New Haven. Then it was London for a while and Paris, but it was difficult in France. She couldn't speak the language, and I refused to take the modeling course she enrolled me in. It didn't matter. Her relationship there failed as miserably as her previous marriages. We went to Stockholm, stayed with my grandmother for a year. I finished high school and moved to Boston to study architecture. That's where my mother lives now."

It was more than she usually told people. Unsure why she'd become so garrulous, Sasha gave her fingers a subtle tug. He released her hand but continued to regard her in an assessing way.

"Did you enjoy living in all those places?"

"I liked the people. I make friends easily, so the moving part wasn't a problem. And who wouldn't love New York, London and Paris?" From an adjacent booth she heard Mandy laugh as she served her customers, and once again, the image of eight murdered women flitted into Sasha's mind's eye. Vexed by her lack of mental control, she released a breath. "Do you have any idea why he killed her?"

Nick had no trouble following her change of subject. "All we've got so far is the obvious physical connection to his previous victims."

Sasha's head spun. Facts and fears overlapped. "I'm sorry, did you say Kristiana Felgard was local?"

Nick's expression gentled. "She was a tourist, Sasha. April said she checked into the hotel late yesterday afternoon. She spoke limited English and was very polite."

Sasha rolled that over in her mind. "Why do you think she came to Painter's Bluff?"

"She could have been a heli-skier. It's a big sport here. She had a helmet and goggles in her suitcase. There's also the ice sculpture festival that takes place at the end of January. Participants are beginning to arrive for that."

"So you think what? That the killer followed her to Painter's Bluff?"

"Or knew her itinerary and arrived ahead of her."

"Are you saying he stalks his victims?"

"I've always thought so."

"Lovely." Sasha sank back into her seat. "That means he could know my schedule as well."

"It's possible."

"I wasn't serious, Nick. I thought you just said this guy wasn't necessarily after me."

"I'm not saying he's been stalking you specifically, Sasha, merely that you fit the profile. If he sees you, you could be at risk. The proverbial two birds with one stone."

Her laugh contained no humor. "Two women with Swedish backgrounds travel to Painter's Bluff at the same time. Your nut gets an unexpected twofer, and you get a golden opportunity to catch him." She watched his eyes. "What aren't you telling me, Detective?"

He regarded her for a long moment. "Kristiana didn't have a reservation."

"Well, that's… Hmm."

"Yeah, very hmm."

Mandy wobbled past in her cowboy boots. She had four steak dinners precariously balanced on her arms.

Before she could evade him, Nick recaptured Sasha's hand. "Are you hungry?"

For him, she thought suddenly, as electric shivers raced up her arm. "I am, actually. I missed lunch."

"Then we'll order. While we eat, you can tell me about your life in Denver and why a beautiful woman like you would prefer to design buildings over clothes."

Feeling suddenly reckless, Sasha leaned closer to him on the leather seat. "It's a deal. And afterward, you can tell me why a gorgeous cop like you chose to devote himself to solving cold cases." Giving in to desire, she brushed her lips temptingly over his. "You can also tell me what kind of a snowball's chance in hell you think you have of talking me into leaving Painter's Bluff."

"S'cuse me, ma'am."

A man bumped Sasha's elbow as he passed her in the second floor corridor. She recognized the stained cowboy hat and charcoal-gray parka, but beyond that didn't take much notice of him.

She couldn't believe it was only ten o'clock. So much had happened since she'd arrived in town, it felt like 3:00 a.m.

Nick Law, a cop who specialized in cold cases, believed that a serial killer was going to target her as his next victim. Hows and whys aside, the fact remained that someone had killed a woman last night. A woman with features similar to her own. A woman, like her, of Swedish descent. He'd left her naked in the snow, inside a snow angel. He'd strangled her. Had he also raped her? Nick hadn't mentioned that, and Sasha hadn't asked. She really didn't want to picture it.

So far, the local newspaper was reporting a death with no reference to a serial killer. There'd been no snow globe left at the scene, or if there had been someone had removed it.

Why?

Nick hadn't been able to answer that question. The sheriff hadn't showed, and Dana had gone home after his wife paged him. He'd murmured something about in-laws wanting him to put his computer skills back to work and join them in Silicon Valley.

Alone with Nick after that, Sasha had kissed him.

Why had she done that? She wasn't Barbara—please, God, not even close. And while Sasha did flirt with men sometimes, she seldom went so far as to touch them. She'd meant to tease Nick, she knew that. What she hadn't intended to do was enjoy herself.

Nick had given her very little by way of a reaction. Whether he'd liked the kiss or not, she couldn't tell, though he had stared at her for some time afterward.

A reluctant smile quirked Sasha's lips. Perversity, it seemed, ran rampant in her family.

She heard footsteps to her left, followed by a woman's voice.

"Evening, Mr. Rush." April, the redhead from the front desk, flashed a high-voltage smile at the man in the stained hat as he stood outside room 23. "Truck still not fixed?"

The man fumbled with his key. "Maybe tomorrow." He jammed it hard into the lock, glanced in Sasha's direction and nodded. "'Night, ladies."

April patted her heart. Her voice dropped as she approached. "He's so Gary Cooper."

Sasha had to force her own key into the very old lock. "All I saw was a hat, facial stubble and a sheepskin collar."

April paused for a chat. "This is his third night here. Not on purpose, mind you. His truck crapped out on him two miles south of town. How are you for towels?"

"I'm good. Listen, if Max Macallum's looking for me, tell him I'll talk to him tomorrow, okay?"

"Got it." When the door to room 23 gave a faint creak, April hitched up her breasts and offered a sugary, "Sleep well, Mr. Rush." To Sasha, she whispered, "Think I'll rent *High Noon* tonight."

"Right now I couldn't stay awake through the opening credits."

"Have you seen it?"

"Once, when I was five."

April gestured at Sasha's hair. "You should watch it again. You're totally Kellyesque."

"Sorry?"

"Rent the movie. Gary Cooper, Grace Kelly. You'll get it. You're beautiful in a Princess of Monaco way. Not the type we usually see here in Painter's Bluff."

"I heard Skye Painter was a bombshell in her time."

"So they say. At this point, she's more of a character." April patted Sasha's arm. "You look done in, hon. Get some shut-eye. Tomorrow should be a decent day, although forecasters are talking blizzard by nightfall. Sleep well."

"I'll do my best."

As she started across the threshold, Sasha thought she heard a sound like a raspy breath. When the door to room 23 clicked shut, the sound stopped.

"Weird," she murmured. And made a point of bolting her own door behind her.

He locked himself in, hid away. No prying eyes could find him here. Trembling all over, he pressed his forehead against the door.

He couldn't deny it anymore. The monster that had lived inside him for so many years was back. It had grown into a vicious, spiky-tailed demon. Sometimes it vanished like smoke. Other times it snarled and scratched and whipped its tail around until he had to let it out.

It crawled to the surface, so close he could feel its heart beating against his ribs, feel its hot, greedy breath on his skin. He pictured her face, heard her voice. Tossing his head back, he breathed out the hatred through his nostrils.

He'd killed her many times already, but somehow she always came back. He needed to kill her again, do it properly this time. Then, finally, his pain might end.

He visualized the beautiful blonde, imagined her preparing to climb into her soft hotel bed. Removing her clothing, piece by piece. Removing her false halo and wings, perhaps for the last time.

He raised his forehead from the door. And heard the monster chuckle.

Chapter 3

"So what's the story, Nick? Gotta be something more than pictures of cold female bodies bouncing around in that head of yours. You gonna share, or just sit there staring at a corpse all night?"

Sheriff Will Pyle was growing impatient. Nick saw it on his face, heard it in his voice. Pyle got annoyed when people died in his town. So far in his four-year term of office, only twelve had. Two of them had been heli-ski accidents, eight had gone from old age or disease, one man had committed suicide. Kristiana Felgard was a blot on Pyle's record and he didn't like it, not one bit.

Surprisingly, though, he didn't seem to resent Nick's being there, or the fact that Dana had placed the call to Denver without consulting him.

Pyle was a big-boned, beefy man of sixty-two. He'd been a state cop in Illinois for over thirty years before coming to Painter's Bluff in search of a quiet life. Until last night, he'd had it. Though he and Nick had crossed paths on several occasions during Pyle's term, this was the first time in an official capacity.

Straddling an outdated swivel chair, Nick rearranged the photos on the sheriff's desk. "You took a lot of shots, Will."

The sheriff removed his gun and holster. "Old habits, Nicky. We cover our butts. Got a mix of digital, Polaroid and good old Kodak film. Even took videos under floodlights. We did our best to preserve the site, but January being what it is and us not really equipped for such an undertaking, there's not a whole lot left up there." He stretched his back, raising his arms overhead. "You want coffee?"

"Black, two sugars."

"Two?" Pyle snorted. "You lose your toughness in the city?"

"I used to take four."

"Sissified city cop." Pyle hunted through a cupboard for the sugar. "Can you even ride a horse?"

"Bareback through the snow to school, just like my daddy and his daddy before him."

Another snort, this time of laughter. But Pyle sobered as he poured the coffee. "What do you make of this unholy mess?"

Nick picked up a graphic shot. "Nothing good so far. I see blood on the snow here. Besides the strangulation bruising on the victim's neck and the rope burns on her wrists and ankles, she was unmarked."

"Noticed that."

Nick counted the spots of blood. There were four in

the snow and another on a jutting rock near the victim's left shoulder. "Talk to me about the blood."

"We collected samples and sent them to the county lab for analysis. Should have the report in a day or two. Be great if it matched up with the DNA samples you got from the guy who attacked that woman in Aspen." Pyle searched for stir sticks in his desk drawer. "How long you been working this case, Nick?"

"Nine months."

"On one cold case. Don't you find that kind of police work frustrating?"

"Yeah, it's frustrating, but someone has to make sure the victims and their families don't slip through the cracks. They deserve justice, Will, to say nothing of the perps who deserve to be locked up."

"Point taken, but a job like yours'd drive me to drink. Strand of hair here—no match. Drop of blood there— useless DNA. No witnesses, no way to place a suspect at the scene. You must have an endless supply of patience to go over a file from a thousand different angles."

"Think of me as a dog looking for a bone to chew on. He'll sink his teeth into the smallest one and stick until something juicer comes along."

Pyle chuckled. "Dana says you could've been a cowboy. You have a ranch waiting for you when your daddy retires. Instead you're riding herd on a bunch of dusty corpses. I'm sure the families are grateful, Nicky, but in your boots I'd have taken the cattle, hands down."

"Give me ten more years and I might agree with you."

Pyle handed him a chipped mug. "Here you go, sweetheart, two sugars. Now let's take a break, and you can fill me in on this architect my deputy's been babbling about all night. He spotted her checking into Skye's hotel. She as DDG as he claims?"

"Drop-dead gorgeous?" Nick caught his bottom lip briefly between his teeth. He could still feel the way she'd nipped him earlier. "Yeah, you could say that. She's definitely a beauty—long legs, long blond hair, blue eyes…"

"Blue like the lake up at Painter's Lodge, swears my deputy. Or the ocean around a tropical island."

"Your deputy watches too many travel shows."

"Nah, his mom writes poetry. When he acted up as a kid, she'd sit him in a corner with a book and make him read."

Nick used his laptop to enlarge a section of the imprint near the victim's head. "He set something down here, Will. From the impression and the displaced snow around it, I'd say it was knocked over."

"Snow globe, you figure?"

"That'd be my guess." Nick glanced up. "Do the Sickerbie boys spend much time at Painter's Rock?"

"No reason for them to in the winter. Besides, they'd have screamed like girls if they'd seen a dead body. They'll swipe their mom's bank card and do it up at McDonald's, but they'd have reported this, Nick, not left her there for Hank Milligan to find. Poor old guy nearly had a coronary, and he doesn't carry a cell phone. He had to hike all the way back to town to report it."

Nick highlighted the patches of blood only a few inches from the imprint. He suspected the drop on the rock might be the key. "Did Milligan disturb the site?"

"Hank might be old but his eyesight's better than mine. Knew what he was looking at twenty feet away. Didn't have to get close to know she was dead."

"What's the ETD?"

"Anywhere from 11:00 to 3:00. Sorry, Nick, that's as good as our doc could do. The country medical examiner might be able to shave a few hours off either way." Slurping coffee, Will picked up a clipboard. "We're running the out-of-towners now. So far, they're clean."

"He won't be into other crimes. We'll have to link him either to the victim or to the scene in another way. When did Kristiana Felgard arrive in the States?"

"Seven days ago. Her passport says she flew into JFK. We've asked the New York police to look for relatives, but that'll take time."

Nick brought up a map of Sweden. "She came from Hallstavik. That's near Stockholm." Where Sasha had lived for a year with her grandmother. "Where did she go after New York?"

"You'll have to give us a bit of time. We're checking out the airlines, railroads and bus companies."

"How did she get to Painter's Bluff?"

"Rental car from Denver."

"Backtrack from Denver. Find out how long she was there. Contact her next of kin in Sweden."

"Yes, sir," Pyle mocked, and Nick's lips moved into a smile. The sheriff slurped more coffee. "You staying with Dana?"

Nick switched to an old file. "I've been invited. I'll see. Fawn's parents are in town. They already have a full house." Sitting back, he regarded the screen. "If this guy sees Sasha, we're screwed."

Pyle grunted. "Man, I gotta get a look at this woman. How old do you figure she is?"

Nick didn't have to figure, he knew—her age and probably a number of other details she'd prefer to keep private. "Twenty-nine. She's the youngest one-third of a partnership that got rolling just under three years ago. They're building a clientele and a reputation, but architecture's a tough business. This job for Skye Painter is important. I doubt if dynamite could blow Sasha off it."

The outer door opened and closed while Nick contemplated Sasha Myer's face.

Pyle's all-pro deputy rushed in ruddy-cheeked. "We got it, sir." He looked from the sheriff to Nick and back. "The snow globe. We found it smashed in a trash can behind Annie's Barn."

Someone was using a jackhammer in the hotel hallway. Sasha lifted her face from the pillow and tried to remember if April had mentioned any construction work in the hotel.

The hammering became a series of thumps, and she realized someone was banging on her door. That was never a good thing in the middle of the night.

"Okay, I'm coming." She pushed herself upright. "Stop pounding holes in my door." Her robe had slipped to the floor. She had to search for it in the dark because she couldn't remember where the light switches were.

The pounding stopped when she twisted the knob and yanked. "What?" she demanded. Then groaned. "Oh, God, not you. No offense, Detective Law, but go away."

He brushed past her and began to prowl the room. "Don't you use your viewer?"

"My what?" She turned, noticed the small peephole in the door. "If I had, I'd have added the security chain, not opened up. Why are you here?" She hunted for a clock. "What time is it?"

"Six o'clock."

Not as early as she'd thought. Combing her fingers

through her hair, she forced her mind into function mode. "There's no one under my bed or in the bathroom, as you can see. I had the dead bolt on all night, and I didn't hear a thing."

He paused by the window, surveyed the building across the street. "Do you always sleep with the curtains open?"

Not usually, but she'd been too exhausted to notice. She ignored his piercing gaze and tightened the belt of her white terry robe. She needed coffee badly. However, since there was only a mini fridge in the room, she settled for orange juice.

"Look, Nick, I know who you're searching for, but why are you doing it in my room?"

He left the window. "The murder didn't go according to plan, Sasha. We found the snow globe."

So things were going from bad to worse. "Where?"

"Behind Annie's Barn. It was broken."

"And that means…?"

"Something screwed up."

"Mostly for Kristiana Felgard, as far as I can see. Maybe she fought him and broke the globe."

"I doubt it." His gaze swept the room from corner to corner, halted on her leather backpack. "Is that all the luggage you brought?"

Even half-asleep and lacking caffeine, she could laugh. "No wonder you're not married anymore. How many women do you know who travel with only a single backpack?"

He shot her a quick look, and she wished she'd at least had time to brush her hair.

"I've met a few."

"Most of them were probably planting trees and

couldn't tell you what day of the week it was." Sasha took a long drink of the juice. "Skye wants us to stay at the lodge while we're here."

He moved closer, and she fought an urge to sidestep. "We? As in you and who?"

"Me and Max, I imagine. Not me and a serial killer, I shouldn't think."

Nick took the bottle from her hand, set it down. Catching her arms, he brought her forward. "The problem is, Sasha, you need to think all the time. You're not doing that."

"I just woke up, Nick. I'm not used to being so defensive this early in the day."

There were flecks of gold in his hazel eyes. And a night's worth of stubble on his face. Marveling at the beauty of his features, she touched a finger to his chin. "You haven't shaved. And you're wearing the same clothes as yesterday. You haven't been to bed, have you?"

"I grabbed an hour of downtime at the jail."

She blinked in surprise. "You slept in a jail cell? That is devotion."

"We discovered traces of blood on the globe."

Because he was still gripping her arms, she refused to shiver. "Hers or his?"

"Not hers. We don't know yet if it's his. There was blood at the scene, as well."

"Lovely." A thought struck her. "Should you be telling me this?"

"Why, are you planning on running to the local newspaper with your scoop? You have a right to know certain aspects of the case."

"And you think because the killer messed up, he'll want to fix his mistake... Oh, hell." She released a breath.

"That's exactly what you think, isn't it, and what *he* might be thinking, too."

With his thumbs, Nick stroked circles on her upper arms. "Tell me Denver's starting to sound good to you."

"It is." She raised her head, firmly defiant. "But I'm not going back. Come on, Nick," she said, at the flicker of vexation on his face. "Would it matter if I did? If he wants to kill me—" this time she did shiver "—he'll simply follow me and do it wherever. In an alley, or a park, or someone's front yard. Snow's snow, and he's murdered women in several different cities and towns."

"You're missing the point, Sasha."

"No, I'm getting it loud and clear. Look, would you mind letting me go? Thanks," she said, when he dropped his hands.

He didn't move away, and Sasha was so intrigued by her response to him that she didn't, either.

"Why did you come to my room, Nick, at six in the morning?"

"I thought about coming at two. Better?"

For some reason, the faint spark of humor in his eyes settled her.

"I'll tell you what," she said. "I'll only go up to the building site during the day, and I'll come back to the hotel before it gets dark. I'll make sure Max is with me, and I won't talk to strangers, either here or there. Does that work for you?"

"Do I have a choice?"

"You could arrest me."

"Love to. Why don't you assault me, and we'll go from there?"

"Handcuffs and everything? You're kinky as well as mysterious, Detective. I love it."

"I had a feeling you would."

"If that's a comment on my character, I'll caution you to reserve judgment. I'm not usually a flirt, but my mother preached what she practiced, and as much as I hate to admit it, one or two of her bad habits stuck."

He placed his hands on Sasha's arms again. This time, however, he simply slid them up and down to draw her in.

Captivated as much by his gaze as his touch, she offered no resistance. She let him ease her hips against his, and shifted her attention from his eyes to his mouth.

Although her immunity to most men's charms was unparalleled, she suspected Nick would be a different story. As if to verify that fear, alarm bells began to clamor in her head. She planted her palms on his chest. "No, Nick, wait."

He stopped with his mouth a tantalizing inch above hers. "What am I waiting for, Sasha?"

She realized the fist she had wrapped in his shirt was hauling him toward her rather than pushing him away. "I have no idea." And, smiling, she yanked his mouth onto hers.

"A serial killer? Here? In Painter's Bluff?" An agitated Max raked his fingers through his hair. "I don't believe it. People said a woman died up at Painter's Rock. No one mentioned the word *murder*. Sasha, we need to—"

"Drive up to the site and do the job Skye hired us to do," Sasha finished for him. She tossed her pack in the back of the Land Rover. "You can ride with me if you want to."

"Not a chance. Two vehicles are better. I've heard Smoking Gun Pass is tricky."

"And steep," Sasha recalled. "Skye said to use chains."

A man in a navy-blue parka began making his way across the street. Sasha spied the badge and wondered what obstacle he was going to place in her path.

"You Sasha Myer?"

She nodded, slammed the door. "You must be Sheriff Pyle. Dana mentioned you last night."

"I'll bet he did. You seen Nick today?"

Seen, argued with and kissed. "He checked my room for intruders at the crack of dawn. Didn't find any."

"Give us time." The sheriff's surprisingly astute gaze shifted to the man at her side. "You'd be Skye's engineer, then."

"Max Macallum." He held the hair out of his eyes with a gloved hand. "Is it true you're looking for a serial killer?"

"Just a murderer at this point. We'll get to the serial part later." The sheriff's smile had a wolfish edge. "You sure are pretty, Ms. Myer."

"Sasha, and thank you." She glanced past his shoulder. "Where's Nick?"

"Questioning out-of-towners. He wants one of my deputies to keep an eye on you."

"Why doesn't that surprise me?"

"I decided to do it myself."

She'd half expected this would happen, but it was still worth a protest. "I have a rifle, Sheriff. It's licensed and in good working order. Nick doesn't seem to grasp the fact that I don't need anyone riding shotgun for me. I can take care of myself perfectly well."

Pyle made a sign of negation. "Nick and I agreed. It was either me or Dana, and I won the toss." He moved closer. "This is one mean dude we got here. It's possible he's killed eight women so far, and if he has, there's no reason to think he'll stop. You look a lot like the last victim. This is a small town. I'm willing to bet he's taken notice."

"I feel so reassured." Sasha felt eyes boring into her head and, without turning, said, "Stop gaping, Max. It's a long story that involves blond hair and Scandinavian ancestry. He won't come after you."

Max cleared his throat. "Should we maybe try to contact Skye and explain the situation?"

The wind kicked up, lifting Sasha's hair beneath the ice-blue hat her grandmother had knitted for her last Christmas. "I've tried to call Skye four times this morning. Her service says she's out of range. Let's do our jobs and let Sheriff Pyle and Nick do theirs."

Max opened his mouth, then closed it and slumped. "I'll get my keys."

He looked so miserable that Sasha gave his back an encouraging pat as he trudged past. "It'll be fine."

The sheriff emitted a grunt that might have been a chuckle. "You want reassurance, talk to our cold case investigator. The Snow Globe Killer only goes for women. Like the lady said, you're safe enough."

"Unless his aim's off," Nick remarked, coming up behind them.

"I'll be back," Max promised Sasha, edging away. "Phone Skye again while I'm gone, okay? She won't expect you to risk your life for the sake of a resort."

Sasha ignored him and turned her attention to Nick. His expression was impassive as usual, and showed no sign of the kiss she'd given him this morning. "I don't need a babysitter, Detective."

"You're going to tell me you can shoot a gun, handle treacherous driving conditions and defend yourself against all comers, but so could Belinda Nordby. She was the fifth victim. And a cop," he said before Sasha could ask. "She'd been one for seven years. This isn't a game, Sasha."

She didn't flinch, but countered with an even, "I talked to my partner Regan Streete after you left this morning. She wants me to come back to Denver. She says Tommy can work with Skye."

"But you said no."

"Tommy designs inspired office buildings, but he's a techno geek who doesn't quite grasp the concept of fusion between structure and land, and I don't think Skye wants the MGM Grand up here."

"What about Regan?"

"She has a condo development and two restaurants on her plate. This is my project, Nick. I do hotels and houses."

From the sidewalk, Sheriff Pyle grunted, "You're not going to talk her out of it, Nicky. Best to let me go up there with her while you ask your questions down here."

She sent him a quick smile. "You see? Even the sheriff understands me."

Before she could move, Nick boxed her between himself and the Land Rover. It both amused and frustrated her to discover that she actually felt breathless.

With his eyes locked on hers, he lowered his head. "Don't try losing him in Smoking Gun Pass, Sasha."

"You can't lose someone in a mountain pass, Nick...." She regarded him through her lashes. "Can you?"

"Stick to your route. And your promise. Back before dark, agreed?"

She considered teasing him, but then she pictured

Kristiana Felgard in a cold room and nodded. "Don't worry, Max won't want to stay even that long."

"And you know Max how well?"

"We had our company Christmas parties together."

"That's it?"

"He borrowed some liquor from our bar."

"So he's a close friend then."

She offered Nick a sweet smile. "Let's just say I know him better than I know you."

Sliding his hand under her chin, he held her firmly in place. "Max Macallum was here in Painter's Bluff when Kristiana Felgard died."

Sasha didn't move or pull away. "So was your sheriff. And Dana. And Gary Cooper down the hall from me."

Nick's gaze dropped to her mouth before returning to her eyes. "You can work with Max, Sasha. That doesn't mean you should trust him."

"What about you, Detective? You said a cop was killed. Maybe it took another cop to do it."

"Maybe it did."

He ran his thumb lightly over her lips. She'd rather he'd used his mouth, but even a misplaced wish wasn't going to deter her.

"I don't trust easily, Nick, and I always watch my back. It's one of the few good lessons my mother taught me." Partly because he continued to stare, but mostly because she wanted to, she bridged the small gap between them and gave him a kiss. "I promise, I won't trust anyone." She kissed him again, then stepped away. "Not even you."

Chapter 4

"You kissed her?" Dana shook his head in amazement. "You've known her less than eighteen hours, and you kissed her? You don't kiss women you've known for eighteen days, sometimes eighteen weeks, once even eighteen—"

"I get it, Dana." In the sheriff's private office, Nick searched for and located Will Pyle's clipboard. "It's out of character for me."

"It's off the map for you. Lacey—"

"Is remarried and living in Michigan with a man who's not a cop. Subject dead. Move on."

His warning tone had no effect on Dana. "You're a puzzler, Nick. Getting involved with a potential victim. What's the deal with that?"

"She's not going to be a victim."

"Calmly stated, but so far your questions have struck

out. And Will's like a bull in a china shop with his interrogative techniques." Dana frowned as Nick started out. "Where are you going?"

"Mountain House." A scan of the second sheet on the clipboard revealed that only a handful of the people staying there had spoken to the sheriff. "I've done Annie's Barn and most of the Hollowback Inn."

Hauling out his gloves, Dana jogged along behind him. "April said there are climbers heading up the north side of Hollowback. Party of five."

"When did they leave?"

"The morning after the murder."

"Does she have names?"

"Names and Visa card numbers. They rented climbing gear." Dana sucked in a sharp breath as Nick pushed through the door. "Man, it's cold."

Clouds scudded across an already gray sky. Nick watched them bunch together. "Snow's coming."

"It's been that kind of year. We've had three major slides already. One missed Skye's lodge by less than five hundred feet."

Nick's eyes traveled up the mountain. "Where's the building site?"

"Five miles west of the lodge. That engineer's got his work cut out for him. The pass alone'll confound him for months. All the roads except one snake back to the same spot. If I didn't know better, I'd swear old George Painter planned it that way." Dana crunched along beside Nick in silence, but the sideways looks he darted were telling. Out of respect for a friendship that stretched back thirty years, Nick caved.

"There's something about her that feels familiar to me, Dana. My father's ranch foreman is a Native American—Blackfoot. You know him. He believes in spirits, transfiguration and old souls reborn. I was fascinated by the idea as a kid. I thought I'd outgrown it as an adult. Guess not."

"Well that's unexpected."

"What, that I'd believe in anything spirit related?"

"That you'd admit it." He opened the hotel door. "Details to follow, I hope."

Nick had left his gloves in one of the jail cells—not smart with the thermometer heading toward minus ten. He blew into his hands as April hastened over from the front desk.

"Here's your updated list, Detective Law." She stood close enough to press her breasts into his arm. "There are only seven men who were here the night of the murder, plus the five out climbing. Mr. Phlug is ninety-two and traveling north to Montana with his grandson, Dr. Phlug. They're both really nice. James Peebles is more surly, no idea why. Mr. Rush—well, he's just plain hunky."

Nick's brows went up. "He's down the hall from Sasha Myer, right?"

She pressed closer. "Don't you love cowboys?"

"Since I was a kid," he agreed with a grin. "I've already talked to three of these guys," he told Dana. "You do the Phlugs. I'll take Peebles and Rush."

April bumped his arm. "Mr. Rush isn't here right now, Detective. He's over at Harvey's Garage. His truck broke a kingpin. He's been on Harvey's case to replace it. I don't mean in a nasty way. Mr. Rush is very polite and quiet, kind of skittish, but I figure that's shyness." She ran her gaze up and down Nick's body. "It's totally sexy."

"Room 23," Nick read from the sheet.

"Across the hall from Ms. Felgard." April shuddered.

"It's creepy, isn't it? One minute alive, the next gone. Poor thing. She was quiet, too. A sweet little mouse."

"Uh-huh. Look, phone Harvey and tell him to stall this Rush guy."

"Sure." She hesitated. "Why? I mean, he's the nice one. It's Mr. Peebles who's— Okay, I'm going. Stall. Shouldn't be a problem for Harvey."

Dana peered over Nick's shoulder. "Anthony Rush. Telluride, Colorado. Do you have a hunch about him?"

Nick skimmed the list again. "Not particularly. I just don't want him leaving town, and it looks like he's paid his bill."

Dana ran a finger across the sheet. "Hasn't checked out, though."

"We'll see."

Nick felt revved, but then he always did when a cold case came to life. One thing he enjoyed doing was interrogating people. Anticipating the moment, he arched his brows. "Wanna watch?"

"I've had breakfast. I can handle it." Nick heard the sympathy in Dana's voice as he added, "For his sake, I hope Anthony Rush can, too."

"I read on the Internet that a woman died near Painter's Bluff." Barbara overrode a cloud of static to reproach her daughter. "How? Where? And what does Skye Painter have to say about it?"

"Not sure, Painter's Rock and nothing yet," Sasha lied. The signposts in Smoking Gun Pass had vanished, if they'd ever been there, forcing her to use the map on the dash to locate the proper access route. With various roads and tons of snow, it was a complex endeavor.

"Sasha…"

"Look, Mother, I'm driving. Now's not the time."

Barbara was undaunted. "Is Skye Painter going through with the project or not?"

"I'm sure she is."

"So I can tell Donald you're still working for her."

She wouldn't ask, she promised herself. Wouldn't ask. "Who's Donald?"

"He writes for well-known women's magazines. I told him about your job and he was so impressed he wants to do an article on you."

"But you'll rate a strong mention, I'm sure."

"That's not the point."

Sasha could have pressed, but why bother? It would only spark another argument.

"I'm flattered, Mother." She traced the road on the map with her finger. Behind her, the rearview mirror showed only snowdrifts and white-tipped trees. How could she have lost both Max and the sheriff?

"I e-mailed you last night," Barbara said above the static. "You didn't answer."

"I was too tired to switch on."

"Now why is that, I wonder? Did you go out partying? Honestly, Sasha, you and your brother—"

Slapping her phone closed, Sasha tossed it aside. She considered pitching it in a drift when it rang again.

Without looking, she flipped it up. "What now, Mother?"

"Let me guess. You've got issues." Instead of her mother's annoyed tone, she heard Nick's humorous greeting.

Sasha tilted her head from side to side to relieve the tension in her neck. "This day just keeps getting better and better. In case you haven't noticed, Nick, it's not dark yet." Still, the encroaching snow clouds cast a dull gray shadow on the road ahead. Tired of fencing, she asked, "You didn't call to nag me, did you? Because my mother's already done that. I'm not in the mood to be polite."

"So that's a no to dinner then."

"You just want to make sure I come back to Painter's Bluff as promised."

"You really aren't in the mood to be polite."

A laugh slipped out. "Doesn't anything rile you, Detective?"

"You don't want to see me riled, Sasha. Seven o'clock?"

It would be well past dark by then.

"Okay, seven's good. Now, hang up. I want to let my mood simmer for a few more miles."

"Drive safely."

"I always do," she said, and ended the call.

She managed ten, maybe fifteen seconds of broody silence before she noticed headlights approaching through the snow. Not the Sickerbies this time. These lights were higher off the road, and much more powerful.

Whoever was driving, however, had apparently gone to the same school as the Sickerbie boys. The vehicle barreled through the ruts in the middle of an already tight road.

"This has not been my week," Sasha muttered. And for the second time in two days she yanked the steering wheel hard to the right.

"Harvey?" Dana pushed through the stuck office door of the town's oldest service station. "You in here? No? Well, hell, Nick, I don't know where he can be."

Nick made a wary circle of the shop. A gray truck—

probably the Sickerbies'—sat high on a hoist, with an F250 halfway up beside it. He heard a scraping noise in the corner and motioned for Dana to halt.

Eyes combing the shadows, Nick wove a path through the clutter of mechanic's tools. A moan emerged from behind an oil drum.

"Harvey?" As a precaution, Dana picked up a tire iron. "Is that you?"

Nick drew the gun from his shoulder holster. He pointed it at the ceiling as he rounded the drum—and reholstered it a moment later when he spied Harvey's body.

"Over here." Crouching, he checked the man's neck for a pulse. It was strong and steady.

Harvey groaned, his eyelids fluttered. Nick spied a rusty wrench and saw a gleam of blood on the end.

"Help him," he told Dana.

His own eyes were already scanning the garage. With his gun out again, he watched for movement inside the bay. Catching one near the office window, he whipped the gun down.

"Police." His eyes flicked to the bay door. "Move away from the tires."

A tense few seconds passed before a young man in a snow hat and heavy coat sidled out. His hands went up and his eyes widened with fright.

Nick regarded him over his gun. "You're a Sickerbie, aren't you?"

Dana's head popped up. "Randy, what the hell are you doing here?"

"Waiting for our truck." The boy's gaze remained glued to Nick's hands. "I was in the bathroom when I heard a ruckus. I thought it was my dad come to bust my butt, so I stayed inside."

Nick lowered his weapon. "Did you see anything?"

"Not much. A guy. He was wearing a cowboy hat, kinda like my dad's. He was sort of big, but not real heavy. He wanted his truck."

Nick scoured the remaining shadows as he indicated the Ford on the hoist. "That truck up there?"

"Yes, that truck up there," a voice behind him growled. Harvey sat up, supported by Dana, and gave his head a rub. "The guy grabbed a wrench, whacked me when I told him it wasn't ready. Friggin' jerk." He glared. "It isn't like I have a hundred kingpins sitting around my shop waiting to be installed. Had to order one from—"

"What was his name?" Nick interrupted.

"Rush. And that's what he wanted me to do. Rush, rush, rush. Well, I told him off fast enough. Said my piece, turned my back, and bam, he walloped me."

Nick motioned the frightened teenager aside. "Where did he go?"

"How should I know?" Harvey grumbled. "I was out cold."

Randy used one of his raised hands to point. "He took off in a big silver Chevy."

Harvey snorted. With Dana's help, he climbed to his feet. "Didn't make the best choice. I siphoned off most of the fuel out of that truck this morning so's I could flush out the tank. He won't be going far."

Nick reholstered. "It won't take much fuel to get to Smoking Gun Pass."

Dana gave Harvey's arm a squeeze. "Will you be okay if we leave?"

"Hell, I drove monster trucks when I was your age, Dana. I got an iron skull." He scowled at Nick. "What's this guy's problem, anyway? He knock over the liquor store?"

"I doubt it. Come on, Dana." Nick started for the door. "You can run the plate on the Ford while we chase him down."

"Chase who down?" the mechanic demanded. "What's going on?"

Dana jotted the number of the F250's license plate. "Trust me, Harv, you don't want to know."

Lunatics, Sasha decided as her Land Rover skidded to a halt next to a large drift. Didn't anyone around here know how to drive in snow?

The vehicle she'd avoided by mere inches had its back end jammed against the rock face. Irritated, she shoved her door open and hopped out.

"Don't you dare be injured." She secured her cap, reached inside for her gloves. "Except for snake bites and poison ivy, I'm not up on my first aid."

She heard the engine rev, saw the huge tires spin, and hesitated before closing the door. She couldn't see his features, but the body language of the driver suggested that he was extremely upset. He was alternately thumping the steering wheel and grinding the truck's gears.

As she stood there, the back end jumped a little. The gears ground again. He whacked the wheel with his fists.

"Maybe not," Sasha murmured, and remained where she was.

The Chevy's engine roared; the spinning tires threw up fat streams of snow. The man inside reversed, then shoved the truck into Drive. The back end jumped much higher this time.

In her peripheral vision, Sasha spied a vehicle creeping along the road toward the pass. She recognized Max's rented SUV, and released the breath she hadn't realized she'd been holding.

The man in the truck reversed and swung the steering wheel in violent bursts from left to right. Without warning, the box end popped up, the tires made contact with rock and suddenly, the vehicle sprang forward.

Sasha didn't move. If he decided to plow her Land Rover off the road, at least she'd be able to dive away.

The rented SUV crept closer. She saw the sheriff in his 4x4, tight on Max's bumper. Ahead of her, the Chevy truck whipped around in a spray of ice and rock. Sasha glimpsed the driver's face as he glowered through the side window. Then he yanked the stick down and roared away.

It wasn't until he'd disappeared that she realized her heart was pounding. She had to work her fingers from the edge of the door.

Max braked beside her, the sheriff behind him. Both men climbed out. Will Pyle cast Max a scathing look as he clomped past.

"What happened, Sasha? Did you and that truck have a run-in?"

She wrestled her gaze from the road. "Almost, but no. It was just really strange. He seemed so…angry."

"At you?"

"More at himself and his truck, I think." Without looking down, she said, "You're ringing."

Pyle pulled out his phone, shot Max another chilly look. "Sheriff Pyle," he snapped. Then frowned. "Dana, is that you? You know what it's like up at the pass. Dana?" He regarded the screen, made a disgusted sound. "Pointless piece of crap. I lost the call. Let's do it this way, Sasha." He turned his back on Max. "I'll follow you, and the engineer can bring up the rear."

It felt good to smile after such a freakish interlude. "Was there a problem?" she asked innocently.

"The slicker spun out on a flat patch of road." The sheriff scowled at his phone before returning it to his pocket. "Next thing I know, he's kissing the side of the mountain. Almost buried the both of us in the snow and rock he unleashed."

Max, who'd remained silent to that point, faced him down. "The tires are bad, and the chains don't fit properly. I didn't get the vehicle I requested from the rental company. And don't even get me started on your roads, Sheriff Pyle. If I'd designed them, they'd be passable summer and winter. By locals and slickers." His expression became apologetic when he caught Sasha's eye. "I tried to phone you after I spun out, but your line was busy."

"Worried mother," Sasha said. "It wouldn't have mattered, Max. The guy in the Chevy came out of nowhere."

"Must have got himself turned around. It's easy to do up here." Pyle examined the back of her Land Rover. "Doesn't look like you hit anything. I'd say you're good to go on, unless you'd rather go back."

She secured her cap. "I'm not a quitter, Sheriff. Come on, Max. You can lead."

"I liked my arrangement better," the sheriff grumbled. "But anything to get up and down before the spring thaw."

His phone rang again. By the time he dipped his hand in his pocket, it had stopped.

"There must be twenty dead spots between here and town." He opened Sasha's door wider. "In you go, missy.

Take the right fork, then bear left. Right again and left."
He bared his teeth at Max. "You hearing this, Mr. Engineer?"

"Loud and clear, Sheriff Pyle. I'll see you at the site,
Sasha."

Sasha supposed this could accurately be described
as a smoking convoy. Sliding in, she eased her Land
Rover back onto the road. And tried not to think about
the fact that the man who'd sideswiped her had taken
the same fork.

It began to snow before Nick and Dana reached the
halfway point to Smoking Gun Pass.

Dana braced a hand on the dash while he used Nick's
laptop and cell. "Okay, I'm in." He typed the license plate
number, winced and waited. "I don't remember this road
being so bumpy. Needs to be properly plowed. I'll talk
to… Hang on, I've got it. Anthony James Rush. City
of residence—Telluride, Colorado. Forty-seven-year-
old white male. Drives an '88 F250. Everything seems
fine here."

"Yeah, if you don't include the fact that he whacked
Harvey Stubbs with a mechanic's wrench and stole a
4x4."

"Well, yes, that. But his driving record's impeccable."
Dana tapped the keypad. "Signal's fading, Nick. Anything else you need?"

"A radar tracking device for Rush would be good.
We're coming up to the fork."

Dana let out a whistle as he closed down. "Man, look
at that overhang. It's enormous. Do you know that in
a bad year, this pass can be closed five or six times by
slides? We've already had to dig out twice since Novem-

ber, and looking at that snow ledge, I say we're approaching number three. George Painter used to set off slides on purpose, thus the name Smoking Gun Pass. He liked to separate himself from the vermin in town."

"Sounds like my father." Nick kept his eye on a large rift developing in the overhang, while Dana watched the other side.

"It'll hold," he said, but his anxiety was evident. "Right turn."

The road twisted and turned, sometimes following the curve of the mountain, sometimes rolling away.

At a hard thump on the roof Dana raised his eyes. "Nick, this isn't good. We could get trapped."

"So could Rush."

"You're not helping me here, old friend. Remember, I have a wife and three kids in town. Left turn."

"I know the pass, Dana."

"Sorry. Nervous." He pointed east. "Skye's lodge is that way. I'm not sure about the building site."

Nick was. He'd drawn the map in his head. Lodge, building site, Sasha, roads. But where was Rush? Would he hide, or try to make it through the pass and into Wyoming?

A clump of ice landed on the windshield. Nick maneuvered around an even larger chunk. "Storm's getting worse." He turned right, drove for half a mile and rounded a sharp bend. A moment later, he braked so hard he almost threw Dana into the windshield.

His friend blinked at the wall of snow and rock sitting directly in their path. "My God, when did that happen? Did you hear anything?"

Nick regarded it for a moment, pictured the terrain and reversed. "Must have come down last night."

"But that's the way through to the other side of the mountain."

An ominous cracking sound filled the air as pieces of ice began to skitter downward.

"Uh, Nick…"

"I hear it."

Easing the truck around a boulder, he glanced at the widening rift. The ground began to tremble. Even the air seemed to vibrate. Ice pellets flew sideways across the hood.

"Nick, I think we're—"

"In trouble."

In the rearview mirror Nick saw a ball of snow bigger than his truck land on the road.

They were ahead of the worst of it, but there was still only one route away from the cracking snow.

"Gonna be fun," he murmured, and tried to remember why he'd left the city.

Chapter 5

"We're stuck, marooned, destined to become a bear's dinner. Or worse, starve." Max shivered in the blinding snow outside Skye Painter's enormous wood-and-stone lodge. "Even if we could get in there, who's to say we'll find any edible food?"

Sasha nudged Max's ribs. "Stop complaining, and be glad Sheriff Pyle knew how to get here."

"It's *The Shining* all over again." Max adjusted his earmuffs. "Wait and see. We'll find a caretaker in there, and he'll be a nut."

"Is he on drugs?" Pyle asked, joining them. "Or just a pain-in-the-butt pessimist?"

Sasha regarded the wide stoop. "I think the word you're looking for is *terrified*." She pointed at the stairs. "Those treads have been cleared recently."

"By the crazy caretaker," Max predicted.

"He also watches too many horror movies." Turning, she shielded her eyes with her hand. "Is that an engine?"

Pyle squinted through the whipping snow. "It's Nick's truck." Relief showed plainly on his face. "Thank God. I think he has a satellite phone."

"It won't work in these conditions," Max said flatly. "The signal needs to reach a satellite. Not likely with such dense cloud cover."

"You're a regular bundle of laughs, aren't you, Macallum?" Pyle waved his arms at the approaching vehicle. "Dana's with him," he told Sasha.

Her lips twitched up. "Looks like the bears are going to feast tonight."

"I can't believe you're making jokes, Sasha." Max batted his arms to ward off the cold. "That was an avalanche we saw back there. Snow and ice and rocks and trees, all tumbling down the mountain, all currently blocking the only road to town."

She patted his shoulder. "Yes, Max, we've grasped the dire implications of the slide. Panicking about it won't make it go away."

She left him to complain as Nick braked his truck behind her Land Rover. Dana climbed out on shaky legs.

"I don't ever want to do that again." He leaned against the door. "It chased us here. An enormous wall of snow. It followed us all the way to Painter's Outlook. My heart's never going to recover."

Sasha forged a path to the driver's door. "What about the pass itself?" she heard Sheriff Pyle ask. "Looked to me like we're cut off that way, too."

"We are." Dana still sounded weak. "My guess would be we're looking at a week, maybe ten days up here. Thank God for Skye's lodge."

Nick had his door open and was rummaging around in the space behind the seat. Sasha leaned against the frame. "So what's the story, Detective? I know you weren't out for an afternoon drive."

He tugged on something that was stuck. "Here, take this." He handed her his laptop and maneuvered himself into a better position.

She peered past him. "Can I help?"

"Not unless you're a magician. Dana wedged my sat phone down here to keep it safe, and it's caught on a spring."

The sight of his very sexy butt in jeans distracted her even under these dire circumstances. Boosting herself up, she started to suggest that she might be able to free the phone with her smaller hands, but instead, she found herself staring over him at an approaching figure.

"My God, there is a caretaker."

"What?" Nick raised his head. "Where?"

"Two o'clock. He looks like a miniature abominable snowman." As the figure drew closer, her eyes narrowed. "I think it's Skye Painter." A frown appeared. "What's she doing up here?"

"Same thing as us for the next week or so."

Sasha heard a thunk, followed by a soft, "Damn."

She leaned over him. "Broke it, huh?"

"Damaged at least." He worked the box free, shook his hand. "It and me."

Sasha saw the trickle of red and stilled his arm. "Don't shake blood on the seats, Nick. You'll attract bears." She struggled with a spark of amusement. "Max is spooked enough already."

In the confines of the cab, Nick watched her as she inspected the cut. She felt her own blood heat because of it, and raised her eyes to his. They were nearly gold and absolutely mesmerizing.

A sigh escaped her. "Honestly, Nick, you could stare down a hungry grizzly, especially if it was a female."

"I'll take that as a compliment." He continued to stare. "Where's Skye?"

"Standing by the front fender. Sheriff Pyle's talking to her."

Sasha took a moment to assess the woman. April was right; Skye Painter was a colorful individual. They'd only met once, but with a person like Skye, once was enough to leave a lasting impression.

Mahogany hair, undoubtedly dyed, spiked pixielike around a thin face with once-fine features. As with Nick, however, it was her eyes that really stood out. They were tobacco-brown, direct and assessing. At seventy-six, she walked tall, and while she might look like a snowman in her ski suit, she was actually a very slender woman.

"He's telling her about the slide." Sasha used a napkin from the glove box to wipe Nick's hand. "Press down for a minute and the bleeding'll stop. I'll bandage it once we're inside."

Skye regarded the row of vehicles, then the sheriff. With a mittened hand, she indicated the lodge.

"We'll take that as an invitation." Nick picked up his sat phone one-handed, checked for his keys and cell, and propelled Sasha out of the truck ahead of him.

"This is a fine mess," Skye was saying in her no-nonsense way. "I have a meeting in Houston three days from now." She zeroed in on the satellite phone. "Does that thing work?"

"I wouldn't count on it," Nick replied easily.

"Well, we'll figure something out, one way or another." She made a shooing motion toward the house. "Move, all of you, into the lodge. You can park and plug your vehicles in the car barn once we get ourselves sorted out. Hello, Sasha, Max, Dana." She halted in front of Nick, gave him a more thorough inspection "Hello to you, too, handsome. Do I know you?"

"Nick Law. I'm a police detective from Denver."

"Huh." She clucked her tongue. "Think I'll be moving to Denver, folks."

"You already have a place there, Skye." Dana held the front door open. "Word is it's a palace."

"My stepson lives in the palace, the no-account pipsqueak." She gave Nick's chest a pat. "Why couldn't I have met you forty years ago? So unfair." The wistful moment over, she eyed him in speculation. "You on vacation, Detective?"

"You didn't tell her about Kristiana?" Sasha sent the sheriff an incredulous look.

"Who had a chance?" The last to enter, Pyle closed the door and began brushing snow from his pants and sleeves. "If you don't already know it, the woman's a motormouth."

The woman also owned a stunning alpine lodge. Sidetracked, Sasha pivoted in a full circle to take it in.

Three of the walls were constructed of planed wood rather than the traditional rounded logs. The fourth and most spectacular was comprised of paneled glass, three thick, solid sheets of it that soared upward a full thirty feet. The fireplace was exquisite, double sided and, unless Sasha was mistaken, a masterpiece of honed granite.

Most of the rooms were sectioned off, to contain the warmth, she assumed. Only the central area remained open. The furniture was simple but looked comfortable, and the dining room appeared to have a view not only of the mountain, but also of a large lake.

"Painter's Pond." Skye followed her gaze. "That's what my great-granddaddy called it. The county prefers Hollow Lake."

"It's beautiful. All of it. Outside and in." Sasha's gaze wandered up a wide set of stairs to the second-floor landing. "The place is huge, and yet it feels wonderfully cozy."

Skye began to unwrap. "You want to see textbook cozy, you hike on over to my great-granddaddy George's shack. I've seen bigger outhouses. Then there's the burrow—it's a cabin built directly into a rise of land. George's brother Sam slapped that together. Their cousin Deacon preferred mud and wood shavings for his hut. Waterproofed it with something, no one's sure what."

"Sounds like the three little pigs," Dana remarked.

"Why are you here, Skye?" Sasha asked. "We thought you were out of town, certainly farther out than this."

"I came to get the place ready for you and Max."

"*You* came to do it?" Max stopped fussing with his coat. "Don't you have staff?"

"I have scores of employees in my business life, but on a personal level, I prefer simplicity." She fixed Sasha with a shrewd look. "Is Detective Nick your boyfriend?"

Sasha smiled. "No." Then she sighed. "Uh, Skye, there's been some trouble." She prodded Sheriff Pyle again.

A chuckling Skye slapped her hand. "You can stop poking him right now. For all Will's experience and, I will say, skill on the job, the man's afraid of me." She gave him a jab of her own. "Aren't you, my dear?"

He surprised Sasha by reddening slightly.

She pulled off her cap and called to Nick, who had his leather jacket slung over one shoulder and was looking through the bank of windows at the lake. "Nick, tell Skye why you came to Painter's Bluff."

"That's Will's job."

At the base of the stairwell, Dana ran a hand around his neck. "I'll do it."

"He's afraid of me, too," Skye said, "but not for the same reason. I like his pretty face, and he knows it."

Dana managed a half smile. "I'm still married, Skye."

"Fawn's a good girl, but she's too obliging. You need a woman who's a force unto herself."

"I need a drink," Will said.

Relief replaced the anxiety in Max's face. "Oh, I'll second that."

"I don't drink," Skye told them. "But the bar's between the dining and living rooms." She held them back with her next statement. "No one drinks till I find out what's going on."

Resolved, Dana jammed his hands in his pockets. "There was a death in Painter's Bluff, Skye. It happened right after you left."

"By death, I assume you don't mean ninety-eight-year-old Pearl Perkins, peacefully and of natural causes."

"No, a much younger woman, a stranger. She was… well, murdered."

"I see. No details, just murdered."

"At Painter's Rock. You know, where your stepson from Denver wanted you to build a restaurant. It wouldn't have worked in such a remote spot. You were right to veto the idea. "

Sasha rolled her eyes. But before she could flesh out the details, Nick spoke up.

"This woman was strangled," he told Skye. "Likely by a serial killer. Dana and I followed a suspect up here, a man named Rush. He stole a truck from Harvey's Garage and appeared to be headed for Smoking Gun Pass. We didn't catch him."

"You were chasing a suspect?" Sasha asked him. "That's why you're here?"

"Anthony Rush. He was staying at Mountain House. He knocked out the mechanic who was working on his truck and stole a silver Chevy with a lift kit."

"He means the chassis is raised up from the wheels," Dana interjected.

"Yes, I know what a lift kit is." Sasha's mind returned to the previous night. "I met him, Nick, in the hallway outside my room."

She saw the muscles in his jaw tighten, but before he could speak, she asked, "You think he's here, don't you? You think he's trapped with us."

"It's possible," Dana replied.

"It's certain," Nick corrected. "The road that leads through the pass was blocked when we got there, and we couldn't have been more than an hour behind the guy. I've seen slides before. The one on the pass road wasn't fresh. The one blocking the road back to town is."

Sasha set a hand on her suddenly constricted throat. "Are you sure he's the person who murdered Kristiana Felgard?"

"What?" Skye's voice had a rusty edge. "Did you say Felgard? Kristiana Lotta Felgard?"

Absently, Nick ran a hand up and down Sasha's arm, but his eyes were on Skye. "You know her?"

The older woman inhaled deeply, breathed out through her nose. "I do. She looks like you, Sasha."

"Yes, I've been told."

"She's—she was a nurse in Sweden. She's never been to the United States before."

Nick kept his hand on Sasha's arm. "Was she coming to see you?"

"If she was in Painter's Bluff, she must have been. She didn't contact me. She might have told someone in her family, but that wouldn't help. Nils, my second husband, was the only one who actually moved away from Sweden. We married when I was fifty-five and he was sixty. He died before our fifth anniversary. I traveled to Sweden twice in that time. That's how I met Kristiana." Mouth firm, features composed, Skye regarded Sasha and Nick. "Like me, Nils had a family before we met. Kristiana Felgard was his oldest grandchild."

"Why did I get out of bed this morning?" Sasha pushed on her temples, where a headache loomed. "I slept one door away from a possible—"

"Probable," Nick corrected.

She shot him a vexed look. "Probable serial killer, and now I'm trapped on a mountain with him. Skye's second husband's granddaughter is dead. Max is flipping out. Dana's running around the lodge, searching for a spot where his cell phone will work because your satellite phone won't, and neither will Skye's two-way radio. And all the meat in the freezer is either venison or rabbit."

It was after seven, and with everyone more or less settled, she and Nick had gravitated to the upper floor of the lodge, where Sasha had discovered a glass-encased deck porch. In her four hours here, she'd unearthed five such secluded areas.

Max had been baffled by her desire to explore. All

he'd wanted was a drink, a pill and a warm place to sit so he could tally up his list of regrets.

Skye, on the other hand, understood perfectly. Like Sasha, she used activity as a remedy for fear. She'd sent Nick and Dana out for logs, assigned sleeping quarters, and pointed out the common bathrooms. Then she'd shooed everyone from the kitchen so she could cook what she called a Medicine Bow Range dinner.

The smell of seared venison had been drifting up the stairs for several minutes. Sasha supposed she might learn to appreciate the taste of deer meat a week from now, but for the moment, she wasn't looking forward to sampling Skye's culinary handiwork.

With his forearms resting on the wood rail, Nick cast her a sideways glance. "Is your rant over?" he asked.

Her eyes traveled to the trees, blowing wildly beyond the lake. "Not quite. We're looking at seven to ten days up here, Nick, and that's assuming we can contact someone on the outside to tell them which roads to dig out. Ten days in the company of a probable killer—and Max, who might drive Sheriff Pyle to commit murder if cabin fever sets in."

Nick's eyes crinkled at the corners. "And I took you for an optimist."

"I am an optimist. I'm just—" her shoulders twitched "—having a moment. A perfectly justified moment, considering there's a killer on this mountain who has a problem with certain blond females." The wind made an eerie moaning sound as it curled around the eaves. "What do you think he'll do now?"

"Try to survive."

"Well, he'll have his choice of shelter." She indicated a flat rise, barely visible through a stand of snow-covered trees. "George Painter's shack is behind that hill. Half a mile west is brother Sam's burrow, and farther out still is cousin Deacon's mud cabin. Skye says there are also two old stables, three disgusting outhouses and four or five other structures she's never explored." Sasha paused. "He'll have a weapon, won't he?"

"I'd guess a gun."

"So he won't starve. Too bad."

"If he's lucky and smart, he won't even have to hunt for food. Skye's third son built a smokehouse somewhere in the vicinity of brother Sam's cave dwelling. Skye thinks there are two deer hanging in it right now."

"Now there's a lovely picture. Thanks for that, Nick."

He kept his gaze on the lake. "For someone who was born in Denver, you're awfully squeamish."

She breathed out a short laugh. "Last time I checked, Denver was a city. Those of us who like wild game—not me—buy it from a butcher shop."

"Does your mother like game?"

Sasha had schooled herself long ago not to react to questions about her mother. She smiled. "Let's just say that no signal on my cell phone is one of the few good things about being trapped."

Shifting position, he studied her features. She liked having him look, liked it even more when he trailed a finger through her hair. "Do you fight with her all the time?"

Her eyes twinkled. "Oh, we don't fight, Nick, that would be uncivilized. We have conflicting points of view on a wide variety of subjects. Barbara Leeds, my mother, is an English teacher. I have no idea why she chose that particular profession, because children irritate her, but there you go. By the time I was thirteen, my streak of perversity was well honed. I'd decided to have ten kids and bring them over to visit her as often as possible."

"Then you grew up."

"You'd think so, wouldn't you?" She heard large branches cracking in the wind. "I'm twenty-nine, but my mother insists I stalled out maturity-wise at fifteen. She's convinced I'm partying my life away in Denver. Pot calling the kettle black really, although she'd never see it that way."

The smile that stole across his lips quite simply took her breath away. He lightly ran a knuckle along her cheek. "So are you a party animal, Sasha?"

"Depends on your definition of the term. If practically living at the office with partners who are polar opposites and threaten to come to blows no less than ten times a week counts, then yes, I am."

"It sounds like you've taken on the role of referee in your firm."

"I'm told I'm a natural. I can handle Barbara, therefore I must be good at dealing with conflict."

"You'd be better off solo."

But she waved the suggestion aside. "Regan is a good friend, and Tommy's a manageable geek. Any big problems I have, serial killers excluded, stem primarily from too much contact with my mother."

"Who lives in Boston."

"You're a good listener." She welcomed the electric chill that feathered along her spine when he grazed the side of her jaw. "Where does *your* mother live?"

"With my father on a ranch near Outlaw Falls. She's kind and generous and keeps her emotions to herself."

Sasha wasn't surprised. "Any siblings?"

"A brother. He's three years older than me."

"Rancher or cop?"

"Firefighter. Los Angeles."

She hadn't anticipated that and laughed. "Don't you just love the way people's lives veer off the paths of greatest expectation?" Spreading her fingers on his chest, she absorbed his warmth. "Skye's really upset about Kristiana Felgard's death. Not that you wouldn't expect her to be, but a serial killer, Nick, a lunatic who actually arranges his victims in the snow and makes snow angels out of their corpses, seems so depraved compared to a bullet in an alley."

"It's an orchestrated act, Sasha. He's murdering the same person over and over again."

Her fingers curled into a fist. "Is there a sexual element to this act?"

"If you mean does he rape his victims, the answer's no. But there is a sexual aspect, otherwise he wouldn't strip them. The method he uses suggests a need for control. He decides when they die, whether to prolong it or do it quickly. He binds their wrists and ankles, and sometimes gags them. They can't fight him. They can only watch him watch them as he cuts off their oxygen supply."

Sasha tried not to visualize the pain and terror, the suppressed struggles, the screams trapped in their throats as eight women's lives had come to a brutal end.

What had Kristiana Felgard been thinking before she died? Had the killer followed her from Denver to Painter's Bluff? Had he gotten off sexually anticipating a new kill? Who was he really murdering?

A shiver worked its way up from her belly. "I don't want to do this any more tonight, okay? I don't want to think about him, or picture him out there while we're in here, and know that even if the need to kill doesn't drive him closer, the cold and hunger probably will. Anthony Rush." She closed her eyes, wished she could shut down her memory as easily. "God, Nick, I saw him. April wanted to sleep with him."

With little effort, nothing more than a hand on her arm, Nick brought her forward. His hypnotic eyes drew her in even deeper. "He can't touch you here, Sasha, not with five people around you. Given the weather conditions and lack of heating in the outbuildings, survival's going to be his main priority for a while."

Because humor helped to offset fear, Sasha tipped her head to the side. "So what's your priority, Detective Law? A real man—you know, one of those crusty Old West lawmen who can tell by a crushed leaf which way the villain went and what color horse he's riding—would be on Rush's trail as we speak, inspecting the terrain and sniffing the air for sweat and gun smoke."

Nick went along with her. "And by the end of a commercial-filled hour, he'd have his man. One shot, bang, villain's dead. No fuss, no blood."

She scraped a light fingernail across the bandage she'd put on his hand. "You law enforcement officers today are such wimps. You can't read crushed leaves, and you bleed when you're cut."

"Yeah, well, it's a soft world out there, whatever you stressed-out business types might think." His gaze slid from her eyes to her lips. "Rush isn't going to hurt you, Sasha." He eased her closer. "He'll be lucky to get off the mountain alive."

Heat replaced humor as her hips simply melted into his. She hooked her arms over his shoulders. "You know this is totally inappropriate, don't you?"

"Did I mention I'm off duty?"

"I thought cops were always…"

The rest of the sentence flew from her head as Nick crushed his mouth to hers. Cold radiated through the glass beside her, but all Sasha felt was a surging fire deep down inside.

Nick took his time, tasting and touching, exploring every contour of her mouth. Pain and pleasure fused, but it was a good pain, a hungry, wanting-more-now ache that promised to take her to new and dizzying heights.

She caught the ends of his hair with her fingers, tugging until he altered the angle of the kiss. Something stirred in her, a familiar chord struck inside a long-buried memory. When she nipped his lower lip, it felt arousing and hot. It felt right.

She rubbed her hips against him, smiled at the bulge in his jeans. "Gotcha going, don't I, Detective? So much for the man and his horse myth."

Nick recaptured her mouth, kissed her so thoroughly that her train of thought simply spiraled away. "What myth is that, Sasha?"

Cupping his face in her hands, she ran her lips over his face, tasting and teasing while her eyes sparkled into his. "Not sure. Something about being alone on the range. I've never been big on Hollywood's version of the Wild West. I prefer…" she trailed off as a beam of light streaked through the window "…the real thing." Her already racing heart leaped into her throat. "What was that?"

He brought his head up, scanned the area around the lake.

"There it is again." She pointed north. "Nick, that's the road we drove in on from the building site." She peered over his shoulder into the darkness. "Do you see anyone?"

"I can barely see the light." With his elbow, he nudged her back. "Stay behind me, Sasha." Drawing a gun from his waistband, he flipped off the safety. "We need to get away from the window."

She saw him in her mind, Anthony Rush, in the stained cowboy hat, outside his room at Mountain House, fiddling with his key while April flirted with him. Sasha saw him more clearly inside the cab of a stolen Chevy truck, banging his fists on the steering wheel and spinning his tires.

Nick took her hand, pulled her from the deck and into the wide upper corridor. But Sasha resisted. "Shouldn't we wait and see what he does? I mean, surely he wouldn't be stupid enough to come up here."

"Why not? He won't know how many people are in the lodge. He'll see the lights and think shelter."

"Yes, but even cold and desperate, he wouldn't charge in without checking the place first. He's a stranger here. For all he knows, a family of lunatics might own this place."

"In which case he'd fit right in."

"Antisocial lunatics, then." She batted at Nick's hand. "Stop pulling me."

"Stop dragging your feet."

"I'm not dragging anything, I'm being careful. It's dark in this hallway, and Skye has a lot of furniture waiting to be put in storage." They squeezed past a tall bench. "This lodge is seven years old. Why is this stuff still here? Ouch." She rubbed the shin she'd knocked into a chair.

"Will," Nick shouted down the stairs. "Dana. Someone's outside."

Sasha heard a scuffle of feet, followed by Will Pyle's gruff, "Which side?"

"Approaching the front of the lodge." Nick turned to Sasha. "Are you okay?"

"Bruised. Keep going. The light's getting really close."

"I see it." Dipping his head as they descended, Nick squinted through the row of lower windows. "Find Max and Skye. Keep them together."

"Nick, you're not—"

"Yes, I am." He didn't look at her but continued to search the snowy landscape. "And no, you can't come."

"I wasn't going to ask you that."

"Yes, you were." He halted, wrapped his hands around her upper arms. "You want to come because you hate doing nothing."

How could he know her so well after only one day? "I can shoot."

"I know you can."

"Then I should—" She eyed him in sudden suspicion. "What do you mean, you know? How do you know?"

Whatever explanation he might have offered never emerged. A beam of light funneled through the front window and skimmed across the staircase where they stood. It landed on Skye, who was wiping her hands on a dish towel, then flickered and went out.

"Nick," Sasha whispered in his ear. Then she froze as a shot blasted through the night.

Chapter 6

Nick kept Sasha behind him on the stairs. "Stay here, stay low, stay away from the windows. Don't follow." Catching her chin, he added a quiet, "Don't argue."

"I want a rifle, Nick."

Nick didn't oblige her, but Skye did. "Here, you can use my Mach 70." She handed Sasha the rifle, then threw a switch, plunging the ground floor into virtual darkness. Only three emergency lights remained on. "There's also a sawed-off shotgun in the gun cabinet, but as we're all aware, they're not entirely legal in these parts."

"Not in any parts." Nick shoved his own gun into his waistband, located his pack near the door and stuck two extra clips in his back pocket. Picking up his jacket, he motioned Dana to the side entrance. Will Pyle was already in position at the front.

Max, who'd been dozing on the sofa, sat up when

the doors opened and a blast of icy air rushed in. "Wh- what's going on?"

Sasha reached over and set a hand on his mouth. "We have a visitor." When Max didn't react, she moved her hand. "Do you know how to shoot?"

"I can use a bow and arrow, courtesy of a sexy in- structor at Camp Potoomie, in southern Wisconsin." He pushed the hair from his eyes. "Is that what this is about? Someone's trying to get into the lodge?"

"If it's the man who killed Kristiana, I owe him one." Bent low, Skye crept toward the front window. "Come on, Sasha. We'll blindside him."

"Are you calm?" Sasha asked Max.

"I took a tranq earlier. They're strong. I'm thinking I could pop this guy myself right now."

Sasha joined Skye near the front door. "Do you see anything?"

"Nick, for a minute, then nothing." She rested the barrel of her shotgun on the door frame. "I should have thought to bring my dogs. They love it up here, and they're part wolf. They'd tear an intruder's arm off be- fore he could cock his pistol."

Sasha spied a movement at the base of the porch. "Over here," she said. "That's not Nick or Sheriff Pyle."

Skye used her sleeve to wipe the glass. "He's wear- ing a cowboy hat."

"So was Anthony Rush the last time I saw him."

Sasha made a visual circle of the window. Her palms were damp. That meant her adrenaline level was rising. She forced herself to breathe normally.

She saw the movement again and glanced at Skye. "Do these windows open?"

"Double latch at the top, left and right. Squeeze them together and heave."

Tucking the rifle under her arm, Sasha located the latches. "Bigelow and Dunn designed this lodge, didn't they?"

"You know their work?"

"I know they always use these stupid windows. Dunn's brother manufactures them."

"Well, I don't want them in my new resort." Skye pinched the fingers of both hands to demonstrate. "You need to squeeze the latches together."

"I am."

The glass had steamed up from their breath. On the other side of it, loose snow whipped into a miniature funnel cloud. The shadow that had been huddled at the base of the stoop vanished for a moment, then in a sudden surge of motion, erupted from the darkness and clattered onto the porch.

"Door," Skye hissed. "Did we lock it?"

"Nick did." At least Sasha hoped he had. She raised her rifle as a precaution. And aimed it at the door as the knob began to rattle.

Logic dictated that their visitor was hidden somewhere on the perimeter of the lodge. He'd be desperate and therefore unpredictable. With luck, he'd also be hypothermic.

A light tap on Nick's shoulder didn't distract him. He remained crouched behind a large pine, while Dana hunkered down at his side.

"There's nothing in the back. Pyle checked the woodshed, and I did the other two entrances."

Nick nodded. "The car barn's locked, and there's no way for anyone to get under the porch."

"So where'd he go?"

Nick made another sweep. For a brief instant, the wind died and the snow stopped swirling. No moon or stars broke through the clouds, but enough emergency light trickled out of the lodge for him to make out certain shapes in silhouette.

Overhead, the trees creaked and swayed. Ice pellets, dislodged from the branches, skittered down the slope of the lodge roof.

"Maybe he died." Dana's teeth chattered. "I would if I'd been out in this cold for five hours. Remember, Nick, Harvey said the Chevy Rush stole didn't have much gas in the tank. No gas, no running engine, no heat."

Nick thought he glimpsed something near the base of the porch. Unfortunately, the wind gusted up, lifting the top layer of snow and spinning it into a cone.

Nick's eyes narrowed. "He's not dead, Dana. He's right there."

"Where? All I see is— Nick, wait. Nick!"

But Nick was already making his way toward the intruder. In cowboy boots, a bulky coat and a hat, the man clambered up onto the porch. He grasped the doorknob with both hands, cursed and began kicking, first at the latch, then at the window next to it.

Nick heard glass shatter and saw the man shove a hand inside. Two seconds and one shot later, he yanked it back out. Snarling obscenities, he made a dash for the far end of the porch.

At the sound of gunfire from inside the house, Nick used one of the snowdrifts as a ramp to catch the rail and vault over. The man slowed just enough that Nick slammed right into him. His wet cowboy boots slipped, and with a yelp, the intruder crashed into the lodge.

He came up swinging, but missed. Nick smiled and shoved his gun in the man's neck.

"Hope you're not feeling twitchy, pal, because my hands are cold and liable to slip on the trigger." He heard the distinctive sound of a rifle being pumped inside, and saw Dana and Will rushing up the stairs. "Tell Sasha I got him. Tell her his hand is nicely grazed, and get her to open up."

"Is it Rush?" Pyle gave the door a thump.

Nick stared into the hostile brown eyes set in an unfamiliar face. "No, but that doesn't mean he isn't a killer."

"I didn't kill no one." The man's words were badly slurred. He smelled like he'd been sleeping in a landfill for a week with a whisky bottle cradled in his arms.

Sasha gave their smelly guest a wide berth en route to the kitchen, where they sat around the table.

"My truck broke down," the intruder mumbled. "I was moving some stuff out of my shack over on the ridge when the slide hit. Tried to get through the pass, but it was snowed in, so I headed for the lodge. That's when my truck packed it in."

Max waved a hand in front of his nose. "So this is a Sickerbie."

"One of eight," Sheriff Pyle confirmed. "Name's Bo. His wife's Molly. We call her Mo. Bo and Mo and their six little hellions. Didn't know you had a shack on the ridge, Bo. What do you use it for?"

The man's head went down. "Storing stuff."

"Like stolen whiskey?" Nick suggested. "The liquor store in Painter's Bluff was robbed two nights ago, Sickerbie, did you know that?"

Bo's head bobbed up. His bloodshot eyes glittered with malice. "I never stole nothing."

"My mother's a teacher," Sasha said. "'Never stole nothing' is a double negative. Means you did steal something."

He glared, but clearly didn't understand.

Skye sat down next to Bo. "The ridge and everything around it for miles belongs to me, Bo. If you have a shack up there, you're trespassing, and I'll be pressing charges. But that's a minor issue compared to murder." She leaned in, and her voice seemed to drop an octave. "Someone killed my stepgranddaughter, and whoever it was, wherever he is, he's going to pay for that."

It was too much for Bo to process. He clenched his injured fist in his lap. "I never hurt no one—and don't you be listening to Mo if she tells you I did. She's clumsy is all." His mustache quivered as he appealed to Dana. "You know how it is, Mayor."

"What?" Dana's stricken expression verged on comical. "Why are you talking to me? I don't have any idea how it is, although it sounds like Sheriff Pyle should be paying your wife a visit."

"Friggin' outsiders." Bo glowered at Sasha. "She shot at me, and not one of you gives a damn."

Sasha arched a brow. "You were trying to break into the lodge, Mr. Sickerbie."

"You can be arrested for attempted B and E," Nick said. "You were carrying a hunting knife and a .45—which probably isn't registered." He reached out to Bo's bloodstained sleeve and pushed it up. "This large gash on your left arm appears to be a few days old. We found blood at the scene of a woman's murder two nights ago. Do you have an alibi for that time? We know your boys don't. They were out joyriding on stolen gas."

Bo's mouth compressed into a thin line. "You can't prove nothing against my boys."

"Actually, I can. Townspeople love to point fingers at local baddies. There were three witnesses at the filling station."

Bo's neck turned a dull brick-red; his eyes and his mustache twitched. The bandage Skye had tied around his grazed hand popped open as he balled it into another fist.

"I never hurt no one," he said through his teeth, all fifteen of them, Sasha noted in distaste. "You can't say I did, 'cause I didn't. I got rights, even up here. I say nothing to you, you got nothing on me. So I'm shuttin' up."

Standing, Sasha avoided the venison stew simmering on the stove and made a slow circle of the room. Bo Sickerbie's smell had infiltrated even the corners. His hostility was evident. So were his nerves.

She perched on the edge of the table beside Nick. "Do you like snow globes, Bo?"

His mustache jerked to one side. "You ask crazy questions, lady."

"That's not an answer," Nick said.

"I ain't saying nothing to her."

Nick kept his expression pleasant. "Okay, you can talk to me, then. Where's your truck?"

Bo seemed to be searching for the trick behind the question. Unable to find one, he muttered, "Can't say for sure. I got turned around. Maybe out near the old Martin place."

"Which I also own." Skye looked him over. "You need

a bath, Bo, with hot water and plenty of soap. You can use the tub down here." She stabbed a finger at Will and Dana. "You two watch him, make sure he does the job right."

Dana grimaced. "You're all heart, Skye."

"As a public servant, Mayor Hollander, it's your job to maintain law and order and keep the rest of us from gagging on our food."

Bo's weasel-like features grew menacing. "Man's not meant to smell like roses."

Sheriff Pyle curled his lip. "It's either that or you sleep in the car barn. Your choice, Sickerbie."

Bo hesitated, actually appeared to think about it. Sasha struggled with a laugh, then reminded herself that nothing about this situation was remotely funny.

"Right, then." Skye slapped her thigh as she stood. "Plenty of fresh clothes upstairs, for Bo and everyone. Dinner's in thirty minutes. Bo sleeps with Sheriff Pyle."

"Now wait a minute." Pyle puffed up. "I'll make sure he's clean for the sake of my nose, but I'm not sleeping with him."

"Same room, separate beds. My lodge, my beds, my decision. Remember, you're a public servant, too," she added when he opened his mouth.

Pyle shot Nick a dark look.

"Clean him up, Will," Nick suggested. "We'll question him again after dinner."

Sasha tapped Nick's arm. "Why question him? It's Anthony Rush you want, not some ornery drunk who stashes stolen liquor in a shed he doesn't own, on land that isn't his. He doesn't even know what the word *stalk* means, and while I'm sure he's an abusive man, he doesn't strike me as obsessive. Mean yes, and a drunk, but the only person he's fixated on is himself."

"I know."

"So why...?"

Nick regarded the man across from him. "Because even mean, abusive drunks can have friends. In town and out."

Dinner was a grim affair by anyone's standards. Spruced up but scowling fiercely, Bo Sickerbie slumped between Max and Sheriff Pyle.

Sasha ate as much of the venison stew as her stomach would allow. Unfortunately, the soft jazz Max chose as background music didn't help anyone's digestive process.

Outside, the snow, lashed by a nasty wind, struck the windows and doors. Max was right. At this rate, they might not make it off the mountain until June. Of course, most of them would be dead by then, because someone's sanity was bound to desert him long before that.

Sasha helped Skye clean up after the meal. As a favor to their hostess, she hid the jazz disks in the firebox. Then, leaving Nick, Dana and Sheriff Pyle to theorize cop-style, she made her way upstairs.

Skye had given her the best room in the lodge—out of sympathy for her situation, Sasha imagined. Shaped like an L and with its own private seating area, it boasted a queen-size sleigh bed, a large slate fireplace and a cherrywood armoire that housed a number of electronic gadgets.

Her private bathroom had a limestone shower, a spa tub and a comfy divan. Books sat on floor-to-ceiling shelves and ran the gamut from self-help to classic early American.

Best of all, though, because she hadn't unloaded her Land Rover at Mountain House, she had her suitcase and all her clothes with her.

It was after midnight by the time she'd showered and dried her hair. She considered watching a movie, but what she really wanted to do was find Nick.

Did he truly believe the Snow Globe Killer had a friend in Painter's Bluff? It seemed a little too coincidental to her, but maybe he'd simply been trying to get a rise out of Bo Sickerbie.

If that was his goal, he had fallen short. Bo hadn't uttered more than two words all night. Except for the muttering he'd done when Skye had bypassed his wineglass at the dinner table.

Dinner... Too hungry to contemplate sleep, Sasha swung her robe on and, using the built-in night-lights as a guide, headed downstairs.

The lodge was silent, almost eerily so. She was tempted to tiptoe across the floor, but knew that was silly. She wanted food, not to make off with Skye's silverware.

Halfway to the kitchen, she detected a small sound and paused. She didn't have to look to know. Letting her head fall back and a fatalistic smile cross her lips, she continued on.

"Do you ever sleep, Nick?"

His voice emerged from the shadows. "The sofa's comfortable, and I had a feeling you'd be back down before breakfast. Three mouthfuls of venison stew wouldn't constitute a meal in anyone's mind. There's pasta in the cupboard over the stove."

Amused that he'd read her so easily, she selected a hanging pot and filled it with water. "I see you boarded up the broken window."

He stood and approached her with his customary agility. She noticed at once that he'd showered and shaved. His hair was damp, and he wore a midnight-blue T-shirt with his jeans. She sighed. Why did he have to look so damn good all the time?

She rummaged above the stove. "How's your prisoner, Detective?"

"Snoring loudly. Will's wearing earplugs." She felt Nick's gaze on her body, but his eyes locked on hers when she turned. "Do you always wear things like that to bed?"

Surprised, she glanced down. "Like what? The negligee, the robe or—" a teasing smile blossomed "—the cowboy boots?"

Her black silk negligee was short, the red-and-black silk robe long, and the black boots had three-inch heels. Her mother would be appalled.

"I use what I have on hand, Nick. Skye gave me a pair of fuzzy pink slippers that look like bath mats with eyes. I think they're supposed to be cats. My grandmother wears fuzzy slippers. I'm not ready for that yet." Sasha faced him across the island counter, set her elbows on the butcher-block top. "One thing I could do, though, is alter my appearance."

Suspicion crept in. "How, I'm afraid to ask."

"I went through the cupboards in my bathroom and discovered three boxes of Mahogany Luster hair color." She examined the ends of her own hair. "If I'm not a blonde, would the Snow Globe Killer still be interested?"

"Still interested, but really pissed off."

"And here I pictured myself looking like Catherine Zeta Jones for a few months. I have a vivid imagination and many unachievable wishes on my list."

"You're a beautiful woman, Sasha. You don't need any physical-enhancement wishes on your list."

Vague humor faded to a sigh when she thought of Kristiana. Skye said she'd been beautiful, inside and out. "What did you mean earlier, Nick, when you said that even serial killers can have friends?"

"I meant someone could be helping him."

"Someone up here, helping Anthony Rush who stalked a woman from Denver to remote little Painter's Bluff? That's a stretch, isn't it, not to mention an incredible co-incidence?"

"If he really did stalk Kristiana to Painter's Bluff, then, yes. If she was a random strike, then it's no stretch at all."

Sasha placed her hands flat on the counter. "Nick, I'm too tired to put your theory through its paces. I thought you believed that Rush stalked Kristiana here. Now you're saying he didn't, or might not have? That he could have come here for whatever reason to hook up with someone, and seeing Kristiana simply brought out the beast, so to speak?"

"That about covers it."

Dragging herself onto a high stool, Sasha attempted to sort her thoughts. "You think Bo Sickerbie might know Anthony Rush?"

"It's possible."

"He'll never admit it if he does."

"Not without the proper inducement."

"So we what, threaten to crush a body part unless he confesses?"

"I could tell him you want to use him for target practice."

"Ah, yes, then there's that little mystery." Still on the

stool, she poured pasta into the bubbling water. "How did you know I could shoot? Have you been Internet spying on me?"

He smiled. "Step away from the stove, and I'll answer you."

"That's a yes. Why? I don't have a criminal record."

He trapped her hands before she could grab the boiling pot. "The first time you ran away from home you were nine. The state police found you hitchhiking west on the highway. At eleven, you stowed away on a westbound train. A year later, you made it to Denver by plane. The FBI showed up on your father's doorstep. They would have arrested him for kidnapping if you hadn't confessed."

"I asked how you knew I could shoot. I know what I did as a child."

"I'm getting to that. After a B and E at your mother's home in London, she stated that she disliked guns, wouldn't have one on the premises. Perversity, Sasha. Your mother hates guns, so you learned to shoot. You learned so well, you became one of the top junior skeet shooters in Kent."

She bared her teeth. "I hate computers."

"How many times did you run away?"

"None of your business." Then she shrugged. "Seven. Four of my attempts weren't reported. Barbara sent her own bloodhounds after me. She could do that because for two and a half years she was married to a private investigator."

Nick stroked the back of Sasha's hand. Such a simple act, such an erotic sensation. Her whole arm tingled.

"Why did you do it?"

She couldn't take her eyes off his long fingers. "Do

what? Oh, run away. Barbara wanted to control me. My brother, Angus, too, but me most of all. She saw herself in me. All the dreams she'd missed out on, I could fulfill for her. I'm not sure I even wanted to be an architect. I only know my mother didn't want it. It's like a reverse control thing, which makes me crazy when I think about it, so I don't." She sent him a level look. "Unless someone forces the issue. And FYI, I was the best junior skeet shooter in Kent. The boy who won the competition had a father with royal connections. He missed two of his targets. I didn't miss any."

"You didn't miss Bo Sickerbie, either."

"He'll heal. If you're interested in my opinion, Nick, I still think Bo's a drunk who's of no use to anyone, particularly a serial killer whose goal is to murder again and again until the demon that's driving him is satisfied."

"Or until he gets caught."

"Or that."

"It was a theory, Sasha, a possibility. As a cop you learn not to close doors. Assumptions will screw you every time, so once in a while you toss out a wild idea."

Sasha had a wild idea of her own right then, and it had nothing to do with Bo Sickerbie, serial killers or friends.

She leaned in again, turned her hand over in his. "Did I mention that you have amazing eyes?"

"I used to stare down cranky bulls as a teenager."

"Now you stare down thieves, killers and women."

A ghost of a smile appeared on his face. "Not too many women these days."

"I find that hard to believe. I mean, come on, Nick, you're a cop, you're gorgeous, you don't appear to have any weird fetishes or phobias."

Lifting her hand, he brought it to his lips, kissed the

tips of her fingers. "You know what they say about appearances."

"That sounds so cryptic. I love it." Her teasing tone resurfaced. "Let me see if I've got you figured out. You were shy as a child, and although you overcame the problem as an adult, you're still the quiet kind. You sit in a corner during a party, drink beer or wine and observe your fellow partygoers."

"Whereas you prefer to dance and socialize."

"I love to dance. I also make the rounds, converse politely and flirt a little, but nothing serious. You want to see a party maven, watch my mother circulate at a black-tie affair sometime. She came to one of my company Christmas parties in Atlanta, and went home with my CEO."

"Sounds embarrassing."

"I quit two weeks later and moved to Philadelphia. But Denver's better. Last Christmas…" She trailed off as an earlier memory popped into her head. "Max."

Nick linked her fingers with his. "What about him?"

"He was talking to Anthony Rush at Mountain House."

His eyes sharpened. "Where?"

"In the lobby, while I was checking in."

"Was it a friendly chat?"

She went over it in her mind. The talking, the gesturing, the interruption. "Not especially. Damn."

Curling his fingers lightly around her jaw, Nick brought her mouth up to his. "Don't worry about it, Sasha. Max doesn't strike me as a good liar."

She smiled against his lips. "That's an assumption if I've ever heard one. You don't know what he is, and as you pointed out this morning, neither do I."

"So we'll wait and see." The kiss he gave her was hot, hard and completely mind numbing. Sasha swore she saw stars for a moment, then realized it was one of Skye's glittering night-lights. Still…

"You do that very well, Nick." So well she wanted to do it again. Instead, she ran a thumb over his lower lip. "But the pasta's ready, and my stomach's in control right now. Just promise me one thing."

"That I'll let you have the bigger plate?"

"So close. Promise you won't question Max without me."

"Deal." He slid his lips over hers as he spoke. "So long as you promise not to use the hair dye in your bathroom."

The temperature dipped as the night wore on. Luckily, one of the cabins, a muddy-looking structure with one window, and a door attached with rawhide strips, had a fire pit in the corner. Someone had spent time here, if not this winter, then last. There were logs piled next to the pit and a stack of yellowed newspapers beside it.

It would do for the night. He'd eat the candy bars in his pocket, sip the whiskey in his flask, clean his gun and maybe even sleep. He wouldn't get caught.

He heard his mother's disdainful "Humph" behind him and swung to face the door.

His flashlight revealed a bare room, but that meant nothing. She could appear out of nowhere, had done it countless times when he'd been young. There she'd be, breathing down his neck, smelling like mouthwash and vanilla. God, how he'd hated those smells, and her. No wonder his father had abandoned them.

He laid his candy bars, four of them, out on a dusty

bench. Shining the light on the fire pit, he began stacking twigs.

Tomorrow would be better. The dark was always a problem. In daylight, the shadows vanished and with them any possibility of his mother sneaking in to spy on him.

He didn't realize he was holding a dried twig until he snapped it in two. He heard her derisive snort and brought the pieces up like knives.

"Go to hell," he shouted. "Go there, stay there and leave me alone."

"Stupid boy," she whispered in his head. "You've been alone for years. Ever since the day you killed me."

Chapter 7

"This is ridiculous." Max paced back and forth like an arcade duck on Skye's boat dock. "If you brought me out here to freeze a confession out of me, then we're all going to die, because I don't know what the hell you're talking about. Come on, Sasha, you can't seriously believe I'd be in cahoots with a serial killer. I design road systems. I'm in line to become a partner."

Nick could see that Sasha felt bad for starting this. She set a hand on his arm. "I know you're not in league with him, Max, but Detective Law doesn't. Answer his questions truthfully, and we can all go back to the lodge."

Max pulled down the earflaps on his hat and stomped his feet. "I told you, I don't know the guy. He asked me for directions to a smoke shop. I guess he thought I was a smoker."

Nick hoisted himself onto a pylon. "So instead of

going to the front desk, which would have been logical, one guest asked another guest for information. Sounds unlikely to me."

"I don't care how it sounds, that's how it was."

Sasha gnawed on her lip. "What else did he say, Max?"

"The usual things. I mentioned that there wasn't much to do at night in Painter's Bluff. He agreed, said he hated small towns, but that's where back roads lead, so you always wound up staying in one at some point."

Nick watched his face. "Did he mention knowing anyone there?"

"No, but he asked about renting a truck, wanted to know where I'd gotten mine."

"Did he seem nervous?"

"Maybe some. I wasn't paying close attention. Believe me, if I'd known he was a serial killer, I'd have been shouting for the sheriff." Max wiggled gloved fingers to check his circulation. "Sasha, tell him you were three days late, and that if you'd arrived as planned, we'd have been up here at Skye's lodge, far away from Mountain House and Anthony Rush. I wouldn't have been there, so he couldn't have asked me for directions, and we wouldn't be having this conversation."

"He has a point," Sasha agreed. "I was late getting to town."

Nick considered for a moment, then made a subtle head motion. "Go on back to the lodge, Macallum."

"If you want to do something," Sasha suggested, "you could try fixing Skye's two-way radio."

"Dana's working on that." Mollified by her encouraging tone, Max shoved his hands in his pockets. "But maybe I can help him."

Nick hopped from the pylon. "Actually, we'll go back with you."

"Oh, goody, a police escort. I feel so privileged."

Sasha watched Max clomp away. "You know, I *was* late arriving, and he does have an excellent reputation as an engineer. We've hurt his feelings, suspecting him. Let him pay us back and brood awhile." She pulled a second pair of gloves from her pocket. "Why are we going back? I thought you wanted to search for Rush."

"I do." Nick studied Max's receding figure. "Will and Dana are going to help us. Unless you'd rather stay inside with Skye."

"Thanks, but I've had enough indoor time today. I showed Skye my blueprints and told her to flag what she wants me to change. She'll be immersed for the rest of the day."

"Tell her to keep her shotgun on the table."

"Don't you think that's a bit drastic?"

"Maybe." Nick cast a thoughtful look at the boathouse behind her. "But I talked to Will last night. Before he met his wife, Molly, twenty-five years ago, Bo Sickerbie had a girlfriend named Leanne. Apparently they had a volatile relationship. Two days before her seventeenth birthday, Leanne's body was discovered in Painter's Creek."

"I feel like a nineteenth-century outlaw heading up to Hole in the Wall." Sasha drew in a deep breath. She almost had to trot to keep up with Nick's longer stride. "The coats are cool, though. And Skye even gave us black earmuffs and Stetsons." To match the long black sheepskin coats, courtesy of their hostess, that would keep them warm, even in the biting wind.

Nick glanced sideways. "Yeah, thank God we're co-ordinated."

Sasha held her hat on as the wind gusted. "You don't have to be sarcastic, Nick. I'm only making conversation so you won't think about the cold, and I won't think about Anthony Rush. Are we checking brother Sam's burrow first or second?"

"First, if we can find it. Will and Dana are searching the buildings closest to the lodge." Nick squinted at a distant structure that had tilted a good fifteen degrees over the years. "That could be one of the smokehouses Skye mentioned."

"If it is, I'll stay outside. I don't want to see a deer carcass hanging from the rafters."

"It's food, Sasha, sustenance. Survival."

Ignoring him, she repositioned the shoulder strap of her rifle. "Skye says there's a farmhouse over the rise and about half a mile west. Her father used to store salvaged wood and tools inside."

"Smokehouse first, then burrow, then farmhouse."

Sasha's footsteps slowed as they approached the tipped structure. She swung her rifle down. "I'll stand guard."

Nick smiled. "Coward."

"City girl," she reminded him, and leaned against the outer wall.

It took him only a few minutes to explore the interior. "Any deer?" she asked when he emerged.

"Three, but no sign of an intruder."

Sasha used the end of the rifle to push her hat up. "I told Skye about Bo's dead girlfriend. She was living in Denver at the time, but she remembers hearing about it. She said Leanne had been seeing some guy from Virginia Dale that year. Story was she'd dumped Bo six months earlier, but Bo, being Bo, wasn't prepared to be the dumpee, so he'd show up wherever she went, often drunk and invariably looking for a fight. The sheriff arrested him twice for threatening to pound the guy's face to a pulp and feed it to his daddy's pigs."

"Then he married Molly and created six kids in his own image."

"Well, hey, isn't that what procreation's all about? My mother thinks it is, and in case I haven't mentioned this, she's never wrong."

"Lucky mother." Nick nodded to the right. "Burrow's this way."

Snowflakes drifted down from the gray-white sky. Sasha caught one on her tongue, then saw Nick looking at her and laughed. "You did play in the snow as a kid, right?"

"Dana and I had a few snowball fights."

"I bet. How did you meet him?"

"When I was six, I bloodied his nose on behalf of my female cousin. He pulled her pigtails and stole her lunch box."

"A defender of the public even then."

"There were two first grade classrooms at our school. Dana kept sneaking out of his and into mine. He used to hide behind me. I didn't blame him. Every boy in school had a crush on my teacher, Miss Miller. No one liked Dana's teacher. She smelled like liniment and had a mustache."

"Lovely sensory image, Nick. So as boys tend to do, after you fought, you became best friends."

"Until we were twelve. Then his family moved to Denver."

"But you kept in touch."

"He visited his grandparents in Outlaw Falls every summer. We got our first case of poison oak together."

"That's so touching." The snow grew deeper the farther they ventured into the woods. "Do you know his wife?"

"Yeah, I know her. I was best man at their wedding."

"Is she like your ex-wife?"

He gave a soft laugh. "Well, that's subtle."

"Hey, I'm up to my knees in snow. I don't have the energy for subtle. If you don't want to answer, you can just tell me to shut up. My brother does it all the time."

"Are you close?"

"Absolutely. Angus and I are best friends, allies and coconspirators. My mother thinks he's in Europe right now, but he's really in Australia. By the time her European sources inform her that he's nowhere to be found on the Continent, he'll be in Malaysia. At which time I'll tell her he left Europe and went to Australia."

Nick made a quick but thorough scan of the surrounding area. "You live in a complex world, Sasha."

"Unlike you, whose life is an ongoing process of sifting through the remnants of unsolved crimes, searching for any speck of dust or dandruff that shouldn't be there." At his sidelong look, she held up her hands. "Honestly, Nick, I admire your dedication, but it has to be a bit of a drain on your emotions."

"It has its moments."

Except for the crunching snow, they walked in silence for several hundred yards. When Sasha spied a door set into a hillock, she assumed they'd found the burrow.

"My ex's name was Lacey," Nick remarked out of the blue.

Curious, Sasha slowed her footsteps. "It's a pretty name."

"She's a pretty woman. We were married for three years. One was good, two were rocky. She couldn't be a cop's wife."

"More women probably can't than can, Nick. Sheriff Pyle's wife couldn't handle it. And he couldn't handle her. Something about a domineering attitude, but we didn't delve too deeply into that."

Nick's expression went from mild surprise to amusement. "You talked to Will about his marriage?"

"Actually, he talked to me—while you were talking to Bo, and Skye was admiring Dana's butt."

"I didn't need to hear that."

"So I guess you don't want to know what she thinks about your butt." Sasha endeavored not to pant, but the snow was over her knees now. "Will said his wife left him after he took a bullet for the third time."

"Injuries happen. It's an occupational hazard."

"Have you ever been shot?"

"Once."

Sasha' s breath stalled in her throat.

"A thief got me in the shoulder while he was stealing a car."

She set her jaw. "I hope they put him away for a very long time."

Nick inspected the hillock from all angles. "They didn't have to." Leaning close to her ear, he asked, "Are you coming in this time?"

Unsure how to respond, she merely nodded.

The door opened inward, which saved them from having to dig out the area in front of it. Clearly, no one had been inside the place for years, possibly decades.

Sasha picked up a rusty coffeepot and dangled it by its handle. "Ptomaine must have been rampant in the nineteenth century."

Nick roamed the single large room. Even with the door open and a smoke hole cut through the hilltop, they needed flashlights. He angled the beam upward, circled it. "A cave would have been more hospitable."

"Everything they drank must have tasted like metal." Sasha examined an old tin cup. Two dead spiders and a large claw dropped out when she turned it over. "I'd bet you my commissions for a year that cousin Sam never married."

Nick leaned over her shoulder. "If you're finished examining the dishes, we can go. Rush hasn't been here. I want to see the farmhouse you mentioned."

"It couldn't be worse than this place." She was tempted to bury her face in Nick's neck and inhale, but she quelled the urge and simply escaped. "Skye said the farm was due west of here." She looked up as they emerged. "Which would be a helpful direction if we could see the sun. Where's west?"

Nick chuckled. "Not a Girl Guide, huh? Have you even tried camping?"

She swung the rifle strap onto her shoulder. "Twice with my father. He called me a good sport, and took me to a hotel for dinner."

"I'm impressed."

She waited until he secured the door before grabbing the front of his black coat and yanking his head down for a kiss. "You're not yet," she said with a challenging twinkle. "But before we get off his mountain, Detective Cowboy, you will be."

* * *

Skye's half a mile turned into a mile and a half. Nick wouldn't have made the trek, except he knew Rush must have taken shelter somewhere last night. And if he hadn't, there was always the chance they'd stumble over his frozen body.

Sasha kept pace with seeming ease, which was a good act since her stride length was at best three-quarters of his. Nick admired her for not complaining or even asking him to slow down. He did so, anyway, as they began a steep uphill climb.

He knew two things: they had to find Anthony Rush. And Nick had to stop kissing her. It was becoming a habit, a bad one that felt incredibly good, but was screwing up his brain and punching the hell out of his emotions.

He heard her murmur something, and glanced over. "Problem?"

"Not at all, because, as I've been telling myself for the past half mile, I go to the gym, I go to the gym, I go to the gym. Are you sure this is west?"

"House should be at the top of the hill." His lips curved. "I talked to Skye, too."

Her laugh made his stomach muscles tighten and his throat go dry. So much for self-restraint.

Swinging her rifle down, she used the butt end as a walking stick. "Are hills bigger in the northern part of Colorado than they are in the south? No, don't answer that. I go to the gym."

He shortened his stride a little more. "Lacey didn't like working out. She hated being hot and sweaty."

"You should have told her gyms have shower rooms. Anyway, I'm not especially hot right now."

He frowned. "Are you cold?"

"Relax, Detective. I'm fine. I want to slide back down this hill, though."

"I'll see what I can arrange. What is it?" he asked when she stopped walking and stared.

She pointed ahead. "The house."

Hidden behind a clump of trees, and a hundred yards away, it was in critical condition. Nick marveled that it was still standing.

"I don't see any footprints," Sasha noted.

"So if he's up there, we can be sure he didn't approach from the east."

She sighed. "You just don't like conversation at all, do you?"

They trudged onward, and when they emerged from the trees she halted again, this time in surprise. "Wow. My mother's Smoky Mountain relatives live in nicer shacks. Oops." She sent him a wicked smile. "I'm not supposed to talk about them. Tennessee cousins, on her father's side. Her cousin's daughter showed me how to make grits for breakfast one day. My mother never forgave her."

"What were you and your mother doing in Tennessee?"

"Her father, my grandfather, died. He wanted to be buried with other members of his family. I think in spite of everything, she loved him, so she went to the funeral, simple as that."

At the front of the house, less than a third of the front porch and only two of the outer steps remained.

"These look…" Kicking off the snow, Sasha tested her weight on the lowest one. It snapped in two beneath her foot. "…really unsafe."

Nick eyed the warped door. No one had used this entrance recently. "Let's try the back."

"Rush weighs more than you do, Nick. Twenty pounds more would be my estimate. One wrong step on a board that has either wet or dry rot, and he'd be on a fast track to the cellar."

"The wood out here's been exposed to the elements. It might not be as bad inside."

"Uh-huh." She gave him a nudge from behind. "Your theory, not mine. You go first."

Nick spotted a side entrance partway around the house. The door opened with a solid shove and led straight into what had once been a large country kitchen. A wood-burning stove, undoubtedly used for cooking, stood on the far wall. A tangle of harnesses and several mildewed blankets sat on top of it.

Sasha explored the room with care. "If you erase all the dirt and cobwebs, it's like stepping out of a time machine and into the past." One of the flat burners shrieked in protest as she twisted it free. "Can you imagine baking bread in this monstrosity?"

She opened a nearby door. "I think I found the pantry," she said, rooting around the dust-encrusted shelves. "Personally, I'd have stayed in Boston or St. Louis or whatever city I happened to live in, and waved goodbye to the departing wagon trains. God help me, I sound like my mother, but I really couldn't have handled such a rustic life."

Nick meanwhile found a door of his own. Shining his flashlight, he inspected the narrow ladder staircase. It couldn't be the only way up to the second floor, he reasoned. There had to be a central stairwell somewhere in the middle of the house. Still, he decided to take it.

"I'm going up," he called back. "Don't fall through any floors while I'm gone."

"No problem. I'll stand here and try to figure out why Skye's father put twenty bottles of dirt in the pantry cupboard."

Smiling slightly, Nick tested the bottom step. The treads felt solid enough. However, two steps from the top he heard the wood split, and swore. The handrail held for a fraction of a second, before it cracked as well.

The last thing he saw as he plunged downward was the sawtooth edge of the broken step rushing up to meet his face.

Sasha heard the prolonged crack and the series of crashes that followed.

"Nick?" Scrambling to her feet, she rushed to the door of the stairwell and braced her hands on either side. "Nick?"

Panic clawed at her, but she reined it in and, pulling out her flashlight, started upward.

"Nick?" She wouldn't sound frantic, she promised herself. "Where are you?"

She zigzagged her beam over the treads. When it landed on the broken one, her stomach dropped. "Oh God."

Using the more stable outer edges, she climbed. She called his name, but received no response. On the last unbroken step, she knelt—and felt the wood sag precariously under her knees.

"Nick, are you down there?"

Afraid to breathe, she peered into the black hole. Her flashlight revealed nothing but broken beams, a crisscrossed maze of them, so many she couldn't see to the bottom.

"So there must be a basement," she reasoned.

Scrambling up, she hurried back to the kitchen. Could she access the cellar from inside? Given what she knew about Colorado farmhouses, it seemed unlikely. But a new owner might have altered the structure at a later date.

Something, possibly a floorboard, creaked loudly in another area of the house. "Nick?" His name echoed through the silence that followed.

Another creak reached her, this one much closer.

Hope rippled through her. She picked her way across the kitchen, planted her hands on the swinging door— and watched it land on the floor like a felled tree.

The dust cloud that sprayed up all but choked her. Eyes watering, she stepped over it.

"Nick, are you out here?"

The boards stopped creaking, but something banged hard to her left. Pressing the heel of her hand to her heart, she shot an accusing look at the loose shutter that continued to slam against the outer wall.

"I really hate derelict houses." Dropping her hand, she used her buoyed adrenaline to combat fear. "Where are you, Nick? I swear, if you're hurt and I have to hike back to the lodge for help, I'm going to…" Fear won out, and she released a shaky breath. "Please don't be hurt."

A short hallway led from the front of the house to the rear. At the end, she spied a promising door.

Because the knob was missing, she had to stick her fingers through the hole left behind. "Nick?" She tried again.

Still no answer.

She needed both hands to shift the door even six inches, although she had no idea why. If anything, it appeared to have shrunk with age. Or maybe it never had fit properly. Anchoring herself, she gave a mighty tug.

It popped open as if it hadn't been stuck, surprising her. Her own momentum sent her stumbling backward. She regained her balance and grabbed the edge before it could swing closed.

"I really hate old buildings," she repeated.

Then her heart leaped into her throat as a man's face sprang from the shadows, and a pair of hands snaked out to grasp her arms.

Chapter 8

Everything swung in large black circles, the basement, the broken boards, the beam from his still-illuminated flashlight.

Pieces of wood clattered to the ground when Nick sat up. His breath steamed around his face, adding to the disorienting effect. He'd fallen from the roof of a bunkhouse when he was ten, had fractured his arm and four ribs. He couldn't remember being in any more pain then than he was right now.

He felt something wet and sticky at his hairline and knew it was blood. But he'd had deep cuts before. He'd focus, figure out where he was, and get the hell out of here so he could find Sasha.

Standing with difficulty, Nick bent and breathed until the dizziness threatening to undermine his balance subsided.

Sasha was upstairs. She'd be looking for him. His head came up; the fog in his brain cleared. He'd noticed something before he'd fallen, at the top of the staircase. Footprints, several of them in the dust, as if someone on the second floor had considered using the ladder to descend, but decided against it.

Still bent, Nick breathed out one last time. They could be Rush's prints. If they were, and the man was still here, Nick had walked Sasha straight into a trap.

Fighting the dizziness, he swept his light around the space. He'd fallen through a grid work of old beams and boards, probably hammered in place to shore up the sagging floors and walls. The house was a death trap. Perhaps in more ways than one.

He located an interior hatch on the third sweep. There were no stairs leading up to it, only another crisscrossing welter of beams that a child might enjoy scaling, but not a full-grown man who was still seeing stars.

Dropping the flashlight in his pocket, he caught hold of the first beam. It groaned but held.

Surprisingly, the two-by-fours worked better than a ladder. Nick used a fist to knock the hatch back, and hauled himself through the opening.

"Sasha?" Moving his jaw from side to side, he cleared his throat. "Sasha, where are you?"

Years of working the Chicago Homicide Division kicked in. He picked up the muffled scrapes and shuffles of a struggle in progress. Where? On his knees, he held himself perfectly still and listened. Somewhere at the rear of the house, he realized and, drawing his gun, took off at a run.

The sounds grew louder. He heard a man grunt, followed by Sasha's stifled gasp. Of pain? Nick swore and forced his legs to carry him through the living room toward a darkened hallway.

He made it to the opening, had just positioned himself to make a one-eighty swing, when footsteps began to pound across the floorboards.

Nick gripped his gun, spun out. "Police."

A man barreled into him, shoved hard and kept going. Off balance, Nick managed two shots. One embedded itself in wood. He had no idea where the other went.

He swung back, ran down the hall. "Sasha?" Fear created an icy lump in his throat. He recognized it even if he couldn't remember feeling it before. "Where are you?"

"Right here."

She appeared so suddenly that he almost knocked her over.

"What…?" He caught her arms and a portion of his breath. "Are you all right?" He inspected her face, pushed back her hat. "He didn't hurt you?"

"He hit me." She ran her own hands through his hair, looked frightened when her fingers came out red and sticky. "You're bleeding. Nick, I heard a gun. What happened? Did he shoot you?"

"It was mine." He calmed himself in order to calm her. "I'm fine. You're fine. He's gone."

"It was Rush." She searched the pockets of her jeans for a tissue, couldn't find one and wound up using the cuff of her white top to dab at his forehead. "Don't move. Let me see. That's a deep cut."

"You said it was Rush," he prompted, stilling her hands. "Where was he? What did he do?"

"He was behind a door, the basement door I thought, but it was a closet of some kind. I couldn't get it open at first, but then I did, and there he was. He grabbed me. I kicked him and he threw me against the wall. Then he grabbed me again, and I fought him. That's when we heard you. He started to drag me with him, maybe to use as a shield, but he let go when I kicked him in the leg. I think I pulled out some of his hair. We should go look."

Nick held her in place. He wanted her to stand still so he could check her again for injuries. "Don't worry about the hair. We can't test for DNA up here, anyway."

"What if he gets off the mountain?"

Nick lowered his head. The dizziness had returned. "He won't get off. I might have shot him, I'm not sure. Doesn't matter. He's as trapped as we are."

Hauling her up against him, he dropped his cheek against her hair and ordered himself to breathe. Rush was gone, and Sasha was safe. Nick could live with any other problems.

"I thought you might have been impaled on a beam."

He felt her trembling, and tightened his hold. "It would have made for an interesting headline."

"Oh, really catchy." He heard the reluctant amusement in her voice. "Colorado Farmhouse Kills Cold Case Detective." She bunched her fingers in his hair. "Can we go now?"

"Yeah, we can go." He kissed the side of her neck. "Just as soon as we find something to use for a sled."

They really did slide down the hill. Not for fun, although in spite of herself Sasha enjoyed the ride, but because sliding conserved energy. By the time they staggered back to the lodge, night had fallen.

As much as she wanted to, Nick refused to let her make a fuss over his wounds.

"It's a cop thing," Skye remarked wryly. "Men are

complete babies most of the time. Unless they're cops. Then they're superhuman. My first husband's brother was a physician. He said it astounded him how many injured officers wouldn't take their full recuperation entitlement. Broken leg, no problem. Put me in a walking cast, and I'm good to go. Your boyfriend could have multiple cracked ribs, and the only person who'll ever know about them is him."

"We'll see about that." Sasha leaned her elbows on the kitchen table and pushed on her throbbing temples. "Why is it, Skye, that when something dramatic happens you don't feel it until the drama's over and you're home and safe?"

"Human defense mechanism. When we're safe, we can feel. Until then, we react."

"I wouldn't mind feeling a little less right now." Sasha was silent for a moment. "He's not my boyfriend."

"Bit of a delayed reaction, wouldn't you say?"

"I'm running on half power. It slows down the rest of the functions."

"Similar to air generators."

Concern crept in. "How much fuel do we have?"

"Oh, plenty." Skye opened and closed cupboards. "There's a large holding tank under the car barn, as well as several drums of propane. I just prefer to conserve my resources whenever possible." She chuckled. "As for my commodities, specifically money, I'm a bit less miserly. I didn't hire you, Sasha, because of your company's rates. A business associate recommended you."

"Regan told me. Not that we're complaining, but we've never quite figured out how your associate got our name. Did he say anything to you?"

"Nothing except you're talented and forward thinking, you pay attention to details, and you listen to your clients' wants and needs."

"That's some recommendation."

"The designs you showed me today are dead-on, if you'll pardon the term. I'm looking forward to working with you." Having said that, she pawed through one of the upper cupboards. "Someone around here likes brown beans and pears. And tomato juice."

Sasha's smile felt a bit surreal. Must be the aspirin. She'd taken five so far, and they hadn't made a dent in her headache. "You did tell us to help ourselves, Skye."

"And I meant it. I'm probably more attuned to children than adults. Ice cream, cookies and chips go first when my grandkids visit. Then it's soda, frozen pizza and—"

"You have frozen pizza?" At Skye's raised eyebrows, she chuckled. "My mother says I have the taste buds of a twelve-year-old. She's not far wrong."

Skye jotted down items. "There are pizzas, ice cream and even French fries in the storage shed. We'll call it the tweenage larder. Take a couple of canvas sacks and load up whatever you want."

Sasha pocketed the list. "Shed's behind the car barn, right?"

"It's the building with the white door. My youngest grandson's idea. He figured that since all the outbuildings were constructed to resemble miniature log houses, the doors at least should be painted different colors for identification purposes."

"Sounds like a designer in the making." Sasha removed the long black coat from a peg and twirled it on.

"Take a hat," Skye reminded her, still going through cupboards. "The sacks are in the mudroom bench. And you should take one of those." She nodded at the gun cabinet. "A pistol will probably do."

"Skye, don't you think—"

"Why don't we ask Nick what he thinks? I believe he's upstairs butting heads with Will."

"Just what he needs, more shots to the head." She used the key Skye had given her to unlock the glass cabinet, and chose a sleek black gun. To coordinate with her ensemble, she reflected with a smile. Hat, boots and gloves on, she left the lodge through the side door and crunched through the snow toward the storage shed.

Finally, the moon and stars had come out. Black clouds tipped with silver drifted across the night sky, but not enough of them to blot out an almost full moon. The air smelled fresh and crisp, and the wind had dropped from a blustery twenty to a barely perceptible five miles an hour.

Sasha picked out the Dippers as she walked, and Orion's belt. The sky was breathtaking in the western mountains, much more so than any other place she'd lived. Too bad her mother had never appreciated it.

Then again, had Barbara ever appreciated anything? Or anyone?

Shaking the depressing questions away, Sasha located the white door. She hoped belatedly that it wouldn't be locked, because Skye hadn't given her a key. Setting a hand on the knob, she twisted. And only paused a moment when she remembered Anthony Rush's face popping out at her back at the farmhouse.

But that had been another place and time. Marshaling her defenses, she gave the door a firm shove.

Nothing and no one appeared. Unfortunately, the light inside was minimal at best, a single low-watt bulb that didn't fully illuminate the crowded room. She knew the shed was composed of three similar rooms, running in a straight line from front to back. Naturally, the freezer and food stores were in the third.

Sasha picked her way across the floor. For some reason, likely residual nerves, her skin began to prickle. Silly, she told herself. Rush wouldn't come here. He'd be a fool to venture so close to the lodge.

On the other hand, the shed door hadn't been locked, and if bears grew bold when threatened with hunger, why not people?

"Don't," she ordered herself. "Rush isn't a bear, he's a man, with a brain." Her footsteps slowed. "A murderer, with a twisted brain." And halted. "A cold-blooded killer, with a homicidal brain."

She needed to lose those thoughts right now, to remain calm and think clearly. There was no danger for her inside a building that stood only a few dozen yards from the lodge. One scream, and Nick would come running. If she knew that, so would Anthony Rush. She hoped.

She twitched her shoulders to shed the prickles on her skin. Despite her best efforts, however, the eerie sensation lingered, that feeling of being watched, of something evil lurking in the dark. Shadows loomed everywhere, in all the corners and several of the spots between. There had to be fifty crates in the room, plus an equal number of human-size burlap bags. She also counted four stacks of tires and five or six mountain bikes.

Her boot heels made a flat sound on the wooden floor. She thought she heard a click ahead of her and paused midstep. Then the door behind her creaked softly, and she spun.

Dana jumped, held up his hands. "Whoa, hang on,

Sasha, it's me." His eyes glued themselves to the gun currently aimed at his head. "I saw you come out here. I didn't think you should be alone."

She lowered her weapon a bit, breathed out a gusty sigh of relief. "I saw Anthony Rush's face when you walked through that door, Dana."

He pushed her shooting hand down. "Aim that at the floor, okay? The thought of a bullet anywhere below the waist scares the hell out of me."

She barely smiled. The tension in her arms was making her tremble all over. Then she remembered the other sound she'd heard, and spun in the opposite direction.

"What is it?" an edgy Dana demanded.

"I heard a click before you came in."

He came up alongside her, regarded the door ahead.

"It might have been ice on the roof." She kept the trigger cocked, wished her heart would slow its frantic beating. "Falling ice could sound like a click, couldn't it?"

"Hey, I'll accept anything that isn't connected to Rush."

Sasha was just beginning to breathe normally when the sound reached her again, a tiny snap that might as well have been cannon fire. "Okay, now that definitely wasn't ice."

Dana ran nervous palms along the sides of his coat. "I guess we have to look, huh?"

She stared, incredulous. "Why?"

"I don't know. What if it's Rush?"

"Well, I don't want to meet him again, do you?"

"Are you nuts? I'm no hero. You're right, let's do the smart thing and go get—"

In her peripheral vision Sasha detected the movement just as Dana did. Long fingers clamped on to her arm.

Whirling, she came up short, with a muffled gasp and a curse that hissed out through her teeth. "Nick!"

He pressed a hand over her mouth, shook his head at Dana for silence and nodded forward. "Someone's back there."

Sasha pried his hand away. "We know that. We were coming to get you."

"We were," Dana confirmed in a whisper. "It could be Bo we're hearing, though. I was watching him, but he fell asleep, so I decided to work on the radio. When I went to check on him fifteen minutes ago, I couldn't find him."

"Go back to the lodge," Nick said in Sasha's ear. "You wanted to a minute ago," he reminded her, when she huffed.

"Only to find you. I'm not a coward, Nick."

"I don't know. You let a killer get away earlier today."

She should have been irritated by his teasing tone, but it was so unlike him that she actually felt a smile bubble up. "Don't tell me I'm rubbing off on you, Detective. Using humor in the face of fear? I wonder if that attitude won wars."

"I doubt it." His response was dry.

A protracted scrape had Dana's hands balling at his sides.

"That sounded like a window sliding upward," Sasha warned.

Drawing his gun, Nick tapped the mayor's shoulder. "Stay behind me." He gave Sasha's waist a cautioning squeeze. "Both of you. We'll go in fast."

As it turned out, they went in so fast the middle room passed by in a blur. Sasha glimpsed machinery, and very nearly got tangled in a bale of barbed wire. She offered

Dana a grateful smile for helping her unhook, and ran after Nick to the final door.

He kicked it in, braced and took aim. "Police!"

She knew he intended it as a warning, but couldn't see that or anything else stopping Rush. Desperate people took desperate chances.

Frigid air slapped her cheeks from across the room. "He went through the window, Nick." She regarded the double latches. "No wonder he made so much noise. Those things are impossible to open."

Nick gave the corners of the room a cursory inspection before climbing out and hopping into the snow. He switched on his flashlight. "Stay here. I'll be right back."

Dana seemed prepared to obey, but Sasha jumped out after Nick.

"Have you gone deaf since this afternoon?"

"No. What I've done is learn that, one, there's some kind of creepy connection between Anthony Rush and creaking doors, and two, I tend to run into him when you're not around. He could be anywhere, Nick, and I'd rather be the hunter than the hunted."

"We won't be hunting far in the dark. I only want to know which direction he took." He looked around. "Keep your gun out and your flashlight on. Stay behind me."

"Yes, I've got that one memorized." She ran her beam in a straight line toward the lake. "The footprints lead that way."

Nick glanced through the window. "Dana, go back to the lodge and tell Pyle what we're doing. Make sure Skye locks all the doors and windows."

"Okay, but don't go out on the lake. Skye says there are already cracks in the surface."

The moon reflected off the snow, illuminating every

open expanse between the shed and the lake. Only a dense copse of trees to the east remained in darkness.

Sasha trotted up alongside Nick. "There's a stream that feeds the lake and flows through those woods. Since most of the snow's blown off the ice, Rush wouldn't have to worry about leaving footprints. He could find the frozen stream and follow it into the trees."

"Looks like that's what he did." Nick regarded the tracks, which ended at the edge of the lake.

"Skye told me those woods go on for miles at this altitude."

"Good to know."

Curious, she tilted her head. "Do you skate?"

He studied the ice, seemed to register the question as an afterthought. "I played hockey for a few years."

"On lakes?"

"Occasionally."

"Would you recognize unsafe ice if you saw it?"

"Not at night."

"So Rush might fall through, after all." She shivered, rubbed her arms. "Problem solved."

As she'd anticipated, Nick's attention shifted to her. "You're more bloodthirsty than I would have thought."

"What you mean is I'm self-centered and unfeeling because I could actually wish another human being dead. But I wouldn't wish him dead, Nick, if I thought he'd be caught and no one else would die. I wouldn't even wish it if I was the only one in danger. But I think everyone up here is at risk. If he could murder eight women for his own twisted reasons, why not a lodgeful of people in order to survive? If he can be captured, fine. If not, and someone has to die, I hope it's him. Can we go back now?"

"Yeah, we can go back."

Nick caught her hand before she could turn, and pulled her into his arms. Tipping her hat back with his finger, he kissed her.

It wasn't a long kiss, it wasn't greedy or hot or hard. But she felt it down to her toes. And that was saying something, Sasha reflected, because she'd worn the wrong boots and her feet were numb with cold.

His hands made a long, slow slide down the sides of her body. Both her heart and her stomach made the slide with them.

When he lifted his head, she had to remind herself to breathe.

He touched his nose to hers. "I wasn't serious about you being bloodthirsty. I understand how you feel. But I think we're all operating on an assumption. We're taking for granted that Rush is the serial killer."

It seemed like a fairly safe assumption from Sasha's point of view—although at the moment, and still reeling from Nick's kiss, her mind was a trifle hazy. She coaxed it into gear and took a necessary step back. "He bolted when you started asking questions, Nick. He was staying in the room directly across from Kristiana Felgard at Mountain House. He arrived in town right before she died. He has a gash or something on his right hand, and…" She trailed off, tapped a finger on his shoulder. "I didn't mention that before, did I?"

"A gash?" Nick stared straight into her eyes. "Are you sure?"

"I am, yes. I don't know how that slipped my mind. His hand was wrapped in a rag when he grabbed me. It slipped during our struggle. I saw the cut. It wasn't new, but it looked nasty."

She could almost see Nick's mind processing the information. The expression in his eyes went from intense interest to speculation, to calculation.

She arched a brow. "Do you still think we're making assumptions about him?"

"We are, but they're sounding more and more valid."

"So that guilt I was feeling for what I said about possibly wanting him dead was totally unnecessary."

"I wasn't trying to make you feel guilty, Sasha. You were frightened. It's a natural reaction."

"Uh-huh. Tell me, is Psychology 101 a prerequisite at the police academy?"

"You're not the only one who went to college, you know." His gaze skimmed the lake. "You're right to believe he'd kill for food and shelter. Will and I talked about it earlier. Knowing how close Rush is and how desperate he's become, we decided that as of tonight one of us is going to stand guard inside the lodge while everyone else sleeps."

"You think it's gone beyond serial killings now, don't you?"

"To a point. One thing I'm sure of is that no matter how many of us he picks off first, he'll make certain you're the last one left alive."

He'd missed her. He could have had her tonight, could have hauled her into the woods, found a patch of virgin snow and choked the air from her lungs. But instead he was alone and cold, so very, very cold.

The monster snapped its angry jaws inside him. He tightened his own in response. Interference wouldn't be tolerated again. Next time he'd do it and to hell with anyone who blundered in.

He pictured her in the snow where she belonged. A beautiful blonde on the surface, with a heart of ice inside. How could an icy heart beat? How would that heart feel when a portion of it was chipped away? Would it melt or stop beating altogether?

He had no answer for that, wasn't even sure the questions mattered anymore. He felt confused and alone up here, cut off from all but one of his lifelines. He needed to eat and sleep, to restructure and regroup. The monster must allow him that much.

"Be patient," he said to soothe it. Then, closing his eyes, he rocked back and forth until it tumbled into a fitful slumber.

Chapter 9

Will took the initial night watch, because Sasha was convinced that Nick had a mild concussion, and sleep was the best remedy for it. Too bad sleep came with dreams, and every dream he'd had lately invariably descended into a nightmare.

Since it didn't seem fair to dump all the unpleasant tasks on Will's shoulders, Nick and Dana agreed to take turns babysitting their prisoner. Not that Nick believed he'd run, but the possibility existed that Bo was in league with Anthony Rush. In fact, Dana thought Bo might have been trying to help him tonight.

"How do we know it was Rush in the storage shed?" he demanded as the two men lounged in the den. "It could have been Bo. Maybe they have some kind of sordid history. You and I went to school together, why not Sickerbie and Rush, as well?" His hands became props as the idea expanded. "Maybe Rush killed Bo's teenage girlfriend for him. Stabbed her and tossed her in the water. Rush could have had a thing for her that Bo never knew about. I wonder if she had blond hair?" He blew upward at his own curls. "Are you with me on this, Nick?"

"Not really."

"But it makes sense, doesn't it? Well, okay, why not?"

"Because after you lost him tonight, Skye discovered Bo in her son-in-law's bedroom, going through his closet. Looking for money'd be my guess. That was about the same time we were outside in the shed."

"Ah, well, so much for the inner sleuth. Truth is, I can't even tell when one of my kids is lying to me. Fawn, either. I hate to think what'll happen when the young ones go through puberty. Our boy's into everything now. No shelf is safe. We bought a big lockbox before Christmas, some ancient chest the former mayor was selling. The key's one of those old-fashioned deals, unwieldy, but it has a solid lock. That takes care of Bobby. As for Jessica…" He took a sip of beer. "Did I mentioned she has a crush on you? Just turned twelve. She's what they call a tweenager now. Anyway, she thinks you're totally hot, like a rock star."

"Great, now I'll feel uncomfortable every time I set foot in your house."

"Don't worry, it'll pass by summer. She'll move on to one of the neighbor's kids."

"Or one of the Sickerbie boys."

"Well now there's a comforting thought. Thanks a lot, old friend." Stretched out on the floor in the den, Dana watched the flames in the fireplace flicker and dance. "Man, I can't believe we're thirty-six already. Where does time go, Nick?"

"Don't look at me. When I get buried in a cold case, time eludes me."

"Do you ever see Lacey?"

"Once, about six years ago."

"She still hate the cop scene?"

"Now and forever. We got married too young, Dana. I was twenty and heading for the police academy. She was naive as hell. We both were."

"Fawn and I married young. Hardly even knew each other when we walked down the aisle. You'd known Lacey for what, three years? When it's right, it's right. Lacey never felt right to me."

"Thanks for the retrospective. Do you have any other belated advice to offer?"

"No, just a smug smile from time to time and the hope that you'll eventually settle down."

A brief silence reigned between them. Dana closed his eyes, folded his hands on his chest. "You know, Nick, I never did understand what drove you to become a cop. Why not a rancher like your dad?"

He was spared the necessity of answering when Sasha shoved the door open and strode over to grab him by the front of his T-shirt. "Bed, now. Will's on guard, and Bo's looking like a cartoon weasel salivating outside a full henhouse. Except his hens are liquor bottles, and Skye says the lock on the cabinet's only so strong."

Dana yawned and stretched. "You sure you don't want me to play watchdog tonight, Nick?"

"Thanks, but I'd rather get it over with."

Sasha tugged. "If you're feeling generous, Dana, Max is looking for a chess partner."

"Thanks, but I'm a lousy chess player. No poker face.

Anyway, it's getting late. My eyes start to cross after eleven."

"You see? Dana knows how it works." When she pulled again, Nick relented with a vague smile in his friend's direction. "Midnight comes, people go to bed. Sun rises, people wake up."

"Cops have different inner clocks than regular people. I worked the night shift both in Chicago and in Denver, Sasha."

"Then you're out of sync, and it's time you got back in. Cold case detectives need to work during the day so they can cross-check old leads with other daytime workers."

"All you need is a good Internet connection and the proper access codes to check anything these days."

"Did I mention that bruised ribs hurt a lot when someone rams a fist into them?"

With a smile dancing in his eyes, he held his arms out to the sides. "Go on, take your best shot. I worked a cattle roundup one fall with four fractured ribs. Pain and I are old friends."

Holding his gaze, she drew her arm back for the punch. And only halted an inch before she made contact.

"You're lucky, Nick. I was really tempted."

"But far too sweet to follow through."

She gave his stomach a jab for good measure. "There's nothing sweet about me, Detective Law. I'm convinced I was Ma Barker's sister in a former life."

"In this one, you're a princess."

"It's a clever illusion. My mother's gorgeous even now and with only one small surgery to her credit. Talk to most of her former husbands, though, and the word *viper* tends to crop up. Surprisingly, that's an illusion, too. Took me years, but I finally figured it out. Strip away the facade and what you're left with is a woman who's painfully insecure."

"Looks like I'm not the only one who minored in psychology."

"Sheer desperation drove me to that conclusion." Behind him now, she pressed her hands to the small of his back. "Keep going. Up the stairs and turn right."

"Left. I'm with Bo tonight, remember?"

"Trying not to, actually."

Not a single floorboard creaked in the lodge. Skylights and large unobstructed windows allowed moonbeams to shimmer in. Although impulse was a rare thing for Nick to experience, let alone act on in his personal life, he trapped Sasha's hand when she would have turned, and drew her through an ancillary hallway to a space that was as much a narrow sundeck as a room.

Skye called it her gallery. The portraits that lined the interior wall chronicled the lives of her colorful forefathers. Across from the paintings, a bank of windows stretched for forty uninterrupted feet.

Sasha's tolerant amusement gave way to awe as they entered. "Wow, I missed this when I was exploring yesterday." She backed up for a better view of the largest framed oil. "That has to be George Painter, Skye's great-grandfather. Trader, fur trapper, rancher, town founder and benefactor."

"Hermit, accidental father, fortunate man." Going with the impulse, Nick draped his arms over her shoulders from behind. "Did you know he had a mail-order bride?"

"That would be the woman in the portrait beside him." Head cocked, Sasha studied the black-haired female with the severe expression. "I have a great-aunt who wears that same stern look every day of her life. I hope it doesn't happen to me."

"It won't."

"It could." Facing him, she let her hands slide around his waist, so she could hook her thumbs in his back pockets. "I saw a picture of her when she was young. My mother and I both take after her."

"We have softer lives, Sasha. Better food. More enjoyment."

"Right." She tipped her head farther back to stare into his eyes. "Like all that fun I had this afternoon and again tonight. By the time we get off this mountain, Nick, I'll be ten years older than I was when I left Denver. Unless I bump into Anthony Rush again. Then I might not get off at all."

Although his insides clenched at the thought, Nick schooled his features and regarded her through his lashes.

He didn't feel dizzy now as he had earlier, but he sure as hell felt something. And it was burning a hole in his gut, to say nothing of his defenses. Maybe impulse wasn't the best thing for him, after all.

He saw the smile that stole across her lips. "Something funny?"

"Probably not from your perspective." She ran her fingers through his hair and along the side of his neck. "You don't want to like me, do you, Nick?"

"It complicates things."

"You like Dana."

When he merely stared, her smile became a laugh that melted something way down inside.

"I mean," she clarified, "that you're willing to invest in a long-term friendship with him. You could have cut those ties years ago, but you didn't. Why?"

"Sorry, my psych class didn't extend to analyzing old friendships."

"What about forming new ones?"

He set his thumb on her chin just below her bottom lip. He was tempted to say to hell with it and dive in, but he held off a moment longer. "We're not necessarily new, Sasha."

He didn't know if she would understand his meaning or not. He wasn't sure he understood it. Campfire stories related to him by his father's Native American foreman should have been relegated to the realm of myth years ago. That he'd resurrected them lately both frustrated and intrigued him.

She stilled her hand on his cheek. "Are you talking about old souls?"

"I know someone who believes in the possibility."

"What do you believe?"

He was done with believing, and with thinking. He wanted to feel, to dive into an unfamiliar ocean and see where he surfaced.

Because it was so completely out of character for him, he hesitated another moment, watched her eyes watch him back. Then with a single, swift movement, he hauled her upward and let his hormones take over.

It was like being tossed into a whirlpool, a long, liquid spiral that sucked away his defenses one by one and encouraged him to kick deeper until he reached the spinning center.

She tasted like red wine and sex. The flavor of her shot into his bloodstream and straight to his groin. For years, his emotions had lived an uneventful life in the shadow of his work. Now they pulsed and pounded and practically punched their way out, through one crack, then another and another.

Her tongue slid over his, and he heard the purr of pleasure deep in her throat. He pulled her closer so he could feel her entire body, from the breasts that crushed against his chest, to her hips and thighs where they pressed into his. The skin at her waist was soft and silky and cool. He took his time exploring, let his fingers trail slowly upward and his mouth deepen the kiss.

Her heart beat hard and fast, a match for the drumbeat of his own. He saw himself stripping off her clothes, making love to her on the gallery carpet. Wondered how it would feel to abandon logic and reason and simply go with the hunger inside him.

Vague thoughts formed and faded in his head. She moved her hips in a seductive rhythm against him, dug her fingernails into his flesh and very nearly sent him over the edge.

He broke off, breathing hard, knew he had to before he lost himself completely in her. And if not that, then because they were standing in a public part of the lodge.

"Whoa." He curled his fingers around her arms, rested his forehead against hers while he harnessed the remnants of his self-restraint.

She kissed him again, a light touch that feathered outward to his ear. When he sucked in a breath, she took advantage of the moment and bit his lobe. "I don't like 'whoa,' Nick. Kiss me again."

His breathing didn't want to steady. "Sasha…"

"Stop being a cop, Detective, and loosen up. Be bad." She nipped his lower lip, then licked the hurt and smiled against his mouth. "No one's looking. No one's up here."

He managed a faint smile. "No one that we can see."

One more kiss and he raised his head, let his hands take a final slide over her hips. "We're standing in front of a window, Sasha. The moon's up. The woods are behind us."

"Spoilsport." But her eyes traveled past him to the glass. "I wouldn't mind being observed if I thought it was by a normal person. With Rush, it's perverted."

Even distracted, Nick noted the sudden shift of shadows in the doorway. With a soft, "Don't move," in Sasha's ear, he reached a hand behind him for his gun. Whipping his arms around her, he aimed it at the center of the largest shadow.

"Drop the knife, Bo," he said calmly, "and step out where I can see you."

"Sickerbie was spying on you? And carrying a knife?" An appalled Max stomped snow from his boots as he entered the kitchen where Sasha sat. He had a bucketful of tools and her cell phone in his hands. "Still no signal," he said, handing it back. "Which leaves us with the two-way radio, since no one up here has a clue how to repair a damaged satellite phone. I'll work on it today if Dana will let me near the thing. What did Nick do?" he demanded in the same breath.

Sasha licked raspberry jam from her thumb as she ate her toast. "What you'd expect. He told Bo to drop the knife and talk."

"What did Bo say?"

"He likes to whittle."

"Are you joking? In the middle of a crisis, he wants to hack on a piece of wood?"

"Just telling you what he told us."

"Did you buy it?"

"No, but then I don't know the man. Maybe whittling's one of his hobbies. I gather Bo has multiple…talents. He used to distill and sell his own hooch until the state police caught on to him."

"After which he started stealing other people's hooch."

"If we're lucky, maybe we'll stumble across his stash. Nick said something about going up to Painter's Ridge today. That'll be after we search the Martin farmhouse and a handful of other places Skye's been remembering since we got here." Sasha gave the bucket a tap with her toe. "Who's better at working on the radio, you or Dana?"

"He's more skilled with electronics, but I win for inventiveness. No matter what happens, it's an old device. Skye should have replaced the thing years ago."

"You gotta love hindsight, don't you?"

Max's expression soured as Nick came down the stairs. "I don't gotta love *him*. Good luck today, Sasha."

She enjoyed watching Nick approach. His long, rangy stride and slim hips coupled with the memory of last night's kiss had her mind spinning in wicked little circles. And it wasn't even 10:00 a.m. yet.

"So," she asked him, "who's going where and doing what with whom?"

"You, me and Will are going up the mountain via cousin Deacon's mud hut."

"More mud. You take me to the nicest places, Nick."

The side door opened and closed. Skye came in, dusting off her arms and batting snowflakes from her hair. "There's more white stuff coming down." She unbuttoned her coat. "I had a good sniff around the storage shed. Food's missing all right. I brought up six big cans of that pop-top ravioli and there are only three left. Ditto the baked beans and a bag of Brazilian coffee, which I happen to love. Also juice, peanut butter, crackers and several packages of the jerky my son-in-law insists on sticking in my stocking every Christmas."

A slippery tendril curled its way through Sasha's chest. "So someone here really is helping Anthony Rush—or Rush himself got into the storage shed last night. Nick?"

"Six of one, Sasha."

"You're such a comfort in a time of mounting panic."

"Just doing my job." He glanced at the counter. "Speaking of food, did you pack some for our hike?"

She finished off her toast. "We stuffed all three backpacks with food and supplies."

"I hope you're not planning to spend the night on the mountain." Skye waved an arm at the blanket of clouds outside. "Those are filled with snow, and even if the temperature has gone up several degrees, it'll still be damn cold up on the ridge. Oh, by the way, did I mention there's a hunter's cabin about forty minutes from here?"

She'd mentioned so many structures lately that Sasha had lost count. "Is it habitable?" she asked.

"It does the job—which is to say it serves as an emergency shelter for anyone who needs it."

"Anyone, as in Anthony Rush?"

Skye chuckled. "It's not much of a hideout. Too exposed. But it's there, so you might want to have a look-see on your way back. Now as far as that goes, you leave the ridge no later than three, you hear?"

They had no choice but to hear, since Skye reminded them all the way out the door and halfway into the woods.

Sheriff Pyle hitched up his pack and tuned her out. "She's a good woman, but too much like my ex for us to get on. Four years to my credit as sheriff, and I still feel like I'm on probation with her. She says I'm out, the townsfolk'll vote me out, no questions asked."

Sasha considered the sheriff's remarks as they trudged along one of the better-defined paths. "Does she have any Swedish or Finnish ancestors?"

Pyle made an uncertain motion. "George Painter's wife might have had some Scandinavian blood."

Sasha recalled the stern-faced woman in the portrait. "George's wife had black hair and olive skin."

"Her mother was Spanish," Nick said. "The Latin genes won out."

"You've done your homework, Detective Law."

"There's a library on the second floor. Lots of family info to be had. For example, George's cousin Deacon had four wives."

Sasha rewound her knitted scarf. "No biggie. My mother's had five husbands."

"At the same time?"

She laughed. "Okay, cousin Deacon wins. Was he a follower of Brigham Young?"

"No, just handsome and horny. He had ten kids and still died alone up here in his mud-and-sawdust hut, which, by the way, he built when he was sixty-three."

"It's nice to know the rich and powerful are as dysfunctional as the rest of us. I wonder what Rush's family is like."

Nick shifted his pack. "Thirty minutes on the Net and I could find out."

A beefy man with twenty extra pounds on his belly alone, Sheriff Pyle puffed slightly as they walked. "We might get lucky, Nick. Dana thinks there's hope for the two-way radio."

The mountain rose sharply to their right and dropped

into a deep chasm on the left. Sasha hoped for all their sakes that cousin Deacon's hut was straight ahead and on relatively level ground.

"What's your father's ranch like, Nick?" she asked, partly because she was curious, but primarily to keep Anthony Rush's image out of her head.

"Big."

"Yes, well, so's this mountain. I was thinking in more specific terms."

"He raises cattle, horses and chickens, but the cattle are his lifeblood. He has ten ranch hands led by a seventy-five-year-old foreman whose name is Dan Running Bear Greeley."

"The old-souls man?"

"That's him."

Pyle breathed out a grunt. "My ex believed in reincarnation. Told her friends she'd be back in another body and they should keep watch for her."

Sasha regarded him in surprise. "Your ex is dead, Will?"

"Yup. Didn't I mention that? Had a heart murmur all her life. Not long after the divorce, it gave out on her."

She set a hand on his arm. "I'm so sorry."

"Me, too—about her dying, anyway. About the split, not at all. I say people with heart conditions shouldn't make things worse by trying to run other people's lives. You'd have said it, too, if you'd met her." He sucked in a bolstering breath. "How much farther to Deacon's hut, Nicky?"

Nick nodded toward a band of snow-coated pines. "It's right there."

Sasha surveyed the ramshackle building, which was

hardly larger than her father's garage. "I guess you'd call that a utilitarian structure, huh?"

"It's more than that, Sasha. See all those half-filled holes in the snow?"

She did and smiled when comprehension dawned. "Footprints?"

"Recent ones." Nick's eyes took on an anticipatory gleam that sent a chill of excitement through her blood. "On your guard, people. Cousin Deacon's had a visitor."

Someone had indeed been staying in Deacon Painter's hut. The evidence was scattered all around, from candy bar wrappers to an empty whiskey bottle to a stack of burned logs in the fireplace.

Nick crouched by the hearth, rubbed a fragment of charred wood between his fingers and thumb until it turned to ash. "He wasn't here last night."

Pyle plopped down on a raised bed of mud and shrugged off his pack. "What'd you and Skye put in these things, anyway, Sasha? It feels like I'm carrying a load of bricks."

"Food and supplies, Will, and we distributed the weight evenly."

"Put more sugar in your coffee," Nick remarked, still examining the hearth. "Keeps your energy level high."

"I'll make a note." The sheriff exhaled and stood. "Okay, our boy's gone. Must have found better digs." He cast a baleful look at the boxy room. "Wouldn't be hard to do."

Sasha followed his gaze. "You didn't see brother Sam's burrow or the death trap farmhouse. This place is homey by comparison."

Will snorted. "How long d'you think Rush has been gone, Nick?"

"Twenty-four hours, give or take. How far to the Martin farm?"

"A good hour."

"You okay with that?" Nick asked Sasha.

"No problem. I go to the gym, remember?"

He remembered. And he hadn't been asking her so much as Will, whose physical conditioning had obviously slipped since he'd worked for the state police.

It was an arduous slog over snow, ice and rock. The farmhouse, which stood on a small plateau, was backed by trees, a mountain stream and still more rock.

With each step, Nick noticed, the sheriff fell farther behind. He glanced at Sasha beside him. "What's in his pack?"

"Bread, biscuits, some jerky and a stick of butter. I think Skye also added two containers of juice."

"That's it?"

"Well, extra gloves and socks, a survival blanket and some matches." She gave the sheriff an uneasy look over her shoulder. "He is a little…thick around the middle. You should slow down."

"Uh-huh." Nick made a long sweep of the trees and surrounding ridges.

Sasha looked with suspicion from his face to the trees and back. "Is there something you're not telling me?"

"Yeah." He returned his gaze to hers. "I'm hungry."

"Second that." Pyle caught up at last. He shed his pack, worked the kinks from his shoulders. "Let's eat."

"After we check the house," Nick told him.

Pyle curled his lip. "I hate youth."

"You're not ready for a rocking chair yet, Will." Before he could object, Nick seized his backpack. And was more than a little surprised by the weight.

"I've got it," Will said quickly, and slid the straps back on his shoulders.

"You sure?"

"'Course, I am. I'm not as fast as you, but I can still get the job done. Now go. I'm right behind you."

They walked a few minutes before Sasha bumped against Nick's shoulder. "Why do you have that expression on your face?"

"There's no expression, Sasha. I'm thinking."

"About Will?"

"Yeah." He glanced back. "His pack's got more than bread, juice and socks inside."

"Maybe he added another gun for backup."

"Guns don't clink."

She stared. "You think he's packing glass? Like a couple of bottles?"

"Maybe bottles," Nick agreed in a mild tone. "Maybe a bottle and a glass globe."

Chapter 10

Sasha liked Will Pyle. She didn't want to suspect him of anything. Besides, what did having glass in his backpack really prove? Only that Nick was as guilty of making assumptions as everyone else.

Because of the way the snow had drifted, they approached the Martin farmhouse in a roundabout fashion. The structure had withstood the ravages of winter extremely well in her opinion. Despite being empty three years since old man Martin's death, all the doors opened and closed with ease, stairs and floors appeared sound, and even with a thick layer of dust and far too many cobwebs, the few remaining pieces of furniture were in good condition. Unfortunately, there was nothing to indicate that Anthony Rush had been there and no reason to linger once they'd eaten their lunch.

"Don't even think about it," Sasha warned Nick when

the sheriff went outside. "If he did have a globe in his backpack, would he leave the thing here so you could find it?"

"That's not his pack, Sasha, it's mine." Nick hoisted it, adjusted the straps. "He took his with him when he left."

"Oh." She sighed. "I guess that's not good."

"I thought you didn't want me going through it, anyway."

"I don't. Your cop mentality's rubbing off on me. In my world, you don't suspect a person of being a criminal simply because he or she feels a little proprietary about a certain possession. You couldn't dynamite my mother's purse out of her hands at a party. She even carries it while she's dancing."

"What about when she's teaching?"

"She locks it in her desk. She doesn't trust staff rooms."

"Or the people who use them?"

"Okay, so you can add paranoid to her list of problems. One thing I'll say in her favor, she knows how to make her students listen and learn." A smile danced in Sasha's eyes. "Kind of like your Miss Miller from first grade. The kids are dazzled by her beauty, and she knows it."

Nick gathered up the refuse from their lunch. "Did you ever consider becoming a teacher?"

She crushed the empty juice boxes. "Not a teacher, not a model, not a cop."

"How about a small town sheriff?"

"Stop it, Nick. Will Pyle is not a serial killer."

Nick stuck the Stetson back on her head, flicked a finger down her nose. "I didn't say he was."

"Then why do you think he might be carrying a snow globe around with him?"

"We've been through this already. Food went missing last night. If not Rush, then another person stole it. It's possible Anthony Rush is being helped by someone at the lodge."

"Yes, but I thought you meant someone as in Bo Sickerbie."

"Still a prime contender."

She seesawed her head to ease the tension in her neck. "Am I really supposed to believe there's even the slightest chance that Will Pyle could be working with Anthony Rush?"

"Your best bet is to believe that anything's possible, and don't trust anyone."

"Not even you and Skye?"

That gleam she'd noticed earlier reappeared in his eyes, except this time he pulled her up against him and directed it entirely at her. "You can trust me to keep you safe, Sasha, but not in any other way."

Her heart stuttered. For a moment she actually stopped breathing. It wasn't until she felt herself becoming light-headed that she shook off the sensation.

His eyes were so damn sexy, she thought, then sighed when Will clomped back in.

"Sorry I took so long. You ready?"

Still holding her captive, and with his eyes on hers, Nick nodded. Sasha could have sworn for a moment that he was reading her mind. Then he smiled and gave her waist strap a firm cinch. "We're heading southwest, Will, to the ridge. You can lead the way."

The jut of land that was Painter's Ridge towered above the river below. At this time of the year, it looked like little more than a tall cliff, but with the snow gone and water rushing along at its base, Nick imagined the view would be spectacular.

"I haven't seen Bo's truck yet." Sasha sheltered her eyes with her gloved hand and scanned the distant snows-cape. "All I see up here is trees."

"And Bo's shack."

"What?" She searched again, saw nothing. "Where?"

Thirty feet away, Will jabbed a thumb over his shoulder. "Green roof, brown base, in the middle of those big spruces."

It took her two more sweeps to separate the building from the trees. "That's Bo's?"

"Odds are good," Nick said. "Ten minutes and we're there. Ready, Will?"

"Just walk."

Nick kept Sasha directly in front of him. Did he suspect Pyle of aiding and abetting a killer? Not really. Was he willing to risk Sasha's life on gut instinct? Not a chance.

Fifteen minutes later, she was jiggling the padlock on the narrow brown door. "The way he's got the place secured and camouflaged, he might as well stick up a sign up that says Beware! Stolen Merchandise Inside."

Nick removed the rifle from her shoulder. "With Bo, it's more likely to read Keep Out or Die. Stand back."

Holding the weapon waist high, he aimed and fired. The blast echoed through the woods for several seconds.

"Makes you realize how alone you are, doesn't it?" Pyle observed.

Nick said nothing, merely flipped off the lock and booted the door open.

Sasha started to laugh the moment she stuck her head

inside. "My God, how many times has the Painter's Bluff liquor store been robbed?"

Nick ran his gaze over the stacks of crates and boxes. "Bo didn't steal all of this in Painter's Bluff." He pried the lid off one. "Looks like it's mostly hard stuff. Sickerbie obviously knows his customers' preferences."

"He's gonna know the inside of a jail cell for a long, long time," Pyle growled. "He's got enough Jack Black in here to send the whole town on a bender for six months."

Nick saw nothing to indicate that Rush had been inside the place. The lock had been new, secure and unmarked.

Pyle continued to grumble. "I'm gonna twist that weasel up like a pretzel and throw him in Skye's root cellar for the duration. Beats on his wife, steals liquor—what else has he been up to that I don't know about?"

Sasha dropped one of the dusty bottles back in its box. "I don't think he murdered Kristiana Felgard."

"Score one for the weasel," Pyle said. "Could still be doing favors for the killer, though. What do you think, Nick? D'you see Bo as a murderer's accomplice?"

"I can see anyone that way if I try hard enough." Catching Sasha's eye, Nick tapped his wrist and mouthed the word, "Time."

She held up four fingers, then five more: 4:05 p.m. If they left now, they still wouldn't reach the lodge until well after dark.

"We have to go, Will," he said when the sheriff started looking through more boxes. "You can figure out what to do with Bo later."

"Gonna string him to a bedpost until he confesses, is what I'm gonna do."

Sasha took his hand. "We're leaving now, okay? Use

your nasty thoughts about Bo to fuel your muscles for the hike back."

They'd made a loop around the Martin farmhouse, so their route back to the lodge would be a different one. Nick visualized the uphill climbs and slippery descents that Skye had spoken of, and calculated that the return trip could easily take two hours.

Will held his own for the first portion of the trek, but he began to labor when they reached a series of icy slopes. Nick kept Sasha close, and an eye on the sheriff, ten feet behind them. He did a double take when he saw Will dig a vial out of his pocket and shake a pair of white tablets into his palm.

Sasha glanced up when he swore softly.

"He's taking pills."

"If they're caffeine-based, I wouldn't mind a couple myself." When Nick shot her a level look, she sighed. "Do you want me to ask?"

"You think he'll tell you?"

"Never know until you try." She dropped back and offered the man a smile that Nick himself would have been hard-pressed to resist. "Are you feeling all right, Will?"

"Breathing's tight. It'll pass."

"Can you take something for it?"

Pyle launched a visual dagger at Nick. "Already did. You hear that, Nicky?" he challenged. "They're pills for my asthma." A gravelly chuckle broke through. "Saw you looking. You thought I was into heavy drugs, didn't you?"

"It crossed my mind."

"City cops," Pyle scoffed. "Everything's black or white. You—"

The last word exploded from his mouth as his foot

slipped on an icy rock. Sasha made a grab for his arm, but only caught his backpack and only for a split second. The rock shot out from under his boot. Nick saw his hands fly up and his body crumple. Then he was somersaulting down the slippery incline, and there was nothing anyone could do to stop him.

Dread coiled in Nick's stomach. Holding Sasha's hand, he helped her with the difficult descent toward where the sheriff had landed.

"He's not dead," she maintained through stiff lips. "He can't be dead."

But he didn't move even though his face was buried in a snowdrift.

"Will?" Nick shed his pack, knelt and felt for a pulse. Thankfully, he found one in Pyle's neck.

"'s my ankle." The sheriff's voice was a bleary mumble.

Sasha breathed an audible sigh of relief. "Can you move?" she asked, while Nick examined the bones of his right leg.

"Think so." Lifting his head slightly, he blew out a series of short pants. "Other leg, Nicky."

He continued to pant, rearing up when Nick reached his left ankle.

"Nothing else hurts?"

"I think I took one in the gut, but other than that, I'm okay."

"There's no blood," Sasha confirmed. She tugged off his backpack and set it aside. For Nick's benefit, she held up her wrist. Even upside down and in fading light he could see that it was after five o'clock.

They got Will turned over amid a stream of grunts,

groans and creative swearing. Nick propped his leg up on one of the packs.

At Will's feet, Sasha said, "I know how to make a splint, Nick. Three pieces of wood should do, and strips of cloth to bind them."

Nick wiggled the sheriff's boot off. "He won't be walking on it no matter how well we splint the bone."

Pyle leaned forward, rubbed his shin above the injury. "Don't say that, Nicky. Could be it's only a bad sprain."

"You want to hike uphill in the snow on a bad sprain?" Nick surveyed the area. It was surrounded by small rises on three sides, but it still felt exposed. "We need to find shelter."

In his mind, he juxtaposed their location on the mental map he'd drawn earlier. Skye had rattled off a list of buildings this morning. Were any of them near here?

What little light remained in the sky winked out, leaving them in almost total darkness.

Sasha clicked her flashlight on. "One of the few camping things I can do is make a fire. You bind Will's ankle, I'll find some kindling."

But Nick, who'd gotten his bearings now, shook his head. "I'll start the fire. That old hunter's cabin Skye talked about should be around here somewhere. I'll see if I can find it."

That would mean leaving Sasha alone with a man he only hoped he could trust. But with Will injured, he didn't have many options. Eyes narrowed, Nick said, "Keep your gun ready, Will, and don't let Sasha out of your sight. If Rush hurts her, you won't want to see me again."

"I'm five feet away from you, Nick." Sasha rocked

back on her heels. "I can hear every word you're saying. I can also take care of myself."

"Four eyes are better than two in the dark." He pulled his gloves on with his teeth and motioned her to the side.

Will snickered. "Wants to give you a big he-man kiss before he rides off into the sunset." He winced. "Did we bring a medi-kit?"

Sasha hunted through her backpack, extracted a canvas pouch. "Yes, we did, thanks to Skye. It's for hikers, so there should be lots of emergency goodies inside."

Will's lips were turning blue, Nick noticed, and Sasha had to be cold as hell. That she hadn't uttered a word of complaint was one of the many things he loved about—

His eyes shot up. Love? Had he just thought the word *love?*

It had to be a Freudian slip. He was a cop with a failed marriage and little or no social life. What the hell did he know about love?

He heard Sasha's exclamation of delight, and set the question aside.

"This is great. These metal things are splints. You'll have to buy Skye dinner for this, Will."

Still off-kilter, Nick forced his mind to work. Although he didn't want to waste time starting a fire they might not need, he also couldn't be sure how long it would take him to locate the cabin, or if he'd even be able to find it in full darkness. While Sasha dealt with Will's ankle, he gathered kindling, set it over the napkins from their lunch and lit the paper.

It took some coaxing and carefully directed blowing, but the flame caught and slowly ignited the wood. When he felt certain it could support more, he broke off a handful of birch branches and crisscrossed them over the fire.

"There." Sasha sat back to evaluate her handiwork. Will's foot was still propped on his backpack, but it appeared more stable. "Not bad, huh?"

Nick smiled into the fire, warmed his hands over the top. "Looks good to me, Nurse Nightingale. You still with us, Will?"

"I could use some of that whiskey we found in Bo's shack. Or, uh, maybe—" he cleared his throat "—one of the beers in my backpack."

Sasha's brows went up. "You brought beer?"

"Three," Pyle confessed. "Figured we could drink 'em on the way back to the lodge. That juice we had at lunch has no kick. A beer'll keep the blood flowing."

"He brought beer." Sasha was close enough that Nick could see the amusement on her face. She leaned forward. "Was it bottled beer, Will?"

"No other kind," he told her.

She smiled broadly. "Bottles clink, Nick."

"Yeah, they do—unless they're broken." He gave Will's good foot a tap. "I smelled malt when I went to check your pulse. My guess is they didn't survive the fall."

Satisfied that the fire would continue to burn, he climbed to his feet and took Sasha with him into the shadows. He hesitated, then gave up trying to separate his emotions. Wrapping his fingers around her neck, he kissed her long and hard.

Her lips were as chilled as his. So was her cheek where his knuckles grazed it. "I'll build up the fire before I go and leave you some wood. If I'm not back in an hour, you'll need to break off more branches." The flickering firelight allowed him to see her eyes. There was fear in them, but along with it he recognized the glint of determination. "Keep your rifle ready."

She worked up a smile. "Take my flashlight as a backup, Nick. If the batteries in both lights die, just listen and you'll hear me singing. It's a lesson my father taught me as a child. Whenever I got lost, I was supposed to sing."

Nick's lips twitched. "I had no idea you were so talented. Architect, paramedic, fire builder, singer."

"Yes, well, don't applaud too loud. My vocal range is extremely limited. On the other hand—" the glint became a twinkle as she moved enticing hips against him "—I have other skills that more than make up for it."

When she caught his bottom lip between her teeth, Nick felt his heart drop straight into his groin. It took every scrap of self-control he possessed to tear his mouth away.

"Feel better now?" she asked.

"I feel hotter, that's for sure."

"Hot's better than scared." She stepped back, handed him her flashlight. And with a defiant spark of humor in her eyes, began to hum an old Johnny Cash song.

"It's spooky in the woods after dark, don't you think? On a mountain, with critters prowling around and no way to see them until they're practically on top of you?" The sheriff rested his gun on one upraised knee and smiled crookedly at Sasha. "Just thought I'd say that and get it out in the open. You scared?"

She sat cross-legged in the snow, as close to the fire as she could get, and fed long birch branches to the flames. "More like terrified. I feel sorry for any critter I spot, because in my current state, I'll be totally trigger happy." She held out a bag to him. "Do you want another cookie?"

He made a disgusted sound. "You can't make a meal out of Oreos, Sasha."

"I can," she said, and dipped her free hand into the bag. "At least for one night."

"You and Nick sure as hell are a pair. Sugar, cookies, it's a wonder either of you sleep."

She rolled the package down and used the tab to secure it. "I don't want to sleep right now. Nick's been gone for forty minutes. He might be lost, or hurt, or—" Stopping herself, she stuffed the bag in her pack. "He might have met a bear."

"Doubt it. A cougar maybe, or a mountain lion."

"Or Anthony Rush?"

"That's gloomy talk. You've been spending too much time with your friend Max." Will shifted position, grimaced, but worked his butt around until he'd made a comfortable dent in the snow. "You been an architect long?"

She fed larger branches to the fire. "Eight years."

"Nicky's been a cop since he was twenty-one."

"Did you know him back then?"

"Nope. We met four years ago, right after I was elected sheriff. He came up to see Dana. Now Dana having already been mayor for two years, me being recently elected and Nick being on the Denver force, the three of us decided to do a little day fishing at a hole outside of town." He slapped his thigh. "'Course, I was in better shape in those days. You get complacent when life's easy."

Sasha counted the branches beside her and decided she'd need to cut several more in order to keep the fire at its current level. Humor kindled when her gaze fell on the knife Nick had left behind. Seeing it jammed in the ice, blade down, struck her as absurdly funny somehow.

Will rearranged himself again. "If you have a joke you're keeping to yourself, I wouldn't mind hearing it. I'm getting ice blisters sitting here."

"No joke." She tapped a restless palm on her rifle, pulled her Stetson lower so it met her upturned collar. "I was thinking about my mother. She'd be horrified if she knew I was out here. The daughter she raised was supposed to be genteel. I should be having dinner with a doctor or a lawyer or an accountant, not hacking down branches and listening for wild animals."

"Is she as pretty as you?"

Sasha smiled. "Everyone says I look like her. And she looks like her mother, and the daughter she expects me to have will look like all three of us. That's the Barbara Leeds plan. Keep the line going until one of the daughters gets it right."

"Gets what right?"

"Whatever it is that's wrong."

"You're losing me, Sasha."

"That's okay. My mother lost me years ago."

"Why do I hear amusement rather than disdain when you talk about her?"

"Because I decided when I was very young that I wanted to stay sane. You can't do that if you're always trying to measure up to someone else's standards, their expectations." She shoved her sleeve back, angled her watch toward the fire. "It's been fifty minutes, Will."

"I know."

She exhaled. "We need more wood."

"Know that, too. Tell you what. You score the branches

and snap 'em off, and I'll break them into manageable-size pieces." He patted her boot as she stood. "He'll be fine. I gave him a hard time today with the pills, but Nick's a good cop, one of the best I've met."

She dusted snow from her coat. "You're only saying that to make me feel better."

"Actually, I'm saying it to make *me* feel better. I was a cop in Illinois before I came here. Saw a lot of felons and a lot more felonies. I never came up against a serial killer. You gotta think a certain way to catch those kind of people. Case goes cold, you get creative. One thing I know about Nick—though I'll admit, I don't know much—he's solved more than one cold case since he came back to Colorado. Chicago would love to have him back. Denver Homicide would love to have him, period. But the captain who heads the cold case investigation team isn't about to let him go. That's the talk, anyway." He yanked the knife free, wiped the blade on his sleeve. "We're not completely out of the loop up here."

But they were almost out of firewood.

Sasha hitched the rifle over her shoulder and headed for a medium-size birch tree. Score the bark, snap the limbs. Keep a wary eye out for animals, both feline and human.

"You wanna maybe hum another song?" the sheriff called out. "Then I'll know you're okay."

She chose Queen and belted out the lyrics with gusto.

Chuckling, Will broke the first branch she tossed over. "I feel like I'm in a hockey arena."

The song dwindled off as her eyes combed the darkness. "I wish I did. I keep thinking we've tumbled into a snow globe, and no matter which direction we go, there's no way out. We'll just keep circling back to the same spot for the rest of our lives."

"That's nerves talking. We'll get out of here, all right."

She'd have an easier time believing that if Nick was with them. Easier still if she could rid herself of the sensation that something with very large eyes and a very chilly soul was watching them.

"Paranoid," she murmured, and grasped another branch.

"You're not singing, Sasha."

Searching her repertoire, she selected the "Small World" song from Disneyland. Singing was good. It was definitely better than thinking about how badly her jaw ached from not letting her teeth chatter.

The snow had developed a thin top crust that crunched when she walked. Bare branches clacked overhead. The pines rustled. For a split second, she thought something stirred to her right. Then the pine trees rustled again, and all the shadows shifted.

She whooshed out a breath. Behind her, Will broke more branches. It was a specific sound, repeated over and over again. Which was probably why she noticed the sound beneath it so clearly.

Her knife blade froze in place. Heart knocking, she strained to hear.

Snap. Will broke a branch. Snap. Another one. And a third. Then, somewhere in the darkness beyond the fire, she detected a stealthy crack.

Very slowly, Sasha brought her hand down. She held the knife at her side, but tightened her grip on the handle. Was she imagining things?

A protracted squelch from above had her pulse rate

tripling. "Oh, hell," she whispered, and backed toward the fire. "Will…?"

"Do you know any Willie Nelson?"

She slipped the rifle from her shoulder, continued backing up. Something, perhaps a boot, made a rubbing sound as it lost traction for a moment.

The shadows on the second rise seemed thicker than the ones on the edges. It wasn't Nick up there, and it wasn't a mountain lion. Dropping the knife in her pocket, Sasha switched the rifle to her right hand.

"We've got company," she said softly.

"I heard it," he replied in an undertone.

"He's behind you."

"They always are." Louder, he said, "That'll be enough wood for a while, Sasha." He worked himself around on his good knee. "Think I'll take care of a little business behind that boulder. Can you watch the fire?"

She dragged her eyes from the shadow. "Yes, sure. Do you need help?"

"Just keep singing."

She hummed something, made herself skirt the fire as if inspecting it. Was Anthony Rush here, watching them? It had to be him, didn't it? And no matter how casual she acted at this point, unless he was a complete fool, he must realize she'd heard him.

"Now would be a really good time for you to come back, Nick," she whispered under her breath.

The darkness altered on the hill. Sasha gnashed her teeth, curled her finger more firmly around the trigger.

If she could see him, she could shoot him. On a less promising note, he could probably see her quite clearly right now.

She eased away from the flames, bounced slightly

in place as an outlet for her screaming nerves. "Where are you, Nick? I know I said I could take care of myself, but I'm not used to fending off invisible serial killers."

Then she recalled what Nick had said about Rush wanting her to die last. That meant Will was the one in immediate danger.

She glanced at the boulder. "Will, are you okay?"

"Working on it," he answered, and she suspected he was angling for a clear shot. "How's the fire?"

"Still burning."

As her eyes adjusted from firelight to darkness, she spotted a silhouette within the shadows. Seconds ticked by. The silhouette crouched, then slowly crept downward.

"Damn." When she heard the unmistakable sound of feet in the snow, Sasha abandoned pretense and shouldered the rifle. "Get back here, Will," she shouted. "Whoever it is, he's coming down."

Chapter 11

Nick located the hunter's cabin thirty minutes after leaving Sasha and Will. It sat in plain view on an open stretch of land near the crest of a large hill. He had to agree with Skye—it would be one of the worst places on Hollowback Mountain for a person to hide. But a faint orange glow from inside told him someone—could only be Anthony Rush—was doing precisely that.

Nick approached from the east side, heard nothing and risked a look through the window. Empty. A scan of the interior revealed no cupboards or closets, just a single door, four windows and a fire burning low in the hearth.

He decided to go for it, ducked under the window and kicked the door open with his foot. Moving his gun from side to side, he went in, but still no one appeared.

"Okay, so what are you up to, pal?"

Nick could think of a few things, none of which would keep Rush occupied for long.

With his ears attuned to the smallest sound, he prowled the room. He spied the food first—full cans of ravioli, beans and pears, and others that were empty tossed under the bench. A bag of coffee had been torn open and sat next to a stovetop coffeepot. A large bottle of vodka stood between two cots, one of which had a pair of rough blankets heaped on it.

Nick took a moment to check the exterior, then used the tip of his gun to poke the blankets.

When he hit something hard, he nudged the wool aside, saw the shape of the object inside and gave a short laugh. It wasn't a snow globe as he'd thought, but an unopened bottle of brandy. Whoever had bought this had very expensive taste.

An ember popped in the fireplace, but beyond that the cabin remained silent, with only the wind whistling softly through the rafters and his own footsteps on the rough wood floor.

He noticed the canvas strap on his second tour of the room. It looped out into the light from the shadows under the bench. Snagging it, he tugged until the bulky pack slid forward.

Facing the door, he unzipped the top, pawed through jeans, shirts and underwear. Nothing exciting there, he reflected. No snow globe, no more booze, only a shaving kit containing a blade razor, nail clippers and—his brows went up—a mustache and goatee. Now this at least was a little more interesting.

But not half as interesting as the documents he discovered in the second zippered compartment. It was a small bundle, wrapped in plastic and secured with two elastic bands.

Nick glanced at the door before opening the package and shaking out the contents. There was a recently issued U.S. passport and two Colorado driver's licenses. The first license belonged to Anthony Rush of Telluride, Colorado; the second and older of the pair carried the name Jason Watts. The photos on both were identical and matched the one in the passport, which also claimed to be the property of Anthony Rush. Unlikely, Nick thought, that the passport photo would be exactly the same as those on the licenses.

"What else have you got in here?" he wondered aloud, and wasn't surprised to tear open a brown paper bag and discover a wad of twenty, fifty and hundred dollar bills. There was no sequence to the serial numbers, and the condition varied from nearly new to old and faded.

More embers popped. Nick rewrapped the documents and money and stuffed them in his coat pocket. Then he zipped the pack and pushed it back under the bench.

By his internal clock, he'd been here almost ten minutes. Why hadn't Rush returned?

With the question nagging at him, he crossed to the north window. And felt his throat muscles seize when he spotted the glimmer of light below.

It was the fire he'd started before leaving Sasha and Will. If he could see it, so could the occupant of this cabin.

Gun out and swearing, Nick bolted for the door.

"Will?" Sasha kept her rifle shouldered and her mind off the fear that wanted to paralyze her. "Did you hear what I said?"

"I heard you." He laid a hand on her arm, eased himself around at a ninety-degree angle from her. "Where'd he go?"

"I don't know. He was coming down the slope, but he stopped."

"Could be he saw your rifle."

"Maybe." Though she was far from convinced. She nodded at a rocky incline. "He might be over there. A chunk of snow rolled down a minute ago."

"Sizing up the situation," the sheriff judged. "We need to be farther from the fire."

Sasha thought they were far enough away, but with Will leaning on her, she fell back another fifteen feet.

The minutes crawled past. "And so we wait." Her vision kept blurring, but that could be due to the drifting smoke. Or blinding fright.

"It's a game, Sasha," Pyle said. "Predator and prey. Always hated it myself, but the rules aren't ours to dictate. Predator has the advantage every time."

"That's not reassuring, Will." Her finger on the trigger felt twitchy. She relaxed her muscles and listened. Predators had nerves, too. The advantage couldn't all be on their side.

Another sixty seconds ticked past. Will leaned more heavily on her shoulder. It would end, she told herself. Rush couldn't play this game forever.

"What was that?" Will's grip tightened.

"A branch moved in the fire," Sasha said, although she'd nearly jumped out of her skin at the sound. "Are you sure we shouldn't do something? Let him know we know he's up there?"

"And then what? Start shooting? Don't know about you, but I'm not ready to die tonight if that doesn't work."

He was right. They had to play the game.

More snow tumbled down. Sasha blinked smoke from her eyes. She heard the strange rubbing sound again—snow on boots that couldn't gain a proper foothold. Was the wearer descending the hill?

"There!" she exclaimed softly. "I see his outline."

Will waved his gun at the smoke. "Think maybe you're right. He's sneaking down. Damn." He took aim. "You ready?"

"No." She squinted through the scope, saw more gray than black and wished the fickle wind would gust up.

Untended, the fire collapsed. It sent up a shower of sparks that startled Sasha and made the silhouette pause. Bent low, he swung to his left.

Will lowered his gun hand. "Wait a minute now." A clatter of falling rocks and ice erupted on the rise. "Knew it." He gave Sasha's shoulder a hard downward thrust. "Don't move."

She couldn't move, almost couldn't breathe with most of his body weight bearing down on her.

At the sound of gunfire Will hauled her back, or rather stumbled and simply took her with him. Sasha landed on her backside in a drift as another shot rang out.

Who was their shadow man shooting at? The obvious answer hit, and she scrambled to her knees. "Nick!"

The sheriff rolled over, puffing. Sasha planted a foot in the snow. Should she shout or remain silent? She chose middle ground, aimed her rifle skyward and squeezed the trigger.

The man—she saw him now—wheeled toward the fire. His gun snapped up and down. He bared his teeth. She held her breath and tracked his movements with her rifle. But he faded in and out of her sights.

"Stand still," she whispered as he vanished into the darkness yet again. A moment later, the sound of a struggle reached her. Panic swelled. "Nick?"

She jerked her rifle sideways, heard the sheriff growl from behind, "Fire again. I lost my gun when I fell."

Sasha angled the rifle upward and shot another bullet into the air.

Rush made a furious sound, like a battle cry. As he stumbled through a weak pool of light, he snatched a knife from inside his parka and went for Nick's chest.

With terror beating a frantic tattoo inside, Sasha brought the rifle up and fired directly over Rush's head.

He ducked, whirled toward her on his heels. She saw Nick tackle him, saw Rush kick free and stagger back. But even off balance, he didn't go down. He barely slowed down.

"Why do the mean ones never have glass jaws?" She quelled the trembling in her arms and took aim again. Then Nick dived in, and she had no shot.

"Move," she urged him. "Just a little to your right."

But he didn't, and a moment later both men vanished into the darkness.

"Damn." She would have started forward, except she felt a rough tug on the bottom of her coat. Looking down, she realized Will had a strong hand clamped onto the hem.

"You're not going anywhere, missy."

She tugged. "I can help him." However, her bravado faded at the absurdity of the statement. "I hate doing nothing."

"So do I. Doesn't make charging in half-cocked the best decision."

"But—"

"You're staying put, and that's final. I'll arrest you if I have to."

Fear and frustration warred with logic. Logic won. "You're right, I know you're right. It's just…difficult."

"No more so for you than for me."

She could have argued, but something in that potential argument frightened her almost as much as Anthony Rush. "It's okay. You can let go now."

"Sorry, I don't trust you."

Peering up the hill, she knelt beside him. "Did you see where they went?"

"To the far side of the rise."

"You don't seem very worried."

"No need to sound so disapproving, Sasha. Nick'll have the advantage."

"Rush is heavier."

"Nick's younger. He's also trained."

"That's bull, Will. Rush could be trained, too. From the street, by the military, as a mercenary." She would have continued if she hadn't spied the strain on the sheriff's face. He'd gone very pale. "Come on, let's get you back to the fire."

"Appreciate it."

Sasha listened closely, but heard nothing except the crackle of birch and the occasional shifting of branches. Biting her lip, she limped with Will to the edge of the fire, collapsing on her knees as he settled in.

The hat came out of nowhere. It flew over her head to land on the snow in front of her.

It was Anthony Rush's stained cowboy hat, and its appearance was followed by a silky whisper that flowed directly into her ear. "You forgot the cardinal rule, pretty lady. You didn't watch your back."

* * *

She recognized the voice.

If her muscles hadn't momentarily locked, Sasha would have rammed both elbows into Nick's stomach. Instead, she let her head fall against his throat.

"You almost gave me a coronary."

She felt his lips move into a smile that died when he said, "I couldn't hold him. He's hurting, but he's tougher than I expected." An arm snaked lightly around Sasha's waist. "Are you all right?"

"Defibrillating now."

"Rush didn't trust your shooting."

She turned her head until her mouth was almost on his. "Smart man."

Will gave an awkward cough. "You two aren't going to embarrass me, are you?"

Nick's smile reappeared when she nipped his lower lip. "Depends how easily you embarrass."

Groaning, the sheriff let his head bob. "What a hell of a night this has been."

Will was right. It was hell. In fact, Sasha couldn't remember a night that had ever passed as slowly.

They considered going up to the cabin since Nick doubted Rush would return, but decided the difficult climb would be too much for the sheriff. Instead, they remained by the fire and kept an eye out for any movement above.

They were packed up and ready to leave by dawn. Nick jury-rigged a stretcher out of pine branches, tape and gauze. They had cookies and jerky for breakfast and by 7:00 a.m. were making their way back to Painter's Lodge.

Nick had showed them the passport he'd discovered in the cabin, as well as the two driver's licenses and the cash. He said he had a theory, but he refused to delve into it until he had a chance to blow up Rush's photo on his laptop.

Whatever. Sasha had been so happy to see him alive and unharmed that she didn't care what any of it meant.

Almost ninety minutes of slogging through snow and ice brought them within sight of the lodge. Bundled from head to toe, Skye and Dana met them as they passed George Painter's shack.

"Heaven's looking out for you," Skye shouted above the wind, which had picked up from a slight breeze to twenty miles an hour in the last fifteen minutes. "Bad weather's moving in fast." She helped Sasha hoist her side of the makeshift stretcher. "I figured you'd survive, but I have to say I'm awfully relieved to see you."

"Ditto." Sasha smiled her thanks at Dana, who grasped the heavy branch and shooed her out of the way.

They didn't try to converse for the rest of the trip. As the wind grew stronger, Sasha's limbs grew heavier. Nick might be able to function on zero sleep, but she was a zombie at this point.

Max greeted them at the door. "Bo's been prowling like a caged tiger. He won't be happy to see you."

"He'll be downright miserable when I'm back on my feet," Pyle promised from between Nick and Dana. "Abusive, thieving weasel. What the hell kind of example is he setting for his sons?"

Normally, Sasha would have jumped in and agreed, but to do so meant she'd need to think, and right then even the simple task of speaking was beyond her.

"Bed," Nick said, and steered her toward the staircase.

"Bath," Sasha countered, as a pair of hands guided her up.

They weren't Nick's hands, she realized with a sense of bleary disappointment. However, as long as they weren't Anthony Rush's either, she was grateful.

Rose-scented water steamed around her. She heard Skye's voice, but not distinct words. Sasha's world felt blissfully dreamlike, soft and white, like snow without the cold.

Bubbles frothed. Something warm and honey flavored slid down her throat.

"Sleep," Skye ordered from a great distance.

"Nick...?"

"Is next on my bully list. Don't worry, Sasha. I'll get him into bed if I have to sit on him."

Amusement bloomed for a moment, then slipped away as she drifted into a deep, deep sleep.

She saw Nick's face, felt herself reaching for him. So gorgeous. So easy to want. Too easy to love.

Oops, bad idea. Mustn't fall in love. Barbara wouldn't approve. Or would she? A cop in the family might be a good thing in her mother's eyes.

A sea of silky blue surrounded her. Her mother's image came and went. Sasha wanted Nick back, but what appeared instead was a silhouette, the half-formed shadow of a man whose features she couldn't make out, watching her through cold, colorless eyes.

"Soon," she heard him whisper.

He leaned in close, but the darkness was too thick for her to see him. She glimpsed a tiny orb in his hand. Inside it, snowflakes fluttered and danced around a delicate blond angel. The angel held a harp, but if that was harp music she was hearing, the instrument had been made in hell.

Metal clinked against metal, like jingle bells, with a much harsher cadence.

"You're going to pay, Sasha Myer." Hot breath poured over her face. "I'm going to squeeze the life out of your body. You'll be dead, and she'll suffer because of it. I'll watch her icy heart break…."

"Nick?" Blinking sleep from his eyes, Dana made his way through the living room. "My God, do you ever sleep?"

"I slept when we got back."

"Uh-huh, for two hours. I counted. Will and Sasha haven't surfaced since they went upstairs this morning. Oh no, wait, we're talking yesterday morning now. Do you know what time it is?"

"Yeah, I know what time it is." Nick kept his eyes on his computer monitor.

"It's after two. That's a.m., my friend."

"Where's Bo?"

"Snoring upstairs. Can't you hear him?"

Nick listened and offered his friend a smile. "Sounds like a chain saw." He hit Enter and studied the image on-screen. "I've seen this guy before."

Dana joined him at the kitchen counter. "That's Rush, right?"

"The other name I've got for him is Jason Watts."

"Does it matter what a serial killer calls himself?"

"It bothers me."

Dana gave his head a resigned shake. "It would."

Pushing his laptop aside, Nick flicked through a stack of files.

Dana watched for a moment, then went to the cupboard and removed two mugs. "Did Skye tell you I got static on the radio today, and under it, I think, a voice?"

"Can you transmit?"

"We'll have to clean up the static first. I'll work on it later." He held up a mug. "Coffee?"

"Mmm."

"Are those the files of the dead women?" He spun Kristiana Felgard's picture around. "She's lovely, even in death. It's such a waste. Do you have any idea why Rush is doing this?"

"I didn't get a sense of the guy while I was fighting him, Dana. Only that he was desperate to escape."

"Was he going for Sasha?"

"With Will there? I doubt it."

"So you did get a sense of him."

Nick sat back and rubbed gritty eyes. He'd been awake too long, wasn't thinking clearly. "Maybe I did," he conceded, "on a subconscious level. There's a lot going on in my head right now. I can't separate it into manageable pieces. Don't skimp on the sugar, and you can lose the yuck-face. I need energy."

"Eat a power bar. Or did Rush steal our supply of those as well?"

While his friend rattled on about the merits of carbs over sugar, Nick let his mind wander back to the cabin. He ran the list of foodstuffs and liquor, and didn't like how it added up.

"Hey." Dana snapped his fingers. "You still with me?"

"Thinking." He took a long drink of coffee and shut down his computer. "Something's not jibing, but I can't figure out what it is."

Except he was positive he'd seen Anthony Rush, aka Jason Watts, somewhere before.

"I'll check on Sasha, then grab some downtime. By the way—" polishing off his coffee, he made a vague head motion toward the stairs "—your chain saw stopped buzzing several minutes ago."

Sasha awoke with a thud and a gasp. Because the quilt was wrapped around her body, it took her a few confused seconds to realize she'd fallen out of bed.

Shoving the hair from her face, she struggled to untangle her limbs. "Haven't done this since I was seven."

As she wriggled free, she noticed the first rays of dawn creeping over the horizon. Then she heard the sound of smacking lips, followed by a quiet groan.

"Skye?" Climbing to her knees, Sasha stared at the woman lying prostrate on the window seat. Her arms were folded over her sawed-off shotgun, and she was snoring softly.

Touched and amused, Sasha started to laugh. She had to bury her face in her quilt to smother it.

Skye Painter was standing guard for her. The woman owned banks and supermarkets. She raised cattle, bought and sold properties. She was planning to build a luxury resort on Hollowback Mountain, most of which she also owned. And yet here she was, fast asleep on a window seat, with a gray blanket draped over her and an old family shotgun in her arms. It was hysterical.

Or *she* was, Sasha thought, wiping her eyes with her fingers. God, she needed coffee. She also needed to find Nick.

A quietly as possible, she slipped into her silk robe

and cowboy boots. With laughter still tickling her throat, she cracked open the door.

Nothing and no one stirred. But she felt something. A tingling sensation feathered along her spine. The tingle became a jolt when a man's hand closed around her ankle.

Chapter 12

If her heart hadn't been stuck in her throat, Sasha would have roused everyone in the lodge with her scream. Instead, she kicked free and stumbled away, prepared to fight. Until…

"Nick?" She pushed the hair from her face, regarded him in disbelief. "Are you crazy? What are you doing outside my door?"

He used his wrist to rub what had to be a very sore hip. "I'm here because Skye's inside, and she insisted you needed to sleep, not, as she put it, set the damn bedsheets on fire."

"Skye said that?" Her irritation momentarily forgotten, Sasha made a sound of amusement. "I like that."

"Why did I know you would?"

She massaged her throat as if to coax her thudding heart back into place. "A thousand freaky nightmares weren't enough. You have to go and scare another decade off my life. My hair's going to be snow-white before this is over." Suspicion moved in. "Why aren't you getting up?"

"Enjoying the view." He trapped her foot before she could take aim again. "I'm also waiting for feeling to return to my hip. Did you talk to Skye?"

Sasha thought about securing the belt of her robe, but decided not to. More of Barbara's influence perhaps. "She's still asleep. Why?"

He stood, held out his hand to her. "I want to show you something."

This wouldn't be good. He'd gone from totally male and admiring her bare legs to clinical cop in less than five seconds. Although he did slide his knuckles across her collarbone before propelling her down the hall.

She heard a rough sawing sound coming from behind one of the doors, and made a face. "I know it's your turn to watch Bo next, Nick, but is there any point? It isn't like he can leave the mountain."

"Say that again once we get downstairs."

It wasn't an answer, but it was all he would give her until they reached the main floor.

"Okay." He stood her in front of the liquor cabinet behind the bar. "Can you open that?"

She'd known this wouldn't be good. She gave the latch a twist. "No."

"If you shake it?"

She did. "Still no."

"Do you see any scratches on the lock?"

She bent to look. "Not a one."

"And we know Skye's been using the lodge's perimeter alarm system ever since Bo showed up."

"Yes."

"Last question. Do you know where Skye keeps the key for this cabinet?"

"In the cupboard next to the sink with all the other keys, including the wine fridge." She pushed on a blood vessel that throbbed in her neck. "What's missing, Nick?"

"A bottle of Napoleon brandy. Very old, very valuable. Very much something Skye remembers putting inside this cabinet."

The pulse in Sasha's throat began to pound in time with the blood vessel. "Is she sure none of her relatives drank it at Christmas or on New Year's Eve?" The expression on Nick's face had her sighing. "That's a yes."

"She brought it here from Denver for a friend who's coming to Painter's Bluff to judge the ice sculpture contest. Right now, it's in the old hunter's cabin up on the ridge."

"So someone here is helping him." Sasha dropped onto a bar stool. "I don't suppose there's the slightest possibility that I'm still upstairs dreaming." At Nick's level expression, she shook her head. "Didn't think so. Well, it isn't Skye, or Dana or Will. It shouldn't be Max, but it could be Bo. He's being monitored, but not twenty-four hours a day."

"Bo wasn't in the storage shed the night before last."

"And Dana was with me, and Will was…somewhere. Skye sent me out, so it wasn't her.… It wasn't Will," she maintained, at Nick's quick upward glance.

"That leaves only Max, Sasha."

She opened her mouth to protest, then closed it again. "He did borrow some vermouth from our Christmas party supply. But aid and abet a serial killer? I'm sorry, Nick, I can't see it. His firm is rock solid, and he's got an excellent reputation. He designs road systems—overpasses, viaducts, even underground tunnels. He and his partner engineered an incredible double cloverleaf for a Houston freeway two years ago."

Nick zeroed in on the kitchen cupboards. "You said Skye told you she was missing some pears."

"She did, yes. I take it you found pears in the cabin."

"Three jars."

"I still think it's Bo. We heard Rush in the storage shed, and Bo took the pears and brandy. You also mentioned vodka, so maybe he stole some of that as well."

"If I'm Bo, why not simply point Rush up to my shack on the ridge?"

"Because Rush didn't want to stray that far from his food supply, besides which, he doesn't know the mountain. What if he got lost searching for Bo's stash?"

Nick's lips quirked. "That's very logical, Sasha."

"Thank you. You don't buy a word of it, do you?"

"I think it could be Bo."

"So why do I feel like your mind's in overdrive and still deducing?" Because she wanted to touch him, she moved close enough to run a finger along the line of his dimple. "What nefarious thoughts are running through that gorgeous head of yours, Detective?"

The quirk became a smile. Catching her elbows, he brought her forward on the bar stool. "Nefarious, Sasha?"

"Yeah, you know, sinful, wicked, iniquitous, base."

"I'm sinking lower by the second." He blew the hair from her forehead, ran his thumb over her cheekbone. "I've seen Rush somewhere before."

Her heart gave a hard thump. "In one of the serial killer's victims files?"

A ridge formed between his eyes. "I went through

them. There's no photo of a suspect, or anyone associated with the women, who looks like Anthony Rush."

"If that's his name."

"My guess is his real name is Jason Watts."

"Because that was the name on the older driver's license?"

"Older and still valid. Same photo as the one in his passport."

"Which wouldn't be the case if the ID was genuine. Which means it's fake—probably." She smiled. "See, no assumptions. I'm getting better."

"You're getting something," he agreed, then hitched in a breath when she slipped from the stool to bump her hips against his.

"Getting you hard, I hope. Making you hungry. Making me hot." She looped her arms around his neck, tilted her head at a provocative angle. "If Skye won't let us set the damn sheets on fire in my room, maybe we should go to yours."

"Reading my mind, angel— What?" He stopped his mouth half an inch from hers. "Why did you tighten up?"

"I had a dream." She tried to cast it off, but shuddered instead. "You said angel. It reminded me."

"Sorry, bad choice of words."

Her fingers bunched the shoulders of his shirt. "I dreamed that a man—Rush—said he was going to make me pay. I saw an angel inside a snow globe, but it was small globe, the size of a large marble. The angel had a harp, and I heard music. Except it was more like a jangle of metal, so it didn't fit the image." She ran a finger over his throat. "For a moment, Nick, I felt his hands on me. He was shaking, like he wanted to strangle me, but he held himself back. He said when I was dead someone else would suffer. Then suddenly he was gone, and the dream changed."

Nick held her arms, looked into her eyes. "Are you sure you were dreaming?"

"Pretty sure. I think Skye gave me a sedative—not that I needed one to sleep. But it had to be a dream, Nick. Rush couldn't have gotten into my room."

It didn't ease her mind that the concern in his eyes intensified. "Did you see his face?"

"No, not really, but I wouldn't see Rush, would I, because I really don't have a good picture of him in my head. To me, he's pretty much a stained cowboy hat, whiskers and leathery skin. A stereotypical cowboy... What is it?" she prompted when he didn't speak.

"Nothing. A feeling. I need to figure out where I've seen him."

"It was a dream," she insisted. "For the sake of my sanity, Nick, tell me that's all it was. No way could Rush get inside the lodge."

"No, he couldn't," Nick agreed. But his gaze traveled up the stairs, unsettling her. "Unless someone let him in."

The monster thrashed and roared. It inflated, threatened to burst out of his skin.

"Not yet," he begged it. "Not until she's alone, and no one can interfere."

Someone had come dangerously close to interfering last night, but he'd gotten out as he'd gotten in, through her bedroom window.

A snicker welled up, blotting out fear. Security systems were so easily disabled. He wondered how many people really knew that. A little ingenuity, and it was done. He could come and go at will, and no one need ever know.

Of course, they'd figure it out when she was dead, and they saw a snow globe sitting next to her naked body.

Oh, now there was a moment to be savored. That one and all the others to come. The tears. He couldn't wait to see the tears. And the devastation. Daughter dead, mother destroyed.

For the first time in its life, the monster would dance with glee.

Dana slouched in Skye's office chair, drank coffee and glowered at the two-way radio. "How can it almost work one minute and be dead the next? I heard static, Nick, I swear I did, and a man's voice. He said something like, 'Heading out now.' But when I came in here this morning, there was nothing."

Nick noticed a movement in the doorway and saw Bo standing there with a smug smile on his face.

"You like radios, Bo?" he asked mildly.

Both hands went up. "I wasn't nowhere near the thing." He tapped his nose. "But I can sniff out trouble sure enough."

Nick kept his expression pleasant. "So what have you sniffed out lately?"

The smile stretched. "Not a damn thing. Skye says to tell you she's making flapjacks for breakfast." He gave a mocking salute. "See you downstairs, Detective Law, Mayor Hollander."

Dana pushed a knuckle into his temple. "No offense, but I'm glad he's your burden tonight, Nick. He's been eating garlic lately, whole cloves of it. It seeps into your brain, makes you dream about big garlic-headed aliens with snow globes in their hands." He rubbed his eyes and sighed. "Have you seen Max this morning?"

"He's talking road systems with Skye."

"He should be talking radio with me. It was so close to working. There has to be a way to get it back."

"Keep trying. I'm taking Sasha up to the hunter's cabin again."

Dana swiveled his head, incredulous. "Are you out of your mind? That's where Rush is. Or was. She's far safer in the lodge than in a serial killer's lair."

"He won't be there." Nick checked his gun. "I want to see if he left anything behind."

"And you think Sasha's better off with you up there than down here with us? That doesn't make me feel very secure, Nick."

"It's not supposed to." Nick shoved a full ammo clip in place and holstered his gun. "Leave Max with Skye, okay? Work on the radio yourself."

There was nothing inside the hunter's shack, not even an empty can. The fire was cold, the cots were bare, the blankets were gone.

"You had to figure he'd move on." Sasha tested one of the thin mattresses for comfort. "These aren't bad, actually." Her eyes teased him. "Can we be kinky and spend the night here?"

Nick poked around under the bench. "That's not kinky, Sasha, it's crazy."

"I don't know." She bounced again. "If it were my turn to sleep with Bo, I wouldn't dismiss any alternative, reasonable or otherwise. Skye figures the plows should be halfway through the blocked pass by now, unless more snow came down after the initial slide." With one last bounce, Sasha stood. "Nick, what exactly are you looking for?"

"Anything that shouldn't be here."

"You took his ID and his money. I'd say you got the important stuff."

"Uh-huh."

She took a passing swat at his hat. "I could have been playing chess with Max, or tweaking my plans for Skye's resort, but no, I let you talk me into coming back out in the snow and cold with you. And what do I end up doing? Babbling to myself because you want to inspect every dust bunny in the cabin."

"Dust bunnies tell stories."

"Hair and skin particles, DNA. I know. But you were the one who told me that the hair I yanked from Rush's head at that abandoned farmhouse wouldn't do us any good up here. Why did we really came back, Nick? Did you want me out of the lodge because you're worried that Rush's accomplice is going to do something you won't foresee?"

"I wanted you where I thought you'd be safe."

"And if Rush decides to ambush us here?"

Still crouched, Nick scanned the empty room. "Better the devil you know." He frowned. "What's that?"

Sasha bent low, followed his gaze to the fireplace. "I'd say it's a charred log."

Nick was up and moving before she finished the sentence. "It's like being with Sherlock Holmes," she muttered, but straightened and joined him. She glimpsed a partly burned scrap of paper. "What is it, Nick, a label? More ID? A gum wrapper?" Then she spied the letters ARTEGENA and the name Hotel Blanca, and curiosity shimmered. Wrapping her coat around her legs, she crouched beside him. "If that's the Hotel Blanca in Cartagena, I know it."

Nick studied the scorched remains of a matchbook cover. "You've been to Colombia?"

"Twice. We didn't stay at that particular hotel, but it's a big white building with bronze-glass windows. Really impressive. Not so much architecturally but aesthetically. It just sort of hits you in the eye."

"Huh."

"That's it? That's all you have to say?" She couldn't contain her laugh. "No, 'I wonder what this is doing in a cabin where Anthony Rush was staying'?"

"I imagine he used the matches to light his fire."

"There's also a good chance he got the matchbook from the Hotel Blanca in Cartagena. And yet Mr. Rush's passport is a convenient blank."

"Whereas Jason Watts's passport might tell a very different story."

She set her chin on Nick's shoulder. "So if this matchbook does in fact belong to him, what was he doing in Cartagena? None of the women killed by the Snow Globe Killer came from there." Her brows went up. "Drug importer or dealer maybe?"

"Always possible."

"Not someone you'd want to double-cross."

"You never want to double-cross a major-league dealer."

"Are we going to tell the others about this?"

"Our clue, our secret. For now." He ran a thumb over the burned edges. "Are you up to searching George Painter's shack?"

"Well, now that you've piqued my interest, yes." Since Nick was so temptingly close, she kissed him, then sat back to muse. "Rush is a man of many faces. I didn't expect this one. Could a blond female have screwed up a major drug deal for him, and that's what's behind all the deaths? Or maybe she exposed him, and he's using different names so he can continue dealing without anyone realizing who he is."

"Or he could be running and simply needs a false identity."

"My idea's more cloak-and-dagger, more underbelly of the drug world. I like it better than yours." When he didn't respond, she jiggled his shoulder. "You're really bothered that you can't remember where you've seen him, aren't you?"

"Yeah."

Because she wanted him to lighten up before she started feeling frightened again, Sasha kissed his ear. "Relax your mind, and it'll come to you. It works for me. Case in point—remember last night when I told you I've never really gotten a good look at Rush's face? Well, now I'm seeing a scar, a long, fine scar across his chin." Despite her best effort to beat it back, fear crept in. "The freaky thing is, Nick, in my dream I saw Rush's chin quite clearly. There was no scar on it."

Of course, dreams meant nothing, Sasha reminded herself for the rest of the day. It could have been a smear of dust she'd seen on Rush's face. It didn't matter anyway, because he hadn't been in her bedroom last night.

George Painter's shack turned out to be as empty as the hunter's cabin. Unfortunately, that allowed them plenty of time to return to the lodge for dinner.

Cursing and grumbling, Will hobbled downstairs on a set of makeshift crutches. Bo smirked throughout the meal. Max and Dana accused each other of damaging the radio.

"It was working," Dana insisted. "I heard a voice."

"So did I," Max countered. "Just because I jiggled a few wires after you left doesn't mean I killed it. The thing's obsolete."

"That's enough." Skye sounded annoyed. "We'll blame my son-in-law for insisting that old equipment is better than new, and me for listening to him. That's Dana's wine, Bo," she snapped. "Hands off."

Bo sneered. "Can't get drunk on one glass of wine."

"You won't be getting drunk ever again if I have my way." Pyle stabbed a finger at his plate. "Eat your rabbit stroganoff, and shut your damn trap."

Could the atmosphere be any more charged? Sasha wondered. Cabin fever was setting in, and unless he was very careful, Bo would soon be bearing the brunt of his fellow captors' deteriorating tempers.

Transferring her stroganoff to Nick's plate, she blocked the sound of the howling wind outside. Ice pellets pecked at the windows, and even the lodge's chimney refused to draw properly. Smoke billowed into the living room at intervals and gave the air inside a gray, foggy texture.

"Movie night," Skye announced after coffee and dessert. "Who wants to choose?"

Max did the honors. While Sasha didn't mind his selection, she sensed she was in the minority.

"Daughter and mother switch bodies." Pyle elbowed Sasha as he picked up his crutches. "Why do I think you'd love to be in that position?" He turned to Nick. "Talk to you upstairs?"

Lifting Sasha's wrist, Nick regarded her watch. "Too

early to tuck Bo in for the night." He kissed her nose. "Have good dreams this time, huh?"

"I'll try."

The credits rolled before 10:00 p.m. Skye was already snoring in her chair, and Max had fallen into a wine-induced stupor. Sasha removed the disk, shook her companions awake and visualized soaking in a hot tub.

It would have been more fun to have company, she thought as she poured lavender bath gel into the water. But Nick was on Bo patrol, which meant that any sexual fantasies she might have—and she'd had more than her share lately—would have to wait.

She tried not to remember that fantasy and reality were two entirely different things. She wanted Nick in her bed, wanted his hands on her body and him inside her. But what would happen after that? Where would it lead? Where could it lead?

Nowhere.

She made an angry slash in the air when her mother's face popped into her head. What did Barbara have to do with Nick—or with anything in her life?

Why did Nick have to be watching Bo?

The bath lost a portion of its appeal, but she stepped into the water regardless, listened to Keith Urban and wished she'd brought some wine.

Wind rattled the eaves outside. Ice tapped at the windows. Her mind began to drift.

Images formed slowly, with no hard edges or sense of fear. There was snow, billowy soft beneath her, and Nick's hands on her skin. Long fingers skimmed over her breasts to her waist, and farther down, until he slipped between her legs and began stroking her into a frenzy.

She was gasping, arching up to meet him, when everything around her changed. Cold took over from heat. The hands that touched her were no longer Nick's. These squeezed her throat so hard she couldn't breathe. She heard the pounding of her own heart. There was no air, only a man's face in the shadows above her.

For a moment, he bore down harder. Then he laughed and reached up. Whipping the scar from his chin, he stretched it into a garrote and wrapped it around her throat.

"Tonight you die," he promised in a harsh whisper. "No assumption there, Sasha Myer. That's cold, hard fact."

The temperature dipped to five degrees. He couldn't take much more of this. Waiting, always waiting. Hiding, skulking in the dark. Listening to his mother squawk at him every time he managed a quiet moment.

"It's no fun to suffer before you die, is it?" she taunted him. "You made me suffer, then you killed me. You deserve to be here." Her voice became a sarcastic drawl. "Poor, stupid Anthony Rush."

"Shut up," he shouted, and blocked his ears. "Go away. Leave me alone."

"Who the hell are you talking to?"

The question struck him like a blow to the jaw. He whirled, gun in hand, had to breathe through his teeth many times before he could pry his finger off the trigger.

His visitor's cheeks paled. "Are you all right?" he managed to ask.

"Idiot. How can I be all right? The city cop took my ID and my cash. You have to get them back."

"I can't. You know I can't."

"Then you'll have to get more. That cop's not taking

me in. I'm not going to prison. You throw him off my scent or I swear, you'll be going down with me. Do it," he growled, sensing an objection. "If you want to get off this mountain in one piece, Cousin, you'll do exactly as I say."

Chapter 13

Sasha surged upright, splashing water and bubbles on the bathroom floor. It took her several seconds to orient herself and calm her racing heart.

"I've got to stop doing this." She breathed out, let the nightmare break apart and reality sink in. It had started so well—her and Nick and the heady promise of sex. How had Rush managed to sneak in?

No more baths, she resolved, and reached for a towel on the warming rack. Only showers. You couldn't fall asleep in the shower.

Wrapping herself in her white terry robe, she drained the tub and set her mind on another room down the hall. She wasn't going to think about Anthony Rush. She wanted a more tantalizing dream. She wanted a tall, gorgeous cop with incredible eyes, amazing hands and God knew what else. She wanted Nick.

Shoulders squared, she opened her bedroom door. And slammed face-first into a man's chest.

Nick caught her arms before she could leap back. "It's me." He redirected the knee aimed for his groin. "Only me."

The shaky breath she blew out surprised him. He'd expected her to give him a light jab in the gut for scaring her. Truthfully, he wished she'd done that rather than collapsing against him as if something or someone else had done the scaring.

"What is it?" He nudged her far enough back to capture her chin and tilt her head up. "Was someone here?"

"Only in my imagination. It's a delayed reaction. When I ran into you, I was running into Rush. I dreamed about him again." Nick felt the chill that rippled through her. "I was in the bathtub, and you were with me."

"Sounds good so far."

"I thought so. But then you mutated into him. He ripped off his scar and tried to strangle me with it."

Nick ran a comforting hand along her back. "I blew up the bottom half of Rush's face on my computer tonight. There's a faint white scar on his chin."

"Oh, good, so my powers of detection under duress are intact. Why am I dreaming about him, Nick? And why is he still a shadow in my dreams? I know what he looks like now. I memorized every feature today from the photo you showed me." It relieved him to hear vexation rather than fear in her voice. "Why did he wrap his scar around my neck?" She raised her head. "I hate weird dreams."

"Is there any other kind?"

The barest hint of a smile crossed her lips. "I've had

a few lately, and Rush had no part in them." To demonstrate, she moved her hips against him.

The action drew a swift surge of heat to Nick's lower body. It fascinated him how quickly she could go from being terrified to seducing him so completely that he almost forgot how to swallow.

Her eyes danced. "I've had some pretty erotic dreams since I arrived in Painter's Bluff. Even more since we got snowed in."

His gaze lingered on her mouth. He wanted to dive in and devour her. But he needed to be sure she was no longer frightened.

"You want to get into the details of your dreams, or leave them to my rather limited imagination?"

A knowing gleam entered her eyes. "I don't think anything about you is limited, Detective." She walked her hands up and over his shoulders. "I was coming to find you a moment ago. Now suddenly, here you are." Her lashes fell halfway as suspicion slipped in. "Why are you here? You weren't going to sleep in the hall again, were you? Because you're supposed to be on Bo patrol and…" She halted, glanced down. "Is that glass I'm feeling? Ahh." Her smile returned when she spied the wine.

"French Bordeaux, 1972."

Teasing fingers threaded through his hair. She kissed the corner of his mouth, made his head spin. "What about Bo?"

"Will showed up fifteen minutes ago to relieve me. His idea." Nick inhaled her scent, gave in and nuzzled a slow path down the side of her neck. "I didn't argue."

"So we're…mmm." Her arms tightened around him when he raised his head. "No, don't stop. That was a good mmm."

"I'm not stopping." He kissed her temples, her eyelids, her cheekbones. "I'm working my way toward the best part."

When he finally reached her lips, he felt them turn up into a grin. "If you think this is my best part, I'm gonna blow you away, Nick Law."

The fire inside begin to rage as he fed on her mouth. For once in his life he didn't care where he wound up when the night was done, as long as he wound up with her.

Sasha hadn't expected a single, albeit spectacular, kiss to consume her, but it did.

Shock jolted through her bloodstream. Emotions, needs, desires—everything jumbled together, then fused in her head. She wanted him with a breathlessness she couldn't remember experiencing before.

His tongue in her mouth brought a dozen wicked thoughts to mind. It wouldn't just be sex, couldn't be that simple between them. This was Nick, and although the desire to be reckless was strong, Sasha also felt a burning need for more.

That was a distant thought, however, floating in a place way down inside her head. If she went there now and really thought about it, she'd scare herself to death.

Better to go with the moment and damn the consequences. For tonight.

Nick's mouth made her crazy. She wanted to drink him in, to absorb him, because touching was no longer enough. She backed into her room, heard him kick the door closed with his foot.

"Put the bottle down," she managed to say in a thready voice. "I have candles."

He smiled against her lips. "Seriously?"

"Tahitian spice. My mother gave them to me for Christmas."

"And you brought them to Painter's Bluff?"

Her fingers tugged at the hem of his black T-shirt. "I do have some romance in my soul, you know."

"Uh-huh."

When his dimple appeared, she couldn't resist slicking her tongue over it.

"What happened to Ma Barker's younger sister?"

"She has her place. This isn't it." His T-shirt dealt with, Sasha turned her attention to his jeans. Why were top buttons always impossible to open?

Nick appeared to have his own agenda. Ignoring her attempts to strip away his clothes, he circled her waist with his hands and lifted her up. Eyes glittering, but intent on her task, she wrapped her legs around his hips and let him reach for her mouth.

There was something between them, had been from the day they'd met. Something, as he'd suggested, that had more to do with souls than sex. Was that what was buried in her mind? If so, this was no time to be calling it up.

She continued to work on his fly. "Stupid jeans." She tore at the button, heard it fly across the room. "Oops." She tugged on the zipper. "Good thing you have extra clothes. Otherwise everyone here would know what we're doing."

"Most of them think we've been doing it all along."

"Really?" For some reason, the notion delighted her. "In that case, let's bang around a lot, give their imaginations something to work on."

The zipper released. Mission accomplished, she set

her hands on his shoulders. "How's your blood pressure, Detective?"

"Explosive."

She wriggled against him, then gasped with pleasure when he closed his mouth over her breast.

Exquisite pain shot through her, arrowed from breast to thigh. Her breath came in spasms. She dug her fingernails into his shoulders and laid her forehead against his hair.

Cool air flowed across her skin. It carried the scent of spice and soap and clean male flesh. His hair was like silk where it brushed her throat. He lowered her onto the bed but kept his mouth on her.

Sensation spiked through her from every direction, meeting in a swirl of desire between her legs.

Shivers rocked her body. Anticipation and delight spun like glittery snowflakes in her head.

She slid her hands over his skin, savored the satiny smooth texture and the ripple of muscle beneath it. A surging cramp of desire had her stifling the moan that would have emerged. With a final flick of his tongue, Nick removed his mouth from her nipple and blew teasingly on the damp flesh.

He'd almost sent her over the edge already, and they'd only begun.

Grabbing a handful of his hair, she yanked. "This isn't fair. I want to do the seducing."

His looked straight at her. "You are," he replied, and even by candlelight, she could see how dark his hazel eyes had grown.

He let him remove her robe while she tugged off his jeans. Another onslaught of emotions whipped up inside her. Reaching out a finger, she traced the line of his arousal. He was beautiful.

When he would have pulled her against him, she set a hand on his chest. "My turn," she murmured and, sliding down, took him in her mouth.

His reaction was automatic, a harsh intake of breath and a sudden stillness that spoke far more eloquently than words.

She used her teeth and tongue to explore him. There was something vaguely decadent about wanting a man so much. This wasn't casual sex. This felt important. And very, very right.

"Ah, okay." His hands gripped her arms, hauled her upright.

She saw the strain on his face, set her hands on his shoulders. "Only okay, Nick?"

"Incredible." He managed a deep breath. "Euphoric."

"Better." She swayed into his hips, kept her eyes on his face. His groan came out with a laugh.

"Do that again, Sasha, and my self-control's history. We need to slow down."

Yet even as he spoke, his fingers were sliding along her inner thigh. Her breath hitched. She felt them enter her, and made a strangled sound.

"I don't call that slowing down."

His eyes glinted in the candlelight. "We'll call it prolonging the moment then." And lowering his head, he replaced his fingers with his tongue.

There was nothing more to be done, nothing more she could have done except hold on and enjoy the ride.

She fell back onto the sheets. The heat that had been simmering inside for days enveloped her. She pressed her palms to his arms and let her head arch on the pillow.

He was all smooth flesh and lean, wiry muscle. He made the darkness go away, made her drunk and dizzy. Sensation after sensation ripped through her. She raced upward, knew she was heading toward that wonderful precipice. She'd never been this high before. The fall was going to be spectacular—and potentially heartbreaking.

It didn't matter. She dug her fingers into his skin, arched her hips now as well as her neck. And welcomed the climax that shuddered through her in a fierce tidal wave of color and light and wild, raging sound.

"Wow," she gasped when she could speak. "Now, that was totally not fair."

He nuzzled the skin of her belly all the way to the underside of her breast. Following the sensitive curve with his tongue, he murmured, "Night's young, Sasha."

He sounded like she felt—maybe not quite as breathless, but certainly thunderstruck. And just a little too damned pleased with himself.

She dragged air into her lungs, wriggled out from under him and, with absolutely no resistance on his part, shoved him onto his back. "My bed, Nick, my rules. We're going to—"

He cut her off with an openmouthed kiss that rolled right through her body as he pulled her up to straddle him.

He was hot and pulsing, and she wanted him inside her. Though she was still reeling from her initial climax, a deeper, more desperate need began to build. A person could die from this; she was sure of it. Too much desire, too many screaming emotions, not quite enough Nick.

Leaning in, she caught his lip between her teeth and bit down. In the same moment, she took him in her hand and squeezed.

"It's called exquisite torture, Nick."

His eyes were dark with emotions she couldn't begin to read.

"I know what it's called." And in a move so swift she almost missed it, he lifted her up and slid inside.

She made a shocked sound, then simply gave up and went with the wonder of the moment. She felt shaken from head to toe. Nick was beautiful in the half-light. She could have ridden him all night.

Matching her rhythm to his, she delighted in each thrust. She tossed her head back and let him drive her up and over. She felt a primitive need to cry out, but they weren't alone in the lodge, so she breathed through it. Breathed until she was sure her galloping heart could handle the strain.

Still inside her, Nick caught her hips. "Say my name, Sasha. I want you to say my name."

Her muscles had gone limp and oddly numb. "Can't speak yet," she managed to gasp. Then she yelped and moaned when, lightning quick, he simultaneously thrust deeper and opened his mouth over hers.

It was several seconds before she could form a coherent thought. When she did, her eyes glittered. "Do that again... Nicky."

A faint smile appeared. He looked winded and drained and completely staggered by his release. "As soon as I can move, I will."

"Baby steps," she teased, and splayed her fingers across his rib cage. "Start in the middle and work outward in both directions. I'll show you."

And in a deliberately seductive fashion, she began to gyrate her hips.

* * *

Three hours later, Nick was surprised he could remember his name. If Sasha hadn't teased him by saying it over and over again, he might have worried that he'd blown out his brain.

She'd fallen asleep in his arms, with her head pillowed on his chest and her hair tickling his chin. She had, he reflected, an amazing body. She'd known exactly how to make love to him, had known every button that needed to be pushed, every emotional tail that needed to be tweaked. She'd made him feel things he'd never felt before, things he still didn't understand—or entirely trust.

If a part of him accepted the Native American philosophy he'd heard as a child, another, larger part was fully prepared to shoot it down. You couldn't fall in love with someone in a matter of days. It had to be lust; on both sides, it could only be physical.

He'd keep thinking that until he convinced himself. Or until he talked to his father's Blackfoot foreman. It amused more than unnerved Nick to realize he'd prefer to believe the old man.

Sasha shifted next to him. He almost laughed at his body's instant response. They'd made love three times in three hours. He couldn't possibly have the strength to do it again.

Eyes closed, she murmured lazily, "Don't move, Nick. Not a single muscle. I go to the gym, but I'm not Wonder Woman. I may never ride a horse again."

"I'll take that as a compliment."

Her sigh stirred the hair on his chest. "You want to hear something freaky? I can't remember what day it is. I've been lying here trying not to think about making love with you again, and suddenly it hit me, I don't know if it's Wednesday, Thursday or Friday."

"It's Friday."

"Well, you could compliment me back by at least pretending not to remember."

He chuckled a little. "I only know because it's Dana's oldest son's birthday in seven days, and he's afraid he's going to miss the party."

Easing away, she levered up on one elbow. "Skye thinks we'll be out of here by then. I don't know why she thinks that, but I'm willing to trust her." Sasha used her index finger to draw a circle around Nick's nipple. "The same way I trust you, only without the sexual aspect."

"Uh-huh."

Humor flitted across her face. "You're such a talker, Nick. Is that the cowboy way, the cop way, or both?"

"It's my way." He kissed the back of her hand, dropped his gaze to the shadowy *V* of her breasts. "Just like it was yours to take me on a sexual roller coaster ride and get my head so messed up that Bo Sickerbie could strut in here, steal my wallet and your purse, and I'd probably let him strut right out again, because I'd rather make love to you than chase after him."

"So we're agreed, it was incredible."

"Unless you can think of a more powerful word, yeah, it was incredible."

"Oh, I have lots of words. Daughter of an English teacher, remember?" She transferred her attention to his navel. "I can't imagine what she'd make of you."

Nick trapped her wandering fingers. "Sasha, tell me what happened between us didn't have anything to do with your mother."

Her eyes glimmered briefly. "I'd never take a lover to

spite my mother, Nick. Or to please her. I went out with a boy she chose for me when I was fifteen, and I promised myself that same night I'd never do it again."

"Geek?" Nick guessed.

"Jock. Jerk. My mother's always been into that type. She figures I should follow her example. Instead, I follow my instincts." She glanced away. "And my heart."

The candles she'd lit had burned themselves out, and only the memory of a fire glowed in the hearth. They'd made love, drunk wine and made love again. And again. Like Sasha, Nick had gone with his instincts. But he still had to wonder if those instincts had been fueled by something deeper.

"Oh, hell," he sighed into her hair.

Even in darkness, he glimpsed the amusement that replaced the momentary uncertainty in her eyes. "I'm trying really hard not to develop a complex here, Nick."

"That 'hell' was self-directed. I'm the one with the complex."

"If you mean complex as in character, I agree."

"Hey, I'm an open book compared to a lot of people."

"Yeah, guys like Leonardo da Vinci and Franciscan monks."

"Monks live extremely simple lives, Sasha."

"Life without sex can't possibly be simple." Pushing back the covers, she leaned over the edge of the bed. "The wine bottle's here, but I have no idea what happened to the glasses. We'll have to be barbaric and swill it."

He watched her wriggle her luscious butt back into place, and thought about taking a bite.

As if reading his mind, she dangled the bottle in front of him for the first sip. "Talk to me, Nick. I said your name—actually, I think screamed it once or twice—so you owe me. Even a token will do."

He took the bottle from her, couldn't quite wrestle his gaze from the dips and curves of her body. "If you want coherent speech, you'll have to cover up."

"No problem." She went for the edge of the mattress again and came up with his T-shirt. It covered her to midthigh, which, figuratively speaking, was better than nothing.

He took a long drink to soothe his raw throat. "Okay, what do you want to know?"

"Whatever you want to tell me."

Shirt or not, he could see the delineation of her breasts. Was that called obsession? "We've dealt with my not great marriage, and you know how I met Dana. What's left?"

"Depending on how you look at it, over twenty-five years. You hung out with Dana from age six to twelve, married Lacey for three. You rounded up cattle with fractured ribs, went to college—no idea which one— fished at a local hole with Will and Dana and showed up in Painter's Bluff the day after Kristiana Felgard was murdered. That's not much to know about a man I just made love with."

"Three times."

"Exactly."

He leaned against the headboard. She sat cross-legged beside him. Snow drifted through the darkness, but while the wind had died down, the gusts still contained enough bluster to bow the larger trees.

He watched huge white flakes dance beyond the window. "I don't spend much time with people these days. There's my partner, Ray, but he's considered eccentric.

He lives in a trailer outside Denver with his father, who's a retired marine, and a kid who used to live on the street. Outside of him, there's no one."

"No woman, huh?"

He shook his head and couldn't help the smile. "Not yet."

"So I'm picturing a solitary man."

"I was trying to put a more positive spin on it, but yeah, I am. I spend a lot of time on my computer."

"Don't you have to question suspects?"

"That's work related. Ask questions, get answers, get out. There's nothing gregarious about it."

She poked a finger into his side. "I'm not going to ask the obvious question again, Nick."

"Why a cold case cop?"

"You don't have to tell me." She inched the hem of his shirt up, sent him a purposely flirty smile. "No pressure."

He debated between flipping her onto her back or baring a small part of his soul. The first was tempting, but she deserved the second.

"I worked with a detective in Chicago Homicide." He swirled the wine, took a sip. "I didn't like him. He was obnoxious, loud and sarcastic. But he was good at his job. He had an ex and a daughter named Lynda. She was eleven when she went missing."

"Missing," Sasha echoed with vague horror. "At eleven?"

"It's a difficult age." Nick's mind vaulted backward, as if the crime had happened yesterday. "She might have run off, she might have been taken. Whatever the case, she turned up dead. A restaurant owner found her body in a Dumpster six weeks after she disappeared." He looked away. "She'd been raped. I can still see her face. She looked totally innocent. She was totally innocent."

"Did you get DNA samples from the rapist?"

"We got all kinds of samples. None of them was a match for any of our suspects. We had every male member of her family tested, neighbors, even one of her teachers. We investigated her death for three years. There was nothing, no clues, no witnesses. The last person to see her alive was a cashier in a video store. He said she came in to return a movie. He saw her riding out of the parking lot on her bike. It was eight at night, two days before Halloween."

"Are there many gangs in Chicago?" Sasha asked. Then she waved him off. "Stupid question. They're everywhere, and I'm sure you looked into it."

"Gangs, cults, the drug scene, prostitution."

"My God, Nick, she was eleven."

"It's the new twenty. She didn't seem street savvy, but kids have fooled people before, especially their parents."

"Been there," Sasha said softly. "How did her father handle it?"

"Badly. He went from being an obnoxious jerk to a shell of a man in less than two months. He died in February of the next year."

"Of grief or a bullet?"

"High speed chase, but it was the grief that brought it about. He stopped being a good cop because he thought he'd been a bad father."

"And Lynda's case went cold." At Nick's level look, Sasha sighed. "That's when you decided to become a cold case investigator."

"Three years later, but yeah. Her death was the

clincher. When the team in Denver was being put together, I was invited to join."

"Did you ever…" She let a hand motion complete the question.

He knew what she meant. Had he ever found Lynda's killer. "No. Sometimes there's no resolution. Other times, a case springs back to life."

"Example, the Snow Globe Killer."

His expressive eyes captured her troubled ones. "I promise you, Sasha, you're not going to be a victim."

"And I'll bet you hardly ever make promises, do you?"

"It's a rare thing."

Leaning forward, she hooked her fingers around the sheet. "Why is it," she wondered aloud, "that I find that quality so incredibly erotic all of a sudden? Doesn't make promises, but he's killer sexy in bed."

He said nothing, merely watched her inch closer.

She touched the side of his mouth. "Did I mention that I love dimples on a man? Because I do… Ahh!"

He had her on her back so fast, it drew a laugh.

"So much for the gentle art of persuasion." Crossing her arms, she caught the hem of his shirt and tugged it over her head. "I take it you're up for more fun."

"Yeah, I'm up for it." He captured her wrists, pinned them on either side of the pillow. "This time I think we should take a page out of Skye's book and set the damn sheets on fire."

Minutes ticked by like hours, hours like days. Three o'clock came and went. He had to be careful not to slip on the icy roof. However, the pitch was shallow on this side, so all he really needed to be was quiet.

He used a penlight to peer through the first window.

Two beds, two bodies, both asleep. That was the bothersome city cop taken care of. Switching off, he made his way along the roof, past three more windows to the far end.

He felt for the snow globe in his coat pocket. There it was, his beautiful, bitter token, smaller than usual, but adequate. And of course he had his weapon.

Fingers flexing, he paused for a moment to anticipate and savor. But the monster was pushing hard. It didn't want to wait.

Sweat broke out on his brow. His heart thudded.

"This one's for Mommy," he whispered. And eased the window, rigged to open for him, upward in its track.

Chapter 14

It was Nick's turn to dream.

He was in Chicago, or maybe it was Denver, walking down a stinking alley. He heard people breathing in the shadows, and rat feet scrabbling inside garbage cans. A burst of frigid air assaulted him. He saw the Dumpster ahead, but didn't want to look inside. They'd found an eleven-year-old girl here once. What would he find tonight?

Will Pyle's young deputy appeared beside him. In his palms, he held the smashed remains of a snow globe. The angel's head was missing.

"Something's not right, Nicky." Pyle's voice boomed out from his other side. "Why does Rush's face seem so familiar to you? D'you think he's on a most-wanted list?"

No, Nick didn't think that. It was something about the shape of the jaw and maybe the eyes.

"I'm out of practice noticing details," Pyle admitted. "Used to look at people closely all the time, but I only see the ones that matter these days." He clamped a hand onto Nick's arm as they drew alongside the Dumpster. "You don't want to look in there, son."

But Nick knew he had to, and when he did, his stomach gave a violent lurch. He stumbled backward, bent over and breathed through his mouth. He felt something vile and black swimming in his head. She wasn't dead. He wouldn't let her be dead.

Another blast of winter air struck him like a blow from behind. He heard a scraping sound and more breathing.

And then he woke up.

Sasha heard Nick's voice. It sounded hushed but urgent. Her eyes flew open. Why couldn't she breathe?

"Are you awake?"

He spoke from directly above her. She nodded, pushed at the hand covering her mouth.

"Don't make any noise."

"What is it?" she whispered when he released her.

"Someone's in the room."

She blinked to clear her mind. "Is it Rush?"

Nick was already dragging on his jeans, T-shirt and boots. "Stay there." He picked up his gun, jammed a backup in his waistband.

As quietly as possible, Sasha slipped from the bed, pulling on her own jeans and top.

There were two large windows in the room. The one beside the bed could only be reached by a ladder, but the other window sat directly above a small lower roof. That, she was sure, was the intruder's point of entry.

She banged her shin on a chair, but bit down on her tongue and didn't utter a sound.

Icy air wafted over her skin. A shadow fell on the floor. She glimpsed the intruder, or part of him. He crept forward, halted as if shocked, then backpedaled swiftly.

Nick was on him before he could return to the window. But Rush—at least she assumed it was Rush—evaded by shoving the ottoman in Nick's direction, forcing him to stop or trip.

The knife came out of nowhere, large and gleaming. Sasha ran for the light switch, while Nick went for his gun.

Like a Vegas showman, Rush flung the knife at Nick then, using the sofa as a springboard, he dived out the window.

Nick swore, fired once. Sasha hit the light.

"Get Will," Nick called as he vaulted through the window in Rush's wake.

Sasha wanted to go after him, but she gritted her teeth and ran for Bo's room.

Skye met her in the hall. "I heard a shot."

Sasha had to swallow before she could answer. "Rush broke into my room. Nick's gone after him." She pounded on Bo's door. "Sheriff, wake up!" When he didn't answer, she barged in. "Wake up, Will!"

He croaked like a bullfrog coming to life. "What? What's wrong?"

She shook him with both hands until his eyes opened. "Nick's outside chasing Rush. I don't know how, but he got into the lodge."

"I set the alarm," Skye said from the doorway. "It was on when I came upstairs. Nick checked it while I was getting the wine."

"What wine?" Will raised his head. "What's going on?"

Sasha shook him again. A hibernating bear had nothing on this man. "Nick's chasing Rush." Although she was practically shouting, the lump in the other bed didn't move. It didn't make any noise, either. Suspicious, she regarded the covers. "I thought Bo snored."

Groggy, but clueing in, Will reached over and snatched the blanket away, revealing two pillows and a wadded up fleece throw that had been crudely fashioned into the shape of a body.

Sasha grabbed the front of Pyle's undershirt. "How could you not notice that he was gone?" At his stunned expression, however, she relaxed her grip. "I'm sorry. I'm worried about Nick. Can you walk?"

"I will whether I can or not. Outside, both of you, while I get dressed. Which way did they go?"

"Out the window on this side of the lodge. I don't know which direction they ran." Panic wanted to overwhelm her, but she wouldn't let it. "Rush had a knife. He threw it at Nick. Nick shot at him."

"Hell with clothes." Pyle climbed awkwardly to his feet, started for the door at a hobble. "I can't go gallivanting around in the snow. Let's see your room."

His long johns bagged as he limped double time down the hall and into her bedroom. "This the window?"

"No, it's the other one, in the sitting area."

Snow blew in, coating the sill and the top of the chairs. The curtain panels billowed with every gust of wind.

"Footprints on the roof end here," Pyle observed. "Only one set slip-slides past the other bedroom windows and on to yours. The double set takes off that way, toward the woods. They must've gone down the eaves."

Rush would have been dressed for the cold, but Nick

wasn't. Raking the hair from her face, Sasha made an agitated circuit of the alcove. Where had they gone? Did Rush have a gun? Was Nick going to come back alive?

"Yes, he will," she said out loud. "He will." She spied the knife Rush had thrown. The blade was hidden under the ottoman. Eyes on the handle, she bent to examine it. "Will…"

"Window's been tampered with," the sheriff announced. "Someone's taped the latches so they won't catch. What is it, Sasha?"

She'd been backing away from the ottoman and wound up bumping into him.

"There's blood on the handle of the knife."

"What? Where?" He hobbled to the ottoman, shoved it aside. "Damn!" He ran a hand over his face. "Damn."

There was blood on the blade as well.

"Nick, are you out here? Nick!"

He heard Dana calling, but couldn't really tell from which direction. He felt as if he'd been stumbling around inside a titanic freezer, and somewhere along the line, he'd lost sight of the door.

He knew he was losing blood, not as much as he would have in a tropical climate, but enough to disorient him. Although the cold could be largely responsible for that.

"Where are you, Nick?"

"No idea," he replied, but he knew Dana couldn't hear him. "Just hope Rush is in the same condition."

Nick's breath steamed out as he struggled for air. His left arm felt sticky—or, well, frozen now, but it had been sticky for a while.

"Come on, Nick. I know you're here. The lodge is this way. Follow my voice."

How could a single sound come from a dozen different directions? Nick squinted through the thickening snow but saw only vague outlines of trees and misshapen white boulders that resembled freeze-dried ghosts.

He knew he had some blood left because it pounded in his head, so hard and loud he couldn't think. Didn't matter, anyway. The wind kept billowing up, whipping Dana's voice away.

"Nick?"

Sasha's voice joined Dana's. Nick turned instinctively toward it.

"Come on, Law, where are you?"

Max, too? He must've been out here longer than he realized.

"Please answer, Nick," Sasha called.

She sounded closer—or was that wishful thinking? He forced his legs to move. The wind geared down for a moment, and he thought he saw a glimmer of light through the blowing snow.

The lodge?

"Nick?" Sasha tried again.

"Here." He blew out a breath, couldn't seem to get enough air back in.

"Nick?" The light intensified, dazzled his eyes. "You need to give me more than one syllable to follow."

The male voices faded out as he concentrated on Sasha's.

"I'm here." He had to bend to breathe now. God, it was cold. He'd done the cool shirtsleeves-in-winter thing as a teenager. Why hadn't he noticed the temperature then?

He made himself move forward. Those were the lodge lights, he was sure of it. The smaller one swinging from side to side ahead of him had to be Sasha.

"Answer me, Nick," she shouted.

"Right here, angel." Bad word. He stood, let his head fall back and the snow dust his face. "Straight ahead."

"Ni—"

This time his name didn't quite make it out of her mouth. He snapped his head up, focused. "Sasha?"

"I'm okay." The light bobbled. "I tripped. Where are you?"

"Where are *you?*"

"Left, go left. My foot's caught on— Oh my God!"

"What?" He couldn't see her. "Sasha, what is it?"

She stumbled out of the darkness, with no flashlight, and a look of terror on her face.

He grasped the arms she threw around his neck. "What?" Her light still shone where she'd dropped it in the snow. It beamed across a low boulder. "Are you hurt?"

"I— It's—"

He shook her. "Tell me what's wrong. What happened?"

"I tripped." She glanced toward the long rock. "Over Bo. His eyes are open, and he's not breathing. Nick, Bo's dead."

It was controlled pandemonium inside the lodge. Skye stacked logs in the hearth. When Max and Dana returned, Will sent them straight back out to retrieve Bo's body. Nick thawed in front of the fire and let Sasha clean him up.

She soaked off the shirt frozen to his injured shoulder. The wound hurt like hell thanks to Rush's earlier knife-throwing act, but the kiss she brushed across his cheek took away some of the sting.

"I'm glad you're okay," she murmured.

"He needs stitches," Skye stated, looking over his shoulder. "I'll get the kit."

"Kit?" His head might be buzzing, but he recognized a threat when he heard one. "You're not sticking needles in me, Skye."

Sasha sighed. "If she doesn't, you'll bleed to death."

"Liar."

"All right, you'll have a scar."

"Already got one." Couldn't see it, but it was somewhere in the vicinity of his right shoulder. This new one would simply balance it off.

"Men." Sasha pressed a glass to his lips. "Here, drink up. Skye says this whiskey's so strong you wouldn't feel cannon fire."

Sounded fine to him. He swallowed, felt the burn strip the air from his lungs, and wondered vaguely if he'd ever breathe normally again.

Woozy but determined to stay alert, he set his eyes on Sasha's face. Her life was at stake here. Bo Sickerbie was dead. Sasha wasn't going to join him.

"Better now, Nicky?" Pyle settled his bulky frame on the hearth. "Fire's hotter than hell. Should get your blood production up pretty quick."

"Sleep wouldn't hurt," Sasha added, but smiled when Nick caught her gaze. "Yes, I know, there's no time."

Nick turned to Will. "You shouldn't have sent Max and Dana out to get Bo's body. It's too dangerous with Rush still running around loose."

"Body's less than a hundred yards from the lodge, Nicky. By morning, Rush might've dragged Bo off, and we'd have squat."

While Nick saw the logic in his argument, he also

knew how determined Rush was, and apparently how insane.

The room took on a hazy texture. Not a good sign. Resting his arms on his knees, Nick dropped his head forward and exhaled slowly.

He needed to think. Something felt wrong, but for the life of him he couldn't grasp it.

Faces drifted through his mind, with Rush's front and center. He hadn't seen it on a poster, but that niggle of familiarity lingered.

The front door opened, and Dana clattered in. "We put Bo in the car barn. It's close to the house and alarmed."

Speaking of alarms… "The perimeter alarm was on before I went upstairs tonight, Dana," Nick said through the pounding in his temples. "It was locked in, and Skye's the only one who knows the code."

"Bo must've gotten hold of it somehow." Pyle massaged his ankle. "Skye says he snooped through every drawer, cupboard and closet in the lodge."

Sasha shook her head. "It's not written down anywhere, Will. Only Skye has the numbers."

"Then Bo figured it out."

"Not a chance," Nick said. "One of Skye's techno-geek grandchildren installed the thing. It's state of the art. Bo didn't have the brain power to tamper with such a sophisticated system."

"The dumb-ass bumpkin thing could've been an act," Pyle countered.

Could've, might've. Nick pressed on his burning eyelids. "Check the alarm, Dana."

Skye marched in with a long, lethal-looking needle sitting on a bed of white cotton.

"You've got to be joking." Nick stared up at her. "You're not stitching me with that."

"Did he drink the whiskey?" Skye asked Sasha.

"Every drop."

He looked from woman to woman, then closed his eyes and gave a short laugh. "I don't believe this. You drugged the whiskey?"

"Skye's idea," Sasha whispered. "You won't sleep for long. I only let her give you half a dose."

"Of what?"

"Don't worry, Nick. I never put the people I love at risk. I'll be here. You'll be fine."

People she loved...

The words echoed in his mind. Dana's grim announcement, "Someone's been screwing with this alarm," stopped the echo and brought Nick's head up.

"Screwing with it how?" he demanded, hanging on. "Tell me fast, Dana."

"The lights are working, making it seem like the system's up and running. But it's all for effect. The alarm itself is completely disabled."

"Bo didn't do it," Nick said for the tenth time since he'd woken up. "He wasn't computer savvy enough to pull it off."

"I agree." Sasha had her fingers hooked in his waistband in an effort to keep him on the bed. "Come on, Nick, you were only out for three hours. It's midmorning. Skye says you have to be careful not to tear your stitches. And you can't possibly have recovered from last night yet."

He cast her a wry look. "What part of last night are you referring to, Sasha?"

"All parts." She tugged on his belt loop when he went to stand. "Can't I at least feed you soup and say 'Poor baby' before you go charging off after the bad guy?"

"Try it when I have the flu. Injuries just piss me off."

"Nick…"

"Bo's dead, Sasha."

She refused to let go. "You could be dead, too. Bo must have been helping Rush. Maybe Rush told Bo how to disable the alarm. But Bo did something, or he screwed something up, or maybe he just pissed Rush off. The alarm wasn't really on, Bo knew it, ran outside while all the commotion was unfolding upstairs, and Rush whacked him with a rock. Dana even found the rock next to Bo's body. If Will can buy the scenario, why do you need to complicate it?"

"It's too easy, too neat."

A sigh escaped. "I knew you were going to say that."

"Which means you must have thought it yourself." He worked a fresh T-shirt over his head, let her tug it into place.

"I did," she conceded. "But sometimes neat and tidy is simply the way a situation turns out. Listen to me, Nick. I got mugged once in New York when I was seventeen. I had three hundred dollars in my purse. Not smart, I know, but it was a birthday gift from my uncle, so what could I do? Anyway, the mugger had a knife, and he grabbed my purse. After he took off, I saw something on the ground. It was his wallet. His name and address were inside. He got arrested, and I got everything back except for my three hundred dollars."

Nick's eyes narrowed. "You got mugged?"

She smiled. "That was way back at the beginning of my story. Did you happen to catch the ending?"

"The mugger dropped his wallet. Why?"

"Because he was a klutz, I imagine."

"So you didn't fight him at all."

"Of course I fought him. I was seventeen. I had two credit cards in my purse, each with a ten thousand dollar limit."

"And the fact that this guy had a knife was no big deal?"

"My mother was the primary card holder, Nick. Payment of those cards was her responsibility. The mugger might have cut me during the struggle, but if he'd gotten away and gone on a spending spree, my mother would have killed me. Not literally, but close enough that it was worth the risk. Besides, everything worked out fine. Very neat and easy."

"Right." He stood with care, didn't sway as he looked around for his gun.

Reluctantly amused, Sasha opened her bedside drawer and handed it to him. "Didn't register at all, did it? My story." She waved a dismissing hand. "No relevance whatsoever."

"I don't believe Bo disabled the alarm."

"What about Rush? Maybe Bo snuck him into the lodge early on, and he did the disabling."

"Where was Max last night?"

"Max?" She had to realign her mind. "I'm not sure. After we found the bloody knife, there was a lot of confusion. I was trying very hard not to panic. Skye started banging on doors and shouting. I helped Will get downstairs. Then I ran back up for my boots, grabbed my coat, gun and flashlight, and went out looking for you."

"I heard Dana's voice first," Nick told her, "then yours, then Max's. Were you together at any point?"

"No. I heard Dana, too. He was somewhere to my right. Max was on my left. I couldn't see either of them. I headed for the trees, because that's the direction Will said the double set of footprints went."

"Uh-huh."

When he didn't elaborate, Sasha asked, "What's the problem now?"

"No problem. Questions. This should add up for me, but it doesn't."

"So you're going to what? Take the alarm apart? Grill everyone in the lodge? Search for Rush again? Because if that's the plan, you'd better rethink it fast. You were stabbed last night, remember?"

A smile crossed his lips. "I'm still bigger than you, Sasha."

"One punch in your shoulder and I'd have you flat on your back."

His dimple appeared, melting her. "You can have that any time. Except now."

"Always an exception." She caught his good arm. "What are you going to do?"

He trapped her chin in between his thumb and fingers. "I'm going to take a good, long look at Bo's body."

Sasha left him to his task. Some things were simply beyond her. Instead, she talked about the new resort with Skye, had a lesson in bread baking and retaped Will's injured ankle.

"Nick's making mountains out of molehills in my opinion." The sheriff grimaced. "That's too tight, Sasha."

"Sorry." She unstuck the tape. "He's not convinced Bo was helping Rush."

"Why not?"

"Because he's Nick, and simple doesn't work for him. I'll give him another thirty minutes, then if I have to, I'll drag him back in."

Dana came through the side door, shaking snow from his hair. "I swear, I've seen body parts today that I never want to see on any man again. Where's Max?"

"Working on the radio." Sasha tore the tape. "What's Nick looking for, Dana?"

"Whatever doesn't fit."

Will heaved himself to his feet. "Maybe I'll see how he's getting on. I suppose all mountains have to start with some kind of hill."

"Whatever that means." Obviously weary, Dana shed his outdoor gear. Squatting for a moment, he held reddened hands out to the fire. "As a favor to Nick, I trekked back and forth for two hours searching for signs of Rush. There was nothing."

"No footprints?"

"The wind's been howling all day. Any prints that were there are gone now. I checked around the spot where Bo was hit, even dug a little. I found blood from the head wound, but nothing else."

"I thought Nick already had the murder weapon."

"He does. I found the rock last night. It even has some hair embedded in it. But cut-and-dried..."

"Doesn't work for Nick."

"His father's the same way. Grandfather, too. And then there's the old ranch foreman."

"The old-souls man."

"That's the one. Most of Nick's friends who met him were a bit intimidated. You always had the feeling he was trying to see inside you. Sometimes when he'd stare at me, I'd swear I could feel him crawling around in my head. It was spooky as hell."

"So that's where Nick gets it."

"Hey, for a cop it's a good thing."

Sasha repacked the medi-kit. "Was he always like this, Dana?"

"Pretty much. He's into details. Personally, I think you can be too into them, but you'll never convince Nick of that."

"How can you be too into details?"

Dana drew an air canvas. "Imagine if you examined a painting with a magnifying glass. You'd see the individual brushstrokes, but in doing so you'd miss the big picture. I see a homicidal maniac at large on Hollowback Mountain. Nick sees unanswered questions."

"God, that sounds like my mother. She questions everything and everyone. Especially me. Then she picks the answers apart."

"I knew a girl like that once," Dana remarked. "Is your mother emotionally distant?"

"Yes."

"Supercritical?"

"I haven't done anything right in twenty-nine years."

"Inconsiderate of people's feelings?"

"Very. But she's my mother, Dana, and I still love her in the deep-down child-parent way." Sasha had to push hard on the lid of the medi-kit to close it. "So who's your vixen?"

He set his elbows on his knees, rubbed his eyes. "I think her real name was Dorothy. Everyone called her Dolly. Nick knew her. She was sixteen, we were ten. We had serious crushes on her. One day, Nick gave her a yellow rose. She pricked her finger on a thorn, and threw it back in his face. I took the safe route and gave her a candy bar. She called me a stupid little spud and said she was allergic to chocolate."

"Ah, well, she's probably divorced, stressed out and miserable now."

"Hell no." He dropped his hands. "She married Nick's cousin from Outlaw Falls. They live on a fifty thousand acre ranch in Texas, have no kids and tipple liberally."

Sasha laughed. "No poetic justice there. Does Nick ever see her?"

"Not at all. But he does make a point of sending her a single yellow rose every year at Christmas."

Nick heard the big door grind open and closed behind him. He didn't need to look to know who it was.

"You're sitting on the hood of my Land Rover, staring at a dead body." The suspension gave slightly as Sasha climbed up next to him. "Hate to tell you this, Detective, but that's weird."

"I'm thinking."

"Also weird when done while staring at a dead body." She peered closer. "A body that's starting to look a little scary. Still…" Her tone gentled. "No matter what Bo did, he was the father of six children. Probably not the best father, and I'd guess a really rotten husband, but I can't help feeling a tiny bit sorry for him. No one deserves to die the way he did." She fell silent for a moment, then nudged Bo's arm. "So is this rigor mortis then?"

"More like cold storage. He's starting to look like an alien from the Sci-Fi Channel."

"Is that the kind of alien who rises from his slab and terrifies everyone around him before tearing them to shreds?"

Nick kept his eyes on the dead man, but had to admit he liked having Sasha beside him. "Bo's not going anywhere, except into a box."

"Lovely thought. Can we do that soon? Because seeing him laid out on the workbench like this is really freaky." When Nick didn't answer, she asked, "What are you thinking out here that you couldn't think just as easily and a lot more comfortably inside the lodge?"

He caught his lower lip between his teeth, still feeling queasy from the aftereffects of the pill Skye and Sasha had slipped him in the whiskey.

"I found something zipped inside his coat pocket."

"Presumably not the key to his shack on the ridge."

"That was there, too. But the pocket lining was frozen, as if it had gotten damp at some point."

"Which means?"

"He might have discovered this object in the snow."

"Could we spin that down into something more specific? What is this object?"

He debated, then reached into his jeans. He would have felt her shock even if she hadn't caught back a sharp breath.

"It's a snow globe." She stared at the tiny orb in his hand. "And I'm guessing it was meant for me."

Chapter 15

"It's exactly like the globe I saw in my dream." Sasha wove an angry path among the vehicles in the car barn. "Except it wasn't a dream. He was there, was going to kill me, would have killed me." She frowned. "But he didn't. Why not?"

"That's the night Skye decided to watch you. She must have interrupted him." Nick wanted Sasha to hold on to the anger, not let fear chase it away. "You're alive, and he won't get another chance to touch you." He snagged her as she passed him, pulled her into his arms. With his face buried in her hair, he said, "If he does, I'll kill him where he stands."

"Rush was in my room, Nick. He brought a snow globe." He felt her shudder and tightened his arms. "Why such a small one?" It was no bigger than a cherry tomato.

"He was on the run. It's probably all he had. There's

dried glue on the bottom, which means it was likely attached to something else."

"Like a Christmas ornament? So, what? Rush has a fixation with Christmas?"

Nick wished he had answers for her. "He probably has half a hundred fixations, none of them healthy."

She drew back and looked up at him. "Are you going to tell the others, or is this our clue, our secret, too?"

He recalled the matchbook they'd found among the ashes in the hunter's shack, from the Hotel Blanca in Cartagena. *Didn't fit,* a voice in his head whispered. What did tropical Cartagena have to do with a serial killer who left his victims in a snow angel? Too many of the crucial puzzle pieces were skewed.

"We'll let them in on this one," he said in the end.

She studied his features. "What's wrong, Nick?"

His brows came together. "I don't know. Things just don't add up. Colombia plus drugs doesn't equal serial murders and snow angels."

Sasha glanced at the slab where Bo was laid out. "Maybe it's too much, trying to figure out a puzzle while standing beside a corpse. Can we go back to the lodge?"

"Is everyone there?"

"Far as I know. Dana and Max were snapping at each other over the radio, and Will limped back in about fifteen minutes before I came out. Skye was cooking dinner." Sasha forced her lips into a smile. "Hasenpfeffer. I'm going to be a lot thinner by the time I leave this mountain."

As long as she was alive.

Nick chased away the thought and pinched her chin. "I'll make you mac and cheese later. You ready?"

"To take a fifty foot walk through the snow, in the

dark, with a killer who's gotten into the lodge at least twice, thrown a knife at you, killed Bo Sickerbie and is probably popping blood vessels as we speak because his snow globe is missing? No, I'm not ready." She squared her shoulder, cast a quick look at Bo. "But I'm not planning to die, either. Not like he did, and not like Kristiana Felgard. I won't be a serial killer's snow angel."

Sasha's nerves were scraped raw. For two nights she only slept because Nick was with her. For two days she only ate because they sneaked downstairs at midnight and cooked up whatever came to hand that didn't contain rabbit or venison.

"Seven minutes on high, and these cheese and pepperoni things will be done." Elbows on the counter, Nick loaded two frozen wraps into the microwave. "Sasha, how can you have lived in Paris and like this stuff?"

"They have the same stuff in Paris. And I'll eat escargot, just not Bambi or Thumper."

"Not even going to ask."

When he straightened, she saw him roll his injured shoulder. She poured two glasses of wine, handed him one and started for the stairs. "That needs to be redressed. I'll be back."

"You've got five minutes."

To Sasha's mind, no creaks on the staircase gave the lodge a spookier air than a whole haunted house full of creaks and groans. She'd have to mention that to Skye, maybe design a few loose boards into the new resort.

As she passed one of the balconies, she noticed that the stars were out. Unfortunately, the wind remained brisk and clouds loomed on the horizon, like a veil of impending doom.

Turning left, she counted doors. The supply closet was the seventh on the right. However, when she got to the fifth, she heard a noise and paused.

It wasn't a footstep or a rustle of fabric, and it definitely wasn't the wind. No one slept in this wing, and Bo was gone, so it wasn't him snooping through drawers.

It wasn't Anthony Rush, either, she told her thudding heart. The alarm was on and functioning. Nick had seen to it.

A prickly chill swept over her skin. Should she get Nick or go on?

The sound came again. It reminded her of a very long month she'd spent at her uncle Paul's cabin in Bow Lake. He'd still used a television antenna, and the few channels he'd received had been as much static as picture.

She regarded the door. Wasn't this the radio room?

She stepped closer, heard it clearly this time. Static, followed by an incoming voice. Male or female, she couldn't tell.

But the voice on this end belonged to a man.

"Max?" she called softly. "Are you in there?"

Voices and static vanished.

She twisted the knob, hesitated when she discovered the door was locked. "Max?"

No one answered, but she knew what she'd heard. Someone was in this room.

Someone like Anthony Rush?

She jerked her hand away, retreated several hasty steps. Bo could have given Rush a key. Rush might have gotten in here tonight before Skye set the alarm.

Unnerved, Sasha retreated several more steps.

"Sasha?"

Skye's whisper had her heart shooting into her throat.

Pressing a fist to her chest, she willed it down. "You know, I wasn't a jumpy person until I came up here."

"I know the feeling." Skye set a hand on her waist. "Why are you staring at that door?"

"I heard static."

Skye tried the knob. This time the door swung open.

Sasha murmured. "It was locked a minute ago."

"Hello?" Pausing on the threshold, Skye felt for the light switch. "Is someone here?"

Sasha heard the click, but no light came on. "Not liking this." She took Skye by the arm. "We should get Nick."

But Skye stood her ground. "We know you're in here, and the only way out is through this door, so whoever you are, you might as well show yourself."

"I'm getting Nick." Sasha ran down the corridor, spied Nick at the top of the stairs and grabbed his wrist. "Someone's in the radio room."

Because no hallway on the second floor ran in a straight line, it took them several seconds to reach the room. They were halfway there when the alarm began to shriek.

Nick reached the door first. Sasha skidded to a halt behind him. She saw Skye lying in a heap on the floor and ran to her. A fierce stream of wind blew through the open window.

Nick went straight to the opening.

"What's going on?"

Will Pyle hobbled in, almost tripping over Skye. Off balance, he staggered into the chair and wound up falling heavily against Nick. By the time Nick got him back on his feet, Skye was moaning and struggling to sit up.

"Don't move," Sasha told her.

"Oh, God, not again." Dana came up behind Sasha and knelt.

"He blindsided me. Hit me with the radio receiver, I think." Skye probed her head with the tips of her fingers. "Can't believe I'm actually seeing stars."

"Was it Rush?" Dana asked Nick.

"Could've been." Nick closed the window as Max appeared in the doorway, obviously frightened.

He knelt down next to Sasha while she tended to Skye. "I believe I'm going to resign from this resort job. How about you, Sasha?"

Behind them, Dana made a sound of disgust, forestalling her reply. "How come every damn time I almost get this radio working, I come back and find it dead?"

"I heard static," Sasha said. "And voices."

Nick turned from his examination of the window frame. "Voices on one end or both?"

"Both."

"She's adamant about that," Skye inserted.

Nick considered. "Max, go downstairs, and press the reset button on the alarm. Dana, leave the radio for tonight."

"What about Rush?" Will demanded. "Aren't you going after him?"

"Not in the dark."

In the process of helping Skye to her feet, Sasha shot him a skeptical look. She said nothing, however, and with an arm around the older woman's shoulders, guided her back to her bedroom.

It took a full hour to settle everyone down. Sasha made sure Skye was asleep before she returned to her own room. Nick came in ten minutes later, handed her a box of Cheerios and checked both sets of windows.

"Honey Nut. I feel so spoiled."

"I'd have brought something sugarcoated, but I figured this was healthier."

"Don't tell my mother, but I lived on cereal in college." Sasha fought with the plastic liner for a moment, then subsided onto the window seat. "Nick, what's going on? Not that I wanted you to, but why didn't you go after Rush? He couldn't have had much of a head start."

"He didn't have any start at all."

She set the box on the sill. "Okay, now you're scaring me. What's the deal here?"

Planting his hands on her shoulders, Nick turned her toward the window. "Footprints," he said in her ear. "Do you see any on the roof?"

"Outside my window, no, but—" Her eyes snapped up, and she pivoted her head. "There were no footprints? But that means…"

"It was a ruse. Whoever you heard in the radio room opened the window. But he didn't escape through it."

A war raged inside him. It had to be done, he knew that. The monster was salivating, licking its lips. So close. He'd come so very close so many times. But always, he'd been thwarted.

Good, a voice praised deep in his head. Good, because what he was doing was wrong. It was false. It wasn't his true will.

Such a weak voice, though, far too feeble to combat the much larger cry. She deserved to die. She must die. He must kill her.

Ah, but he'd lost his snow globe. Would it be enough to kill her and leave her exposed inside an angel made of snow? He didn't know, and the monster was too busy smacking its wet lips to answer him.

He needed to think. Was there time for that? The city cop was on his scent. One slip, and he'd be caught.

The monster's tail lashed in fury. He felt it breathing fire inside him. He saw her face, heard her laugh, watched as that very first snow globe slipped through her fingers and smashed on the floor.

The angel in the glass had broken. So had the one in his heart. No, she needed to suffer, and here it was, the perfect opportunity for him to make that happen.

No more war in his head. With her death, the wound she'd inflicted might finally begin to heal.

The monster breathed through his nose, saw through his eyes, visualized through his brain.

It was past time for Sasha Myer to die....

Snow clouds blew in and out and in again. The wind was an Arctic gale. Nick prowled the lodge from top to bottom, inside and out. Skye rested, Max and Dana worked without success on the radio, and Will bound his ankle with so much tape he almost cut off his circulation.

Rush wasn't in the lodge. That either meant he never had been, or he'd escaped through another door before the alarm could be reset.

Sasha wanted to believe he'd escaped, because the alternative was that someone else in the lodge had a secret, and she simply wasn't prepared to deal with that possibility. No one was. Except Nick.

He circled the outbuildings five times before dinner. Since he refused to let her out of his sight, that meant Sasha had to make the same number of circuits.

On their sixth trip after dark, she jogged beside him

through the band of footprints they'd made earlier. "You know, Nick, even if someone—say Max or Dana—had gotten the radio to work and was using it last night, that doesn't mean he's helping Anthony Rush."

"Say Max," he suggested. "And what do you think it does mean if not that?"

"People have different agendas. Maybe Max was simply fiddling with the thing, and he managed to pick up another station."

Nick shone his flashlight between the buildings. "And?"

"I interrupted him."

He squinted at the roof. "And?"

"He didn't want us to get our hopes up, so he switched off."

"Have you been taking Skye's painkillers?" Nick ran the beam around the perimeter of the car barn. "Because they tend to dull the brain." Seeing nothing, he moved ahead. "Just because Bo's dead, Sasha, doesn't mean he was the person helping Rush."

She followed him. "Don't forget Bo had a baby snow globe in his pocket."

"Which he could have discovered on the ground."

"Why was he outside if not to meet Rush or help him escape?"

"Because Bo was often where he shouldn't be, and the alarm was disabled. For all we know, he saw Rush escaping and decided to follow him."

"Why?"

"Why not? He went through every closet he could open just to see what he could find. Tracking Rush to his lair could have earned him all kinds of goodies. Charges dropped, maybe even a reward. Don't apply logic to a man like Bo Sickerbie."

"Okay." She held up a hand. "You want Max to be the one who was, who is, working with Rush. How a functioning radio could help a serial killer, I can't imagine, but I know what I heard, so someone was using it. However, none of that explains why we're out here for the sixth time today."

Nick swept the flashlight beam across the snow. "I think better when I'm active. When I stop, I start thinking about you."

"Really?" A blend of surprise and delight brought a smile to her lips. Turning, she walked back to him. "So I'm a disruption to your metal processes, then?"

"You could say that."

She grabbed hold of his coat. "Is there anything I could say that would get you back inside the lodge?"

Lowering his head, he captured her mouth in a hot, hard kiss that, for all its brevity, took her mind on a wicked trip through time and space. "After we've made one more circle."

Her train of thought totally blown, Sasha merely stared. "I think the ground just moved." But her eyes focused when she spied a ribbon of motion between the buildings.

"Nick, it's Rush!" She pointed. "He ran behind the car barn. He's heading for the woods."

"Get back to the lodge." Nick had his gun out and was already racing away. "Tell Skye to set the alarm and not to let anyone near the keypad."

Sasha wanted to object, to follow him, to do anything except go back and wait. But she forced her feet to carry her across the snow and through the front door.

"Sasha, you look as if you've seen a ghost." On form once more, Skye left the book she'd been reading on the coffee table and met her halfway across the floor.

"Where are the others?" Sasha asked.

Dana stopped sorting tools in an open box. "Will's soaking his foot. Max disappeared after dinner." Concern etched his features. "Where's Nick?"

"We saw Rush." She caught Skye's hand. "Nick wants you to set the alarm and watch the keypad."

"Oh, and why is that, Sasha?" Max's voice drifted down the staircase.

"Because he doesn't think Bo..." She trailed off as he descended. He had one hand behind his back and a strange gleam in his eyes. "I don't know," she finished, easing Skye behind her. "You guess."

"Okay." He took another step. "I think Nick doesn't buy Bo Sickerbie as Rush's accomplice. Am I right?"

"Yes, you are," Dana replied. He placed himself between Sasha and Max. "Question is, was Nick right?"

An apology flitted across Max's face, then vanished. His hand came out. He offered them a grim little smile as he cocked the hammer of his gun. "Yes, I'm afraid to say he was."

Rush took several blind shots over his shoulder as he ran. Nick ignored them and continued his pursuit.

Rush wasn't going to escape. The moon and stars were out. The man might be a shadow careening across the snow, but he was a highly visible one.

Accustomed to the terrain, and better outfitted for a chase tonight, Nick dogged him to the edge of the lake. Rush didn't hesitate. He skidded down the bank and onto the ice.

"Think again, pal." Planting his feet, Nick took aim and fired.

Rush stumbled, clamped a hand over his right arm where Nick's shot had clipped him. He switched the gun to his left hand, shot twice, then continued toward the trees.

Nick landed two-footed on the ice. "Stop now, Rush, or you're a dead man."

Rush swore at him but kept moving.

Nick fired again. Rush's left leg buckled, but he refused to stop.

"Next one's in your spine," Nick warned.

Another glance, another wild shot from Rush. But he lost steam as he lost blood, and went down on one knee.

Nick heard the ice crack. Keeping one eye on the surface and the other on his quarry, he approached the winded man.

"Gun down," he ordered, and waited until Rush complied. "Hands where I can see them."

"I'll bleed to death," Rush growled.

"Yeah, well that would be a shame."

Nick cast a wary look over the frozen lake. Why did this feel off to him? Ice cracked again, but it was a distant sound, all but drowned out by the wail of the wind and Rush's labored breathing.

Nick had been a cop too long not to anticipate some kind of resistance. Rush didn't disappoint. He folded over as if catching his breath, then spun on his heel and lunged at Nick's knees. Unfortunately, the ice under Nick's feet chose that moment to snap.

If Rush heard the sound, he gave no indication. He merely bared his teeth and tried to head butt Nick below the waist.

Nick leaped aside, slipped, but didn't go down. Rush twisted around, with his arms outstretched and saliva coating his chin.

It was like fending off a hungry wolf, except that this wolf had a long reach and really nothing to lose by throwing himself at his captor.

Nick saw the ice zigzag around Rush's feet. Crouched near the bank, he aimed his gun between the other man's eyes. "If I don't get you, the lake will. Look down, Anthony."

Rush's gaze dropped. He froze, fingers kinked, breath hitching as lightning-bolt cracks split the ice.

"You have to help me," he spat. "You're a cop. You can't let me fall through."

It was the indignation that did it, caused the mental camera in Nick's mind to click. He saw a shadowy image. It hovered on the edge of his memory, so close he could make out the shape of a face.

The ice cracked again. Nick gestured with his gun. "Step left," he said. "A big step. And another." When Rush hit solid ground, Nick warned, "Run and I'll shoot your other leg."

Blood lay in a black pool where he'd stood. One bullet in the leg and a second in the arm had to hurt like hell, and yet Rush was still walking. It wouldn't be an easy trip back to the lodge.

"I'm not going to prison," Rush snarled. "Just so you know, no one's putting me behind bars. She'd tell you I killed her if she could, but I say it was her own fault she died. She was a drunk, a whore, a junkie. She blames me, but she's wrong."

"Yeah, well, that'll be for a jury to decide. Don't

even think about it," he added, when the man jerked toward him.

Nick knew Rush was itching to make a grab for the gun. He saw it in his dark eyes and the way his mouth stretched out at the corners.

Another click, another near image.

"Walk." He motioned with his gun. "Toward the lodge. You know the way."

Now Rush's lips turned down. "You think I killed that blond woman and that drunk, Sickerbie, don't you?"

"Keep moving."

"I didn't." Rush sent him a hostile look. "Can't say I know who did, but it wasn't me."

"Again, up to a jury to decide."

Rush began to limp. Nick saw the trail of blood in the snow, but still didn't trust him.

"I knew he'd blame me," Rush muttered. His shoulders hunched. "You wanted him to all along. I know you did."

"Who are you talking to?" Nick asked.

Rush twitched. "My mother was a junkie. I'm a dealer. She wanted drugs. I wouldn't give them to her. So she went to someone else. No time to wait for me to test the stuff. Could be good, could be bad. Guess what? It was bad, cut with half a hundred chemicals. She died, then moved into my head so she could remind me forever that I wouldn't give her safe stuff. If I had, she'd be alive now. Still a junkie, but alive, instead of rotting in a box in the ground." He raised his voice. "Isn't that right? You tell him what's real, what's true. I didn't kill you, I didn't kill the blonde and I didn't kill the drunk."

He wheeled around, breathing hard. His fingers wiggled at his sides. Blood dripped onto the snow. "My name's Jason Watts," he said through his teeth. "But you know that, don't you, because you took my license."

"Licenses," Nick corrected. "If not Bo, who got you the fake ID?"

Rush's lip curled. "Sixty-four thousand dollar question, cop. I'll tell you one thing, your pretty lady's not safe where you left her. My cousin's got a yellow streak a mile wide and a bad case of jitters. He knows if you catch me, I'll finger him as my accomplice. The way I see it, he should be hitting the panic button anytime now—for all the good it'll do him."

The click came with a light this time. The eye color was similar, but it was the shape of the jaw that did it. Erase the beard, and the features were identical.

"Coming clear at last, huh? Figured it would. Good old cousin Max. A little high-strung, a little unpredictable. Scared to death that something might happen to destroy his fat-cat lifestyle. You gotta watch those ones, cop. They got funny things going on in their heads. Me, I was lousy in school. I deal drugs. But Max was lousy in school, too, even worse than me. So you gotta wonder, don't you, how he got to be an engineer." Rush's grin grew evil. "Assuming he really is an engineer, and not something totally different. What do you think, cop? Is it Grandma you're seeing in that bed, or a wolf looking for a luscious bit of female to pounce on?"

Nick's gaze flicked to the lodge. His mistake and he knew it. Rush's fingers balled. Emitting a sharp feral cry, he launched himself at Nick's gun hand.

Chapter 16

"Move away from the rifle cabinet, Sasha." Max descended another step. "Dana, out of the way."

"No."

"Don't be a hero." Max snorted out a laugh. "You don't fit the part. Nick does, but then I understand Nick's not here. He's gone after Anthony Rush. Trust me, my cousin's a handful. A basket case, but tough as hell. Lucky for me, I'm tougher."

And yet his hand was shaking, Sasha noted through her shock and fear.

Skye stepped forward. "What's this all about, Max?"

"Survival. Mine. I was already coming to Painter's Bluff. Anthony—we'll call him that because it's how you know him—needed help. He was on the run, said all I had to do was give him money and a few pieces of fake ID. We agreed to meet in town. We'd keep it casual, and off he'd go to the Canadian border. Unfortunately, his truck broke down, and he was stuck."

Sasha regarded the gun. "Max, why are you helping a murderer? You'll be charged as an accessory if your cousin—if Rush—escapes. Turn him in, and you can swing a deal."

"I won't go to prison," Max maintained.

"Well, pointing a gun at us probably isn't the best way to achieve that goal." She ran damp palms along the legs of her jeans, watched Dana dip his hand into the toolbox. "We all have family problems, Max. Your cousin's just a little more extreme than most."

"I'm not going to prison."

"Who says you'll have to?" Skye asked. "Stop this nonsense here and now, and we'll all vouch for you."

"Skye has clout," Sasha reminded him. "So does Nick. Will and Dana, too." She spied Will at the top of the stairs, saw Dana's hand come out of the box. "Put them together, and there's a good chance you'll avoid serving any prison time at all."

Max's arm wobbled. "I didn't think he was a killer. Bad, yes, and I'm pretty sure he hears voices, but I just figured he was running drugs up from Colombia."

"Which makes helping him okay?" Dana challenged from the side.

He had both hands behind his back. From Max's point of view, he would appear to have his thumbs hooked in his pockets, but Sasha saw the small hatchet dangling between his fingers.

"Why didn't you confide in me?" Skye pressed. "I've got two ruffian grandsons of my own."

"You do?" Max's hand fell a few inches.

She shrugged. "As Sasha said, we all have our family secrets."

"Put the gun down, Max," Dana advised. "It's obvious you don't want to hurt anyone."

The barrel dropped half a foot. "I don't. I panicked tonight. I can feel it. Nick's going to catch him…" He squeezed his eyes closed. "My cousin knows things about me that can't be made public."

"Like the fact that you hustled your way to a degree in engineering?" Skye suggested.

Max gaped. "You know about that?"

"I wasn't plopped onto the planet yesterday, my dear. When I learned which member of the team your firm was dispatching to Painter's Bluff, I did a little digging. One can't be too careful with one's trust these days. There were, shall we say, blips on your college records. Allegations—never proved—about you hiring people to sit your exams for you."

Sasha stared. "You knew that, and you let him come to Painter's Bluff anyway?"

"I wanted to see what he could do. The real world isn't all about college degrees."

Will was almost on him.

However, whether due to a sound, a movement or simply the sense of having someone behind him, Max whirled. He knocked Will's gun hand with his own. As one of the weapons clattered over the railing, Dana sprang.

"Get the rifle," Skye shouted, but Sasha was already there and tugging on the gun cabinet door.

It was locked. Exasperated, she grabbed a screwdriver out of the toolbox and smashed the glass. She heard feet thud on the staircase, an "oomph," of pain, but she kept her focus and reached in to turn the lock. She was closing her fingers on the butt end of a rifle when she heard Skye gasp.

"I don't think so, Sasha," said a voice from directly behind her. Something sharp jabbed into her neck. "Back off, Skye. Over on the stairs with the others. I think you know it won't take much for me to kill her. And the rest of you as well."

Sasha was too startled to swallow, too frightened to move. Not Max, was all she could think. Not Max or Rush or anyone she would have suspected.

"Catching on at last, are you, angel?"

Her attacker sounded calm, but she knew, even with her mind wrapped in a haze, that he would do exactly what he promised.

He'd kill them, and then he'd kill her. Just as he'd killed Kristiana Felgard and seven other women before her.

Nick dragged Rush back to the lodge, with one hand bunched in his coat collar and the other jamming a gun under his chin.

They'd fought for five minutes in the snow before, finally, Rush had collapsed. Nick felt blood slithering down his arm from his shoulder. He'd torn his stitches. His opponent had two bullets in him. Seemed like a fair trade to him.

"What are you doing?" Rush demanded when Nick hauled him into the car barn and forced him to his knees beside Bo's body. "You can't leave me here with him." He struggled to stand. Nick pressed a foot to the back of his leg, while he opened his truck.

"Get the cuffs out of my glove box," he ordered.

"I didn't kill them."

"Shut up and find the cuffs." Nick had to prod him to make him move. He figured he had about a minute's worth of strength left in his injured arm.

"I saw the woman," Rush muttered. He pawed through the glove box. "I went to a place called Painter's Rock to meet Max. She was there, all laid out and dead. I didn't see the glass globe at first. I fell. The glass broke, and I cut myself. I got rid of the globe in town, but that's it. That's all I did. Well, other than the drug thing. Outstanding federal warrants for smuggling and trafficking. But I've never killed anyone, not ever."

"Uh-huh." Thank God the cuffs weren't locked. "Hands behind your back."

"I didn't kill her."

"So manhandling Sasha in that farmhouse was what, a come-on?"

"I wanted out, that's all, just away from you so I'd still have a chance to escape."

Nick secured the second cuff, breathed out.

"You can't leave me here," Rush declared, outraged. "There's no heat. I'll wind up like the drunk."

"Another person you didn't kill."

"Why would I bother?" Rush spat back. "I didn't know him, never even saw him until we got snowed in."

"Tell it to a judge." Nick gave him a firm nudge. "Come on."

"We're going inside?"

"Unless winding up like Bo's starting to feel good to you."

"I didn't…" His head gave a violent jerk. "Get out!" he roared.

If he hadn't done this same thing five or six times

on the way here, Nick might have been surprised. As it was, he simply tapped Rush on the back and steered him out the door.

"You killed yourself," Rush mumbled all the way across the snow. "Why won't you leave me alone?"

Because his hands were busy, Nick kicked the door. "Open up, Skye, it's me."

When no one answered, he tried again.

"Great friends," Rush chided. Apparently, he'd returned to his usual self.

Nick didn't like the sensation that stirred inside him. He gave Rush a shake. "Were you in the radio room last night?"

"What, do I look crazy? Max brought me food and supplies. I've been holed up in a mud hut ever since you rousted me from that cabin."

Nick didn't want to hear that. Even more, he didn't want to believe it.

"How does your cousin feel about blond females?" When Rush didn't respond, he placed his mouth close to the man's ear. "Answer me, Anthony, or I might have to shoot you again for attempting to escape."

"I'm not—" The air rattled from his lungs. "No, Max doesn't like blond females. I'm not convinced he likes any females. Satisfied?"

"Not quite. Has he ever murdered anyone that you know of?"

"No, but then he's never been desperate before. Hard to say what a man'll do when he's pushed too hard."

He ground out the last five words. Nick ignored him and tried the door handle. It was locked.

Fear spiraled through his system.

"Stand back." He set Rush aside and fired at the lock. It didn't ease his taut mind that the alarm failed to go off.

He bulldozed Rush inside. "Sasha?"

No answer. And more disturbing, no sign of her—or any of them.

Nick moved swiftly. Unlocking one of the handcuffs, he slapped it around the oak banister.

Rush's lips peeled back from his teeth. "Maybe I was wrong about Max. Either that or one of your bunkies is playing a game of his own."

"Sasha!" Nick called again as he took the stairs to the second floor.

He checked her room first. It was empty. So were Dana's, Will's and Skye's. And the snow globe was missing from the safe in Skye's office where he'd put it.

Rush was arguing with his mother's ghost by the time Nick returned downstairs. He glanced at the gun cabinet, saw the smashed glass and ordered his mind to slow down, back up, reevaluate.

Rush was on the run. He dealt drugs. The feds were after him. He'd needed money and fake ID to cross the Canadian border.

He'd been in Painter's Bluff the night Kristiana Felgard was murdered. He'd known he was going to be questioned. He'd panicked, stolen a truck, raced up the mountain and wound up trapped with the rest of them.

But Rush was not a murderer.

Nick spotted the open toolbox, then the smears of blood on the stairs, floor and wall. Sasha's blood? He couldn't, wouldn't let that thought in. He needed to believe the murderer had taken Sasha and locked the others away.

Or killed them.

"Told you I didn't off anyone," Rush shouted. "You've been hunting the wrong guy, cop. It was a wolf in Grandma's bed, after all."

Nick tuned him out, scanned the eerily silent room. He'd been away for at least forty minutes, chasing Rush, cuffing him, fighting. In that time, someone had taken Sasha and disposed of the others.

Taken her where? His mind flew through the possibilities. To the woods? Unlikely. This killer preferred open spaces. And there was a great deal of open space on Hollowback Mountain.

Nick scanned the kitchen counters, the parson's bench, the tables. He saw nothing out of the ordinary. It wasn't until his eyes lit on the staircase that he noticed the set of keys on one of the treads.

Keys?

Homing in on them, he crossed the floor.

The fob jumped out at him, a hollow metal circle with a spot of dried glue and a snapped piece of wire inside—perfectly shaped to accommodate the base of a miniature snow globe.

Nick went through the key ring by key, searching for a number, a tag, any clue at all. He flipped over the last key and a wave of black bile rushed up from his stomach. This wasn't possible. He wouldn't believe it. But the old-fashioned key, green with age and use, taunted him. The key to an ancient chest, now used to lock up valuables from the curious hands of a little boy.

The conversation replayed in Nick's head, loud and clear. There could be no mistake. His worst nightmare was playing itself out.

The key grew larger in his hand. So did the empty fob. The fob that had once held a miniature snow globe.

Nick closed his eyes, forced acceptance. He opened them, stared out at the night.

Where had he taken her? When had he left? How long would he wait?

Nick pictured Sasha in the snow, sucked back a breath and checked to be sure he had both of his guns.

Rush shouted in his wake, "You go out there, and I'm as good as dead. I'm a person, Law. I matter, too."

Nick heard the words, but didn't care. He ran for the rise behind the lodge. It was the best vantage point in the area.

All he needed was a glimpse of light or motion, a footprint, a sound. All he could see was Sasha being laid inside a snow angel.

Dead at the hands of his oldest friend.

The wind swooped and swirled. It sent stinging pellets of snow up into Sasha's face.

"Dana—ouch—I can't see."

He held her by the hair, kept the barrel of a gun—Will's gun—jammed into the side of her neck.

"You fight me, you die," he promised, and licked her ear. When she wrenched her head sideways, he laughed. "I love doing that. I love that I can finally tell you I love doing that. Oh, Barbara," he crooned, "I can't wait to watch you die."

"I'm not Barbara," Sasha said through chattering teeth. "My mother's—"

"Half of what you are," Dana retorted. "You die, part of her dies. But first she hurts. Her precious daughter, so much like her that she could have been cloned, will be dead."

"Dana, please…"

"You're the best one, you know," he whispered. "Not a substitute, the genuine article. I've waited for this moment for so, so long. Do you know what I had to go through to set it up? Not the avalanche, that was a fluke. But you being here, Skye knowing who you were, even the associate who recommended you to her—all my doing."

"You arranged this?"

"Oh, yes. I wangled and finagled, I made phone calls, called in favors from people who know people who know Skye very well. The associate in question liked your work—another lucky fluke. Skye wanted a resort. Mayor Hollander approached her and said, 'I heard your friend Jonah Weiss went to Beat, Streete and Myer for his recreational home. Why don't you talk to him, possibly get the same woman to design your resort?'" Dana screwed the gun barrel deeper into her neck. "I put a great deal of faith in your ability, Sasha. You could have failed me. But then I reminded myself that if worse came to worst, I knew where you lived. I could simply snatch you if need be."

"Why didn't you?" She wanted to tug on his wrist, but settled for trying to prevent him from yanking her hair out by the roots.

"Well, I didn't want to get caught, now did I? Besides, I like making plans. I relish anticipation. I love to kill Barbara. I do it over and over and over again—in my head and in reality."

"But for a long time you stopped killing her."

She felt the sudden tension that thrummed through his body. "That was nothing. A lapse or two. Sometimes it seems… It was nothing. They were pauses, gaps."

She needed to beat back her terror long enough to understand what he really meant.

Lapses and gaps.

"Are you saying you don't always want to kill her?"

He shook Sasha so hard a swarm of pinpoint of lights appeared.

"Killing her is all I think about. The lapses are a weakness. They're not mine."

Confusion dulled the edges of her fear. "You contacted Nick after Kristiana Felgard died, Dana. You asked him to come to Painter's Bluff."

"I shouldn't have. It was stupid, weak." His lips moved, his teeth didn't. She felt the vibrations of hatred radiating from him. "She laughed at me. Your mother laughed at me!"

"I'm not my mother."

"She smashed my snow globe. There was an angel inside. I was going to give it to her. Better than an apple, I thought. But when I told her how I felt, she laughed and pushed the globe back at me. When I wouldn't take it, she let it go, let it fall to the floor and break. She said it was an accident, but it wasn't. She smashed my heart. Now I'm going to smash hers."

Sasha's mind scrambled backward. "My mother was your teacher?"

"Ninth grade. I was fourteen. She was beautiful…. Stop dragging your feet."

He hauled Sasha through the snow, heading where she had no idea. The trees maybe. Or the lake.

"You had a crush on her."

"I loved her. She was gorgeous, just like you." He slid the gun under Sasha's chin, set his frozen cheek against hers. "I wanted to be teacher's pet, but she liked Randy

Wales. Running back on the varsity team. He never gave her a snow globe. I was pretty, too. Why didn't she love me?"

"She didn't love Randy Wales, Dana."

"Stop arguing with me. I know how it was. You don't." He gave her hair a vicious jerk. "I saw you in Denver three years ago. It was Christmas. You were shopping. She was with you. It was like seeing her in a mirror, except you're younger. You are as Barbara was when I fell in love with her."

Think, Sasha ordered herself. What could she do? Not get hysterical was a good start, but it wouldn't save her.

Nick. He could do something. Dana would listen to him—if he could find them.

Frightened, but determined, Sasha freed her right hand, slipped it into her pocket. She felt the extra gloves inside and worked one of them out. Dropping it onto the snow, she started a trail for Nick to follow.

"Dana, I'm not Barbara. Neither are any of the other women you've taken."

"Ooh." He made an amused sound now. "Are you saying I should kill your mommy and not you?"

"You shouldn't kill anyone."

His tone grew dreamy. "I killed her for the eighth time the night before you arrived in Painter's Bluff. I didn't plan to, but suddenly, there she was. Blond and beautiful. I knew it had to be done when I heard her laugh. All this time, and I can still hear Barbara laughing at me."

"Kristiana Felgard—"

"Had Swedish blood. And blond hair, like silk." He blew lightly on Sasha's hair. "Cobalt-blue eyes. No wings or halo, but angels don't wear those things on earth, right? Especially defrocked angels. Oh, yes, I saw Barbara in Kristiana Felgard quite clearly. The rage came over me, and that was it."

"But you're married. You have three kids. You're the mayor of Painter's Bluff. People look up to you. Barbara's not worth losing all of that."

"Barbara's not worth anything," he replied, and kissed Sasha's ear. "That's why I kill her. She dies, I go on. But all the other women were pretenders in the end."

"And I'm not?"

"No." He nuzzled her neck, his hot breath steaming against her skin. Sasha thought she was going to be sick. Instead, she breathed out and dropped another glove.

He was taking her through the trees, toward a small hill with a broad, flat top. She dug in her heels. "Dana, please don't do this."

"She broke my snow globe."

"She did. *I* didn't."

"She told me to go home and not bring her any more gifts. She knew I loved her, and all she could say was go home."

Sasha bit her lip at the sound of his voice. It had gone from a lover's croon to an embittered rasp in the space of one sentence.

His next kiss punished—and caught the corner of her mouth.

He made noises when he inhaled now, long, scratchy sounds that matched the eager anticipation in his eyes. She watched him lick his lips, and shuddered from the inside out.

"Gonna do it, Barbara," he whispered, and with a final groping kiss, threw Sasha onto the snow. "Gonna hurt your little girl. Gonna make her beg. And then…" Still gripping the gun, he surged forward to land on his knees in front of her. "I'm gonna make her dead."

Nick spied a movement below the rise. Winded from the steep uphill run, he searched the darkness. And detected the outline of a man and a woman.

Sasha...

He only managed a brief glimpse before Dana dragged her into the trees, but it was enough. There must be a clearing in there, someplace Dana knew about that he didn't.

But he would. Nick glanced at the blood covering his wrist and glove. If it was the last thing he did, he was going to stop Dana Hollander from killing the woman he loved.

Do it, the monster raged.

Poised to spring, Dana ran his tongue over his lips.

"Dana, listen..." Sasha pleaded.

Tell her to shut up!

"Shut up!" Dana barked.

She attempted to scramble backward. Dana caught her ankle. The monster cackled.

"Don't worry," Dana promised. "You'll be dead before I make the snow angel."

She pried at the fingers holding her. "I'm not Barbara."

"We've been through this," Dana warned.

Use the gun.

"Don't make me shoot you, Sasha."

"I don't want to die."

"She broke my snow globe," Dana cried. "She laughed at me."

"I've never laughed at you."

Shut her up!

Dana abandoned the gun and went for her throat. The foot she planted in his chest shocked him. Air exploded from his lungs.

As he trapped her leg and yanked her forward, her heel rammed his shoulder and pain radiated through his collarbone.

Knock her out!

With a wounded-animal cry, Dana lunged at her throat. "Gotcha!" he breathed, as he wrapped his hands around her neck. He only stopped squeezing when he heard a telltale click beneath the wind. Flipping over, he brought Sasha onto his lap.

"Hello, Nick."

The gun was right there, next to his hip. Smiling slowly, he grabbed it and raised the barrel to Sasha's throat. "Impasse, old friend." The monster's tail smashed the regret that wanted to rise. "You can't shoot me without shooting her." His smile widened. "So who's it gonna be, Nick? Who dies first tonight?"

Nick wanted to feel regretful, or guilty or surprised, but he felt none of those things. Fear for Sasha's life was the only emotion that registered. It clawed at his insides and caused him to hesitate when he knew he should have pulled the trigger.

All he had left now was talk—and the scraps of a fantasy friendship.

He went with the obvious. "Let her go, Dana."

"Well, uh, no. Stand up!" Dana barked at Sasha.

On his feet and shielded, he began hauling her down the hill. Nick saw the ice at the bottom. It was the mountain stream that fed the lake.

"You don't seem shocked, Nick." Although Sasha stumbled against him, Dana remained upright and dragged her onto the frozen stream. "Give me a hint. How'd you figure it out?"

"Your key ring."

"Ah, right, the missing fob. Stupid of me to drop those. I heard them fall when I whacked Max. That was right after I shot and clobbered Will. You want my opinion, Nick, Pyle's past it. Move your feet, Sasha. We're not skating here."

But they were heading for the lake.

"Blame it on Barbara, Nick." He stuck the gun in Sasha's throat, made Nick's stomach clench. "Beautiful Barbara Myer. Ninth grade English. Angel to behold, but a monster inside. Well, now I'm the monster, and someone Barbara loves is going to die."

Nick kept his eyes on Dana, only on Dana. "You'll die, too, old friend. Is that what you want? Is killing Barbara through Sasha worth forfeiting your own life?"

Dana didn't answer, but Nick could see that the tension coiled inside was causing him to tremble.

"Why did you contact me?" Nick asked.

Dana's eyes darted toward the lake. "It was a moment. They happen from time to time."

So there was a part of him that resisted the murders. "What makes the moments happen?"

"Weakness… Stop fighting me, Sasha. Barbara needs to suffer."

"Barbara laughed at you, Dana. I never did." Sasha dug her fingernails into his hand as he pulled her onto the lake. "Why do I need to die?"

"Because it'll hurt her. Because it might heal me."

Nick maintained the gap between them. "Do you want to be healed?"

"Or course I do. Wouldn't you? You know what it's like, Nick. You remember Dolly. You gave her a rose, I gave her chocolate. She laughed at us."

"Actually, she shouted at us."

Dana growled. "I didn't love Dolly." He gave Sasha a yank that made Nick's throat constrict. "Barbara was everything."

"What about Fawn and your kids? What are they?"

He scowled. "I contacted my assistant by radio, told her to tell Fawn not to worry, to tell the kids Daddy'd be home soon."

"Did you tell her that Daddy had a job to do first? That he needed to kill a woman before he could come home? That he'd killed one before he left home, and seven others before that? That he'd killed a man a few nights ago?"

For a moment, Dana appeared stricken. Then his features iced over. "Bo spied on me. He saw me break into Sasha's room the night you were there. When I jumped from the roof, I must have lost the globe. He found it, came after me. I had no choice but to kill him."

"Problem solved, huh?"

"Bo's no great loss."

"That was the second time you'd broken into Sasha's room, wasn't it?"

"Skye interrupted me the first time. She'll pay for that. As far as the radio room goes, that was easy. I heard Sasha at the door. I hid, then decided to let her in. Skye opened the door while Sasha ran to find you. My plan formed. I'd hit Skye and make it seem as though I— Rush—had escaped. That's when good old Will blundered in. I was behind the door during the commotion. Easy as pie to blend in after that."

"How many people have you murdered, Dana?"

"Only the eight women. One got away, remember? And then there was Bo. Of course, the number's going to be a lot higher before I leave this mountain. I'll need to get rid of Max and Will and Skye and you. Rush, too, but he's going to come out the villain. A little strategically placed blood, the testimony of a stellar eyewitness— me—and he'll rot. Maybe not for the previous deaths, but for all the ones up here. And, poor me, I'll have to suffer from survivor's guilt for the rest of my life."

Nick recalled the story Rush had told him. It had been his blood on the snow next to Kristiana Felgard's body. Dana couldn't know it, but his plan actually had a chance of succeeding.

"Got him thinking, didn't I?" Dana whispered loudly to Sasha. "Looks like in this case, the cop'll just die alongside everyone else, and the bad guy'll get away." He kissed her neck. He would have kissed her lips but she wrenched her head to the side and avoided his mouth.

"Is she good in bed, Nick?" Dana murmured. "Does she have her mama's fire? Her passion? Her nasty nature?"

Emotions too fleeting to identify raced across his face. Nick followed him farther onto the ice and scrambled through his memory for a weapon. Only one sprang to mind.

"You had a great wedding, Dana," he said softly. "Remember it? You and Fawn and all your friends and family. We stood there, melting in the sun, hungover as hell from your stag, and really needing food. Then Fawn walked down the aisle, and you said it was going to be a new start for you. Everything would be better now. You were going to move forward."

Dana blinked, slowed his footsteps. "Did I say that? I don't remember."

Nick moved closer. "You said you loved her, said you wanted kids."

"I did love her—do love her, and my kids. Jessica has a crush on you."

"I know."

"She's twelve, already twelve…"

Nick lowered his gun, held out a hand. "Let her go, Dana. It's my turn to have a stag and be hungover on my wedding day. You can be my best man."

"I can… No!" The fury boiled up so swiftly Nick barely had time to react. He dodged the bullet Dana fired, rolled and came up in a crouch near the bank.

"She dies, Nick, and so do you! No more tricks. No more talking. I want it done! I want…" His face screwed up into an agonized mask. "No!" he rasped, and drew a painful breath. "No!"

To Nick's shock, he thrust Sasha forward and grabbed his head. She ran, or attempted to. But Dana's expression altered again and he caught her by the collar, jerking her so hard that they both landed on their knees.

He snaked an arm around her throat. "I have to do this," he wailed. "She has to die. I won't be better until she's dead."

One shot, Nick thought. All he needed was a split second when Dana moved out from behind her.

Nick's palms were sweating. He heard the faint sound of ice cracking. Dana breathed hard through his mouth. His features contorted. Sasha pried on his arm. She made brief eye contact with Nick, then jammed her heel into Dana's shin and sent his foot out from under him.

Dana fell, took her with him. The gun flew from his hand and slid across the lake. The cracks grew louder, closer.

"Dana, the ice is breaking," Sasha shouted.

He grasped her left arm, yanked it hard behind her back as they stood. "I don't care." Fury brought a flush to his otherwise stark-white face. "Maybe I need to die with you, huh? What do you think, Nick? Is that a good ending? Stop struggling, Sasha!"

"I'm not going to die."

As she spoke, she twisted sideways, and Nick had it—his shot. He fired a bullet into Dana's shoulder.

Stunned, Dana snapped his head back. He staggered, dragged Sasha with him. She couldn't untangle herself from the claw that was his right arm.

When the two of them crashed onto the ice, it gave an ominous crack. Long shards arrowed up as the frigid lake swallowed them.

Nick launched himself forward. Cursing Dana, the winter and everything else he could think of, he whipped off his coat. Then, lying flat on the unbroken ice, he worked his way toward the hole.

He heard thrashing, and ground his teeth. If Dana was holding her under, Nick would never be able to save her.

Unless he went in after her…

He was on his knees and ready to dive in when he heard Sasha shout, "No, don't, Nick! He's—he's gone. Don't."

Torn, but prepared to trust her, he dropped back to his stomach and threw his long coat toward her.

"Can you catch it?"

"I think so." Ice and water splashed as she shed her own coat, then she tugged on the bottom of his.

"Don't try to climb out," he told her.

But she knew what to do. Ease up slowly, stay flat and let him pull.

Sixty heart-pounding seconds later, she was out and safe beside him on the bank.

He wrapped both his coat and his arms around her, set his forehead against hers and breathed, really breathed for the first time since he'd seen Dana holding her.

"He pushed me," Sasha said into his shoulder.

Nick wiped the wet hair from her cheek "You mean he tried to push you under?"

"No." Her head came up and she looked into his eyes. "At first he dragged me down with him, but then he stopped. I saw his face change, Nick. He said, 'Get out,' and he pushed me up onto the ice."

Chapter 17

"It's over. It's really over." It had happened so fast that Sasha still couldn't believe it. "He's gone."

Nick collapsed beside her on the bank. A quick but thorough search of the broken ice had brought them nothing. No cries for help, no flailing water, no sign of Dana anywhere. Some blood on the edge from the bullet in his shoulder, but that was it. That and a tiny, half-frozen snow globe.

Huddled inside Nick's coat, Sasha regarded the jagged ice in front of her.

"I'm so sorry, Nick. I know that sounds inadequate, but I really am sorry. I feel…" She searched her jumbled emotions, couldn't seem to separate them from her residual fear. "Responsible, I guess. Like I should have seen something, or felt something, or just known."

Nick glanced up at the night sky as he stood and drew

her to her feet. "Big Bear," he said, and indicated the constellations. "And there's Little Bear. My father's foreman used to call me Little Bear. I should have picked up on his feelings. He was always on guard around Dana, and vice versa."

"Old souls can be bad as well as good."

Nick's gaze slid to her face. "You're not responsible, Sasha. Dana was obsessed with your mother. He hated her, killed women who reminded him of her."

"I know, but it was me, Nick. All along, it was me he wanted. It's terrifying to realize that, and I think it does make me a little responsible. Kristiana Felgard's dead because I arrived late in Painter's Bluff."

"That's called an unfortunate circumstance. Dana did the killing, not you." Nick gave her a gentle tug. "Come on, we've done all we can here. We need to get back to the lodge, find the others and build a fire."

"He locked them in the cellar. Dana shot Will in the arm while he held a hatchet on me. Will charged in anyway. Dana knocked him out. Then he clubbed Max—who, despite his involvement with Rush, deserves some credit. He ran in after Will. Poor Max, he panicked and pulled a gun on us when you went after his cousin. I don't know where he thought he could go, but I guess that's panic for you."

"What about Skye?"

"Bruised cheekbone. Dana backhanded her with his gun—actually, with Will's backup gun—right before he fired at Will." Sasha pressed on her temples. "I can see it all vividly and probably will for the next year in my dreams."

She was in Nick's arms before she realized what was

happening. One minute they'd been walking, the next he'd spun her around and hauled her up against him.

"He could've killed you, Sasha."

"But he didn't. And right at the end, I don't think he wanted to. At least some part of him didn't."

"I'll try to remember that," Nick murmured into her hair.

She rested her head against his cheek. "All this because my mother broke the snow globe he gave her in the ninth grade. Bo Sickerbie and eight innocent women are dead. Why do they do that, Nick? Kill people other than the one they really want? Not that I want my mother dead, but why didn't he go after her?"

"I imagine he couldn't bring himself to do it."

"You mean the old expression 'love is akin to hate' has some validity here?"

"You heard him, Sasha. He thought killing you might be enough to heal him."

"So he knew he was sick."

"That's why he called me after Kristiana Felgard's death. Part of him wanted the killings to end. I've seen it before."

Sasha touched a finger to his mouth. "Just not in a friend."

"No, not in a friend."

"Did I mention how really sorry I am about this?"

"Once or twice." His lips curved into a reluctant smile. "You don't need to look so stricken, Sasha. We were old friends more than we were good friends. And between you and Dana, it was no contest."

"What about Fawn and their kids?"

"Yeah, well, that's going to be tougher to deal with."

Sasha's brow knit. "How did you find us? I dropped

my gloves for you, but I didn't really expect you to find them."

"I saw Dana hauling you into the trees. Then I saw your gloves and realized he was heading for the hill near George Painter's cabin."

She started to speak, but stopped and stared. "Nick, you're bleeding!"

"Just noticed that now, huh?"

"You tore your stitches."

"You took a dip in the lake. What's your point?"

It felt good to laugh, even if the amusement behind it was strained. "You realize, don't you, that when the rescue crews get here, they're going to find a very battle scarred group of people?"

"They're also going to find a drug runner who's wanted by the feds. I cuffed Jason Watts aka Anthony Rush to the banister. I hope Skye's up to digging out a few bullets tonight."

"After she restitches your shoulder."

"You're awfully bossy for a woman who almost…" Eyes closed, he blew out a breath. "Hell, I'm a cop, and I still can't say it."

"You don't have to. I was there."

When she shivered, Nick nudged her toward the lodge. "We need to get back before you freeze and either Will or Rush bleeds out."

"What about Max?"

"Not my decision. He was helping a drug dealer, not a murderer. He might be able to cut a deal."

"He said there were no bullets in his gun."

"Easy enough to verify."

"I think he really was trying to repair Skye's radio. He wanted to get off this mountain. So did Rush. It was

Dana who wanted to keep us here—or, well, keep me here. I imagine every time Max came close to repairing the circuits, Dana sabotaged them."

"With one brief time out so he could send a message to his wife."

"So, you see, there was some good in him. I mean, obviously, there was a lot more bad, but— Nick, the bad was already there before he met my mother, right?"

Nick halted her again. "We'll both be hypothermic at this rate, but you need to understand, Sasha, that what happened wasn't your mother's fault. She could have been nicer to Dana as a child, but the sickness was inside him when he met her. She simply gave it an outlet."

"I suppose." They stood only thirty feet from the lodge, and Rush's furious shouts reached them from inside. "So what's *his* deal?"

"He thinks his mother's living inside his head. He says she says he killed her."

"Did he?"

"I doubt it. He'll be talking to a few shrinks before he goes to trial for drug smuggling."

"So the matchbook was relevant, if only to Rush and his Colombian drug source." In an effort to allay some of the sadness swamping her, Sasha nipped Nick's bottom lip. "I love doing that. You always look so surprised."

"I'm not used to having women bite me—at least not since I left Homicide."

"Mmm, I'll be wanting details on that before the night's done." Her eyes teased. "I'd also like to know what you meant when you said you wanted to have a stag party of our own."

"Heard that, huh?"

She kissed him. "Would it help if I told you I love you?"

He looked from her mouth to her eyes. "Makes it easier for me to say it back. I love you, Sasha." He slid his thumb over her lips. "I never thought I'd say that, never thought I'd feel it. Never would have believed it could happen so fast."

"Yeah, well, meet my mother, then say it again."

"I'll meet your mother, Sasha. And you can meet my father's foreman."

"Deal." Her eyes sparkled as Rush's voice rose to a shriek. "I'm not scared of him, you know."

A vague frown appeared. "Who?"

"Your father's foreman. I'm not my mother. I have my own soul, my own history."

"History's done, Sasha. We start from tonight and move forward."

She kissed his upper lip this time. "Case closed, Detective?"

"Just needs one more thing," he said. And lowering his mouth to hers, he set his personal seal on all of it.

* * * * *

Alana Matthews can't remember a time when she didn't want to be a writer. As a child, she was a permanent fixture in her local library, and she soon turned her passion for books into writing short stories and, finally, novels. A longtime fan of romantic suspense, Alana felt she had no choice but to try her hand at the genre, and she is thrilled to be writing for Harlequin Intrigue. Alana makes her home in a small town near the coast of Southern California, where she spends her time writing, composing music and watching her favorite movies.

Books by Alana Matthews

Harlequin Intrigue

Internal Affairs
A Wanted Man
Waterford Point
Body Armor
Man Undercover

Visit the Author Profile page at Harlequin.com.

A WANTED MAN

Alana Matthews

Chapter 1

"I gotta make a pit stop," Billy Boy said.

U.S. Deputy Marshal Harlan Cole sighed and glanced at his prisoner in the rearview mirror. It was one thing after another with this guy, and he was tired of listening to him.

Billy Boy Lyman had spent half the drive moaning about his cuffs being too tight, the cruiser being too cold, then he started blathering on about how the courts and the Marshals Service had him all wrong. That he was an innocent man caught up in something way over his head.

When Harlan reminded him that he'd tried to rob a bank, put a gun in the teller's face and threatened to pull the trigger, Billy said, "My *partners* were the ones with the guns. I didn't even wanna *be* there—you know?"

"Uh-huh," Harlan muttered, then spent the next two hours listening to Billy Boy's tale of woe, the majority of which was little more than a sorry attempt at justifying the commission of a very serious crime.

Now, true to form, he was making noise about having to "pick a daisy," as Aunt Maggie used to say.

"I'm serious," Billy told him. "I really gotta go."

"Can't it wait until we get to Torrington?"

"Not unless you wanna be mopping up this backseat."

Harlan sighed again and looked out at the night sky and the empty road rolling under his headlights. He had picked Lyman up at the Criminal Justice Center in Colorado Springs, after waiting the good part of an hour for the prisoner to be processed. It had been a long day and all he wanted was to get the man squared away, then head to his motel room and go to bed.

He just wished Billy Boy would shut up. A wish that was likely to go unfulfilled.

This all came with the job, of course. Harlan knew that. The U.S. Marshals Service specialized in fugitive retrieval and prisoner transport, and he'd spent a significant amount of his career chauffeuring dimwits from one jail cell to another. He figured he'd probably heard just about every lamebrained excuse a man could come up with for breaking the law, and normally he wasn't much affected by it. Took it all in stride.

But there was something about Billy Boy that rubbed him the wrong way. The kid couldn't have been more than twenty-two years old, but he had one of those smirky little faces you just wanted to put a fist in. It took every bit of Harlan's impulse control to stop himself from pulling to the side of the highway to give the kid a quick tune-up.

On nights like this Harlan wondered if he should've taken his father's advice and found a different line of work. His father had been a career deputy and when Harlan had decided to follow in his footsteps, the old man had groaned.

"You've got smarts, boy. Use that big brain of yours to make a difference in the world."

But Harlan figured he *was* making a difference. There was nothing more satisfying than taking down a fugitive and helping ensure that the world was a better, safer place. It was just that he sometimes felt as if he were little more than a cattle herder. Even if the livestock he dealt with had a dangerous streak.

Not that Billy Boy was all that dangerous. Just annoying. And the sooner he delivered him to the Wyoming Medium Correctional Institution, the happier he'd be.

"Are we gonna make a stop or what?" Billy asked. "And I ain't talkin' about the side of the road. I like my privacy, and there's bound to be a gas station up ahead."

Harlan glanced at his prisoner in the rearview mirror. "Only on one condition."

"Which is?"

"After you've done your business, you shut your yap and keep it shut for the rest of the ride."

The convenience store was one of those all-nighters with a couple of gas pumps out front. It stood just off the highway, the only sign of life in the vicinity, its fluorescent lights so bright you could see them from half a mile away beckoning late night travelers to stop in for a snack, a cup of coffee and a few gallons of gas.

It was close to midnight and Harlan wasn't surprised to find only a single car parked out front—a battered gray Chevy Malibu he recognized as one that had passed them a few miles back.

Harlan wasn't fond of making unscheduled stops, but he understood how merciless the call of nature could sometimes be. When he worked long transports like this one, he tended to cut back on his liquid intake, but there wasn't much he could do about his passenger. It was up to the previous custodian to make sure the prisoner had been properly "fed and bled" before the trip. Yet despite the long processing time, someone back in Colorado Springs had neglected to do his job.

Harlan parked two slots over from the Chevy, then killed the engine and turned, staring at Billy Boy through the grille that separated the front and backseats.

"You'll wanna watch your step in there. Even a hint of trouble and I *will* shoot you. You understand?"

Lyman smirked. "You ever shot a prisoner before?"

"Once," Harlan said. "And he looked a lot like you."

The smirk disappeared. "You got nothing to worry about with me, Marshal. Like I told you, I'm an innocent man."

"Uh-huh."

Harlan popped his door open and climbed out. Resting the palm of his right hand on the butt of the Glock holstered at his hip, he moved to the back and pulled open the passenger door.

With his own hands cuffed behind him, Billy Boy had to struggle a bit to climb out of the cruiser, but he managed to do it without too much of a fuss. Then Harlan took hold of his arm and guided him toward the convenience store entrance.

When they got inside, Harlan was surprised to find a woman—a girl, really—behind the counter. Places like this tended to hire males for the late shift on the belief that a lone female offered any potential troublemakers a more vulnerable target.

But this particular female didn't look even remotely vulnerable. In fact, despite her youth and obvious beauty, there was a defiance in her expression that was a little off-putting. A look that said, *mess with me and find out.* She probably had a loaded piece resting somewhere under that counter, just in case the class got unruly.

Harlan saw her hackles rise as a buzzer announced their arrival and they came through the door, her gaze immediately shifting to Billy Boy's cuffed hands.

He didn't bother explaining the obvious, and didn't waste any time with chitchat, either. "Restroom?"

A guy in the potato chip aisle at the back of the store—the driver of the Malibu, no doubt—looked up at the sound of Harlan's voice. He glanced curiously at the man wearing cuffs, then went back to minding his own business.

Harlan waited as the girl reached under the counter and brought out a key attached to a wooden paddle. He'd always thought that the necessity for such things was a pretty sad commentary on the state of the world, but he took it from her without comment, then moved in the direction of her pointed finger toward a hallway just to her left.

The hallway was small and cramped with a single door marked Toilet. Harlan shoved the key into the lock, then pushed the door open and gestured Billy Boy inside.

Billy frowned. "Ain't you gonna take these cuffs off?"

"Once we're inside," Harlan said.

Billy looked surprised. "*We*? You're gonna watch me do my business? I *told* you, I like my privacy."

"My mandate is to keep you in sight at all times,

whether I like it or not. You seem to be under the mistaken impression that I should trust you."

"What do you think I'm gonna do? Whack you with my—"

"Just get inside, Billy. I've had about all I can tolerate of you. The sooner we're done here, the better off we'll both be."

"You ain't exactly Officer Friendly, are you?"

"Sorry to disappoint. Now let's get this over with."

Billy Boy scowled but did as he was told, stepping into a room about the size of a broom closet that sported a single toilet and sink. There wasn't enough room inside for both of them, so Harlan moved forward and uncuffed his prisoner, then stepped back and waited in the open doorway.

"You ain't gonna close the door?"

"I'm gonna close your mouth with my fist if you don't hurry it up."

"All right, all right," Billy said, stepping up to the toilet. "Don't get your panties in a wad." He turned his head slightly. "Speaking of which, what do you think of that counter girl? Kinda cute, huh?"

"I think she's way out of your league."

"Yeah? I bet if I treated her right, she'd do anything I told her."

Harlan almost laughed. "Dream on, Billy. Now will you please get to it already? I'd really like to—"

Harlan froze as something cold and metallic touched the back of his head.

"Hands behind your neck," a voice said.

A female voice.

Damn.

Harlan didn't have to see her face to know it was the

aforementioned counter girl. He also didn't have to use that big brain of his to figure out that she wasn't a counter girl at all. She'd no doubt been riding in the battered Chevy Malibu parked outside, along with the potato chip lover. And chances were pretty good that the *real* counter girl—or more likely *man*—was either dead or tied up in a closet somewhere.

Harlan inwardly cursed himself. He'd been at this job for nearly ten years now and he'd just pulled a rookie move. Let the prisoner lull him—or, in this case, *annoy* him—into lowering his guard.

How could he be so stupid?

"Hands," the girl said again. "Now."

As Harlan sighed and laced his fingers behind his neck, Billy Boy Lyman turned around, that infuriating smirk once again adorning his face. He reached forward and removed Harlan's Glock from its holster.

"You were right not to trust me," he said.

Then he brought the gun up fast, slamming it into the side of Harlan's head.

Chapter 2

They found the burned-out shell of the pickup truck parked on the side of the highway about forty miles south of Williamson. It was still smoldering when a highway patrol officer pulled off the road behind it, thinking it was just another abandoned vehicle whose owner had gotten a little carried away.

As soon as he took a closer look, however, he discovered it hadn't been abandoned after all.

There was a body inside.

The medical examiner on scene had warned Callie that what she was about to see would not be pleasant—what people in the trade referred to as a *crispy critter*. And true enough, the sight of that blackened lump on the front seat was one she knew she'd be spending the next couple weeks trying to bleach from her brain.

Despite the damage, the truck's rear license tag had

been spared—an oasis amidst a desolate landscape—and when she called it in, she found out the pickup belonged to none other than Jim Farber, a local rancher.

Considering the fact that Farber hadn't been seen since yesterday morning, the logical conclusion was that *he* was the lump on the front seat.

Callie wouldn't know for certain until forensics did its thing, but she was a strong believer in Occam's razor—that the simplest explanation was the most likely one. After seven years with the Williamson County Sheriff's Department, working crimes a lot more complicated than this, she'd come to rely on that dictum as if it were gospel.

The question, as always, was who had done this and why? Williamson, Wyoming, wasn't exactly known for its violent crime, and the handful of murders Callie had investigated in the course of her career usually led her straight to a member of the victim's family.

That, however, didn't seem to be the case here. Only careful examination would determine the actual cause of death, but whatever it might be, Callie couldn't imagine Farber's wife or either of their two kids pouring gasoline over the family truck and setting it on fire. This was a dispassionate crime, and the Farbers were anything but. It was certainly possible that Callie was wrong about that, but she didn't think so.

A groan pulled her out of her thoughts. "I think I'm gonna be sick," Rusty said, clutching his stomach, his face a couple shades whiter than it had been when they'd pulled up in their SUV a few moments ago.

Rusty Wilcox was a good number of years younger than Callie and hadn't been on the job long enough to build immunity against sights like this. Even Callie was finding it more difficult than usual to shut her mind off to the horror of it all.

But she couldn't let Rusty know this. She was his training deputy, breaking him into the cold, cruel reality of the sheriff's Major Crimes Squad, and it was important to maintain her professionalism at all times.

This wasn't much of a struggle for her, however. Over the years she'd learned to bottle up her emotions, a trait that had soured quite a few relationships.

The truth was, *she* was the dispassionate one. And at thirty-four, she had come to the conclusion that she was destined to spend the rest of her life flying solo. She no longer embraced the dream of a husband and kids and a white picket fence.

She looked at Rusty and could see that he was struggling to hold back the blueberry muffin he'd gobbled up on the ride over, despite her warning that what he was about to see wouldn't be pretty.

"Do it on the other side of the road," she said tersely. "You don't want to contaminate the crime scene."

As Rusty stumbled across the blacktop, Callie went back to her thoughts only to have them interrupted again by a shout from the far side of the pickup truck.

"Deputy Glass! I think I've found something."

She glanced at Rusty, then moved around toward the source of the shout and found one of her crime scene techs crouched next to the passenger door—a grinning, gap-toothed kid named Tucker Davies.

Why did everyone around Callie seem to be getting younger these days?

"Check this out," he said, excitement lighting his eyes as he pointed to a spot just under the truck.

Callie hunkered down and looked. Saw a lump of

half-melted polymer that roughly formed the shape of a handgun. A forty caliber Glock from the looks of it. Just like the one she carried.

Callie immediately understood Tucker's excitement. "Let's just pray the serial number is intact."

"Only one way to find out."

Tucker reached a gloved hand under the truck and carefully picked up the weapon. He pulled it out, studied it, then showed Callie the trigger guard which looked relatively unscathed. "Only a partial, but it might be enough."

This was turning out to be a good day for numbers. First the license tag, now this. And maybe the question of *who* and *why* would be answered much more quickly than Callie had dared hope.

"Let's get it into the system as soon as possible. Hit every database you can think of. I want to know who owns that weapon."

"Might take a while," Tucker told her.

"Then I guess you'd better get started."

Williamson County Sheriff's Deputy Callie Glass was a Wyoming native, born and bred. She'd drawn her first breath on a cold Thursday morning in her mother's bedroom. Her mother was eighteen years old and barely out of high school, screaming in agony as she pushed her first and only child into the world, then promptly passed on.

Some said that Callie's mom might have survived if she'd been in a proper hospital and hadn't been victim to an inexperienced midwife. But there was no way to know that for sure. The hemorrhaging had come on swift and without warning, and the poor girl was dead within minutes of the delivery. Besides, Mary Glass was a free spirit who had never trusted hospitals, and wouldn't have poked so much as a toe inside one—even if her life *had* depended on it.

Callie's father was a kid named Riley Pritchard, who had enlisted in the army a week after he'd found out young Mary was pregnant. The Pritchards were one of the richest families in Williamson, and there was no doubt in anyone's mind that Riley's father, Jonah, had nudged the boy into action, hoping to avoid the possibility of a bastard child claiming heir to their precious family fortune.

By the time Callie was born, Riley had been killed when a base supply struck overturned and crushed him, so the only parent she'd ever known was the woman she called Nana Jean.

Despite being widowed and borderline destitute, Nana had stepped up to the challenge of raising an infant and had done it without complaint.

Most of the time.

What few complaints Nana *did* have, came much later in Callie's life, after a string of romantic disasters had made it clear that her granddaughter's spirit wasn't easily tamed, a trait she had inherited from her mother.

"I just wish you'd settle down," the old woman often told Callie. "Find yourself somebody to share your life with. I won't be around to hold your hand forever."

But Callie was defiant. "Who says it needs holding?"

"Listen, child, you can be the most independent woman on the face of earth, but you still need a little romance in your life. It's been far too long."

"So why didn't *you* ever get married again?"

"Your grandfather was one of a kind. Any man tried

to replace him would only wind up heartbroken, and I'm not about to do that to someone."

"He must've been pretty special."

Nana nodded, a wistful look in her eyes. She'd never been a sentimental woman, so Callie knew that what she was about to say was sincere. "This'll sound like a lie, but I swear to you that up until the day he died, my heart would flutter every time Walter walked into the room."

Callie smiled. "That's sweet."

"Yes, it is, and I keep hoping you'll find someone who does that to *you*. I thought you had it, once, but you're too stubborn to—"

"All right, Nana. I think we're done here."

This conversation was just a rehash of a dozen others they'd had over the past few years, Nana worried about Callie's ever-ticking clock. Such exchanges usually ended with Callie politely but firmly suggesting that Nana let her worry about her own love life. That she had more important things to think about, like putting bad guys in jail.

And *that*, she insisted, was about all the testosterone she was interested in dealing with these days.

"You go on, keep lying to yourself," Nana would always say—a handful of words for which Callie had yet to find a suitable response.

No matter what case she might be working on, Callie tried her best to go home for lunch every day, and today was no exception.

Once the crime scene was squared away and the evidence had been tagged and bagged, she dropped Rusty off at the station house with instructions to make sure

Tucker Davies called her just as soon as he got a hit on the Glock.

Then she drove the mile and a half home, where she knew Nana would be waiting for her with a sandwich and a glass of iced tea.

Their usual routine was to sit and watch Nana's favorite soap. And as the melodrama played out on screen, Callie would invariably start thinking about how old and frail Nana was looking and worry that she might not be around long enough to see how the stories ended.

Today, however, as Callie pulled up to the curb, she was surprised to find a plumber's truck parked in their driveway. Which didn't make sense. They'd had the entire house repiped less than six months ago, and for the money they'd spent, there shouldn't be any need for an emergency visit. Besides, Callie herself usually handled such arrangements, and if there was a problem Nana would have called her.

But when she went inside, she found Nana and the plumber sitting in the front parlor, sharing a pitcher of tea, as if this were nothing more than a social visit.

Although he looked vaguely familiar—about Callie's age and marginally handsome, if you liked the type— she had no idea who this man might be.

Nana took care of that straightaway. "Cal, this is Judith's grandnephew Henry. He just moved to town and I thought it might be nice for him to drop by for a little refreshment."

The lightbulb suddenly went on and Callie remembered where she'd seen him before: in a photograph on Judith's mantel. Judith had been Nana's best friend since childhood.

Callie knew immediately what was going on here and forced a smile. "Hello, Henry, nice to meet you."

Henry got to his feet and shook her hand as Callie shifted her gaze to her grandmother. "Nana, can I speak to you for a moment?"

"Why don't you have a seat, dear? I'll pour you some tea."

"I think we need to talk alone."

Nana reluctantly rose from her chair and followed Callie into the kitchen. Callie could see that the old woman was bracing for a scolding, and she was all too happy to give her one.

As they passed through the doorway, she felt heat rising in her chest and struggled to keep her voice low. "What in God's name are you thinking?"

"He's a nice boy, dear. What's the harm in having him stop by for a glass of tea?"

"Is Judith in on this, too?"

Nana smiled. "Well, I guess she'd have to be, wouldn't she?"

"How many times have I told you, I can handle my own love life. I don't need you and Judith interfering."

"With what? You haven't had a date in six months."

Callie glared at her. "I mean it, Nana."

"Listen, hon, those pipes of yours must be just about frozen solid. Wouldn't hurt to have a handsome young plumber check 'em out. Who knows where it might lead?"

Callie felt her face grow red. "I can't believe you just said that."

"What—you think because I'm old I've forgotten what it's like to have a little—"

"*Stop,*" Callie said, her voice louder and more shrill

than she'd intended it to be. She did her best to calm herself. "Nana, I appreciate your concern, I really do, but please, stop trying to force the issue."

"Dear, if I don't force the issue, I'll be dead before—"

The ring of Callie's cell phone cut her off. Callie took it from her pocket and checked the screen: Tucker Davies.

Already?

That was fast.

She jabbed a button on the keypad and put the phone to her ear. "Tell me this is good news."

"Better than good," Tucker said. "Turns out the Glock has a custom serial number, just like the weapons *we* use, only this one's assigned to the U.S. Marshals Service."

"You've gotta be kidding me."

"I put in a call and found out that one of their deputies lost it last night when the prisoner he was transporting got the better of him. They were headed for Wyoming Correctional, coming up from Colorado Springs."

Callie felt her heartbeat quicken. That prisoner was more than likely her perpetrator. How he'd wound up in Jim Farber's truck was a mystery, but at least they knew who they were looking for.

"I need to talk to this deputy," she said.

"Shouldn't be a problem, since he's already in the vicinity. He's on his way to the station house as we speak."

"Oh? What's his name?"

"Cole," Davies said. "Deputy Harlan Cole."

Callie hesitated, certain she hadn't heard him right. "Say that again?"

He enunciated carefully. "Harlan… Cole."

His words were like a sledgehammer to Callie's chest. If she didn't know better, she'd swear her heart had suddenly stopped dead.

The name was not unfamiliar to her.

Far from it.

And the thought of Harlan Cole walking into her life after all these years made her want to turn and flee. If this was nature taking its course, then she wanted nothing to do with it.

Without warning a bucketful of memories flooded her mind. And while the pain that the name *Harlan Cole* invoked had long been relegated to a tiny corner of her brain, it now sprang forward as if freed from a cage, an untamed and ferocious beast, anxious to devour.

"Deputy Glass?"

Callie had to search for a moment, but finally found her voice. "Thanks, Tucker. I'm on my way."

As she disconnected, she realized Nana was staring at her, concern in her eyes. "What's the matter, hon? You okay?"

Far from it, Callie thought, knowing it would take every bit of her strength to climb into her SUV and drive back to the station house.

Because Deputy Harlan Cole wasn't just a U.S. Marshal. He was a man she had long despised.

He was also the love of her life.

Chapter 3

Harlan had no idea what to expect when he walked into the Williamson County Sheriff's Department.

He was feeling humiliated and out of sorts after last night's debacle, the side of his head still throbbing where Billy Boy Lyman had left a Glock-size bruise.

When he came to, he'd found himself lying in the restroom doorway, the room swaying, his weapon long gone. But what hurt most was the blow to his pride. In the span of less than a minute, he had lost a prisoner, a gun and a sizable chunk of his reputation. All because he'd been stupid enough to lower his guard, and was just biased enough to assume that the girl behind the counter wasn't a threat to him.

Something he'd have to work on.

Whatever the case, he didn't doubt that these mistakes would haunt him for many months to come. And as he pulled into the Williamson County Sheriff's Office parking structure, he had no idea what he was walking into.

The locals would undoubtedly blame him for the death of one of their own, but the question was whether they'd take the professional route and hide their animosity, or—as was so often the case—treat him like a hostile intruder.

The moment he stepped into the conference room, however, such concerns immediately vacated his mind. This could have been a war zone, with bullets flying, and Harlan wouldn't have noticed.

Of the six people sitting at the long table, only one of them—the lone woman in the room—commanded his attention, despite the fact that she refused to look him directly in the eye.

It was none other than Callie Glass.

Harlan's internal alarm bells suddenly went off, and he knew he'd better sit down before he *fell* down. While he would've loved to have blamed his sudden disorientation on his head injury, that was only part of it. The sight of his old college flame sitting not ten feet away from him had thrown him completely off balance.

Was he imagining things? Had the bump on his noggin brought on some cruel hallucination?

No. She was real, all right. As real as a heartbeat. A little older but even more beautiful than he remembered—which, until this moment, he would've deemed an impossibility. He knew she was from Williamson, but he'd never imagined he'd find her here like this.

Not now. Not today.

"Deputy Cole, I'm Sheriff Mercer."

Harlan blinked, then swiveled his head to his left to

find a sunbaked cowboy in a gray suit with a string tie rising from his chair, his hand extended.

Harlan reached out and shook it, happy for the distraction. "Good to meet you, Sheriff. I wish it were under better circumstances."

"You sure you're up to this? Looks like your boy did quite a job on you."

Harlan had hoped that the bruise wouldn't be that noticeable—a symbol of his failure—but it didn't much matter. He'd just have to learn to live with it for the next several days.

"I'll be fine, thanks. But if you don't mind, I think I'll sit down."

Mercer gestured to a chair. "By all means."

Harlan glanced at Callie, then pulled the chair out, as Mercer introduced the people around the table. The names and faces came at him too quickly to process, but when the sheriff got to the only one Harlan really cared about, she finally looked up at him, offering him a curt, professional smile.

Her *eyes* weren't smiling, however. Not even close. And her voice had a clipped, unfriendly tone. "Hello, Harlan."

He nodded. "Callie."

Mercer's eyebrows went up. "You two know each other?"

"Long time ago," she said. "Back in graduate school. We took a couple of criminology classes together."

She'd said this with about as much warmth and enthusiasm as an accountant reciting the tax code. There was a lot more to it than that, but she wasn't offering any details. Which was fine by Harlan. He didn't want to *think* about those details—although he was finding it difficult not to.

Mercer said, "Denver, right? University of Colorado?"

"Right," they said in unison.

They exchanged an awkward glance as Mercer studied them curiously, then sat back down.

"Small world," he said, "but I reckon you two can catch up some other time. Right now we've got business to attend to." He looked at Harlan. "Your supervising deputy says you've got some information to share."

Harlan tore his gaze away from Callie and nodded. He had spent the better part of his morning at the Torrington marshal's substation gathering up as much intel on Billy Boy Lyman as he could find. He hadn't had much sleep since the incident, and his supervisor back in Colorado Springs had urged him to take it easy and let someone else handle the heavy lifting.

But Harlan had refused.

He preferred to clean up his own messes.

When he'd heard that his Glock had been found under a burned-out pickup truck near Williamson—a vehicle carrying the body of a local rancher—he'd made a vow right then and there that he wouldn't rest until Billy Boy was back in custody.

Or begging St. Peter to open up the pearly gates.

"First," he said, "I want to apologize to all of you for making any of this necessary. If I hadn't been derelict in my duties, none of us would be sitting here right now."

He glanced at Callie again but got nothing back. She was carefully examining her fingernails.

"Let's not worry about blame," Mercer said. "The way I look at it, the only reason we're here is because of this boy Lyman."

"Thanks, Sheriff, I appreciate that." Harlan reached into his coat pocket and brought out a small stack of photographs. "I assume you all saw the mug shot I faxed over?"

There were nods and murmurs around the room.

"Lyman's a Nebraska native who moved with his mother to Wyoming when he was sixteen years old. He's been in and out of custody ever since, his latest bust for an aborted robbery attempt at the Colorado Springs Bank and Trust three weeks ago. He was out on parole at the time, and since the courts are backed up, someone on high figured it wouldn't hurt to ship his butt up to Torrington to finish out his state sentence while he's waiting for trial. That's where I came in."

He laid the stack of photos on the table. "We took these from the convenience store's surveillance footage. The main unit was destroyed, but the owner keeps a backup in his office closet."

"How's the clerk doing?"

The question came from a young guy sitting next to Callie. Rusty-something.

"Touch and go, last I heard."

Harlan had found the clerk tied up and shoved into a storeroom, his head caved in by a blow much harder than the one he himself had received. Once he saw the poor guy, he knew that he could easily have wound up in the very same condition. So maybe getting beaned by Billy Boy instead of the girlfriend or the potato chip lover was a blessing he should be thankful for.

Tapping the photos, he said, "These are the two perpetrators who helped Lyman escape. We think they may have been his partners in the bank job, but they were wearing ski masks at the time and managed to get away."

Mercer said, "You run those photos through facial recognition?"

Harlan nodded. "No hits so far, which isn't much of a surprise considering how bad the resolution is." He looked at the others. "We found their Chevy Malibu dumped in a field about sixty miles north of the convenience store. Broken water pump. That's probably where they hitched a ride with the victim. And since people tend to go where they feel most comfortable, I'm hoping they might be local. Maybe one of you crossed paths with them at one time or another."

He slid the photos to Mercer, who picked up the stack and started shuffling through it. Within seconds, something shifted in the sheriff's eyes. "Well I'll be damned. This is getting cozier and cozier."

"You recognize them?"

Mercer didn't answer. Instead he took a photo off the top of the stack and spun it across the table toward Callie. "That face look familiar to you?"

Callie caught it, then dropped her gaze, studying the image carefully.

After a moment, she said, "Looks like Megan Pritchard, but this is a little fuzzy and it's been a while. She hasn't been around much since her last stint in juvie, and that was like—what?—three, four years ago?"

Mercer shrugged. "Give or take."

"So who is she?" Harlan asked.

"Megan Pritchard-Breen," Callie said. "Only nobody uses the Breen part since her mother got a divorce years ago. She's one of our local troublemakers. Sheriff here likes to call her a wild child, but I think he's being polite in deference to the family. Sociopath is more accurate."

"She's also a bit of a fire bug," Mercer told him. "So draw your own conclusions."

"And she's got family up here?"

Mercer glanced at Callie, and Harlan followed his lead, but she once again averted her gaze. He sensed, however, that this time it had nothing to do with their past. There was a different kind of history at play here. An underlying discomfort she wasn't anxious to address. And Harlan had the feeling he was the only one in the room who didn't know about it.

"She's the granddaughter of Jonah Pritchard," Mercer said. "And if you spent any significant amount of time in Williamson, you'd recognize the name."

"Local celebrity?"

"That's one way of putting it, if you like 'em old and mean and wealthier than the crown prince of Tangiers."

"I take it you're not a fan."

"Let's just say the pathology seems to run in the family, only Jonah is a little better at hiding it." He looked at Callie. "And if that *is* Megan Pritchard, I think you know what it means."

She frowned. "You want Rusty and me to go out there."

"I know you've got issues with the old coot, but you *are* the lead deputy on this case."

"Out where?" Harlan asked.

"Pritchard Ranch," Mercer said. "If Meg's in trouble, she'd go to her grandpa for help. Always has, always will."

"Which means Billy Boy might be there, as well."

"That's the logical assumption. So I'd suggest you three saddle up, pronto. We don't have a warrant, but maybe the Pritchards will cooperate."

Harlan nodded, then got to his feet.

"Wait a minute," Callie said, her frown deepening. "You want him to go *with* us?"

Mercer's brows went up again. "Is that a problem? I thought you two were old friends."

Harlan and Callie exchanged another glance, neither of them willing to tackle that one in public, and Harlan could feel the eyes of everyone in the room shifting in his direction. The office gossip line would be buzzing this afternoon.

Mercer tapped his watch. "Tick tock, Deputy Glass. We've got a trio of killers to catch."

Looking like a woman who had just been condemned to a decade of indentured servitude, Callie reluctantly rolled her chair back and stood up.

Harlan knew exactly how she felt.

Chapter 4

"How much farther is it?" Harlan asked.

These were more or less the first words spoken since the three of them had climbed into Callie's cruiser. Now that Harlan had broken the silence, Rusty—who had probably sensed the tension in the air and had been smart enough to keep his mouth shut—gestured from the front passenger seat, saying, "Just up the road apiece. About five or six miles."

To Callie's mind, it might as well be five or six *hundred*. With all due respect to the late Jim Farber and his family, she couldn't wait until this day was over. From Nana Jean's matchmaking to the surprise appearance of a man she loathed and now this trip out to Pritchard Ranch—the *last* place she wanted to go—this was turning out to be a record breaker. All future days would surely be measured against this one.

Callie had never considered herself a vindictive woman. She'd never been one to hold on to a grudge. More often than not she found she could remain civil with the tiny handful of men she'd been intimate with. She had long ago convinced herself that she was a much better friend than lover.

But the breakup with Harlan had been different. Maybe it was her immaturity, or maybe it was the simple fact that she had been so head over heels in love with him. Whatever the cause, she had carried this burning resentment toward him a lot longer than she wanted to admit.

It rarely came to the surface, however. No reason it should. She hadn't seen Harlan in nearly a decade, and had long since learned to get through a day, a week, sometimes even a whole month, without thinking about him. But every time she *did*, she found herself hating him all over again.

She knew, of course, that her anger was simply a way of masking the pain. Not just because of the breakup, but because of the circumstances surrounding it.

She'd bet good money that if the accident hadn't happened, she and Harlan would still be together. No question. But that tragic night had forced such an enormous wedge between them that it was no wonder they could barely stand to look at each other.

Callie didn't think she would ever forgive Harlan for what he'd done. And until today it hadn't been much of an issue.

Now here he was, sitting in the backseat of her SUV, and it took every bit of inner strength she could muster to keep from slamming the brakes and throwing him out in the middle of the highway.

The thing that *really* galled her, however, was that despite her turmoil she couldn't stop thinking about how good he looked. The years had given his face and body an angularity, a solid, rustic dignity that had only been hinted at in his younger days. He'd been attractive back then, no doubt about it, but now he looked as if he'd just stepped out of a movie screen, his blue-eyed Hollywood good looks tempered with just enough real-world ruggedness to make him a genuine human being.

And that was all the more reason to hate him. He should be suffering for what he'd done. Balding and getting too fat and covered in festering boils.

Tell us how you really feel, Callie.

Gripping the wheel tighter, she punched the accelerator and picked up speed.

The Pritchard family had always displayed their wealth without apology. Nestled in the foothills of the Bighorn Mountains, the ranch was seven thousand acres of rolling hills, grassy flatland and a sleekly modern, three-story dream house that was big enough to hold the population of a small third-world country.

As she pulled up to the gate, Callie thought about her connection to the family. Despite the shared blood, she had long ago realized that there really *wasn't* one. Not the kind that mattered, at least. Before she was even born, Jonah Pritchard had made it clear that neither she nor her mother were worth spitting on, and Callie herself couldn't care less about his money.

Everyone in town knew the history between the two families. A few of her friends—including Sheriff Mercer—had urged her to pursue her stake in the Pritchard fortune. When her father was killed, he'd left behind a sizable trust that rightfully belonged to her. But pursuing it meant lawsuits and court hearings and exhumed bodies and DNA tests and a lot of bad feelings all around.

If Callie went forward, she knew full well that Jonah would wage a smear campaign against the memory of her mother. He'd hire a platoon of lawyers and PR flacks to claim the DNA tests had somehow been tainted or tampered with, claiming the girl had slept around like a common whore and that Callie could be just about *anyone's* child.

There was no amount of money that would dull the sting of such an attack, especially in a town the size of Williamson, which had less than seven thousand residents—the majority of whom loved to gossip. And with Nana Jean getting frailer by the week, it just wasn't worth it.

Callie was content to know that she had *earned* her place in this world. And she couldn't help thinking how ironic it was that Megan, the so-called *real* Pritchard granddaughter, had turned out to be a family embarrassment. No smear campaign necessary.

Callie had to admit she'd found a certain satisfaction in this knowledge.

As she pulled her cruiser to a stop, the guard manning the gate came out of his booth and approached her window with a smile on his face. Landry Bickham was a grizzled old cowboy who had been working for the Pritchard family as long as anyone could remember, and Callie didn't think she'd ever seen him without that smile.

"Afternoon, Deputy Glass. You sure you didn't make a wrong turn?"

"If only," she said. "I need to go up to the house. Police business."

Bickham grunted. "You make an appointment?"

Callie just stared at him.

Bickham nodded, then went back to the booth and picked up the phone. Callie knew she could ask him if he'd seen Megan in the past few hours, but there wasn't much point. Landry was loyal to a fault—the secret behind his longevity on the job.

After his call was done, he came back shaking his head, the smile still intact. "Jonah is a little under the weather today, isn't taking any visitors."

"I already told you, this isn't a social call."

Bickham shrugged. "You might try again tomorrow morning."

"Open the gate, Landry."

"I really wish I could do that, Callie, but I've got my—"

Before Landry could finish his sentence, Harlan had his door open and was climbing out. He brushed the flap of his coat back, revealing the star clipped to his belt. "U.S. Marshals Service. Open that gate now or consider yourself under arrest."

Bickham's smile faltered slightly. "For what?"

"For aiding and abetting a fugitive. Or for being a general pain in the butt. Take your choice."

Callie couldn't help feeling a little annoyed by Harlan's intrusion. Didn't he think she could get the job done?

Apparently not.

"Fugitive? What fugitive?" Bickham said. "I'm just following orders."

Callie gestured impatiently. "Do what he asks, Landry. I'll make sure Jonah knows you put up a good fight."

"Is this fella really gonna arrest me?"

"Not if you cooperate."

"All right, then," Bickham said, then shuffled back to his booth and flipped a switch. The gate rumbled and started rolling to one side.

As Harlan got back in the car, Callie hit the gas, shooting forward before he had a chance to sit down and get his door closed.

He yelped, letting loose a string of profanities, and she eyed him in her rearview mirror.

"You okay back there?"

Struggling to collect himself, Harlan shot her a look of annoyance that kept her smiling all the way up the drive.

No, she wasn't vindictive.

Not one little bit.

Chapter 5

Landry Bickham hadn't wasted any time in sounding the alarm.

They were greeted at the top of the drive by Gloria Pritchard, a woman whose beauty had been starkly diminished by years of starvation, alcohol and cosmetic surgery. The result was the exact opposite of what she had intended, her skin stretched so tautly over her sharp bones that she looked much older than her fifty-one years.

Callie only knew her actual age because Gloria and her mother had been best friends in high school. Not that this mattered much. Gloria visibly stiffened at the sight of Callie as they climbed out of the SUV.

Neither of them offered any pleasantries.

"So what has my little darling done *now*?" Gloria asked. The *little darling* being her wayward daughter Meg.

"Is she here?"

"I haven't seen her in a good six months."

"Then what makes you think that's what this is about?"

Gloria smiled humorlessly. "Experience," she said. "I don't need to tell you what a handful that girl has been since the day she was born."

To put it mildly, Callie thought. Megan Pritchard was the devil incarnate as far as she was concerned. But without the brains. Even her own mother had stopped trying to cover for her.

Not that Gloria was the model of a loving parent. Twice divorced and always shopping for a replacement, she paid about as much attention to her own daughter as she might a pet hamster.

Meg's grandfather Jonah, on the other hand, would do just about anything for his girl—whether Gloria liked it or not.

"What about your father?"

Gloria seemed to grow even more tense. "What about him?"

"Has *he* seen her? Recently, I mean. Like the last twelve or so hours."

"I'm afraid I wouldn't know," she said. "This is a big house, and Jonah and I tend to avoid each other as much as possible."

One thing you could say about Gloria was that, despite her family's money and the Hollywood housewife exterior, she was always brutally frank and open about her feelings, even when it meant exposing the truth about their not-so-happy family.

Maybe it was the years of AA meetings.

"You still haven't answered my question," she said. "What's Meg done now?"

Harlan apparently took this as his cue to step forward, reaching into his inner coat pocket as he did.

"Ma'am, I'm Deputy U.S. Marshal Harlan Cole. I'd like you to take a look at this, if you don't mind."

He brought out one of the surveillance photographs and handed it to her.

"Is this your daughter?"

Gloria took a long moment to study the image, then said, "I think so, yes."

Harlan nodded. "You say you haven't seen her in six months, but when's the last time you spoke to her?"

Gloria returned the photograph. "She called me a few days ago. Just to remind me how much she despises me."

"She happen to mention she was headed your way?"

"No," Gloria said.

"Well, we have reason to believe she was, and after last night, she's in the company of at least one wanted fugitive and may well have participated in a bank robbery and a murder." He paused, glancing at Callie as if seeking some kind of approval. She wasn't sure why. He seemed content with running the show. "In light of this," he said to Gloria, "I'd like your permission to search the premises."

Before Gloria could answer, a stern baritone boomed. "I'm afraid you're out of luck, Marshal."

They all turned to find Jonah Pritchard standing in the doorway, a tall man in blue jeans and a dark flannel shirt. He was close to Nana Jean's age, but with none of the frailty. In fact, he was as solid as a twenty-year-old and didn't look even remotely under the weather.

Callie knew she should probably feel something. After

all, he was *her* grandfather, too. But feelings are reserved for those you care about, and she'd have to reach down pretty deep to find anything that resembled an emotional attachment to this man.

"*I* own this house," he said to Harlan, "and permission is definitely not granted."

Harlan stepped toward him now, once again flashing the badge on his hip. "Then I guess you'd be Jonah Pritchard."

"That's right," the old man said.

"Well, I was only asking to be polite, sir, so if you'll move to one side, we'd like to get started."

Callie threw him a look.

Say *what*?

Jonah shook his head. "Without a warrant? If you want to come in, you'll need a judge's signature."

Harlan cocked a brow at him, then turned to Callie and Rusty. "Did you two hear that?"

Callie frowned, not sure what he was getting at. "What?"

"He just asked me if I want to come in. Sounded like an invitation to me."

Uh-oh, Callie thought. So Harlan was one of those. She was a strong believer in procedure and didn't appreciate the cowboys who ignored it in hopes of getting a pass from the courts. She should've realized he was a "Wyatt Earp" the minute he jumped out of her SUV to confront Landry.

But before she could tell him that neither she nor Rusty were about to play along, Jonah stepped aside, moving out onto the wide front porch. Not to invite them in, but to make room for a couple of burly ranch hands who emerged from the doorway behind him.

He looked pointedly at Harlan. "You take one more step in this direction, I'm within my rights to stop you."

Callie watched as Harlan studied the two ranch hands. They weren't carrying weapons, but then they didn't need to.

Harlan said, "Not like this, you aren't. The law doesn't look too kindly on assault against peace officers."

Jonah shrugged. "It isn't too thrilled about illegal search and seizure, either. And it won't keep these boys from putting you three in the hospital." He gestured to his daughter. "Gloria, get in the house. No reason for you to be here for this."

In other words, *get lost.*

Callie could see the resentment in Gloria's eyes. Resentment that went back many years. But Gloria did as she was told. And without protest.

When she was gone, Jonah said, "There's no need for this to get ugly, Marshal."

Now Callie spoke up. "Tell that to Megan, Mr. Pritchard. And to Jim Farber's family. She and her friends left him in quite a state."

"I wouldn't know anything about that."

"Wouldn't you?"

He gave her a look that said he was offended by the remark, but she sensed he was feigning it. Nothing she said could offend him. The old guy was bulletproof.

"Meg decided a long time ago that she wasn't interested in associating with this family," he said. "Not that that's any of your business."

Callie knew that his words were meant to cut much deeper than they did, but after thirty-four years she was immune to him. She'd long been aware that Jonah despised her. By his skewed logic, his son wouldn't be dead if it weren't for her whore of a mother.

The thought of this suddenly brought to surface another part of her life—her years with Harlan—and she wondered for a brief moment if she'd applied her own skewed logic to that situation.

But no. That was different. And she had no desire to wander into any dark alleys right now.

Focus, Callie.

Concentrate on the matter at hand.

"We could clear all this up," Harlan said to Jonah, "if you'd just let us do our job. If you've got nothing to hide, then this conversation is over."

"It's already over," a voice said, and Callie heard the ratchet of a scatter-gun behind them.

She and Harlan and Rusty all turned to find a smiling Landry Bickham holding a pump-action twelve-gauge. He kept it pointed at the ground, but Callie knew he'd use it if the old man gave him the nod.

Her heart started thumping.

This wasn't the direction she'd wanted this afternoon to go.

Harlan turned back to Jonah. "You're making a grave mistake, Mr. Pritchard. I could arrest you for obstruction, right now."

"I suppose you could try," Jonah said.

They were all silent for a long moment, and Callie could see the fury creeping into Harlan's gaze. She'd seen that fury before, when she told him she never wanted to lay eyes on him again.

Jonah gestured. "You go on, now, try to get your warrant. If the judge says I've gotta open up my house, I'll open up my house. In the meantime, you're just trespassing, far as I can see."

For a moment Callie thought Harlan might do something stupid, but he held back. Thank God.

"This isn't over," he said quietly.

Jonah's gaze didn't waver. "I don't doubt that for a minute."

Harlan stared at him a while longer, then his fury seemed to dissipate and he turned, moving back to the cruiser.

Then they were all inside, Callie feeling both frustrated and relieved as she started the engine and watched Jonah and the others go back into the house.

"You think they're in there?" Harlan asked.

Callie wanted to punch him. "Even if they are, unless Pritchard cooperates, there's not much we can do about it right now."

"He's one nasty piece of work, isn't he?"

Callie jammed the car in gear. "Pot...meet kettle," she said.

Then she turned them around and headed down the drive.

Chapter 6

"You know what you are? You're an idiot. An idiot disguised as a fool."

Good old Callie. She'd never been one to mince words, and Harlan could see that she hadn't changed.

Back in the day it had been a trait he'd found endearing. Most of the girls he'd known in college had been hesitant to show their true colors until they had you on the hook. They spent far too much time playing the games they'd learned in high school, and the guys they pursued weren't much different.

But Callie had always been what-you-see-is-what-you-get. Take it or leave it. And that was a large part of what had made Harlan fall in love with her in the first place.

That and the simple fact that she was the single most intriguing human being he'd ever met. Still was.

They were rolling along the highway now, headed toward town, Harlan once again relegated to the backseat while Callie drove and her partner Rusty rode shotgun.

She said, "You do realize you almost got us killed back there."

Harlan looked at her reflection in the rearview mirror. "Don't be so dramatic. Pritchard doesn't strike me as stupid. And technically, he was right."

"You *think*?" Her hands were gripping the steering wheel as if she had hold of his neck and wanted to snap it. "Then what was with all that cowboy nonsense?"

"Just giving the old guy a nudge, see how he reacted."

Callie shook her head. "You haven't changed at all, have you, Harlan?"

"I beg your pardon?"

"Forget it," she muttered.

"No, you opened the box, let's see what's inside."

Callie sighed, glancing at Rusty. He had his cell phone clamped to his ear, speaking quietly into it, pretending not to listen to them.

She said to Harlan, "Maybe Jonah wouldn't have done anything drastic, but there were no guarantees of that. You make stupid moves, you risk people getting hurt. You should know that better than anyone."

Harlan knew a lot of things. Like the fact that she wasn't talking about Pritchard at all.

"Look," he said, "why don't we save the recriminations for another day? Right now we need to concentrate on searching that house. And we need to do it legally."

"That could be a problem," Rusty said, snapping his phone shut. "Sheriff Mercer tells me the judge went out of town for a weekend hunting trip. He's trying to track down another judge in Sheridan, but it could take a while.

Says we might as well grab some chow, then head back to the station house."

Now it was Harlan's turn to sigh. Times like these made him wish real life was more like the movies. Everything happened so quickly on the big screen. Getting a warrant took minutes rather than hours, and the bad guy rarely got away.

He kept thinking about that smirk on Billy Boy's face, and would like to put a fist in it. But as much as he'd like to play the hero and storm Pritchard Ranch, he believed in the letter of the law and knew that such a move was a mistake for a whole variety of reasons.

One thing you quickly learned in law enforcement was the value of patience. No matter what they might say, Justice was neither swift nor blind.

"Maybe the sheriff is right," he said. "I haven't had a bite to eat since yesterday afternoon. By all rights I should be famished."

Callie eyed him skeptically. "You really expect me to sit down and break bread with you?"

"I expect you to be a professional," he told her. "Is that too much to ask?"

Every town has its cop hangout.

Williamson's was a place called the Oak Pit Bar & Grill, a name Callie had always found a bit odd, since Wyoming wasn't known for its overabundance of *Quercus imbricaria*. But she supposed the Cottonwood Pit didn't have the same ring.

As far as she knew, however, there were no trees in evidence here, the indoor barbecue fueled by coals rather than wood. The low lighting and pool hall atmosphere were not to her particular taste, but she couldn't argue with the food they served, and cops all over Williamson County had made the place a regular pit stop.

No pun intended.

Callie didn't want to be sitting in a booth across from Harlan Cole, but she knew he was right. As cruel as fate might be, she was a professional and needed to act like one.

Truth was, she was more concerned about Rusty than herself. Poor guy was caught in the middle of a rich and heated history that he knew nothing about. And as his training deputy, she owed it to him to maintain her composure.

Besides, she was hungry. Thanks to Nana Jean's torturous attempt at matchmaking this afternoon, she hadn't had a chance to eat before she'd been called back to the office.

So here they were, the three of them sitting there awkwardly as they waited on their food, poor Rusty trying to make small talk with two people who clearly had other matters on their minds.

"How long you been with the Marshals Service?" he asked Harlan.

Harlan pulled his gaze away from the sports report on a nearby flatscreen. "Close to ten years."

"You trained at Glynco, right? Out in Georgia?"

"That's right."

Rusty leaned back, took a sip of the ice tea he'd ordered. "I did my basic at the Wyoming Law Enforcement Academy in Douglas, but for a while there I had my eye on Glynco and the Marshals Service. Recruiter approached me while I was still in college." He looked at Callie. "Same with you, right? You almost went federal."

Callie stiffened slightly. "Yes."

"So what changed your mind?"

"Circumstances," she said tersely, but didn't feel like elaborating. Those circumstances were sitting across the table from her.

Rusty gave her room to continue, but when he realized she was finished, he said to Harlan, "So anyway, I decided I'd rather stay local. No chance of being transferred across country, and I like Wyoming. Good place to raise a family. You got family?"

"Brother in California. That's about it."

"Have you always been in Colorado Springs, or do they move you around a lot?"

"I've bounced around a little, but Colorado seems to be the best fit. Been there five years."

"They keep you busy, I guess. Transporting prisoners—that must be pretty interesting sometimes."

"It has its moments," Harlan said. "Especially when one of them smacks you in the head with your own weapon."

Rusty smiled. "At least you've got a sense of humor about it."

"One of my trainers at Glynco always said, you don't find a reason to laugh, you might as well hang it up."

"Amen," Rusty murmured.

Callie was thinking that *she* could use a reason to laugh right now, when someone called out to Rusty— one of the fake-boobed, underdressed cop groupies who rolled in every evening looking for attention. She was standing near an available pool table, gesturing to him with the cue stick in her hand.

Rusty gave her a wave, then turned to Callie. "Citizen needs assistance," he said. "Call me when the food comes."

Callie rolled her eyes. She could just imagine the kind of assistance the girl needed, but this was Rusty's chance to escape the torture and she couldn't blame him. He quickly slipped out of the booth and left them alone.

Harlan watched him go. "I used to be that young once."

Callie scoffed. "You're what—thirty-five? Not exactly Jonah Pritchard territory."

"It'll happen soon enough. Goes by fast, doesn't it? The past ten years are barely a blip on the radar."

Callie had to admit he was right. She sometimes felt as if she had stepped onto a bullet train, the past decade an indistinct blur of joys and heartbreaks and not much in between.

She found herself thinking about the heartbreak that had torn them apart, when Harlan glanced at her left hand and asked, "You never got married?"

She stiffened again. Why was he asking her that? What difference did it make?

"Cops and marriage don't mix," she said.

He nodded. "I found that out the hard way."

She felt a small stab of disappointment. She shouldn't have cared, but for some reason she did. "You were married?"

"Thirteen months," he said. "Lucky number."

"When was this?"

"About a year after you and I split. But I don't know what I was thinking. I knew it was a mistake before it even happened."

"Why?"

His gaze locked on hers, those blue eyes enough to make any woman's legs tremble. Even one who hated his guts.

"Because she wasn't you," he said.

* * *

He didn't know why he'd said it.

The words came out impulsively, a surprise even to him. He could just as easily have told her that he and his ex simply hadn't been in love. But he didn't often think about his marriage, and until this moment he'd never realized that *Callie* was the reason it had been doomed from the start.

Because she wasn't you.

The minute he said it he was plagued by regret, inwardly cursing himself for being so impulsive. He knew how Callie felt about him and she wasn't likely to be receptive to such a statement.

It was no real shock when she sat up slightly, looking as if he'd slapped her across the face.

"What did you just say?"

"Forget it," he told her. "That just slipped out. Don't pay any attention to—"

"You say something like that and you think I'm suddenly going to fall all over you? 'Oh, Harlan, it's so good to see you after all these years. Oh, Harlan, I never should've—'"

"Stop," he said. "This isn't funny."

Callie paused, studying him soberly. "What you did hurt me, Harlan."

"I didn't *do* anything."

"Didn't you? These past ten years may have gone by fast, but they don't change the fact that you're the reason Treacher is dead."

So there it was. The thing that had been simmering between them ever since he'd walked into that conference room. They'd both known it was there, but neither of them had been willing to say it out loud. Until now.

She still blamed him for the accident.

He and Treacher and Callie had been inseparable in college. The *Three Amigos*, everyone called them—a study group that had morphed into a solid, unwavering friendship. And for Harlan and Callie, it became something much deeper.

Treacher had been their best friend, like a brother to both of them, and to say his death was devastating was to understate its impact a thousandfold.

And while Harlan had suspected Callie still blamed him, hearing her express this sentiment with such unflagging conviction—just as she had on their last night together—gave him every reason to get up and walk out of this place without another word.

Instead he said, "I'm not asking for anything from you, Callie. I'm here to catch a wanted man. That's all. And if you have problems with me, I'd just as soon you keep them to yourself." He got to his feet. "Now, if you don't mind, I think I'll get my order to go."

He started to walk away, but thought better of it and stopped, turning back to look at her.

"Just so you know, the reason I said what I said about my marriage is because it's true. I was in love with you, even after you made it clear you wanted nothing to do with me. And every woman I met after we broke up was measured against you. Against what we had before Treacher was killed." He paused. "You may think you have every right to feel the way you feel, but I'm *not* the reason he's dead. If you want to attribute blame, then why not look at the real culprit? Treacher himself."

He expected her say something, but she remained silent. Wouldn't look at him now. And he knew that what he'd just told her hadn't penetrated. The barrier she'd erected was too high and wide and thick, and trying to get through it was impossible.

So why even bother?

Turning, he flagged the waitress and headed across the bar to get his food.

Chapter 7

She was staring at her half-eaten burger when the call came.

After returning to the table, Rusty had given up on her and had taken his food across the bar to sit with the girl with the fake boobs.

Callie hadn't put up much of a protest. She'd wanted to be alone. To think about Harlan and what he'd said.

Because she wasn't you.

There was so much heartbreak in those words that she'd found it nearly impossible to maintain her composure.

How do you react when someone tells you something like that? Someone you once loved so deeply you thought life simply couldn't go on without him?

Do you let go of all the animosity you've nurtured? Do you set aside the pain—the pain he still refused to take responsibility for?

Apparently not, if your name is Callie Glass. And not because you don't *want* to but because you *can't*.

Callie had tried many times over the years, had even thought about getting in touch with Harlan, had often wondered where life had taken him.

But she'd always held back.

Always.

The sting of Treacher's death had ruptured something inside her. A vital organ had been damaged and refused to heal. And every time she picked up the phone, or thought about entering the name *Harlan Cole* into a search engine, she had stopped herself.

She would remember all those crazy late nights when the three of them would get drunk together and talk about the future. Their plans to join the Marshals Service, to request assignments in the same jurisdiction, to raise families in the same neighborhood and have backyard barbecues and birthday parties and cheer their kids on at soccer games.

In short, they were inseparable.

The *Three Amigos*.

And beneath it all was the assumption that Callie and Harlan would get married. Treacher would often smile that crooked smile of his and say, "The two of you were born to be together. God pointed you on a path toward each other from the moment you were conceived."

What they were all witnessing, he told them, was destiny in motion.

A plan perfectly executed.

On hearing this Harlan would pull Callie into his lap and put his arms around her as she leaned back against him, languishing in the heat of his embrace.

"Soul mates," he'd say softly, the warmth of his breath

against her ear. And later when Treacher had gone home, they would lie together on Harlan's bed, making love with an urgent passion that Callie had never since felt.

They both knew that Treacher was right. The bond between them—between all of them—was shatterproof.

Or so they had thought.

They couldn't know that God apparently had different plans. That Treacher would be dead within months, taking that crooked smile and their relationship along with him. That the man who was so convinced that they were meant to be together would become the reason they broke apart.

And when Callie remembered this, she would hang up the phone or close down the search engine and try not to cry.

She didn't *want* to hate Harlan. She just couldn't help herself. Maybe because that hate was the one true thing in her life these days. The one true thing that made her feel alive. Or maybe it was the thing that helped assuage her *own* guilt for not being there that night. For choosing to forego the party because finals were approaching and she felt so desperately behind. After all, if she failed any of her courses she wouldn't get her degree in criminology, and that would screw up the timeline they'd all mapped out.

The irony in this wasn't lost on her. Maybe if she'd taken a short break, just an hour or two away from the books, she could have done what Harlan had failed to do and everything would be on track.

Treacher would be alive.

And she and Harlan would be...

Way to wallow in the mud, Callie.

She shook her head and stared morosely at her half-eaten burger, chastising herself for getting caught up in this nonsense again. She had a *new* life now. A job she did well in a town where she felt wanted. Friends, people who loved her. Nana Jean.

She needed to suck it up and get past this day. Bury her feelings for a while and do what the county of Williamson paid her to do. Help Harlan catch his fugitive and Jim Farber's killer, then say goodbye to the past once and for all.

She had convinced herself that this was exactly what she was going to do, when her cell phone bleeped and she put it to her ear.

"Deputy Glass."

"Callie?"

The voice was familiar. "Yes, who is this?"

"It's Judith, dear. Judith Patterson. I don't want you to worry, but we're on our way to County Memorial and I think you need to meet us there."

"What's wrong?" Callie asked. "What happened?"

"It's your Nana Jean," Judith told her. "She's had an accident."

Callie got to the hospital shortly after Judith and Nana Jean arrived. Judith was guiding Nana through the Emergency Room doorway, Nana keeping a towel clamped to her forehead.

"I'm all right," she said, "it's just a cut. No big deal."

Callie took over for Judith. "What happened?"

"I tripped on that stupid throw rug. Hit my head on the edge of the coffee table. I don't know why Judith insisted I come here."

But when Callie caught Judith's gaze, she could see from her look that there was more to it than that.

A few minutes later a nurse brought a wheelchair and rolled Nana into the exam room and Judith turned to Callie.

"I saw the whole thing," she said. "She didn't trip. She had one of her dizzy spells and fell."

Callie nodded. "That's what I was afraid of."

"There was a lot of blood, too. Thank God Henry and I were there to drive her to the hospital."

Callie glanced out the large bay windows toward the parking lot and saw the plumber lock his van before heading toward the Emergency Room.

Had Nana invited Judith and him back to the house for dinner?

Did she not listen to Callie at *all*?

"It's getting to the point where I don't feel comfortable leaving her alone," she said to Judith. "I'm gonna have to find some kind of solution. Hire a caregiver or something."

"Well, don't say that too loud. You're grandmother's as stubborn as they come and she won't take kindly to some stranger in the house."

Henry the plumber was getting closer by the moment. Callie had no idea if he was in on this matchmaking scheme, but she wasn't interested in yet another awkward moment. She'd had enough of those for one day.

"Well, she'll just have to get used to it," she told Judith, then started in the direction the nurse had wheeled Nana. "I'd better go check on her."

A moment later Callie was standing in a curtained cubicle as the doctor examined the gash on Nana's forehead.

"We'll put a butterfly bandage on it, but you won't need any stitches."

"I *told* Judith it was a just a scratch."

The doctor opened a drawer in a nearby cart. "Well, it's a bit more than that Ms. Glass. She was smart to bring you here. Head wounds tend to bleed a lot and you could have lost a significant amount of blood."

Nana frowned. "Oh, for goodness sake, you'd think it was the first time I ever cut myself."

"Judith had a right to be concerned," Callie said. "Did you tell the doctor about the dizzy spell?"

The doctor's eyebrows went up. "Dizzy spell?"

Nana looked at Callie as if she'd just betrayed a sacred trust. "I see Judith has been flapping her mouth again. So what if I get dizzy once in a while—what's the big deal?"

The doctor took a cotton swab from the drawer. "Dizzy spells are not the kind of thing you want to ignore, Ms. Glass. Especially a woman your age."

"What are you talking about? I'm only seventy-six. It's not like I'm on my deathbed."

"And some of us would like to keep it that way," Callie said.

The doctor nodded. "I think we should check you in for the night and run some tests. Try to find out why you're losing your balance."

"I'm perfectly fine," Nana said.

"This cut on your forehead says different. And I'd just as soon rule out anything serious before I release you."

Nana shot Callie another glance. "See what you've done?"

"Knock it off, Nana. It's for your own good."

The old woman sighed. "I don't see why you feel the need to try to run my life."

Callie couldn't help but smile. "Now you know how it feels."

* * *

It took them nearly an hour to get Nana Jean registered and into a room. By the time the nurse was done fussing with her, Nana had calmed down a bit, reluctantly coming to terms with the idea that she'd be spending the night.

"I hope you don't expect me to eat their food in the morning."

Callie was sitting in a chair next to the bed. "I'll bring you a treat," she said. "One of those cinnamon-raisin muffins from Bartly's Bakery."

Nana's eyes lit up. "Oooh, I do like those. That Edith Bartly knows her way around an oven."

"See? Being here's not so bad."

Nana scowled. "I still say it's a waste of—"

"*No,* Nana." Callie leaned forward and touched her wrist. "Anything that keeps you well is not a waste of time. If something were to happen to you, I don't know what I'd do with myself. You're the only real family I've got."

Callie suddenly felt tears in her eyes, but did her best to hold them back. To see the woman who raised her lying in a hospital bed with an oxygen tube in her nose got her thinking about just how tenuous life could be. She knew full well that, in a matter of seconds, someone you cared about—someone you loved—could go from a filling a hole in your heart to creating one.

She'd had enough of that in her life.

She knew she couldn't hang on to Nana forever, but she wasn't about to let the old woman slip away because of some stubborn, misplaced sense of pride. She could only hope that these dizzy spells were nothing serious.

Nana smiled. "Look at you, getting all misty-eyed. I

don't think I've seen you cry since…" She paused. "Well, it's been a long time."

Callie wiped at her eyes. "Not crying," she said.

"It's all these nasty germs in the air, right?"

Now Callie smiled. "Right."

Nana was quiet for a moment, lost in a thought. Then she said, "I don't tell you this very often, Cal, but since the day you were born, you're the reason I breathe air every morning."

"Oh, Nana…"

"It was hard losing your mom—my sweet little Mary. Seeing the life go out of her eyes right there in front of me. But then I saw that light in you and I knew… I *knew* why I was put on this earth."

Callie gently squeezed her wrist. "Now you're *trying* to make me cry."

"Looks like it's working, too."

There was a sharp knock and Callie swiveled her head, surprised to find Rusty standing in the doorway.

"Sorry to interrupt," he said. "You feeling okay, Ms. Glass?"

"Just fine. Not that anyone's interested in listening to me."

"I'm sure the doctor knows what he's doing," Rusty told her, then shifted his gaze to Callie. "Tried calling you, but I guess they make you turn your phones off in here."

Callie quickly wiped at her eyes and nodded. "Did the judge sign the warrant?"

"Doesn't much matter at this point. We need to get moving."

"What's going on?" Callie asked, sensing his urgency.

"Just got a call from Deputy Cole. He's with Emergency Services. They're headed out to the Pritchard ranch."

"Why? What happened?"

"It's on fire," Rusty said.

Chapter 8

The house was still ablaze when they got there.

The security gate was hanging open, two fire trucks out front, hoses blasting, water arcing toward the flames.

The sky was pitch-black now, the surrounding area illuminated only by the fire, and as Callie pulled her cruiser to a stop, a piercing scream rose from inside the house like something from another world.

Before she could even set the brake, she saw Harlan emerge from his own cruiser and start running. He pushed past the line of firefighters like a man possessed, and headed for the front door.

Callie's heart kicked up.

What on earth was he doing?

She watched in horror as a firefighter tried to grab hold of Harlan, but he spun and slipped away, then hurdled himself through the open doorway, ignoring the shouts of the men behind him, the house now looking as if it might collapse around him at any moment.

Oh, my God, she thought.

He's gone completely insane.

The screams rose again, a woman's voice begging— "Help me! Help me!"—and then Harlan disappeared entirely, swallowed by the fire.

Callie's heart thudded uncontrollably as she and Rusty jumped out of their cruiser and moved quickly to the line of firefighters.

"Why are you just standing here?" she shouted. "You have to go in after him!"

"Are you nuts?" one of the men said.

Then the biggest of them came over to her—an old friend from high school, Phil Dunworth. "That's a fool's errand, Callie. Wind blows the wrong direction, this place is coming down and I won't put my men at risk."

Stunned, Callie looked at the house as the flames continued to grow, her thudding heart threatening to burst through her chest. She couldn't quite believe that Harlan had gone inside there, but he'd once again proven that he was a cowboy and a reckless fool.

Before she realized it, her own feet were moving, heading in the direction of that door as Rusty shouted behind her—

"Callie! What are you doing? Stop!"

But she ignored him and pressed on, feeling a hot blast of air envelop her as she drew closer to the opening. She wasn't quite sure *why* she was doing this, but some buried instinct was tugging at her, forcing her to move.

Then suddenly Harlan emerged from the doorway, his arm around Gloria Pritchard's waist as she clung to him, desperately gasping for air. Her face was blank with shock and her right thigh was stained with blood, soaking through her jeans.

Callie rushed onto the porch and grabbed hold of Gloria, helping Harlan to keep her upright. Then several firefighters joined in, taking Gloria in their arms.

"I think she's been shot," Harlan said.

One of the men nodded as they whisked her toward a nearby ambulance. And as Callie and Harlan moved away from the house, Callie's heartbeat started to return to normal.

Harlan was out of breath, covered with soot and sweat, holding his left forearm in pain.

"You're an idiot," she said sourly.

"And you're in love with that word, aren't you?"

"It was stupid to go in there. You could've gotten yourself killed."

"Why do *you* care?"

She shot him a look. "Oh, come on, Harlan, that's not fair."

"I just did what had to be done," he said. "Now, if you don't mind, I've got some burns to attend to."

Then he picked up speed and continued across the yard to the ambulance.

Less than an hour later, all that was left of the Pritchard ranch house was a pile of charred rubble. A few hot spots still blazed, the fire boys doing their best to keep them down.

Callie stood with Rusty and Harlan, staring at the place in stunned disbelief.

"My God," she said.

The Pritchard ranch was an institution around here, a symbol of wealth and power. And despite what she might think of the Pritchards themselves, to see their home reduced to little more than black ash was both shocking and depressing. She'd never been one to find glee in other people's pain, even if she didn't much care for them.

Sheriff Mercer broke away from a group of firefighters and approached Callie and the others.

"Don't suppose it's much of a surprise," he told them, "but the arson boys are saying this wasn't an accident."

Harlan and Callie hadn't uttered more than a few syllables to each other since he'd emerged from the house with Gloria, and that was just fine with her. But now he said to Mercer, "Megan Pritchard, no doubt."

"Based on her history and the condition we found that pickup truck, I'd say that's a pretty good assumption."

"So we were right," Callie said. "Jonah was hiding her and her friends. Question is, where are they now? And where's Jonah?"

Mercer pointed to a spot near the center of the house, where a black lump could be seen, just barely, near a patch of flames that were struggling to stay alive.

Callie hadn't noticed it before. Another so-called crispy critter.

Oh, Lord.

She swallowed dryly.

"We're thinking he was probably shot, too," Mercer said. "Won't know for sure until the medical examiner gets hold of him. Or what's left of him."

Harlan squinted at the body. "You sure that's Pritchard?"

"Got a witness says it is."

Callie was surprised. "Who?"

"Landry Bickham."

"Landry?" she said. She hadn't seen him in all the confusion. "Where is he?"

Mercer gestured to another ambulance across the tarmac. The first one had already taken Gloria to the hospital. "They found him in the backyard. I took a statement from him while Dudley Do-Right here was getting patched up."

The burns Harlan had suffered were minor, mostly to his hands and forearm. He ignored the jab and turned to Callie. "We're talking about the gatekeeper, right? The one with the shotgun?"

She nodded and Mercer said, "He's been with the Pritchards since high school. Says he tried to drag Gloria out of the back, but the smoke got to be too much for him."

"Is he conscious?" Harlan asked.

"They've got him on a gurney in there, but last I looked he was wide awake."

Harlan nodded and abruptly headed across the tarmac toward the ambulance.

Callie followed him.

The rear doors of the truck were hanging open to reveal Landry lying on the gurney inside, breathing through an oxygen mask as a paramedic tended to a burn on his forehead.

"Mr. Bickham?"

Landry rolled his eyes around in their sockets until his gaze was on Harlan. He reached up and pulled the mask aside, his trademark smile nowhere in evidence. "Still wanna arrest me?"

"Just need you to answer a few questions."

"I already told Sheriff Mercer what I know."

"I prefer to get my information firsthand," Harlan said.

"Can't stop you from asking."

"That's right. So why don't you tell me what happened here?"

"What do you think happened? House burnt down."

"I think there's more to it than that. Where were you when the fire started?"

Landry grabbed hold of the gurney rail and pulled himself upright. The paramedic tried to stop him, but Landry ignored the guy, keeping his gaze on Harlan. "You accusing me of something?"

"Are you *guilty* of something? I mean besides intimidating federal and county law enforcement deputies with a shotgun."

"I never pointed that weapon at you. And I was just doing what Jonah told me to."

"Did you always do what he told you to?"

"That *was* my job," Landry said.

"Did that include helping him hide his granddaughter and her two friends?"

Landry frowned. "What's Meg got to do with this?"

Callie moved up closer to the ambulance doors. "Come on, Landry, you know that's why we were here this afternoon."

"First I'm hearin' about it."

"Somehow I doubt that," Harlan said, "but let's get back to the fire. I'm gonna ask you again, where *were* you when it started?"

"Down at the south stable. Feeding the horses."

"What about the stable hands?" Callie asked.

"Jonah told me to send 'em home for the weekend. Along with the rest of the staff. I'm the only one stays on the premises 24/7."

"Why's that?"

Landry shrugged. "The Pritchards like their privacy. What difference does it make? It is what it is."

"How late does the staff usually stay?"

"Ranch hands do a six to three, house help seven to four, except for the cook, who preps dinner and is out by eight. But they were all gone by noon today, except for the boys you saw with Jonah. And they cut out right after you left."

"Why did he send everyone home so early?" Harlan asked.

"Hard as it may be to believe, Jonah Pritchard don't consult me on such matters. He said send 'em home, I sent 'em home."

It didn't take much to figure out why, Callie thought, but even if he knew, Landry would never tell. His loyalty went beyond the boundaries of death. Jonah may be gone, but he still had family with a reputation to uphold—as sketchy as it may already be—and Landry had been indoctrinated long ago.

Speak no evil.

"Okay," Harlan said. "So you were down at the south stable."

Landry nodded. "It's the one closest to the house—the Pritchards' private stock. Couple of the horses got skittish and I heard shouts, followed by some gunshots. So I figured I'd better get my butt up here. By the time I got to the house, the flames had already started, and when I went inside I saw Jonah on the floor, a pool of blood around his head. No pulse."

"And what about Gloria?" Callie asked.

"Slumped in a corner, looked like she'd been shot, too, but she was still breathing. I tried to drag her toward the back hallway, but I started choking on the smoke. I was about to pass out, so I figured I'd better get out of there and call for help."

Neither Callie nor Harlan said anything, and she could see that Harlan was running Landry's statement through his mind, trying find holes in it.

"And those shouts you heard," Harlan said. "Right before the gunshots. You know whose they were?"

"Not a clue."

"Male or female?"

"Both, would be my guess."

Callie didn't figure there was much guesswork required. Those voices undoubtedly belonged to Meg Pritchard, Billy Boy Lyman and maybe the third man, who had yet to be identified.

It suddenly occurred to her that they may have misjudged Jonah. Could it be that he had been harboring Meg and her friends against his will? That would explain why he'd come on so strong this afternoon. Maybe he'd had a gun trained on him the whole time.

But then that didn't really fit, did it? Jonah Pritchard had never been a man who was easily intimidated, and she couldn't see Meg and a couple of punks forcing him to do much of anything.

Besides, Jonah had always been Meg's number one apologist. So it seemed more likely that he had welcomed the girl into his home, happy to give her refuge in her time of need, even if she was towing a couple pieces of unwanted baggage along with her.

It looked to Callie as if this was a case of misplaced

trust. The question was why had Meg and her friends turned on Jonah? What had gone so horribly wrong?

She doubted Landry would offer any enlightenment. But if anyone could, it was Gloria.

She said to Harlan, "I need to get back to the hospital and talk to Gloria Pritchard."

She turned to go, but Harlan caught her by the crook of the elbow. "Wait a minute."

It had been a very long time since Callie had felt his touch, and she was surprised to find that she recognized it. Remembered it.

Was that even possible?

Gentle yet firm. No intimacy intended, but she suddenly felt as if it were the most intimate thing in the world.

She pulled herself free. "Do you mind?"

"So that's it? You're just gonna take off without me?"

"You didn't seem too anxious to be around me earlier. Besides, this is a murder investigation. Two dead in the span of less than a day, and both murders point to the fire-starting talents of Megan Pritchard-Breen. I hate to break it to you, but your little manhunt is just a sideshow."

"Not if Billy Boy put her up to this."

"You don't know Meg. I can't see anyone calling the shots but her. She's as bullheaded as her grandfather."

"Takes one to know one, I guess."

Callie frowned at him. "What's that supposed to mean?"

"You're about the most bullheaded woman I've ever met," he said. "Something I used to love about you. Now? Not so much."

Callie's frown deepened. "If this is your way of trying

to convince me to let you keep riding shotgun, I think you may want to reconsider your approach."

"At least I didn't call you an idiot."

She huffed at him and started toward her cruiser again, but Harlan caught up to her and once again grabbed her arm. "Callie, I'm not the enemy."

Callie fought off the sudden memory of what he used to do to her with his hands and gave him her best cold stare. "Would you please let go of me?"

He studied her a moment, then did as he was told, Callie saying, "You're on your own from here on out." She continued across the yard, feeling his gaze on her, wishing he would just go away and let her live her life in peace.

But as she climbed into her car and got her seatbelt latched, the passenger door flew open and Harlan sat down next to her.

"I can be bullheaded, too," he said. "So don't even waste your time trying to argue with me."

Chapter 9

It took an hour and a half of surgery to remove the bullet from Gloria Pritchard's left thigh and get her stitched up. She was still in recovery when they arrived.

The doctor told them they'd have to wait until she was transferred to a room before they could question her. She wouldn't be making much sense until the anesthesia wore off anyway.

"How badly was she hurt?" Callie asked.

"Bullet was a through-and-through. Some muscle and tissue damage, but nothing too serious."

"She got lucky," Harlan said.

The doctor nodded. "She'll be sore for a while, and she may have some problems with her lungs, thanks to smoke inhalation, but she should be back to normal in no time."

Physically, at least, Harlan thought. Mental and emotional trauma weren't as easy to shake loose. He and Callie were proof of that. And if Gloria's own daughter—or one of her daughter's friends—had done this to her, the condition was likely to be permanent.

As Gloria slept it off in recovery, Callie went to check on her grandmother, leaving Harlan to spend most of the wait alone. He tried to get comfortable on a plastic waiting room chair, but it was an exercise in futility. And after twenty long minutes of staring blankly at a television screen and leafing through old news magazines, Harlan finally got to his feet and headed down the hallway to Callie's grandmother's room.

He may not be wanted, but anything was better than this.

Back in their graduate school days, Callie had spoken fondly about her grandmother, and Harlan knew that the bond between them was unbreakable. But he'd never had the privilege of meeting Mrs. Glass. Had no idea if she even knew he existed.

Still, when Rusty had told him on the phone earlier that she had been hospitalized, he couldn't help feeling some concern. Callie had grown up without her parents, and the thought of losing her grandmother had to be weighing on her mind.

When he reached the doorway, however, he was surprised to find that Callie was nowhere to be found. He thought for a moment that he'd gone to the wrong room, but the woman in the bed looked eerily familiar. A much older, more delicate version of the girl he'd once loved. The ravages of age had done nothing to erase her beauty, and Harlan knew that Callie would grow old just as gracefully. It was in her genes.

Too bad you won't be around to see it.

This thought slipped uninvited into Harlan's brain,

and while he wasn't sure where it had come from, he had to admit it was accompanied by a sense of sadness. He had always believed that he and Callie would be together forever, but for some reason fate hadn't been in a cooperative mood.

"Are you gonna stand there daydreaming or say hello?"

Harlan blinked and pulled himself from his thoughts. Callie's grandmother was looking directly at him, a wry smile on her thin face—one that Harlan recognized, although it had been a long time since he'd seen it. Callie didn't seem to smile much nowadays.

"Sorry, ma'am. I was looking for your granddaughter."

"She went out to get me a snack. The food here is horrendous." She gestured to a chair. "You want to sit down?"

"No ma'am, I'll just wait here. I'm Deputy Harlan—"

"Oh, I know who you are. Callie told me you were in town."

Harlan stiffened, half expecting her to start shouting at him for breaking her granddaughter's heart and ruining her life, but the old woman kept right on smiling.

"It was a long time ago," she said, "but every email I got, every phone call that girl made while she was away, she must've mentioned you at least two or three times."

Harlan nodded. "She talked about you a lot, too. I'm sorry we never got a chance to meet."

"So am I."

"We had plans to come up that last summer but… things changed."

Her smile faltered. "Well, I guess that couldn't be helped, could it?"

Harlan shrugged. "*Callie* thinks it could have."

The old woman shook her head. "She's a complicated girl, that one. So much like her mother, I sometimes find myself wanting to call her Mary. Probably have, once or twice. She makes her mind up about something, she's apt to hang on to it even when she knows she's being unreasonable."

"Well, unreasonable or not, she made up her mind about me. And to be honest, I didn't handle it all that well. Said quite a few things I shouldn't have. And if I'd known what I was walking into when I came here, I probably would've stayed away."

"Now *that* would've been a shame."

The comment surprised Harlan. "Why do you say that?"

The old woman got up on her elbows now, once again looking Harlan straight in the eye. "I know you two have been busy, but in case you haven't noticed, that girl is still in love with you."

Harlan blinked. "I beg your pardon?"

"You heard me. Child likes to pretend she doesn't give two hoots about you, that you're the reason her life went off the rails, yet despite my best efforts over the past decade, she hasn't met a man she can tolerate. And that's all because of you, son."

Harlan's own words about his ex-wife came back to him suddenly.

Because she wasn't you.

Could Callie have been afflicted by the same malady? Was every man she met measured against him? Against what they'd once had?

Not based on what *he'd* seen.

"With all due respect, Mrs. Glass, I think you're dead wrong about that."

She smiled again. "I may be wrong about the weather sometimes, or who's gonna do what to who on my soaps…but I raised that girl and I know her better than anyone alive. And when I say she's still in love with you, you'd better listen carefully, because I don't want you to blow this opportunity."

"Opportunity for what?" Callie said.

She came up behind Harlan, giving him an annoyed look as she squeezed past him through the doorway. She was carrying a bag of takeout.

"What else?" the old woman told her without a hitch. "To help you catch a killer. That *is* why he's here, isn't it? Jonah and I may have had our differences over the years, but it's a shame what happened to him and Gloria. I guess that's what you get when you raise a bad seed."

"All that stuff I told you is confidential, Nana. I'd appreciate it if you kept it to yourself."

"We're among friends, aren't we?"

Callie shot Harlan a look that pretty much put the lie to everything the old woman had told him. "Colleagues," she corrected. "Even so, you need to learn to watch your tongue. You never know who might be listening."

"I don't think I've revealed any state secrets—have I, Marshal?"

That was a question up for debate, but Harlan said, "No, ma'am."

She looked at Callie. "You see? Always getting hot and bothered over nothing. You need to learn to relax, child."

"And you need to stop telling me that, but I don't suppose you ever will." She turned to Harlan. "Gloria Pritchard's awake and they're moving her to a room. I'll be there in a minute."

Harlan realized this was her not-so-subtle way of telling him to leave, so he nodded to Callie's grandmother. "Nice talking to you, Mrs. Glass."

"Same to you, son. Good to finally meet you after all these years." She showed him another smile. "Don't let your time here go to waste."

"No, ma'am," he said again. Then he was out the door and gone.

Chapter 10

Gloria Pritchard was still groggy, but at least she was lucid. Lucid enough to have tears in her eyes.

"I feel so ashamed," she croaked.

"Why's that?" Harlan asked.

He had waited as they got her settled in the room, and by the time the doctor let him in to see her, Callie had shown up, still giving him the cold shoulder—which wasn't a big news flash.

Even so, her grandmother's words kept tumbling through his brain—

That girl is still in love with you.

But Harlan saw no evidence of this himself. Had to believe that the old woman was delusional. He had long ago concluded that it was too late for Callie and him. That the last train had come and gone.

But what if her grandmother was right?

Did he still feel the same about *her*?

Of course you do, you stupid fool. You never stopped *loving her.*

The thought was a revelation, as surprising as the old woman's words, but was it really true? Did being in Callie's presence stir up feelings that had long lain dormant, or was this simply a case of nostalgia? Of regret over things past that merely created the *illusion* that there was still something between them?

Ten years was a long time. Too long to be thinking about trying to rekindle emotions that he couldn't even be sure still existed.

He was out of practice with Callie. The rhythm they'd once had was gone, and if her grandmother's claim was even remotely true, then he obviously didn't know how to read Callie anymore. Because from all appearances, she was done with him. For good.

But enough of this nonsense. He needed to put it aside and concentrate on finding a fugitive.

He returned his attention to Gloria Pritchard as she struggled a moment, then wiped the tears with the back of her hand. "I should have been honest with you this afternoon. If I had, Daddy would probably still be alive."

It was odd hearing her use the term "daddy." Based on her statements that afternoon, Harlan didn't get the impression that the Pritchard household was a particularly loving one.

"Tell us what happened," Callie said. She was in full professional mode, yet Harlan sensed a tension between these two women, the same tension he'd felt when they'd encountered each other that afternoon. There was something going on here that he wasn't privy to.

Gloria closed her eyes, didn't respond. She seemed

to be trying to muster up the strength to speak, and he wondered if they'd come here too soon.

But from an investigator's standpoint there was *never* a too soon. Every minute lost was a minute wasted.

Harlan gave her time, then said, "Ms. Pritchard?"

Still no response.

He was about to prompt her again, when she finally opened her eyes and said, "It was Megan. Megan and her friends."

"They came to you for help?"

She nodded. "This morning. She and her friend Billy, and another man named Brett something—I didn't catch his last name."

The potato chip lover.

But Harlan wanted to make sure. Reaching into his inner jacket pocket, he brought out the surveillance photos and showed them to her.

"Are these the men?"

Gloria watched as he leafed through the photos, then squeezed her eyes shut again and nodded. "Yes."

"Did they force their way into your house or did Jonah invite them in?"

She looked at him now. "If you knew Jonah, you wouldn't even have to ask me that question."

"But I *didn't* know him, ma'am, so I'd appreciate it if you'd answer it."

She hesitated, then said, "Jonah worshipped Meg. Loved her more than he ever loved me, that's for sure."

"Even when she brought people like Billy Boy Lyman to the house? He's not exactly what most grandfathers would consider boyfriend material."

"Jonah wasn't your typical grandfather."

"Meaning what?"

"It's no secret what the Pritchard family roots are. Even though we've come a long way, and try to pretend we've elevated ourselves, people around here know exactly what we used to be."

"Which is?"

"Outlaws," Callie told him. "They earned their fortune the easy way."

Gloria looked at her, annoyed. "*Easy* has nothing to do with it. That seed money may have bought our land, but our fortune was built through legitimate hard work." She returned her gaze to Harlan. "My great-grandfather was Jeremiah Pritchard. Before he split off and started his own gang, he used to ride with Robert Leroy Parker."

"You mean Butch Cassidy?" Harlan said.

She nodded. "One of Wyoming's favorite sons. But Jeremiah had his fans, too, and there's no denying he helped turn Williamson into the town it is today."

"Oh, brother," Callie muttered.

Gloria stiffened. The malice in her eyes was hard to disguise. "Poor little Callie. Wants so desperately to be part of this family she can't stand the idea that we've actually accomplished something over the years."

"You have no idea what you're talking about," Callie said.

"Don't I? I know you think that just because your slut mother spread her legs for my brother, that somehow makes you—"

"Shut up," Callie told him, and Harlan could clearly see that Gloria's words had cut very deeply. He thought for a moment he might have to hold Callie back, but she quickly got control of herself.

He had no idea what was going on here. Callie had never once talked about Gloria Pritchard in their time together, but it sounded as if there was a blood connection between these two.

Was Callie Gloria's *niece*?

If so, that would make *Meg* Pritchard her cousin. And that was a clear conflict of interest.

"Is there something we need to talk about?" he said to Callie.

"No. Nothing."

But as much as she tried to hide it, he knew she wasn't being straight with him, and behind the quiet anger there was vulnerability in her eyes. A vulnerability he recognized.

She and Gloria spent the next few seconds silently eyeballing each other, until Harlan said, "So what are you trying to tell me, Ms. Pritchard? That because you come from outlaw stock that this somehow made Jonah respect a punk like Billy Boy?"

"Jonah grew up worshipping his grandfather and his outlaw ways. He was always drawn to people who rebelled against authority. People like Billy and his friend. And Megan, of course."

"So then what happened? What went wrong?"

"I'm not sure," she said. "I was upstairs and heard them shouting and when I came down to the living room, Meg had a gun pointed at my father."

"And where were Billy Boy and Brett?"

"They were in the room, too. Billy Boy egging her on, telling her to pull the trigger. I think they may have been high."

"And you have no idea what the problem was? Did Meg say anything? Want anything?"

Gloria stiffened. "What difference does it make? She

shot him, then turned the gun on me. That's all that matters."

"I'm just trying to make sense of it," Harlan said. "If Jonah admired these people and was willing to help them out of a jam, why would they suddenly turn on the two of you? Why would your own daughter want you dead?"

Gloria averted her gaze now. "I wouldn't know."

"Come on, Ms. Pritchard, your mouth is saying one thing, but your eyes are telling me something else altogether. What happened in that room?"

Gloria was silent. Struggling. Then she said, "I think I'd like to sleep now. Could you two please leave?"

"Not until you've answered the—"

Callie touched his shoulder, stopping him. "It's okay, Harlan. I think I may already know."

He looked at her and saw that her anger had abruptly disappeared, her expression now softened by a mix of surprise and empathy, as if something she had long wondered about suddenly made sense.

He waited for her to continue, but she said nothing, turning instead to Gloria. "The rumors are true, aren't they? About Jonah's...preferences."

Gloria frowned. "What would *you* know about it?"

"This town doesn't have many secrets, Gloria. We've all heard the whispers at one time or another."

"That doesn't mean a damn thing," she snapped. "And it certainly doesn't make it any of your business."

Harlan's voice was gentle but firm. "Look, Ms. Pritchard, I know you're hurting, but a murder victim loses all right to privacy the moment we walk in the door. That's the only way we can build a case against a potential—"

"Go away," she said. "Please."

Harlan took a deep breath, then exhaled. "All right, let's put the motive aside for now. What we really need to know is where Meg and her friends were headed when they left. Did they say anything? Give any indication about where they might be going?"

"Maybe you didn't hear me. I'd like to you leave."

"Not until you tell us—"

"Get out," she shouted. "Get out of my room!"

"Ms. Pritchard—"

"Get out!" She pulled herself upright, her IV rattling, her face turning crimson. Tears filled her eyes, spilling down her cheeks as she continued to shout at them. *"Leave* me alone!"

Whatever she was hiding, it was ugly and painful, so painful that she seemed unaware of the wound in her thigh which was starting to bleed, staining her blankets.

Harlan and Callie backed away from her now as the room began to fill with hospital personnel, people in scrubs telling them to go, *now*, as they moved to the bed to try to calm Gloria down.

And as he and Callie retreated into the hallway, Harlan could only thank God that the troubles he'd seen in his own life seemed tame in comparison to what this woman must be going through. The memories they had triggered were ripping her up inside, and even though it couldn't be helped, he felt a twinge of guilt for pushing her.

He looked at Callie, saw the dismay on her face, and thought she must be thinking the very same thing. And despite all they'd been through in their time, Harlan suddenly realized that they were the lucky ones.

Very lucky indeed.

Chapter 11

"That went well," Harlan said. "You want to clarify for me what just happened back there?"

Callie felt sick to her stomach. There had long been rumors about Jonah Pritchard, but she'd never really believed them. She had always thought it was nothing more than vicious small town gossip, whipped up out of boredom and envy.

Yet Gloria's reaction to their questioning seemed to be confirmation of those rumors. Which would explain Megan Pritchard's rebelliousness over the span of her life. If Meg had finally had enough of her grandfather's "attention," then that would surely be a motive to pick up a gun and shoot the old man.

But what about Gloria? Was she complicit in her father's crimes? Is that why she'd reacted so violently? If so, then it was no wonder that she'd been shot as well.

Callie's gut churned. The thought that she shared DNA with these people made her want to throw up.

She and Harlan were back in her SUV, headed to the ranch to pick up Harlan's cruiser, his question still hanging in the air.

"Well?" he said.

"You're a reasonably intelligent man," she told him. "I think you can figure it out."

He shook his head in disgust. "I was hoping I was wrong. Makes me feel a little guilty for pushing her buttons like that."

"Imagine how *I* feel."

He turned to her now, those blue eyes of his studying her as she gripped the wheel. "Gloria isn't the only one keeping secrets, is she?"

"It isn't exactly a secret. It's just not something I talk about."

"Are you ready to talk about it *now*?"

She shrugged. "There isn't much to tell. My mother and Gloria's brother were an item in high school, and she and Gloria were best friends. Until she got pregnant, that is."

"And that was your *mother's* fault, right?"

"Gloria thought so, and never forgave her for it. She looks at me and all she sees is the reason her brother is dead."

"Why? What happened to him?"

"Jonah made him enlist in the army when they found out my mom was pregnant and he got killed in a truck accident. Which is a shame, because Nana Jean says he was the only decent Pritchard this side of Sheridan. Didn't have that air of entitlement the rest of them do. It would've been nice to have gotten to know the man."

Callie had never really missed her parents because she'd grown up without them, but she did sometimes let the "what ifs" occupy her mind.

She looked at Harlan and couldn't be sure, but thought he might be upset by these revelations.

"Is something wrong?"

He shook his head. "It's just that I can't believe we were together for nearly two and a half years and you never said a word to me about any of this."

"It didn't really affect us, and I didn't want to burden you with my family drama."

"That's just it," he said. "It wouldn't have been a burden. I was in love with you, Callie. I wanted to know everything there was to know about you."

She looked at him again—at those blue eyes still fixed on her—and she remembered that beneath his hard exterior he had always had a soft heart. Gentle. Empathetic.

He'd been a kind lover, too. Aggressive but never rough, and always attentive to her needs, physically and emotionally. So of *course* he would want to know everything about her.

That was who Harlan *was*.

Remembering this, Callie felt her heart kick up. She had been in love, too. The kind of love that made her anxious to wake up every morning. To see him. Touch him. Feel the embrace of those eyes. Those lips.

Those hands.

She missed that feeling. Missed the comfort of it. The excitement.

But after Treacher had been killed, all of that had stopped. Grief had consumed her, made her impossible to be around. The circumstances surrounding his death had made her cruel and judgmental and inconsolable. She hadn't wanted Harlan anywhere near her.

Who would have thought that the loss of a close friend could do that to her? To them? Yet it had. And in the process she'd not only lost someone she'd thought of as a brother, but also the man she loved.

Two for the price of one.

Returning her attention to the road, she wondered why she still felt so angry at Harlan.

Did he really deserve her scorn?

Wasn't it time to forgive and forget?

Her feelings for him hadn't vanished—anyone paying close attention knew that. Otherwise she'd be indifferent to him, unwilling to waste any mental bandwidth thinking about him. And it was becoming more and more apparent that Harlan was using up the majority of that bandwidth.

She simply had no choice in the matter.

No choice at all.

Harlan sobered and said, "I guess there's no point in dwelling on the past, is there?"

"I try not to."

"But based on what you've told me, I think you need to consider removing yourself from this case."

Cue the record scratch.

Callie swiveled her head toward him. *"What?"*

"One of the perpetrators is your cousin, Callie. The victim is your aunt. I felt the tension between you two even before Gloria went ballistic. If you keep going like this, your judgment could be impaired."

Callie couldn't quite believe what she was hearing.

So much for forgiving and forgetting.

"You have got to be kidding me."

"It doesn't help that you and I aren't exactly a loving couple anymore. We probably shouldn't even be working together."

"You were the one who wanted to tag along, remember? You can leave anytime you want to."

"I'm serious, Callie."

"So am I."

Harlan sighed. "Look, maybe you and your boss don't see it, but there's a clear conflict of interest here and your involvement in this case is just a bad idea all around."

All right. Enough was enough.

Without even thinking about it, Callie suddenly slammed the brakes, bringing the SUV to a hard stop in the middle of the road.

"Get out of the car," she said.

"What?"

"You heard me."

"You're being ridiculous."

"Maybe you haven't noticed, Harlan, but this isn't Colorado, and there's only one person in this case who falls under your jurisdiction. Billy Boy Lyman. So why don't you concentrate on catching him and leave the rest to the Williamson County Sheriff's Office."

She reached to the armrest and popped the locks on the doors. "Now get out of the car."

Moments after leaving Harlan in the middle the road, Callie started having second thoughts.

What was she doing?

Her actions only proved that he was right about this. That she was too emotionally involved to make smart, rational judgments. Leaving him stranded was not only childish, it was unbecoming of a Williamson County Sheriff's deputy. A senior one, at that.

As Harlan shrank to a pinprick in her rearview mirror, Callie made a vow not to let him get under her skin, then eased off the accelerator and made a quick U-turn.

A moment later she was pulling up alongside him, once again popping the locks as she rolled down her window.

"I'm sorry. That was a stupid thing to do."

Harlan shrugged it off. "We all do stupid things. I shouldn't have been so quick to judge you."

"The problem is, you're right," she said. "I *should* recuse myself." She smiled tersely. "But I'm not going to."

He didn't seem surprised. "You wouldn't be the Callie Glass I once knew and loved if you did."

They both let that percolate for a moment, then she gestured. "So are you just going to stand there gawking at me or get back in the car?"

He gave her a salute, then moved around to the passenger side and climbed in next to her.

They said nothing as she made another U-turn and headed toward Pritchard Ranch. The Bighorn Mountains loomed beyond—a dark, jagged line silhouetted against the night sky.

She thought back to what Gloria had said about her great-grandfather being an outlaw. When Callie was a child, she had heard stories about Jeremiah Pritchard and his gang of thieves roaming these mountains. He was often called the Robin Hood of Williamson County, using the money he'd robbed from banks and trains to help his friends buy land in the area, long before Williamson was what it was today.

It was a legend the Pritchards had traded on for decades. And Callie, knowing that she, too, was related to Jeremiah, had sometimes imagined herself riding with the gang, robbing banks, running from the law and...

A sudden thought occurred to her. "Oh, my God," she murmured.

Harlan turned. "What?"

"I think I may know where our fugitives went."

Harlan's eyebrows raised. "What? Where?"

Callie punched the accelerator and blasted down the road, taking the curve toward Pritchard Ranch. A few moments later she pulled through the gate to find Harlan's cruiser and only a single fire truck parked in front of the smoldering remnants of the house. She pulled in next to the cruiser and killed the engine.

Unlatching her glove compartment, she pulled out a flashlight and said, "Follow me."

Then she had her door open and was out of the SUV, Harlan moving alongside her as she crossed past the fire truck, then flicked on the flashlight and headed down a sloping patch of lawn toward a large wooden structure sitting a few hundred yards away.

"The stable?" Harlan said. "The place has already been searched, top to bottom."

"I know," Callie told him, "but they were searching for the wrong thing."

"What do you mean?"

"They were searching for people."

They reached the stable and Callie threw open the doors, shining her flashlight around until she found a light switch mounted on a wooden post inside. She flicked the switch and overhead fluorescents came to life.

The stable was empty. No sign of any livestock.

"Remember what Landry told us?" Callie said. "That he was feeding the horses when the fire started?"

"Yeah, what about it?"

Callie gestured. "So do you see any horses here?"

Harlan looked around. "You think he was lying?"

Callie shook her head. "This is the Pritchard's private stable, remember? Which means Meg would likely have a horse housed here, along with Gloria's and Jonah's rides. And it looks like someone took them after Landry ran up to the house. Three fugitives, three horses."

Harlan was skeptical. "Or he could've left the doors open and the horses got spooked. They could be anywhere."

"There's one way to find out."

Callie pulled out her cell phone and dialed. A moment later, Rusty was on the line. "Wilcox."

"Rusty, this is Callie. Where'd they take Landry Bickham after we left?"

"Sheriff Mercer released him. He didn't have a place to stay, so I drove him to the Cottonwood Motel."

"Do me a favor and call him over there, then call me back and put us on conference."

"What's going on?"

"I'll explain later," she said, then hung up.

As they waited for the return call, Harlan moved around the stable, poking his head into the empty stalls. Callie watched him, once again thinking how well he had aged. Thinking how he still had that fluid, effortless way of moving, as if he were completely in tune with his body.

Then her cell phone rang, interrupting the thought, and she clicked it on. "Glass."

"Hey, Callie, I've got Landry on the line."

"Thanks, Rusty. Can you hear me, Landry?"

"I hear you," a familiar voice said, and he didn't sound happy. "And I'm seriously thinking about filing a lawsuit for harassment."

"Oh, grow up. I just need you to answer one more question."

He sighed. "Which is?"

"When you heard the gunshots and ran up to the house, did you leave any of the stable doors open?"

"Of course I didn't."

"You sure? Even in the heat of the moment?"

"Is that some kind of sick joke?"

She saw his point, but didn't feel like dealing with his nonsense. "Landry, will you please just answer the—"

"No," he said. "Not even in the heat of the moment. You work for the Pritchards, you learn good habits or you'll be looking for another job. Doesn't matter what's goin' on around you, closing up the stable is second nature, like zipping up your fly after you've done your business."

Thanks for the visual, Callie thought.

"And the horses were here when you left?"

"Of course they were. I said I was feeding 'em, didn't I? What's this all about?"

"Stay on the line a minute. Rusty, you there?"

"I'm here," Rusty said.

"Is Katie Patterson still head honcho over at the Williamson County Library?"

"I think so," he said.

"Good. I need you to track her down and get to the library ASAP. And swing by the Cottonwood and take Landry with you."

"Me?" Landry said. "What do you need me for?"

"Your expertise," Callie told him, then disconnected before he could object.

Pocketing her phone, she turned to find Harlan hovering nearby, not hiding his curiosity. "You ready tell me what you're up to?"

"I already told you," she said. "Finding our fugitives."

Chapter 12

Katie Patterson was not what most people thought of when you said the word *librarian*. At fifty-four she was a twice-divorced bottle blonde with a raucous, tobacco-tinged laugh that had taken more than a few of her patrons by surprise.

Most of her nights were spent at a bar in town called Little Pete's where she regularly debated politics, sports and religion. And if the right man made the right moves, she sometimes wound up sleeping in a bed other than her own.

Katie didn't look, act or talk the way you'd expect a librarian to, but she did have three important things going for her. She was smart as a whip, did her job better than any of her predecessors and everybody in town just plain loved her.

"Got it all right here," she said as she emerged from a

hallway at the rear of the Williamson County Library. It was long past business hours, but she had been happy to open the place up, especially after she found out she'd be helping in an investigation. "Everything there is to know about the Pritchard gang, all in one box."

She let out a husky laugh and dropped a large storage box on the table in front of them. Callie, Harlan, Rusty, Landry and Sheriff Mercer all watched as she pulled the lid off to reveal several documents, yellowed by time, along with a stack of folded maps and an envelope full of archival photographs.

Callie immediately reached for the envelope and opened it.

"You know what you're looking for?" Katie asked.

"Photo I remember seeing when I was a little girl. Pritchard posing for a local photographer."

"That would be Terrance Scarne," Katie said. "Those are his photos hanging in City Hall. He chronicled the history of Williamson for nearly five decades."

Anyone who had gone in to renew their driver's license had seen those photographs. Stark black and white shots of horses and buggies on unpaved streets, back when Williamson was little more than a shanty town.

Callie found what she was looking for and said, "Here it is," then showed the photo to the rest of the group.

It was a posed shot of a tall, unshaven man wearing a dark hat, vest and dungarees, a six shooter slung on his hip as he stared unsmiling into the camera. In the distance behind him was a large wooden cabin, smoke billowing up from a chimney into a cloudless Wyoming sky.

"Jeremiah Pritchard," Katie said. "The Robin Hood of Williamson County."

Harlan didn't seem impressed. "Fascinating. But I'm not quite sure why we're looking at it."

Katie frowned. "This is history, son. Don't need a *reason* to be looked at."

"Unless you have one," Callie said, then pointed to a handwritten caption in the lower right corner:

ROBBERS CANYON 1887

"Is that something significant?" Harlan asked.

Callie nodded. "Robbers Canyon was the Pritchard gang's hideout in the Bighorn Mountains. Nobody outside the family knows where this photo was taken, but some people say the Pritchards have kept the place in good repair. That Jonah would go there sometimes and spend the night, soak in the ambience. Which isn't surprising when you consider his love of his outlaw heritage." She paused, looked at Landry. "I'm betting *you* know something about it, too."

Landry's trademark smile had apparently taken the night off. "Is that what you dragged me here for?"

"I brought you here because I think you're lying to us. I think you know full well that Megan and Billy Boy Lyman were in that house, and this is where they went." She tapped the image of the cabin for emphasis.

Landry scoffed. "If that was true, why wouldn't I tell you? According to Rusty here, they're the ones killed Jonah."

"And I imagine that's troubling to you," Callie said, "but your loyalties aren't just to the old man. You're so used to protecting the Pritchard family secrets that you're no doubt feeling pretty conflicted right now."

She could see that conflict in his eyes, but he was so

deeply indoctrinated that he wasn't about to admit it. Not out loud. "You're out of your mind."

"There's no shame in feeling this way, Landry. You've been with that family your entire life. Your own kin used to ride with Jeremiah Pritchard and you've seen them through births and deaths and divorces, all the time doing what you could to help them out." She paused. "But even Gloria herself says her daughter's out of control. She's the one who told us Meg pulled the trigger."

A flicker of surprise replaced the conflict, but it quickly disappeared. "I don't have to listen this," Landry said, then started away from the table.

Harlan grabbed him by the forearm. "Hold on, Bickham, not so fast. I don't think she's finished."

Landry wasn't a small man, but Harlan didn't seem too concerned about his size. He swung him back around to the table and nudged him forward.

"Floor is yours," he said the Callie.

Callie reached into the box and pulled out the stack of folded maps. There were dates penciled in the corner of each. She found one dated 1888 and unfolded it onto the table.

It was hand drawn, showing Williamson and the surrounding area from a time nearly forgotten, including the acreage that comprised Pritchard Ranch and a good portion of the Bighorn Mountains.

She pointed to those mountains. "Now I know that people have long speculated where Jeremiah's hideout may be, but those who've been adventurous enough to try to find it have never been successful." She looked up at Landry. "But I think you've been there with Jonah. And I think you know exactly where it is."

He eyed her defiantly. "So what if I do?"

Callie smiled. "You're going tell us how to get there."

It took Landry a while to break, but with Harlan once again threatening to arrest him for aiding and abetting a fugitive he finally gave in. He refused to admit any knowledge that the trio had gone to Robbers Canyon—or that they'd been to the Pritchard Ranch at all—but with great reluctance he dropped a finger to the map and showed Callie and the others how to get there.

What they learned was that the trail to Robbers Canyon was nearly a day-long trek, and could only be accessed on horseback.

Sheriff Mercer mentioned the possibility of going in by chopper, but Landry assured him that a helicopter wouldn't have a place to land. Besides, Harlan told them, even if it did, the noise would give them away and they'd lose the element of surprise. Not something he was willing to risk.

"Which once again leaves us with you," Callie said to Landry.

"Meaning what?"

"You can be our guide. Take us in there nice and quiet."

Landry balked. "Now, hold on. I already told you how to get there, and that's about all I've got to offer. You can't force me to go along, and I'm not about to volunteer, so you're on your own from here on out." He looked at Harlan. "And if you wanna throw me in the bucket, so be it. Couldn't be any worse than the Cottonwood Inn."

"How about if we paid you?" Mercer said.

"Paid me?"

"With Jonah dead, you might be looking for a job. Not

a place you want to be in this tight economy, and I'm sure we could scrounge up a little cash for your services."

Landry shook his head. "With all due respect, Sheriff, I'd just as soon take money from the devil himself."

Which, to Callie's mind, was exactly what he'd been doing all along.

Why change now?

They made plans to leave first thing in the morning. Sheriff Mercer, who had a small stable of his own, promised to bring the horses, and they arranged a rendezvous for seven o'clock at Pritchard Ranch.

That would leave Callie just enough time to swing by the bakery and pick up Nana's muffins. She felt a little guilty about taking a trek into the wilderness on the day the doctors would be poking and prodding the old woman, but Nana understood the nature of Callie's job and would insist she go. Besides, Judith would be happy to play stand-in.

As Callie and Harlan headed out to their cars, Harlan said, "Good thinking in there."

They were being cordial now, and she wasn't quite used to it. Had to readjust a little. "Thanks."

"Sheriff says all the road blocks have come up empty, so I'm pretty sure you're right about this. Makes sense that Billy Boy would want to lay low for a few weeks, in hopes we'll get tired of looking for him."

"As if *that* would ever happen."

Harlan grinned. "Billy Boy Lyman has the intelligence and foresight of a two-year-old child."

Callie gestured to the bruise on the side of his face. "That didn't stop him from putting one over on *you*."

It was a good-natured jab and Harlan took it that way.

"I'm laying this one on cousin Meg. I knew she was a force to be reckoned with the minute I walked into that convenience store. I figure she's the one dreamed up Lyman's escape."

"Nobody's ever accused her of being dumb, that's for sure. And if they *are* at that hideout, somebody had to give them supplies."

"You thinking Landry?"

She shrugged. "He was awfully reluctant to help us. And considering Gloria gave Meg up to us in about ten seconds flat, I don't think she's the one."

"Could be Jonah had them set to go before things got ugly."

"True. He would've done anything for that girl. Maybe they had this whole thing figured out days ago. Billy Boy's escape, the trip up to the hideout. But I don't think killing Jim Farber was part of the plan, and that could be another reason Jonah and Meg got into it. He probably didn't know about the murder until I told him."

Harlan nodded agreement. "Whatever the case, I'd bet a month's salary they're stoking up that cabin's fireplace as we speak."

"No doubt," Callie said.

They were quiet for a moment, then Harlan broke off and stepped toward his cruiser. "Wouldn't mind stoking up a fireplace myself. I could fall asleep right in front of it."

"You have a place to stay?"

"I thought I'd head over to that motel. The Cottonwood?"

Callie nodded, then took her keys out and opened up her SUV. She was about to get inside, when she stopped herself, hoping she wasn't making a mistake.

She said to Harlan, "I've been pretty hostile to you and I'm sorry about that."

"I haven't exactly been Mr. Agreeable."

"I hate to see you stuck in a place like the Cottonwood. Why don't you come on over to the house? We've got a guest room you can use."

Harlan looked surprised. "You sure you want to do that?"

"No," she said, "but I'm doing it anyway. You're just lucky Nana won't be there."

"Why's that?"

"She'd be trying to get us all to sit down for tea and sandwiches."

Harlan laughed. "Well, in that case I think I'll take you up on your offer." He gave her an imaginary tip of the hat. "Thank you, kindly, ma'am."

Callie suddenly felt something warm stir inside her. The hat tip was a gesture that the old Harlan made on a pretty regular basis. It was his ode to John Wayne, one of his heroes.

On their first date he'd taken Callie to a revival of the Western *McClintock*. They'd only been study friends until then, but halfway through the movie she saw Harlan quietly mouthing one of The Duke's lines—"You have to be a man before you can be a gentleman"—and she knew she was in love.

She had put her hand in his and leaned her head on his shoulder, and before the night was over, she lay for the first time in his bed, exhilarated by his touch and his complete lack of selfishness. She discovered very quickly that he was both a man *and* a gentleman.

As Callie thought about this, however, the warmth she felt gave way to sadness.

How could she have let that go?

How could she have let any of it go?

"Shall we take your car?" Harlan asked. "Or do you want me to follow you?"

She pulled herself from her thoughts. "I'll drive," she said, then climbed in behind the wheel.

Chapter 13

Harlan didn't quite know what to make of Callie's invitation. The move was unexpected. But then he thought again about what her grandmother had said.

She's still in love with you, you know.

Was there any truth to that?

Part of him wanted to believe it, but a bigger part had serious doubts. She was simply being kindhearted, because, beneath it all, that was Callie. She may have had her stubborn streak, and that hair-trigger temper, but the woman he'd known had been a nurturer at heart. Offering up her spare bedroom was just the kind of thing she'd do. So there was no point in reading anything into it.

Besides, why should it matter to him? He and Callie were long done, and he had his own life in Colorado Springs. True, he'd kept his relationships casual since his divorce, but he didn't often fret over his life as a single man.

He had freedom, could come and go as he pleased. And coming home to an empty apartment was something he'd gotten used to.

But if he was entirely honest with himself, there were nights he'd walk into that apartment and yearn. Not for his ex-wife—that had been a mistake. And not for any of the women he was currently dating.

But for Callie. For that feeling they'd once shared. As if their souls had somehow been connected.

Those were the times he'd root around in his kitchen cupboard until he found a bottle of Jack Daniels. He'd quietly get drunk as he watched the night sky, thinking about all the things he should have said and done back when Treacher was killed. But he'd been too young and stupid—Billy Boy Lyman stupid—and he'd let grief devour him, just as it had devoured Callie.

Harlan sometimes hated Treacher for what he'd done to them, for his irresponsibility. Couldn't he see how much in love they were? What made him think he had the right to destroy that with his reckless behavior?

But if Harlan got drunk enough, he sometimes wondered if Callie had been right. If he'd been more forceful, if he hadn't been distracted by a woman—a major bone of contention with Callie—Treacher never would've gotten behind the wheel of that car and would probably be alive today.

If, if, if…

Sometimes on those nights Harlan saw his best friend smiling at him from beyond the stars, and all the promise in that youthful, charismatic face. And sure enough, Harlan would find himself crying. Drunken tears, but tears nevertheless. Something he didn't like to admit to, but he figured you weren't really a man if you didn't know how to let it loose now and again.

So he let it loose, mourning his losses like a child who has finally realized that his runaway dog isn't ever coming home again.

And the hardest part of all was knowing that when he woke up in the morning, his apartment would still be empty.

Harlan was thinking about these things as they pulled into to Callie's driveway.

"Home sweet home," she said, setting the parking brake.

He studied the house, a modest one-story structure with a rustic feel. It *looked* liked home. Comfortable. Aged, but well-tended.

"You were born here, weren't you?"

"Probably die here, too," Callie said. "This house and Nana Jean are the only constants in my life." She paused. "And the job, of course."

"Of course. The all-consuming beast."

She smiled. "But in a good way."

"Tell that to my face," he said, gesturing to the bruise.

They both laughed as they opened their doors and climbed out, and it was good to hear Callie laughing. There had always been a bright, musical quality to the sound that lifted his spirits. And they needed lifting right now.

Callie jangled her keys and let him in through the front door, then they moved together through a small parlor into a modestly appointed living room, Callie flicking the lights on as they went.

"The spare bedroom is in back," she said, then gestured to a stone fireplace in a corner of the room. "Or you can start that fire you wanted and sleep on the sofa. Your choice."

"No contest," he told her. "Fire it is. As long as I don't wind up like Jonah Pritchard."

"Ugh," Callie said, then pushed him away.

"Bad taste? Too soon?"

"Way too soon."

"So I suppose if I say I want Rice Crispies for breakfast, you'll throw me out of your house?"

He could see that she was about to laugh again, which, of course, was what he'd been hoping for. Cops weren't known for their tasteful humor, and Harlan wasn't any exception. The kind of job they did, humor was often their only relief. Even if it was a bit morbid.

But before he could say anything more, she seemed to sense he was about to crack another joke, and held up a finger.

"Stop," she said, stifling the laugh. "Keep your mouth shut and get to work. I'll grab you some blankets."

So Harlan did as he was told and moved over to the stack of wood next to the fireplace. Shoving aside the grate, he stacked several pieces inside, turned on the gas, then took a long-nosed utility lighter from a basket next to the wood and lit the fire.

It would be a few minutes before the wood caught and he could turn off the gas, so he moved to a rack on a nearby wall that held several bottles of wine. He found a nice Pinot and held it up as Callie came back into the room carrying two blankets and a pillow.

"Quick drink before bed?" he asked.

One of Callie's eyebrows went up. "This isn't a date, Harlan. Don't take this offer the wrong way."

"How could I?" he said. "You're always pretty clear about what you think and feel."

"Maybe not clear enough. Just because we've decided to be cordial doesn't mean this is anything more than two colleagues—"

"It's just wine, Callie."

She caught herself. Smiled. "I guess I've always been too serious for my own good. I'll get the glasses."

She dropped the pillow and blankets on the sofa, then disappeared into the kitchen as Harlan found a corkscrew and opened the bottle.

A moment later she came back and held out the glasses as he poured, a little more generous with the liquid than he needed to be. Truth was, Harlan was disappointed by her insistence that this meant nothing, even though he'd suspected as much. He couldn't stop staring at her, thinking about her body, the way she carried herself. Remembering the things they used to do together. Alone. On his bed.

Maybe the wine would dull his senses a bit.

"To tracking down bad guys," he said, punctuating the words by touching his glass to hers, marveling at how beautiful she looked in the growing firelight.

She stood only inches from him now and he wanted so much to lean forward and kiss her, to taste her lips. But he knew that would be a serious mistake. Instead he drank his wine, nearly downing it in a single gulp.

Callie said, "Slow down, partner, that isn't grape juice."

He finished it off and wiped his mouth with the back of his hand. "I guess I needed that more than I thought I did."

Then he looked into her eyes again and thought he

saw a flicker of desire there. A look he'd seen many times before.

But he couldn't be sure. Especially now that the wine was flowing through his bloodstream. He hadn't been lying about the transparency of her emotions, so maybe what he saw was only the flicker of the fire playing tricks on him. Or his own desire getting the better of him.

He poured another finger of liquid and downed it, then turned and set the glass and bottle on a nearby end table. The wood in the fireplace had caught now, and he crossed to the gas valve and shut it off.

"Guess we'd better get some sleep," he said. "Thanks again for putting me up." He smiled. "And for putting up with me."

"Not so hard," she said. "I deal with criminals for a living, remember?"

Then she finished her glass, set in on the table next to his and bid him goodnight as she left the room.

Harlan didn't think he'd ever been so sorry to see someone go.

It was closing in on three o'clock when Harlan heard the sound.

The sofa was comfortable enough, and although the fire had died down quite a bit, he could feel its warmth. But he'd slept fitfully through the night, still thinking about Callie and his desire to kiss her. To take her in his arms.

He couldn't decide if what he was feeling was real and immediate, or simply the residue of a past that hadn't been completely scrubbed away.

Get a grip on yourself, moron. You're here to do a job and nothing—

The sound came from a hallway on his left—the faint padding of footsteps on wood, and he realized he had dozed off for a moment.

He turned now and saw her silhouetted against what was left of the fire, and in the faint light could see that she was wearing an oversize University of Colorado sweatshirt. Probably the same one she used to wear in the old days. It cut high on her thighs, her smooth bare legs exposed to the night air.

She looked as if she hadn't aged a day since college, and if he wasn't mistaken, there were tears in her eyes.

"I can't sleep," she said softly.

"Neither can I."

Without another word she climbed onto the sofa next to him, pressing her warm body against his, leaning in to kiss him.

As she opened her mouth, the faint smell of her breath wafted past him—a uniquely *Callie* scent that he would know with his eyes closed. Their lips touched and he drew her tongue in, the taste as sweet and inviting as he remembered.

And as they kissed, she snaked a hand down past the blankets, sliding her fingers across the fabric of his boxers until she found him and gently squeezed.

There are those who think that sex is just sex for a man, that he'll sleep with any women he finds remotely attractive. But this wasn't true for Harlan. He wasn't a monk, that was certain, but in all the years they'd been apart he had never found a woman who excited him the way Callie did. He instantly grew hard against her hand, the sudden need to be inside her nearly overwhelming in its intensity.

He wanted to feel her heat envelope him, the memory of it quickening his pulse. He rolled her over onto the cushions and pressed himself against her. Pushing her sweatshirt up, he gently took hold of her right breast and ran his thumb across the nipple, feeling it harden at the touch. Then he lowered he lips to it and she arched her back slightly, pressing into him, her hands searching again, reaching past the elastic of his boxers until she found him.

And he knew that she was feeling the very same overwhelming need. The all-consuming desire. It was as if they had been in a constant state of foreplay ever since he walked into that conference room. He wanted to take his time to please her, but she seemed to be well beyond such concerns, the urgency of her breathing telling him that she was ready for him. Now.

Moving her hands to his waistband again, she pushed his shorts down to free him. She was wearing a pair of silky panties, but she didn't bother to remove them. Instead she pulled them to one side and guided him into her, kissing him, whispering in his ear, "I'm sorry. I'm so sorry."

"No," he said. "It's my fault. It was all my fault."

And he thrust forward like man possessed, electric heat radiating through his body as she writhed beneath him, mewing and moaning with each powerful thrust. He scraped his teeth across her shoulder, her neck, then found her mouth and her tongue again, her quickening breaths in perfect counterpoint to his moving hips.

And just as he thought he couldn't take any more, as if his mind were about to succumb to an explosion of ecstasy, she suddenly looked up at him and said, "Wake up, Harlan. We need to get moving."

Harlan blinked, opened his eyes. Found himself alone on the sofa, his legs tangled in the blankets.

Callie was standing across the room in the kitchen doorway, dressed and ready for work, a cup of coffee in hand.

"You seemed to be having a heck of a nightmare," she said. "You want to share?"

Harlan blinked again, trying to get his bearings. "Did we...? Did..."

"What?"

And then the realization that it had all been a dream came crashing in on him.

"Never mind," he croaked.

"Are you okay?" Callie asked.

Still trying to get his bearings, Harlan nodded. "Fine... I'm... I'm fine."

"Then hurry up and shower. I want to swing by and see Nana before we meet Rusty and Mercer."

Harlan shifted uncomfortably on the sofa.

Easier said than done, he thought.

It would be a while before he could stand up without embarrassing himself.

Chapter 14

"You sure you're okay?" Callie asked.

Whatever Harlan had seen in his dream must have rattled him. He'd been acting funny all morning.

They had been waiting near the charred remnants of the Pritchard house for a good fifteen minutes now, and he'd barely said a word to her since they'd left the house.

"Harlan?"

"Sheriff's here."

He nodded to a truck pulling a long horse trailer as it turned into the drive, Mercer behind the wheel, Rusty riding shotgun. Mercer brought it to a stop and they climbed out, greeting Callie and Harlan with grim nods.

Nobody was looking forward to this ride.

"You try Landry again?" she asked Mercer.

"I would have if he was still around." Mercer dug into his shirt pocket, produced a wooden matchstick, and stuck it between his lips. He'd been trying to quit smoking for weeks. "Hank over at the Cottonwood says he checked out first thing this morning. No mention of where he was headed."

"He didn't look too happy when we left last night."

Mercer chewed on the matchstick as he moved around toward the rear of the horse trailer. "Can't say I blame him. He's known Meg since the day she was born, so I can understand why he'd be reluctant to help us."

Landry was too loyal for his own good. Callie figured he'd spent all these years tending to Jonah Pritchard's every wish, and what had he gotten out of it? She couldn't imagine that he was in Jonah's will. The ranch and the Pritchard fortune would undoubtedly be inherited by Gloria and Meg, and Landry would be left out in the cold.

But Mercer was right. The poor smiling fool felt indebted to the Pritchards and it had been a stretch to think he'd help any more than he already had. Mapping out the trail to the Pritchard gang's old hideout was enough of a betrayal to last him a lifetime. And Callie wouldn't be surprised if he was busy getting an early-morning drunk on.

Mercer took a mobile GPS device from his pocket. "We get up high enough in those mountains, this thing won't be worth squat."

"Terrific," Callie muttered.

The world had grown dependent on satellites and electronic gadgets, and map or no map, she knew this trek wouldn't be an easy one.

Mercer had initially considered attempting an all-out assault, using every deputy he had available to him, but before they'd left the library last night they had decided to keep the team lean and mean. The less manpower involved, the faster they could move.

So it was just the four of them.

This particular stretch of the Bighorns, however, was known to be treacherous territory, which was why a band of outlaws had been attracted to it over a century ago. That it hadn't changed was a testament to how dangerous it could be.

"The main thing we have to remember," Mercer continued, "is to stick together. I don't want anyone getting lost up there."

"Maybe we should try a little harder to find *Landry*," Rusty said. "Appeal to his sense of civic duty."

"Good luck with that."

Fortunately, they were all experienced riders. Landry had furnished them with plenty of landmarks and both Rusty and Callie had done group hikes in these mountains. But today they'd be going well beyond the established trails and once they got into no-man's-land, they'd have be doubly careful.

The only Bighorns virgin in the group was Harlan, but he had assured them he'd be able to hold his own. And despite his odd behavior this morning, Callie didn't doubt it for a minute. She might have her issues with the guy, but he'd always been strong and capable and smart.

"We're wasting time," he said. "What do you say we saddle up and get moving?"

Mercer unlatched the gate of his trailer. The horses—four Morgans from his personal stable—were huffing and shuffling restlessly inside, anxious to be let free. It was a breed Mercer had always sworn by, telling Callie that they were the best trail mounts a man could ask for.

"I think these gals kinda like that idea," he said.

* * *

The Bighorn Mountains were a stretch of the Rockies that spanned two states—north-central Wyoming and southern Montana. The range was a well-known tourist destination for campers, hikers and riders alike, and there were lodges and trails and campgrounds available to anyone with an adventurous streak.

The trail Callie and company were following, however, was not one that was often used. The late Jonah Pritchard had seen to that. It started at the northern part of his property and snaked a good distance up toward Cloud Peak, through what was commonly known as the Cloud Peak Wilderness. The area was controlled by the National Forest Service, but never tell a Pritchard that. Their sense of entitlement stretched well beyond the boundries of any federal mandate.

Robbers Canyon was hidden deep within that wilderness, beyond what anyone familiar with the Pritchard gang legend called the Lost Woods, where the gang had outmaneuvered and sometimes outgunned many a posse.

Callie and the others rode single file along the winding trail, Mercer in the lead, consulting his GPS for as long as it would let him. They all had compasses and photocopies of Landry's hand-drawn map, in case one of them got lost, but so far they were relying on modern technology to get them there.

That would change soon enough, but for the first few hours of the ride, Mercer had shown the way.

As the day wore on, Callie's seat bones started feeling a little sore. It had been a good year since she'd ridden a horse, and not only did she feel it in her butt, she knew that her thigh muscles would pay for it dearly. The ache would set in the minute she dismounted.

Which was bound to be soon, she thought. They'd been riding for over half the day now, mostly uphill, and the horses needed some rest.

As if reading her mind, Mercer called back to them, "There's a creek just around this bend. Might be a good time to water the horses."

"Can't that wait?" Rusty asked. "The sooner were get there the better."

"These gals may be tough, but they need their rest, and I don't figure our fugitives are going anywhere. We'll get there soon enough."

A moment later they rounded the bend and crossed toward a narrow creek that wound past a steep, rocky hillside. They cued their horses to a stop, then dismounted and led them to the water, Callie feeling a burn in her thigh muscles that she knew would be even worse tomorrow. Her legs were trembling slightly, as if she'd just spent the past couple hours making love.

If only.

As Mercer tended to the horses, Rusty found some shade under a nearby tree, then sat down and leaned his back against it, fanning himself. "Could anyone else go for a nice cold beer right now?"

Harlan was still uncharacteristically silent. Unslinging his backpack from his shoulder, he reached inside for a bottle of water and tossed it to Rusty. "It isn't beer, but it'll keep you hydrated."

"Thanks." Rusty uncapped it, then took a long swig and closed is eyes. "Much better."

Callie watched the exchange, noting that Harlan seemed to be doing his best to avoid talking to her. Unable to take it any longer, she said, "So you ready to tell me yet?"

Now came the innocent look. "Tell you what?"

"What's been eating you all morning."

He faltered. "Is it that obvious?"

She glanced at Rusty, then took hold of Harlan's arm and pulled him closer to the hillside. "I haven't forgotten how to read you, Harlan. I know when something's up."

"I guess you would, considering we used to be connected at the hip. Although I'd think you'd be a little out of practice after all these years."

"Like riding a bicycle, I guess. Or a horse." She thought about her aching butt and wondered if there was a suitable analogy there. "So are you gonna tell me, or keep avoiding the question?"

"You may not want to hear it."

She frowned. "Why do you say that?"

"Because it's about you."

She hesitated, but now she was *really* curious. "A statement like that certainly won't discourage me," she said. "So you might as well spill."

Harlan looked down at his boots now, as if what he was about to say was both embarrassing and a little perplexing. Then he said, "I had a dream about you. About us. So real I could've sworn it was actually happening. That's why I was so flustered when you woke me this morning."

She narrowed her eyes at him. She thought she knew where this was headed, but wanted to make sure. "What kind of dream?"

"The kind of dream you don't want me having anymore. You came to me on the sofa wearing that oversize UC sweatshirt you always used to—"

"All right," Callie said. "I think I get it."

"That makes at least one of us."

"What do you mean?"

"I thought I was past all that. Yet here we are, together for less than twenty-four hours, and I'm already having dreams about you. I think that says something, don't you?"

Callie was surprised to discover that her heart had kicked up a notch. She tried to shrug it off. "Like what? That you're a man?"

"Come on, Callie, this isn't about sex and you know it."

"Oh? Then what's it about?"

"Forget it," he said. "I shouldn't have told you."

Too late, she thought, as a bucketful of images tumbled through her head—exactly the wrong *kind* of images. She was supposed to be focusing on this manhunt and all she could see were Harlan's lips and tongue and hands and...

Not about sex, huh? Then why couldn't she scrub these images from her brain? Now the damage was done and she realized her legs were trembling again. Only it had nothing to do with the long ride.

Calm yourself, Callie. For all your talk of forgiving and forgetting, this isn't really what you want. You've moved on. So stay moved on.

But had she? Really?

And if Harlan was having dreams like this, maybe *he* hadn't, either. Maybe they should both be paying close attention here.

But no, there was always that one thing that came between them. That one wedge that she just couldn't seem to shake loose.

Treacher.

Poor dead Treacher.

And the thought of him and everything that had happened that night always had an instant sobering effect on her. Instead of seeing *Harlan's* lips and tongue now, she saw Nicole Bittenger's lips and tongue, doing unspeakable things to Harlan. It was a part of this whole sordid mess she hadn't thought about in a long, long time, but she knew it was the glue that kept that wedge firmly in place.

Harlan had been with someone else when Treacher was killed.

He had always denied that anything had happened that night, but Callie hadn't been able to allow herself to believe him. To trust him. And if you can't trust the man you love, what's the point?

"I think you're right," she said. "You shouldn't have told me. Some things should remain unspoken."

"That's always been the problem, hasn't it?"

"Meaning what?"

"After the accident we spent a lot of time shouting past each other, but we never really sat down and talked about it. About exactly what happened."

Callie hardened. "I know what happened."

"That's the thing, Cal, you *think* you do, you think you have it worked out exactly how it went down, but you never really listened to my side of the story. You pretended to, but you made up your mind about me before I even walked in the door."

"People have eyes, Harlan. They told me what they saw."

He shook his head. "They got it wrong. It was a party, remember? They were drunk and too busy dealing with their own B.S. to pay any attention to..."

He paused, his gaze suddenly shifting to a spot above

her right shoulder. The eyes tightened slightly, then grew wider.

Callie wheeled her head around, looking up toward the rocky hillside. "What is it? What's wrong?"

"I thought I saw something move up there. Someone watching us."

Callie scanned the hillside, looking up toward an outcropping of rocks, using a cupped hand to shade her eyes against the sunlight. She stared intently at those rocks, but saw nothing unusual.

But before she could tell Harlan this, he suddenly grabbed her arm and shouted, "Look out!"

An explosion went off and dust billowed, chunks of the mountain breaking free, the entire hillside soon following, a tidal wave of rock and debris tumbling toward them.

The horses whinnied in terror and began to scatter, the thunder of their hooves drowned out by the rumble of the falling rock.

Harlan jerked on Callie's arm, pulling her out of the path of a rolling boulder.

"Go! Go!" he shouted, and the two kicked into motion, trying to avoid the onslaught.

She heard Mercer cry out in alarm and saw Rusty scramble to his feet as another boulder blasted past the deputy, coming within inches of flattening him.

They all ran, giving it everything they had, as the landslide bore down on them, the rocks and dirt seeming to consume them.

Harlan picked up speed, dragging Callie along with him as she saw Rusty go down, followed by Mercer. She let out a shrill, terrified shriek—

And before she knew it, her world was nothing but

broken earth and stone as the avalanche pulled her and Harlan under.

Then everything was still.

Chapter 15

When Harlan awoke, he was buried beneath the debris. He didn't know how much time had passed, but guessed it was seconds rather than minutes.

He tried to move. No pain. Didn't seem to be hurt in any substantial way. A gap in the rubble was letting air come through, and he could see daylight.

He still had hold of Callie's arm and could feel her pulse throbbing beneath his fingers.

Alive, thank God.

But in what condition?

"Callie?"

Nothing.

Releasing her, he twisted his body, shifting the earth around him until he was able to move his arms. He began pushing rocks and dirt aside and finally broke through to the surface.

"Callie?"

She uttered a faint, muffled groan.

Sounded far away.

His heart pounding, Harlan got to his feet and frantically burrowed through the mound of dirt and rock, tossing it in all directions until he finally found her—still in one piece, but rattled and a little banged up.

Her breaths came in long gulps as she drew in precious air. "...thank you..."

"Are you okay?" he asked. "Anything broken?"

She checked for any serious damage, then shook her head. "I... I—I don't think so."

Harlan pushed aside the rest of the debris and helped her to her feet. He heard more groans nearby and saw both Mercer and Rusty struggling to free themselves as well.

The way that hillside had come down, it was a miracle they were all alive.

"Everyone okay?" he asked.

Mercer grunted in the affirmative as he kicked some rubble aside and stood up, cursing under his breath.

Rusty said, "I think I may have twisted something, but I'll live. How are *you* guys?"

"Mad as hell," Callie said, still breathing hard. She rubbed her elbow as she wheeled around to look up at the mountain. "Who *was* that up there?"

Mercer cursed again, spitting dirt. "Our fugitives, is my guess. At least one of them. Must've come back to see if anyone was looking for 'em."

But Harlan wasn't so sure. "That sounded like a dynamite blast. Where would they get dynamite?"

"From Jonah, no doubt. Old guy was crazy enough to keep some handy. Maybe up at the cabin."

"Does that mean we're getting close?" Callie asked.

"According to Landry's map, we've still got the Lost Woods ahead of us." He gestured. "And I hope one of you still has a copy of the thing, because both it and my GPS are buried somewhere under this slide. I was checking our route when the blast went off."

Harlan climbed up and over the rubble toward the mountain, straining to see if anyone was still up there.

No sign of life.

"Whoever it was, I'm betting they're long gone. Probably started riding the minute they set off the blast."

"He better hope I don't catch him," Mercer said. "It won't be pretty if I do."

Callie looked concerned. "We've lost the element of surprise. What if they take off before we can get to them?"

Mercer dismissed the idea with a wave of the hand. "They take off, where they gonna go? This isn't exactly friendly country, and there aren't any more outlaw hideouts to head for. Besides, whoever did this thinks we're dead. *I* sure would."

"Maybe so," Harlan said, "but we need to move faster. No more rest stops."

The comment must have reminded Mercer about the horses. Looking visibly worried, he scanned the landscape until he found all four of them grazing a couple hundred yards away at the bottom of sloping incline. They looked unfazed now, as if the world hadn't just fallen apart around them.

Mercer let out a breath and said, "Gotta love those gals. Always sticking close to papa. More than I can say for my ex." He looked at the others. "I assume you folks are ready to mount up and go?"

Rusty was checking his right ankle. "Sooner I get off this thing, the better. Looks like it's starting to swell."

"All right, then," Mercer said, then put his fingers to his mouth and whistled. The horses responded immediately, coming toward them in a loping gallop.

Mercer dipped into his shirt pocket and found a wooden matchstick. Stuck it between his lips.

"Let's get after these cowards before they figure out we're still alive."

There's nothing like a brush with death to help you get your priorities straight.

As they continued along the overgrown trail, Callie realized that all this drama between her and Harlan was little more than trivial nonsense.

What did any of it matter right now?

What she needed to do was concentrate on the task at hand. Get the job done and worry about the rest after the killers were behind bars.

But even as she told herself this, she had to admit that when she'd heard Harlan's voice calling to her from beyond the rubble, the relief she'd felt had been palpable.

She thought for sure he hadn't survived the slide, and she couldn't quite fathom a world without him in it. She may not have seen him for a decade, but at least she had always known that he was out there somewhere. Living and breathing. Being Harlan.

And that meant a lot to her.

More than she was willing to say.

When she thought about it, she realized she had been just as happy to see him emerge from that burning house with Gloria Pritchard clinging to him. Even at the height of her anger toward him, that sudden fear of losing him had ripped through her like a dark tide.

If that meant she was still in love with him, then so be it. But she couldn't let it interfere with what they'd come here to do.

No distractions.

She needed to get down to business, and Harlan seemed to be feeling the same way. He had gotten quiet again as they rode along the trail, the Lost Woods looming up ahead. He had taken the lead now, using Landry's map to guide them, and his focus and stolid determination was a comfort to her.

It was also, she was beginning to realize, an aphrodisiac.

Why was she letting him get to her like this?

Concentrate, Callie.

No more personal drama.

There were a lot of legends surrounding the Lost Woods.

Several acres deep, it was a nearly impenetrable maze of ancient Douglas fir that stretched into the sky above them, their high, thick branches exposing only patches of blue. It was said to be haunted by the ghosts of outlaws past, men who had fled here to escape a posse only to find themselves hopelessly lost, and dead within days.

Except for the Pritchard gang, of course.

Others said that the trees themselves would watch whoever entered these woods, tripping them up with their gnarled roots, covering them with branches after they fell, so that their decaying bodies would become part of the earth and never be found.

Callie didn't take much stock in these legends. She

wasn't the superstitious sort. But the moment they rode into the woods, the world seemed to grow darker—not simply the blocking of the sun by the trees, but a kind of kinetic darkness that swirled around them like the souls of angry spirits.

"Lovely place," Rusty said. "Tell me again why I volunteered for this manhunt?"

Mercer huffed a chuckle. "Who says you volunteered?"

"At least tell me I'm getting hazard pay. Somewhere there's gotta be a silver lining to this operation."

"The silver lining is waiting at that cabin," Callie told him. "When we catch the bad guys."

"Spoken like a true training deputy."

She knew he was only half-serious, but he was starting to grate. "And you're talking like a whiny rookie."

"Hey, what do you want from me? I almost got killed back there and my ankle hurts."

"So do my elbow and my butt," Callie said, "but you don't hear me complaining. At least we're still alive."

"And I'd like to stay that way, thank you very much."

She looked at him. "What are you trying to tell us, deputy? You don't think you're cut out for this job?"

"Just blowing off steam," he said.

"Well, blow it another direction. And be grateful we're still in one piece, even if your ankle *does* hurt."

She knew she sounded harsh, but she couldn't help herself. Maybe she needed to blow off a little steam, too.

She softened. "Look, Rusty, I'm sorry, but this isn't much fun for any of us. Once we've got these creeps in jail, we can all go to the Oak Pit and get drunk. I'll even get that cop groupie with the fake boobs to massage your ankle if you want."

Rusty smiled. "You wouldn't have to try too hard. In fact, if the Pritchard Ranch hadn't burned up last night, I think I might've sealed the deal."

Uh-oh. TMI. She was suddenly sorry she'd brought up the subject. "Well, if you do get lucky, I hope you'll keep it to yourself."

His smile widened. "Don't worry, I'll try to limit it to just a few hundred of my friends."

Despite her mood, Callie managed a laugh. Rusty may have been a complainer, and he may have had trouble handling crime scenes, but he wasn't shy and he knew how to make her smile. He was a nice distraction from the gloom surrounding them.

When it came down to it, he was also a good cop. But as his training deputy, she was required to keep that tidbit of information to herself. She needed to help him build his confidence, not his ego.

Up ahead Harlan brought his horse to a halt in the middle of a small clearing and signaled to the others to stop.

"What is it?" Callie asked.

He scanned the woods as they all pulled up alongside him. "Trail ended. No sign of it anywhere."

Callie looked back the way they'd come. The trail had indeed stopped at the edge of the clearing and didn't seem to pick up anywhere else.

"What does the map say?"

"That we follow it through the trees, and when we come through to the other side, we'll be just above Robbers Canyon."

A small spike of concern stuttered through Callie. "So where is it, then? Did we go off course?"

"Not according to Landry."

"Maybe he lied," Mercer said. "Another reason for refusing to come with us." He paused. "Ladies and gentlemen, I think we've officially been punked."

"But why?" Callie asked. "He's just set himself up for an obstruction charge. He could go to jail."

"You think so? He'll just claim he got it wrong, or he forgot. That we were pressuring him too much." Mercer swore under his breath.

"Or maybe he doesn't care," Harlan said. "Maybe he was setting *us* up at the get-go."

"How so?"

"What if that landslide wasn't caused by Billy Boy and his friends at all? What if the one we have to watch for is—"

A shot rang out, echoing in the trees. Mercer grunted and flew off his horse, landing hard on the ground, blood pumping from his upper left arm.

Harlan whipped around. "Down! Everybody down!"

Another shot rang out and they all dove, the bullet striking a nearby tree, splintering wood. One of the horses spooked and reared up, nearly stomping Mercer's head as her hooves came crashing down. Then it and the others scattered, galloping off into the trees.

More shots followed, one after another, the bullets punching the ground around them. Callie grabbed for her service weapon, but it was hard to tell what direction the shots were coming from, and she was too far away for her weapon to be effective. Unfortunately, their rifles were with the horses.

"Callie!" Harlan shouted. "Over here!"

She wheeled around and saw him dragging Mercer behind a tree. There was a momentary pause, then the shots started again as Callie and Rusty followed Harlan and dove for safety. They quickly pulled themselves upright, putting their backs to the tree, Rusty in pain, holding his ankle.

Her heart pounding wildly, Callie peered out into the woods but saw nothing. She glanced at Harlan and Mercer. Harlan had a hand clamped over the wound in Mercer's arm, trying to stop the flow of blood.

"How bad is it?"

"Not good," he said.

"I'm fine," Mercer grunted between gritted teeth, his face about three shades paler than usual. "Give me a gun. I'm gonna shoot this son of a—"

"Quiet," Harlan told him, then cocked his head to listen.

Silence.

The shots had stopped.

He gestured to Callie. "Keep your hand clamped over the wound. I'm going after this guy."

"What? How can you even tell where he is?"

"I'm guessing he's on the move, either getting out of here while the getting's good or looking for a better angle. Either way he's bound to make some noise."

She didn't like the idea of Harlan going out there alone. "Why don't we all just stay right here. Safety in numbers."

"And let him get away? Or worse yet, get into position and take us down? I don't think so." He gestured to the wound. "Take over."

Callie knew she couldn't stop Harlan, and arguing about it would only waste precious time. When he released the pressure, Mercer groaned. Callie quickly took Harlan's place, clamping her hand over the wound.

"See if you can stop the flow," he said. "If he loses too much blood, he's gone."

Callie nodded, then immediately reached down and unbuckled Mercer's belt. She'd have to use it as a tourniquet.

"Good thinking," Harlan said, then got to his feet and disappeared into the trees.

Chapter 16

Harlan had never been in the military, but he was lucky enough to have military training of a sort. When he was nineteen, he and his big brother Sam had gone to a three-week boot camp in Montana where they'd learned the same tactical and evasive maneuvers that were taught in the marines. Not quite the same thing, sure, but it had given him a confidence that would have been sorely lacking otherwise.

After he was recruited by the feds, he'd trained at Glynco and found that much of that training was similar. And in his time with the Marshals Service he'd been in his share of tight situations, including a hostage recovery that had nearly gotten him killed.

In other words, Harlan was no stranger to violence. He may not have encountered it on a day-to-day basis, but he'd seen enough to know how to maintain calm and to focus on his objective: finding the shooter.

He had no doubt that it was Landry out here. The bogus map had sealed that conclusion. And judging by the way Bickham had been so quick to defend Jonah Pritchard yesterday afternoon, to confront three officers of the law with a shotgun, it was obvious where his loyalties lay. Baked-in loyalties, so to speak, and Harlan didn't think Jonah's death had changed anything. Despite what Meg Pritchard may or may not have done to her grandfather, Landry's mission was to protect and defend the family, and he was doing just that.

Harlan moved from tree to tree as quietly as possible, stopping to listen for any telltale sounds—the rustle of bushes, the scattering of birds, the crack of timber.

But he got nothing.

He was almost certain that the shots had come from this direction, but the more time he spent out here, the more he began to wonder if Landry had fled. The man wasn't exactly a young buck, and he had to know that any physical confrontation would only end with him getting hurt.

Harlan was starting to think this was an exercise in futility, when he saw something out of the corner of his eye. Nothing more than a distant glint of light in the trees but it was enough to make him swivel his head and take a closer look.

And sure enough he saw it again, coming from higher ground, inside a clump of bushes. Light reflecting off a mirrored surface of some kind.

Or maybe the glass of a rifle scope?

If so, the shooter was about three hundred yards away up a slight incline, getting a bead on Callie and the others where they hid behind the trunk of that Douglas fir.

Knowing the shots would start up again soon, Harlan

didn't waste any time. He began working his way again from tree to tree, moving as quickly and as stealthily as possible, circling around and behind the shooter's position.

Then taking his Glock from its holster, he crouched low and started inching toward that bush.

But as he got closer, his intuition kicked in and he suddenly realized that he was wrong. The shooter wasn't hiding inside that bush, and the light he'd seen was, in fact, nothing more than a mirror.

A decoy.

And as this realization set in, Harlan felt cold steel on the back of his head for the second time in forty-eight hours.

The barrel of a rifle.

"You'll want to drop that weapon, son."

Harlan cursed inwardly. Landry Bickham was behind him. And Harlan couldn't quite believe that he'd been duped twice in a row. All that training and what had it gotten him? He'd once again let his guard down in a tight situation and that wasn't good. It wasn't good at all.

What the heck was wrong with him?

"You're making a huge mistake here, Landry."

"Oh? How you figure? You folks'll be dead, I'll be alive and Meg and her friends will be able to ride out of here without you people interfering."

"I don't get it. Why are you helping them?"

"I don't see as how that's any of your business."

"Call me curious," Harlan said.

He honestly didn't care about Landry's motives, but he figured the longer he kept the man talking, the longer it would take him to pull the trigger.

"Well, you know what they say about curiosity,"

Landry told him. "And it looks as if it's about to come true for you."

So much for that plan.

Harlan heard the faint rustle of fabric and felt movement behind him and knew it was now or never. Shooting a hand back, he grabbed hold of the rifle barrel and twisted, just as the shot went off. The sound of the blast exploded against his right eardrum, pain piercing it as he turned, swung out hard and landed a solid blow to the center of Landry's face, using his Glock as a club.

Bickham shrieked and dropped the rifle as he stumbled back, grabbing at his broken nose, blood pouring between his fingers, his eyes wide with surprise and sudden horror.

Harlan kicked the rifle aside, then raised the Glock and trained it on him, saying, "One more move and I'll consider it an excuse to shoot you."

But the only move Landry Bickham had left in him was to drop to the ground, sitting in the dirt as he nursed his bleeding nose.

Callie said, "There's no point in holding out on us, Landry. We're gonna find out one way or another."

Harlan was having trouble hearing from his right ear. It had begun to ring, as if he had just come from a sound barrier-busting rock concert, and he wondered if it would ever go away.

Small price to pay for being alive, he supposed, but he'd much prefer to avoid having to wear a hearing aid for the rest of his life, if that was even remotely possible.

Once he'd gotten Landry back on his feet, he had cuffed his hands behind him and escorted the old fool back through the woods to where Callie and the others were situated. Callie had succeeded in stopping the flow of blood from Mercer's arm and he was already sitting upright, his face no longer looking quite as pale as it had been a few minutes ago.

Not that he was the picture of health. They all knew they had to get him to a hospital. And soon.

As Rusty hobbled through the woods trying to rustle up the horses—and a much-needed first aid kit in one of the saddlebags—Callie took charge of questioning Bickham.

"You hear me, Landry? You might as well fess up."

"He broke my nose," Bickham said, a nasally twang to his voice.

"And you tried to kill us. Twice. So pardon me if I don't have a whole lot of sympathy for you."

"Shoulda done it back in that library. Taken that floozy of a librarian down with you."

Callie sighed. "Your not winning any friends here, Landry. You might want to consider being a little more cooperative before one of us hauls off and breaks that nose again."

Landry visibly winced. "I want a lawyer."

"You what?"

"A lawyer. I don't have to say nothin' without one. I know you think I'm stupid—most everyone does—but I got enough smarts to know my rights."

Harlan was a big believer in due process. More than once Callie had accused him of being a cowboy, but he had never been one of those law enforcement types who abused his power in the name of the greater good. He usually played it aboveboard and straight down the line. Collected his evidence the hard way, through good solid police work.

But to his mind today was different. This man had nearly killed them more than once. Had dedicated himself to the task. Not only that, the people he was protecting had torched a vehicle with a man still inside and had done the same to a house after shooting two people. Not to mention they'd started this little crime spree with a fairly solid knock to the side of Harlan's head.

So seeing as how they were out in the middle of nowhere, and about as far from a lawyer as you could get without stepping foot on the moon, he didn't figure the due process really applied right now.

Sometimes a man had to do what a man had to do.

He and Callie exchanged looks, then Harlan said, "Cal, maybe you should see if you can help Rusty round up the horses."

"I'm fine," she told him.

Harlan shook his head. "No, we're talking plausible deniability here. The less eyes see what's about to happen, the better chance we have of Landry's complaint against us not holding up in court."

"What's about to happen?" Landry asked, fear now etching his face.

"Shut up, I'm not talking to you." He looked at Callie again. "I mean it. Mr. Bickham and I need to have a private talk."

Callie didn't budge. "What about Sheriff Mercer?"

"In his condition I figure he's got built-in deniability."

Callie considered this a moment, and he could see the conflict in her eyes. He was half convinced she wouldn't go along, but then she said, "You know what?"

"What?"

"I think I just heard Rusty calling. Sounds like he needs my help."

Harlan nodded grimly. "Then I guess you'd better get moving."

They exchanged another look, and he could see the reluctance in her eyes, knew she wasn't completely in love with this plan of attack, but then she was gone and Harlan returned his attention to Landry.

"You touch me, you'll regret it," Bickham said. It was an empty threat and he knew it.

Harlan didn't respond with words. He casually reached forward and pinched Landry's nose between his first and middle fingers. He squeezed and Landry howled, dropping to his knees, tears popping into his eyes.

"Now, Landry, I couldn't care less about the reason you're here. I figure in that dim little brain of yours there's some kind of motivation at work, but I'll leave that for the forensic psychologists to decipher, assuming you're still alive when we're done."

Landry burbled something unintelligible but Harlan ignored him.

"Now we can take you back to town and get you a lawyer and hope that lawyer will convince you to make a deal with us and tell us what we want to know. But I've been riding a horse all day long and dodging rocks and bullets, and I didn't go through all that just to have to drag your sorry butt back home on the slim chance that you'll cooperate. Especially when one of those bullets has put a man I've come to respect in very serious danger."

Landry was moving his head around now, trying to break Harlan's grip, but Harlan and his brother Sam had seen their share of Three Stooges movies and he'd had a lot of practice with the old knuckle pinch. And judging by the look on Landry's face, fighting it was only making it hurt worse.

After a moment he gave up, now squeezing his eyes shut against what Harlan had to think was pretty unbearable pain.

"So here's what you're gonna do. From here on out, you're gonna shut your mouth unless I ask you a question. And if I ask you one, you'll answer me sincerely and without hesitation. You got that?"

Landry tried to nod his head.

"I'm glad we understand each other," Harlan said, then released him. Landry collapsed to the ground, trying desperately to recover, fresh blood staining his upper lip.

Harlan couldn't help feeling a little bad about it. Under normal circumstances he wasn't prone to violence, and he wasn't particularly proud of what he'd just done. But these weren't normal circumstances and considering what they'd been through, he figured his actions were more than justified.

"You listening to me, Landry?"

"Yes," the old fool croaked.

"Good," Harlan said. "I want to you to lie there for a while, start feeling better. And once we've got the sheriff here squared away for travel, I'm gonna send him and Rusty and Callie on their way. Then you and I are gonna go visit that cabin. No more phony maps. No more ambushes. You understand?"

"Yes," Landry croaked. "I understand."

Harlan showed him a slow smile.

"I figured you would."

Chapter 17

Callie wasn't having any of it.

"No," she said, adamantly. "I'm not leaving. Not now."

They had found Landry's horse tied to a tree several yards from the spot where Harlan had snuck up on him. Harlan had uncuffed him just long enough to get him aboard, then snapped one cuff to the saddle horn and the other to his wrist.

In the meantime Rusty and Callie had rounded up their own horses, found Harlan's first aid kit and tended to Mercer's wound before getting him ready for travel.

Now Harlan was insisting that Callie go with Mercer and Rusty and leave him behind to deal with Landry and the fugitives.

"That's just not gonna happen," she told him.

"You trust Rusty to get the sheriff back in one piece?"

"He can get him within cell phone range. After that he'll call the medevac crew."

Callie wasn't about to let Harlan shove her aside. Not now. She'd already gone along with his blatant disregard for due process and didn't feel particularly good about it, even if it *had* resulted in Landry's full cooperation. To her mind such behavior was a slippery slope, and she could only hope that this had been an exception rather than the rule.

Harlan said, "Considering the amount of time we've wasted, it could be dark before we get to the hideout. I don't think this is a place you want to be after sundown."

"You're not changing my mind, Harlan. This is *my* investigation and I plan on seeing it through."

"It could get ugly."

"It already has," she said. "And in case you haven't noticed, I've managed to survive so far."

Harlan studied her for a moment, and a smile grew on his face.

"What are you grinning about?"

"To be perfectly honest," he said, "I was hoping you'd fight me on this."

"Oh? Why?"

"Despite our bickering, Cal, I kinda like working with you." He sobered slightly. "I'm full of all kinds of regret, and I really wish it could've been this way all along. Lived that dream we always talked about. With or without Treacher."

Callie saw the sincerity in his expression. Knew the words were heartfelt. Tears unexpectedly threatened to fill her eyes, but she struggled to hold them back. She didn't want anyone here seeing her cry.

Especially Landry.

But in that moment whatever animosity she'd felt toward Harlan dissolved. Disappeared. She didn't know how long it would last, but it felt good to be free of it— even if only for a moment.

"So do I," she said softy. "So do I."

It took another twenty minutes to get Rusty and Mercer on their way. Mercer's bandage was bloody, but with the tourniquet still in place, the flow seemed to have stopped for now and he assured them he had enough strength to see himself through to the nearest cell zone. That he could even sit atop his horse in his condition was a testament to his iron will.

"You be good to my gals," he said, struggling with his pain. "They get hurt, there'll be hell to pay."

Callie assured him they would, then watched the two men ride away, hoping against hope that they'd get the sheriff to safety before that wound started to bleed again.

When they were gone, Harlan and Callie mounted their own horses, then Harlan turned to Landry. "Showtime, Bickham. You plan on keeping your promise, or do you need a little reminder?"

Landry's eyes widened slightly, his free hand moving involuntarily toward his nose, as if to protect it. Then he caught himself and scowled. "You better hope nothing goes wrong out there, son. If it does, you're the first one on my list."

"Yeah? How's that working out for you so far?"

"Mark my words. You're a dead man."

Harlan's eyes glazed. "You know how many times I've been told that over the course of my career? I've transported men who'd make you pee your pants if you spent more than five minutes with them. So don't for a second think you can intimidate me, Bickham. If anyone should worry about winding up dead, it's you. I won't hesitate to shoot you, if I have to."

Landry had lived nearly his entire life with the Pritchards, and some of their arrogance had obviously rubbed off on him.

"You're good when a man's hands are cuffed," he said. "But that bruise on your face tells a different story."

Callie cut in. "You know what, Landry?"

He turned, scowled at her. "What?"

"I think I like it better when you smile."

"I'll bet you do," he said. "Everybody does."

He let one spread across his face now, but it was so full of malice that the hairs on the back of her neck prickled.

"Even your mother liked it," he said quietly. "Did I ever tell you I knew her in high school?"

Callie stiffened. "Not that I remember."

"Knew your daddy, too. Even before I started workin' for the Pritchards. He and Mary were quite the couple. But old Jonah, well, he just couldn't abide by some tramp corrupting his perfect little son."

"Call her that again," Callie said, "and I'll shoot you myself."

Landry shrugged. "It's not like I'm the first one to say it. But I never felt any ill will toward her. Truth is, I had a crush on her. If things had been different, who knows? You might be calling *me* daddy."

The thought made Callie want to puke. But then it occurred to her that Landry was only trying to get a rise out of her. Keep her off guard and eventually he might be able to use her discomfort to make a move. She wasn't sure how he'd do it with his hand cuffed to the saddle, but there was no point in taking chances, and she refused to let him get to her.

"Nice try," she said. "But my mother wouldn't have come anywhere near you even if she was dying of thirst and you had a bucketful of water."

"Just shows how little you know. I'll bet that grandma of yours painted a nice little picture."

"I think you need to shut up now."

"You're completely clueless, aren't you?"

"Enough, Bickham," Harlan barked. "Don't make me pull you down off that horse."

Landry swiveled his head toward Harlan. "Hold on, now, I think this girl deserves to know about her family. About her momma *and* her daddy." He returned his attention to Callie. "You probably believe all that nonsense about Riley Pritchard getting himself killed in a truck accident."

"It's the truth."

Landry chuckled. "The truth can be manufactured if you've got enough money. We all learn that every time we turn on the TV. But I know the *real* truth about your daddy, and if you want me to keep it to myself, I'll respect your wishes. Let you go on believing in fairy tales."

Something sour turned in Callie's stomach. She knew he was still playing with her, baiting her, but she also felt compelled to listen. Nana had never told her a whole lot about what had happened to her father, and she wondered if Landry really *did* know something.

"Tell me," she said.

His smile widened, and she wondered why she had never noticed the ugliness behind it. "You sure you want to hear this?"

"Tell me," she said again.

Harlan had good enough sense to stay quiet now. He would instinctively want to protect her, but he knew by the tone of her voice that this wasn't the time to interfere.

Landry said, "Like I told you, your daddy didn't die in no truck accident."

"How, then?"

He waited a moment for dramatic effect. "Boy up and killed himself. Slit his wrists, right there in his barracks."

Callie's stomach flip-flopped and she felt prickles on her scalp. Could this be true?

"How do you know that?"

"Everybody in the Pritchard family knows it."

"I don't understand. Why? Why would he do that? Because his father forced him to join the army?"

"Jonah didn't force him to do nothin'. He cherished that boy. Riley decided to run off on his own. When he found out about Mary."

"Because she was pregnant?"

Landry huffed. "No, he was over the moon about that. You could barely contain the boy. He was gonna be a *father*."

Callie was at a loss. "Then why? Why would he run away?"

"Because six months into her pregnancy, Mary told him the truth."

"About what?"

"That he wasn't your daddy after all. Turns out Mary wasn't a one-man kinda gal."

Callie's gut tightend and he held her gaze, his eyes burning with intensity. He was enjoying this. And despite her skepticism, she had to ask the question.

"Let's assume for a minute that you aren't a lying sack of garbage. If Riley didn't get my mother pregnant, who did?"

Landry showed her his most malevolent smile yet.

"Why, Jonah Pritchard, that's who."

Chapter 18

The world turned sideways.

Callie felt a rush of dizziness slam into her and she nearly fell out of the saddle. She really *was* going to be sick now. Could feel the bile rising in her throat.

She didn't think she'd ever come this close to fainting before, even when she got the news about Treacher. But she was close now. Had to muster up every bit of her will to keep from diving headfirst into the dirt.

Sensing her distress, Harlan nudged his horse up alongside hers and grabbed hold of her arm. "You okay?"

She was trying to control her breathing. Couldn't get enough air to form any words.

"How you expect the girl to be okay?" Landry said. "News like that is bound to trouble *anyone*."

"Shut up, Bickham," Harlan snapped.

"I'm just the messenger. She's the one insisted I tell her."

"I said, shut up. You say another word, I'll pull you off of that horse and beat you to a pulp. You understand?"

"Whatever you say, Marshal."

Harlan glared at him then returned his attention to Callie. The world was starting to right itself now, and she was finally able to breathe.

"Easy, Cal. Just take it slow..."

She knew he must be thinking he'd walked straight into one of Nana Jean's soap operas, but his blue eyes showed nothing but concern and she was grateful for that.

"I'm good," she said. "Thank you."

At least she hoped she was.

The thought that her mother had ever gone near Jonah Pritchard's bed was ridiculous.

Wasn't it?

He squeezed her arm. "Take your time."

She put her hand on his and squeezed back. "No, I'm okay now. I'm fine."

"Well, ain't you two love birds a picture?" Landry said. "Just like Jonah and Mary. Of course, she was a good thirty years younger than him."

Harlan turned, sitting upright in his saddle. "Your nose looks like it stopped bleeding, Bickham. You want me to fix that for you?"

"Anybody ever tell you you're a violent man?"

"I'm not the one running around trying to kill people, remember? Keep flapping your gums and you'll find out what violence really is."

Landry opened his mouth, then immediately closed it again, finally smart enough to heed Harlan's warning.

Something else that Callie was grateful for.

There was no way to know if he was telling the truth about her mother and Jonah, and she could only hope that he was the lying sack she thought he was. But Gloria's unspoken accusation kept tumbling through her head, and that was enough to stir up some doubt.

Of course her mother had been eighteen at the time of her pregnancy, and was known to be a bit of a wild child. Was it possible that she had been attracted to Jonah? Had she been dating Riley, but secretly sleeping with his old man?

The thought sickened Callie, but then that's exactly what it was designed to do. Landry was playing mind games. Trying to exploit a weakness where he saw it, to gain some kind of leverage over her.

But it wouldn't work unless she let it.

And she wasn't about to let it.

She steeled herself and sat upright, refusing to give in to his emotional terrorism.

"Can we get moving now?" she said to Harlan. "The sooner this creep and his friends are behind bars, the better I'll feel."

Once they got started, they rode for another hour, continuing to wind their way through the Lost Woods. They had picked up the trail again, right where Landry had promised it would be, so at least he wasn't taking them on a wild goose chase.

Or so they hoped.

They still had no idea why he'd gone to so much trouble to help a trio of unapologetic sociopaths. It seemed odd to Callie that his loyalty was so strong that he was willing to kill for them—especially after they'd shot Jonah—but she had long ago given up on trying to figure out what motivates criminal behavior. People killed for the stupidest reasons, so in a perverse kind of way, maybe Landry was to be commended. At least he hadn't gutted anyone over a pair of tennis shoes.

Not that this would make Sheriff Mercer feel any better. And Callie doubted it would color a jury's verdict once she testified against the old fool. But on the list of motives for attempted murder, loyalty wouldn't even be close to the top.

Landry obviously felt that someone he cared about was being threatened, and had decided to do something about it. And back in the outlaw days he probably would've had a lot of townsfolk cheering him on, just as they'd cheered on Jeremiah Pritchard.

But the outlaw days were over. Even out here in the middle of nowhere.

Maybe someone had forgotten to tell Landry.

The sun was almost gone by the time they reached the far side of the woods and found themselves on a high bluff overlooking a canyon.

Calling it a canyon was being generous. It was really little more than a crevice in the earth, the mountains on either side rising toward the sky like protective walls shielding it from any but the most observant eyes.

No helicopter would be able to find it. And it was no wonder that none of the posses of the past had ever made it this far.

"Robbers Canyon," Landry said, then gestured to the lip of the bluff where a narrow trail snaked treacherously into the crevice. "It's getting dark. Might want to postpone the rest of this trip 'til daylight."

"How long is the ride?" Harlan asked.

"Ten, fifteen minutes, I'd guess. Never really timed it."

"And what are we walking into when we get down there?"

"Another trail. Five-minute ride around a couple out-croppings before we hit the cabin."

Callie could see the wariness on Harlan's face. They had no real reason to believe this man, and every reason to assume he was sending them straight into an ambush.

Landry sensed Harlan's hesitation. "What's the matter, Marshal? Don't you trust me?"

"We trusted you to draw us a map," Harlan said. "And look where that got us."

"That was before you so kindly reminded me how much I value my life." He gestured to his nose. "And my extremities."

"Doesn't help that you threaten to kill us every chance you get. And tried a few times."

"All true, but you're a man and you know how it is. Gotta put up a good front, make sure your opponent knows you ain't no pushover. Especially in front of a lady. But after this long ride, I've seen the error of my ways."

"Not if you think I swallowed a single word you just said."

Landry snorted. "Good one. I like that." He looked out at the sky. "But the more we jaw, the closer it gets to sundown. So what's it gonna be, Marshal? Yay or nay?"

Harlan looked down at the canyon, then up again at Callie. "What do you think, Cal? Think we should trust this creep?"

"We don't have much choice. It's about the only thing we *can* do at this point."

"Now you see there? That's a smart girl," Landry said. "It's all that Pritchard blood running through her. Even if it is watered down a bit."

Callie swiveled her head. "You're gonna want to knock that off right now."

"You know, you remind me of your mother. She and I used to smoke cigarettes back of the band building at school. Did a little necking now and then, too, although I never did get past second base with her."

Now Harlan chimed in. "Stow it, Bickham."

But Landry wasn't listening. "One day she up and tells me all about her little love affair with Jonah Pritchard. Says he may be older, but he's the kindest, most giving lover she's ever—"

"All right," Callie said, turning to Harlan. "Either we tie this weasel to a tree and leave him up here, or I'm gonna be forced to use my firearm."

"I opt for the firearm," Harlan said, and he didn't sound as if he was joking.

Landry took a look at their faces. "Now wait just a minute."

"What do you say we let fate decide?" Callie said, then climbed off her horse and gestured. "If I find rope in this saddlebag, then that's that. But if it's empty, I'll take that as a sign I need to empty my gun, too."

Harlan nodded. "Works for me."

"Now hold on," Landry said, his gaze going straight to the saddlebag. "This ain't funny. You want me to shut up, I'll shut up. I was just havin' a laugh."

"Too late," Harlan said. "You played your last card and it was a joker."

Callie reached for the saddlebag in question and unfastened the flap. Flipping it open, she shoved a hand inside and pulled out a coil of rope.

"Lucky you," she said. "I guess that joker was wild."

Landry's entire body went slack. He looked relieved but defeated. She was pleased to see that all the fight had drained out of him.

Of course she'd *known* there would be rope inside. She had put it there before they'd left Pritchard Ranch, and Harlan had seen her do it. But if Landry could mess with people's heads, so could she. And she almost felt ashamed by the amount of pleasure it had given her.

Almost.

"Tree it is," she said, then hefted the rope. "Although this might make a pretty good noose."

Harlan nodded again. "That works, too."

"You people are just flat-out cruel and sadistic."

Callie smiled. "That's not it at all, Landry. We just don't like you."

Five minutes later they had him cuffed, gagged and tied to a tree, with a promise that they'd do their best not to forget about him.

The look on Landry's face was one that Callie knew she would cherish for many years to come.

Chapter 19

They decided to enter the canyon on foot.

Despite the growing darkness they knew that their horses were a visual target, and if anyone should be waiting for them, the potential of being spotted was much too high.

Besides, navigating such a treacherous trail in the dark on horseback wasn't exactly a wise move. As much as Callie loved the animals, she figured there was less risk of taking a tumble if she was traveling on her own two feet.

The trail was narrow enough that looking down into the canyon made her heart pound a little. It was a long drop, and a simple misstep could end in disaster.

She and Harlan moved quickly but carefully, using flashlights, but only turning them on when they absolutely had to. It wouldn't do to have Billy Boy or Meg or

Creep Number Three see bobbing lights on the mountainside and sound the alarm.

Callie said, "We better hope Landry doesn't get loose up there."

"Are you kidding me? He'd need the intervention of the Almighty to do it. And I'd rather risk that than risk him giving us away."

"I was just making noise, but I have to tell you, a part of me really did want to shoot him."

"I don't blame you," Harlan said, "all that garbage he was spewing about your mother?"

"You think he was telling the truth?"

"Based on what little I know about Landry Bickham, I'd say that he and the truth have been strangers for a very long time."

"Maybe so, but he sure got me wondering."

"Tell me this," Harlan said. "Does it really make a difference? Father, grandfather, either way Jonah Pritchard is dead, and when he was alive he didn't want to have anything to do with you. If it were me, I'd wash my hands of the whole thing."

"I keep thinking about my mother. Nana Jean has always painted this rosy picture of her and if she had anything to do with Riley killing himself—"

"You'll tie yourself up in knots if you start thinking like that." He took hold of her wrist and they stopped. "But maybe there's a lesson in this. One we can both benefit from."

"What do you mean?" Callie asked.

"Maybe we shouldn't be so quick to believe what people tell us. They embellish, they exaggerate and sometimes they flat-out lie. And everything is filtered through their own experiences, their own prejudices."

"Why do I get the feeling this isn't about my mother?"

"Because you aren't a stupid woman," Harlan said. "I know this isn't the time to be getting into this, but once we're done here, I'd like you to do me a favor."

"And what's that?"

"I'd like you to sit down with me and let me tell you what happened the night Treacher died. Treacher getting drunk, Nicole, the whole nine yards. And I'm talking about the truth, not a bunch of so-called eyewitness accounts by people who could barely stand up straight."

Callie instantly felt the walls going up—the way they always did when she was confronted by that night. But when she thought about all the shouting and the crying that she and Harlan had done in the aftermath, all the accusations, she realized she never really *had* given him his say. Not without a knee-jerk reaction to every other word he spoke.

She had closed him out without apology. She knew that now, and there was no excuse for it. She'd paid dearly these past ten years because of it.

It occurred to her that being so deeply in love with someone was a double-edged sword. There was the joy, the exhilaration, but there was also the fear, the insecurity, the jealousy and anger—all of which stemmed not from the relationship itself, but from a personal lack of self-confidence. The inability to believe that someone can love as much as he is loved back.

The key, she realized, was trust and communication. Listen to each other and don't jump to conclusions, no matter what someone outside that relationship might say.

Callie knew she owed Harlan his chance to explain. And even if that explanation didn't live up to scrutiny, at least she could take comfort in knowing that she'd been *fair* with him. This time.

As they stood there in the middle of that narrow trail, Harlan's hand on her wrist, the darkness gathered around them, she reached up with her free hand and touched his jaw, then leaned forward and kissed his cheek.

"It's the least I can do," she said.

Then he turned his head toward her, put his mouth on hers and gave her a real kiss, before moving past her and continuing on down the trail.

And as Callie watched him, she once again thought about her trembling thighs and knew that what she felt in them had nothing to do with the ride.

Landry Bickham couldn't help laughing.

All his life everyone had looked at him as dumb old Landry, the boy who never could. There may have been some truth to that in school where he'd always had trouble paying attention, but for every ounce of book learning he lacked, he'd earned a pound of street smarts. And he knew a man couldn't get through this life without a fair bit of improvisation.

As incongruous as it might seem—considering he was a sunbaked old ranch hand—unlike Jonah, Landry had never been a big fan of outlaws. Landry's hero, believe or not, was a little Hungarian-born fella called Eric Weisz, otherwise known as Harry Houdini.

If you were to sift through the rubble of the Pritchard home and work your way down to the basement where Landry kept a bedroom, you'd find the charred remains of his Houdini collection. Half a dozen biographies, several how-to books, and even a couple of old silent movies the magician had made to capitalize on his popularity.

It killed Landry to know they were all gone now, but such is life, and they'd be easy enough to replace.

Landry had performed a few card tricks in his time, but he'd never found much fun in it. Oh, he could hold his own in the sleight-of-hand department, but it didn't interest him all that much, unless he could find a way to get something out of it.

His true skill had always been knowing how to read people. To figure out how to manipulate and misdirect them, just like any good magician. He may not have been big on fancy card moves, but he could win a pot with a smile and a wink, or get a woman to lie down with him with a few simple words, or make a self-possessed old coot like Jonah Pritchard think he was running the show.

It sometimes took a fair amount of improvisation, but like Harry Houdini, Landry was good on his feet. He could control a conversation and make a couple of light-weights like Callie Glass and U.S. Deputy Marshal Cole react pretty much the way he wanted them, too.

Once they'd caught him in the woods, he'd known full well that if he pushed them hard enough, they would do exactly what they'd done. Leave him alone up here while they went off to perform their so-called duty. Such as it was.

He had gotten a kick out watching little Callie play her game with him. She was a tough gal when she needed to be—everybody knew that—but she'd never been the type to up and shoot someone just because he'd rattled her cage a bit. It had been fun watching her, however, and he felt a tiny chuckle coming on just thinking about it.

Misdirection and manipulation. Controlling the dialogue and knowing how to get people looking at your left hand when they should be watching the right. Which is why, as Marshal Cole slapped these cuffs on one wrist, Landry was busy using his free hand to pick the Marshal's pocket.

Quickly, deftly and accurately.

And by the time the cuffs were snapped shut behind him, Landry had clipped the key between his fingers in a way that would make his hands look empty. It was a trick old Harry used to do before they locked him in a trunk and dumped him in the river. Or turned him upside down and stuck him in a tank full of water.

Ropes and knots had never been a challenge for Landry, so once the cuffs were off, everything else was gravy. And five minutes after they'd left him behind, he was on his feet and headed for the trail.

People might think he was dumb, all right…

But he was nobody's fool.

They smelled burning wood long before they reached the cabin.

They were close to the second outcropping when smoke wafted in their direction, and Harlan help up a hand, signaling for Callie to stop. Crouching low, he moved to the tip of the outcropping and peeked over the edge of the largest stone.

Callie moved up next to him. With the darkness came the cold, and she could feel it seeping in through the fabric of her jacket. They stayed close, sharing their warmth.

There was a clearing ahead, the cabin sitting about three hundred yards away, looking almost exactly as it had in the archive photo but larger than she had expected. The only thing missing was a desperado staring intently into the camera.

Without cell phone reception or electricity, Callie felt

as if she had been thrown into the past, to a simpler, more primitive time. It was the same feeling she'd gotten as a child, when she and Nana Jean had visited a ghost town near Parkerville which had remained untouched since its abandonment a century before.

A saloon. A blacksmith's shop. A general store. A large old mansion that the tour guide had referred to as a "house of ill repute"—which, to nine-year-old Callie, had sounded like a hospital of some kind.

Like that old town, there was calmness to the air here. A peace. And she suddenly understood why Jonah liked coming here.

"Someone's home," Harlan whispered.

A kerosene lamp hung from a hook in the front window, its yellow light flickering. They watched intently for a moment, then saw movement in the light. A shadow passing through it.

"There's bound to be a back way in," Callie said, then looked at the mountain walls surrounding the clearing. There was some exposure here and there, but plenty of cover, too, which would allow her to work her way around to the rear of the cabin. "Give me about three minutes."

She was about to go when Harlan stopped her.

"No," he said, "Let me do it."

She shook her head. "You're too big of a target."

"And if they spot you, they won't hesitate to shoot you. I won't have that on my conscience."

Callie frowned. "We're both professionals, Harlan. I can handle myself. And since I'm probably half your size, there's less chance they'll spot me."

She could see from his expression that he knew she

was right, even if he didn't like the idea. She heard the reluctance in his voice.

"Three minutes," he told her. "Then I'm going in."

"I'll be there."

"You get yourself shot, I'll never forgive you."

"If I get myself shot, don't expect me to be as stoic as Mercer. I'll be crying like a baby."

"All the more reason not to," he said.

She grinned at him, then climbed down from the outcropping. Staying low, she carefully edged her way past it, keeping her eyes on the cabin as she darted across a narrow stretch of the clearing to a cluster of rocks on the other side.

She hunkered down behind them, eyeing that flickering light, looking for any sign of life in the window. Satisfied that no one was watching her, she stood up again and made another dash, moving laterally toward another group of rocks.

From here she knew it was just a matter of climbing up a small, rocky hillside and around to the rear of the cabin.

Checking the window again, she made her way up and over the rocks and began to climb, moving as quickly as she could, leaping from stone to stone and hoping she wasn't making too much noise.

Less than a minute later she stood in a cluster of trees, looking down at the rear of the cabin. It seemed much bigger up close, with at least two or three bedrooms. There was another window back here, and she knew if she could get close enough, she'd be able see inside.

Checking for signs of movement, she moved into a crouch and slowly worked her way down the hillside until she was only feet from the cabin. She heard voices inside, angry voices, but the sound was muffled, and there was no way for her to identify them.

She made a last quick dash now and was directly below the window. The voices were louder, more distinct. Steeling herself, Callie slowly edged her head up past the window sill and peered inside.

What she saw froze her to the spot.

There were two men and woman in the room. Megan, of course, sitting in a chair by the fire, rocking back and forth like a little kid who had just been severely traumatized and was trying to block out the world.

One of the men was pacing, a kid of about twenty-two or so, the kid from Harlan's surveillance photos—Billy Boy Lyman. The other man was seated at a table, Billy Boy waving the business end of a shotgun at the back of his head. But he wasn't the one called Brett, and Callie couldn't quite fathom what she was seeing here. It put the lie to everything she'd believed about this case since yesterday afternoon.

"Come on, you old fart, I'm losing my patience. Sign the paper and I'll kill you fast. Otherwise you're gonna think I'm the devil himself."

The man in the chair said nothing. Didn't move. Just looked defiantly at Billy Boy.

Which didn't surprise Callie in the least.

The old man in the chair was none other than Jonah Pritchard.

Chapter 20

Billy Boy was becoming more and more restless. This wasn't going at all the way he had hoped it would.

Meg had promised him that the old man would cave the minute Billy threatened to kill her. Said he had a soft spot for her. All Billy had to do was play his part, and Pritchard would give them anything they wanted.

Unfortunately Meg had underestimated her influence over the old man. Turned out he wasn't so anxious to be cooperative after all.

Their plan, such as it was, had been hatched days ago, back when Billy first got the news that the judge in Colorado Springs had decided to ship him up to Torrington while he was waiting for trial. This was shortly after he got tagged for the bank robbery—another one of Meg's brilliant ideas—and Meg and Brett came to visit him at county.

"We're gonna bust you out," she told him. A proclamation that Billy had greeted with some very sincere skepticism.

Meg Pritchard was one of hottest women he'd ever known. Wore that body of hers like it was some kind of weapon, and she was an expert marksman, that was for sure. Shortly after he met her, however—and boy did he remember *that* night—Billy had to admit to himself that not only did Meg have a crazy streak, but was probably not the brightest planetary star in the galactic empire.

The idea of actually breaking someone out of jail sounded like something you'd see on a television show, but Meg was so freaking lovely to look at you couldn't help but give her a listen, even if what she was saying didn't make a whole lot of sense.

"And how do you plan on pulling off this big escape?" he asked. They were sitting across from each other in the visiting room and the guard on duty had made Meg put on an oversize T-shirt for fear that what she was wearing would rile up the inmates. Billy didn't doubt that it would.

"Easy," she told him. "When they transport you up to Torrington, they'll have to take the main highway, right?"

Billy nodded. "I guess so. Most direct route."

"Well, there's a stretch along there that's deader than the moon. Only thing around for miles is this little gas station mini-mart place, stays open twenty-four hours."

"So?"

"So that's where we do it. You pretend you've gotta use the facilities, and we'll be there waiting for you the minute you step foot in that store. Bing, bang, boom, you're free."

Bing, bang, boom, huh?

Billy thought about this genius plan, and knew there were just too many things that could go wrong. "What if the guy doing the transporting don't wanna stop?"

"You'll just have to convince him. Keep talking to him the whole ride, try to get on his nerves. Trust me, he'll be happy for the break."

Billy's skepticism hadn't waned. "I don't know. Sounds pretty dumb to me."

This was when Meg had started to pout. She always looked cute when she did it, but Billy hated it. She'd get all grouchy and start holding out on him and eventually he'd have to give in to her anyway.

He looked at Brett, who had been sitting there silently the whole time. Probably because he was twice as dumb as Meg. They'd all met in juvie a few years back and had been friends ever since.

Billy said, "What do *you* think of this idea?"

Brett shrugged. "Could work, I guess."

That was about as much of a commitment he'd ever get out of the guy, and Billy figured it was enough. Besides, what did he really have to lose?

"All right," he said to Meg. "Let's do it."

Even if it hadn't worked out, the expression on her face had been enough of a reward. Lord, she was hot. If this lamebrained plan had even half a chance of getting him close to what was under that T-shirt again, it was well worth the effort.

And surprise, surprise, Meg had turned out to be right.

The problems started when Billy found out the rest of the plan. This didn't happen until they'd knocked the Marshal out and hit the road in Brett's Malibu. Brett was driving while Meg and Billy got frisky in the backseat—no T-shirts this time—and man oh man, she was looking better than ever.

When they were done, Billy wanted to know where they were headed, where they'd hide, and Meg informed him that they were going to her grandfather's house.

"Now why would we want to do that?" Billy asked.

"Two reasons," she said. "He worships me and he's the guardian of my trust fund."

This was news to Billy. "Trust fund?"

"Fifteen million dollars. Enough money to get us out of the country and then some. Maybe head to Barcelona. I always wanted to go to Italy." Then she offered him a smile so dazzling he had to plant a kiss on those ripe red lips of hers. Of course the sudden revelation that she was the richest woman he'd ever met might have had something to do with it.

Question was, if she had all this money waiting for her, why on earth had she convinced him and Brett to rob a freaking bank?

This chick really *was* crazy.

"So what does this mean, your gramps being guardian of the fund?"

"Means I can't get the money without his signature."

"Will he sign it over?"

"Hah," she said. "Not likely. Not without a little convincing."

"You said he worships you."

"Which is why he won't sign. Figures it's in my best interest to make me wait until I'm thirty before I can collect it."

"Thirty? What's the point of that? Half your life is over."

"Tell me about it," Meg said.

"So how do you plan on convincing him to sign?"

She smiled again, as if what she was about to reveal was the most brilliant scheme any human being on the planet had ever come up with.

"Piece of pie with chocolate ice cream," she said. "We make him think you're gonna hurt me if he doesn't."

Now this was when Billy realized he had a major problem on his hands. Because this was, without a doubt, even dumber than her plan to help him escape. Except *that* plan had managed to work out just fine.

So should he be listening carefully now?

"We show up at the ranch," she told him. "Introduce you as a couple friends of mine. So far so good. Only once we're inside, we make it clear to the old coot that I'm actually your hostage and unless gramps does what you tell him to do, you'll waste me right there in front of him."

"Doesn't making him sign the money over to you kinda give you away?"

"Who cares, as long as I got my money? Besides, it won't much matter at that point."

"Why?" Billy asked.

"Why you think?" she said. "We're gonna kill him."

Billy considered this, and the thought of fifteen million bucks might have been clouding his judgment a bit. "And you really think this is gonna work?"

"He's got all the paperwork right there in his study. He'll sign it in a heartbeat if he thinks he's gonna lose his precious little Megs."

Billy wasn't convinced. "This is a working ranch, right?"

"Right."

"And you expect me and Brett to waltz in there and

start threatening you when he's surrounded by all these people who work for him? I can imagine some of those ranch hands are pretty tough."

"Nothing to worry about," she said.

"How you figure?"

"I've got a man on the inside. He'll make sure the place is cleared out shortly after we get there. He's Grandpa's right-hand man and pretty much runs the show around there."

"Man on the inside," Billy said suspiciously. "This isn't some guy you're sleeping with, is it?"

Meg scrunched her nose at him. "Ew, give me some credit, Billy. He's my real father. Only nobody knows I know that."

"Real father? I thought your parents were divorced. Wasn't your daddy some guy named Breen?"

"Yeah, except he was just a friend of Grandpa's. He was only pretending to be my father because Grandpa didn't want anyone knowing my real dad was some low-life ranch hand."

What the heck?

"You got one seriously screwed up family, you know that?"

"Tell me about it."

"So if your real dad is such a lowlife, how come gramps keeps him around?"

"What can I say," Meg told him with a shrug. "Everybody loves Landry."

Everybody loves Landry, huh? Everybody but Billy, maybe. When they showed up at the ranch, he'd taken an instant dislike to the man. Didn't like the way the guy kept sizing him up as if he was trying to decide whether or not Billy was good enough for Meg—which was a laugh considering how seriously twisted everyone on Pritchard Planet was.

Whatever the case, Megan's plan turned out to be just as worthless as Billy had suspected it was. Old man Pritchard wasn't buying any of it, not from the get-go, and before they knew it a couple of sheriffs showed up towing none other than Marshal Harlan Cole along with them.

All because Meg had gotten the bright idea to hijack a truck, then rob the guy and torch him on the highway.

To Billy's surprise, however, Pritchard covered for them. Then after the cops left, all hell broke loose in the Pritchard mansion and poor Brett wound up dead.

Seemed Landry had some kind of lamebrained scheme of his own, which included double-crossing Meg, Billy and even Grandpa Moneybags with that shotgun he was holding. Maybe he figured he'd just kill everybody, starting with Brett, then blame it on Meg and Billy and pocket that Pritchard money for himself.

How exactly that was supposed to work was beyond Billy's ability to reason, but there it was, a complete mess by any definition. And in all the confusion, Meg and Billy just barely managed to grab some horses and get the heck out of Dodge, taking Grandpa along with them before this Landry fool shot them all.

Now here they were in some remote freaking cabin—Meg's idea again—trying to get Grandpa to cooperate and sign the papers she'd stolen from his safe. But Grandpa was no pushover. Grandpa was probably one of the orneriest, most infuriating people Billy Boy had ever had to deal with.

"Come on, Pritchard, you're what? Eighty-three years old?"

Pritchard said nothing.

"What've you got to live for anyway? Even your own granddaughter wants you dead."

He glanced over at Meg, who had been sitting by the fireplace for a good hour, her head in her hands as she rocked back and forth in her chair. The closer they'd gotten to this place, the more subdued she'd become, as if some very bad memories were coming back to her, and she couldn't quite handle the weight.

Pritchard finally broke his silence. "You don't know what you're talking about," he said. "Megan loves me."

"If you believe that, pops, you are one deluded old cowboy."

"She loves me and she knows it. Always has, always will. Isn't that right, Meg?"

Meg didn't respond to him. Just kept rocking. Billy was really starting to get worried about her.

Pritchard looked at him intently now. "Even if I do sign this paper, it won't mean a thing. You and Meg are wanted by the law. What makes you think she'd even have a chance to get to these funds?"

"What are you talking about? They're hers, ain't they?"

"I always knew that girl wasn't college material, but I never figured she'd hook up with somebody quite as idiotic as you."

All right, Billy thought. That was enough. He ratcheted the shotgun and pressed the barrel to the back of Pritchard's head. "Last chance, gramps. Sign it or die."

"Is that what you want, Megan? You want him to shoot me? You know how much I love you. I've showed you that every chance I got. I've always been your sweet Grandpa J, remember?"

Billy expected Meg to go on rocking, but she surprised him when she suddenly stopped. She looked up at Pritchard, and there was pain in her eyes like he'd never seen before. Like the eyes of a puppy who's been tortured and can't quite figure why.

But there was also heat there. Anger. "My sweet Grandpa J?" she said. "My sweet Grandpa J?"

"Remember you used to call me that when I tucked you into bed at night?"

Billy watched as Meg's face went though half a dozen different emotions before settling on what he could only describe as pure, unadulterated rage.

She jumped to her feet, her face beet red, shouting, *"My sweet Grandpa J?"* Then she looked at Billy like a rabid skunk and said, "Shoot him, Billy!"

Billy took a small step backward. "What?"

"I don't care if he signs the paper. Just shoot him. Pull that trigger and shoot him!"

"What about the money?"

She took a step toward them now. "Did you hear what I just told you? I don't *care* about the money. It's dirty money anyway. A payoff for his guilty conscience. He's a sick, disgusting old man. So just shoot him now, before I take that shotgun and do it myself."

That was when the door to the bedroom flew open and the lady sheriff pointed a gun at Billy.

"Drop the weapon right now, Lyman, or the only one who gets shot is you."

Chapter 21

Billy Boy didn't drop the shotgun. Not right away. And Callie was starting to wonder if he ever would.

She was also starting to wonder where Harlan was. He should've been here by now. She'd waited as long as she could outside the back window, before circling around to one of the bedrooms and climbing in, knowing the closed door would give her cover.

She'd stood next to the door, listening to the two men long enough to get a broad idea of what Billy Boy was up to, and it still hadn't made a whole lot of sense. And since she hadn't seen their friend Brett in the room, she'd assumed that it was *his* body burnt to a crisp back at the Pritchard Ranch. Which meant both Landry and Gloria had lied.

But why? To protect Meg?

If so, then why had Gloria claimed Meg was the one who had pulled the trigger?

Try as she might, Callie hadn't been able to figure it out. And all she'd wanted was to get this whole sordid affair over and done with. Get all these idiots squared away and dumped in a jail cell where they belonged, and let some other poor fool sort through the mess.

Then she could go home, see how Nana Jean was doing and finally sit down with Harlan—where the heck *was* he?—to listen to what he had to say.

That wasn't too much to ask, was it?

But with Megan screaming for Lyman to pull the trigger, Callie had figured she had only seconds to act, so, Harlan or no Harlan, she'd done what she had to do. She'd burst into the room, trained her Glock on Billy Boy and hoped and prayed he had enough brains to be cooperative.

"I mean it, Lyman, drop the weapon. *Now.*"

For a moment there, Callie thought everything would be all right. From the look in Billy Boy's eyes he seemed to know that this was a done deal, that he might as well give it up and take his chances with a jury. And old Jonah looked relieved, even thankful.

But now Meg was shouting even louder, nearly frothing at the mouth. "Don't listen to her, Billy! Shoot him. Shoot that old monster!"

And when Callie told her to shut up and sit back down, Meg scowled at her and charged, coming at her like a ball of intense white heat.

Callie had no choice but to turn the Glock on her and fire. She aimed for the calf, hit a solid piece of flesh and Meg went down to the floor hard, howling in agony.

But apparently this was a deal breaker, because now Billy Boy swung around in a rage and pointed the shotgun at Callie. "What'd you go and do *that* for?"

He was at such close range that the blast would cut her right in two, and as his finger wrapped around the trigger, she went into a dive.

Suddenly Jonah Pritchard leapt out of the chair and tackled the kid, knocking him to floor.

The shotgun went off, shattering a window, and now Jonah was straddling Billy, starting to pound the living daylights out of him. Hitting his head and face over and over again.

Callie rolled and got to her feet and pointed the Glock at them, "Enough!" she shouted. "That's enough, Jonah! I think he got the message."

Jonah stopped and nodded, Billy Boy bleeding and barely able to move, but alive and breathing.

As Callie kicked the shotgun aside, Jonah got to his feet and went to Meg, crouching down to check her wounded leg. The moment he touched her, however, she jerked away from him. "Leave me alone, you creep!"

Jonah said, "I don't know what your mother told you, girl, I don't know how she managed to poison your mind, but I've never laid a finger on you."

"I know what you did," she cried. "I remember it."

"I don't see how that's possible, because it never happened. Not once. Not ever. I'd kill myself before I'd hurt you."

Jonah seemed quite adamant about this and Callie didn't know what to make of him. Was he telling the truth? Had Gloria implanted false memories in Meg's brain just to get her daughter hating a father she'd long resented?

If so, it had to be one the cruelest forms of child abuse Callie had ever encountered.

Jonah untucked his shirt tails and tore off a strip of

fabric, tying it around Meg's leg to stem the bleeding. Then he picked her up and took her over to the sofa near the fireplace and laid her down.

He looked up at Callie. "She's losing blood. We need to get her to a hospital."

He was right, of course, but this wasn't Callie's first concern. She was worried about Harlan. Even after the shotgun blast, he hadn't made an appearance.

So where was he?

The question was answered a split second later as the cabin door burst open.

Landry Bickham stood in the doorway, smiling that Landry smile, a big black gun in his hand pointed directly at Callie.

"Nice to see you again, Cal." He tossed some rope to the middle of the room. "Now it's *your* turn to get tied up."

Callie was at a loss. How could Landry have gotten loose? He'd been cuffed and hog-tied to a tree.

Her heart was beating uncontrollably. And not in a good way. "Where's Marshal Cole?" she asked him.

Landry gestured. "Back there in the dark, taking a little nap."

"Is he alive?"

"I hit him pretty hard," Landry said. "Woulda shot him, too, but I didn't want to attract any attention."

Callie felt sick. Felt tears dampening her eyes. "You son of a—"

"Now, now, Cal, if it makes you feel any better, you won't much care in a few minutes time." He gestured. "You might as well put that gun down. You won't be able to use it. Not before I use mine."

Callie wanted to smack that smile off his face. She hesitated, then crouched down and set her Glock on the floor.

"Now kick it over here," he said.

She did as she was told and he picked it up, stuffing it into his waistband. "Shotgun, too."

Callie stepped over to the shotgun and kicked it in his direction. He bent down and scooped it up, then tucked his gun away and ratcheted a round into the shotgun's chamber. "Now I want you to take those ropes and tie Grandpa and his little love muffin up."

"And if I refuse?"

Landry pointed the shotgun at Billy Boy and pulled the trigger. Billy Boy immediately stopped moving.

And breathing.

Jonah, who was still crouched next to Meg on the sofa, visibly flinched and got to his feet again, staring at Landry in disbelief. "You just killed that boy in cold blood."

"Indeed I did." Landry looked at Callie. "That answer your question?"

His ability to shoot an unarmed man told her everything she needed to know about him. All this time she'd thought *Megan* was the sociopath. But looking at Bickham, she saw nothing behind his dark eyes but emptiness. The body he inhabited contained neither heart nor soul.

Jonah said, "Why are you doing this, Landry?"

"Does it really make a difference?"

"I think I have a right to know."

"A right?" Landry laughed. "Now that's just like you, isn't it, Jonah? You think you have a right to know and do and say just about anything you want. Because you have money. You're the big, rich man with all the privileges."

"You want some of that money? Is that it?"

"Honestly? I couldn't care less. I'm here for Gloria. She's tired of waiting around for you to kick the bucket."

"So that's it, is it? The two of you did this together?"

Landry laughed again. "As you well know, Jonah, this ain't the only thing the two of us did together. And I'm sorry to say that that mental case you're fawning over right now is the fruit of my loins."

"That's no way for a father to talk."

"Father? You never let me be a father to her. You were too ashamed to think some cowboy like me had soiled your bloodline." He gestured. "Callie here knows a little bit about that."

Jonah didn't respond and Callie said nothing.

"Gloria didn't want that little headache anymore than I did. You're the one insisted she be born. And now look what we've got—a murdering psychopath."

Apple doesn't fall too far from the tree, Callie thought.

"I don't get it," she said to Landry. "If you haven't been trying to protect Meg all this time, what *have* you been up to?"

"Trying to finish what we started yesterday afternoon. Claim Gloria's inheritance."

"I don't understand."

"I can see where you'd be confused, all these people trying to muddy up the waters with their own idiotic agendas. But the truth is simple enough. Megan here contacted me and wanted me to help her get her boyfriend out of a jam. And Gloria and I knew this was our perfect opportunity to clean some house and lay the blame on Little Miss Nutbucket and her friends."

"How can you talk like that?" Jonah hissed. "She's your own daughter, for godsakes."

"Didn't we just cover that ground? Keep up, Jonah. Your last few minutes alive, I want you to understand just how much your *own* daughter hates you."

"I know I haven't been the perfect father."

"Perfect father?" He huffed a chuckle. "Ask Callie here something about that. You go and knock up her ma, barely eighteen years old, then pretend like she don't even exist. How far from perfect you think that qualifies for?"

The knot tightened in Callie's stomach but Jonah looked indignant. "Where did you hear that ludicrous story?"

"Where else? From Gloria."

Callie frowned. "You said my *mother* told you that."

Landry shrugged. "So maybe I embellished a little."

"Or a lot," Jonah said. "Don't believe a word of this, Callie. I never went near your mother."

"It don't make a whole lot of difference," Landry said. "In a few minutes you'll all be dead anyway, and Meg and her friends will take the blame so Gloria can collect her rightful inheritance."

"I don't get it," Callie said. "If Gloria's behind all this, how did she get shot?"

Landry smiled. "That was just our way of convincing you folks that our story was true. I gotta say I didn't want her going inside that burning house, but she's a brave little filly, and she figured that would seal the deal."

"Not to spoil your fun, but aren't you forgetting something?"

"And what would that be?"

"Sheriff Mercer and Deputy Wilcox. They know you were the one trying to kill us in the woods."

Landry shrugged again. "They've got no proof Gloria had anything to do with it, and she's all I really care about. That's why I've stayed at Pritchard Ranch as long as I have." He smiled. "Besides, I was only trying to scare you folks off out of concern for Jonah. I knew these psychopaths had ahold of him, and didn't want your interference getting him killed."

"You think anyone will buy that nonsense?"

"You throw enough money at people, they'll buy anything. I may do a little time, but it's nothing I can't handle and Gloria will be waiting for me when I get out." His expression hardened and he gestured with the shotgun. "Enough chitchat. Show and tell is over. I think it's time you do what I told you and start tying these two up."

He stepped backward in the doorway, bent down and picked something up from the porch, then dropped it on the floor in front of her.

It was a large canister of kerosene.

"And when you're done," he said. "my little psychopath of a daughter is gonna start another fire."

Chapter 22

When he came awake, Harlan smelled smoke.

His head was pounding, a sharp wet pain coming from the back of his cranium, the night air cutting into it like a rusty blade.

He groaned involuntarily, and a voice above him said, "So you're alive after all. Guess I didn't hit you hard enough."

Landry Bickham.

Hands grabbed Harlan's jacket collar and Bickham started dragging him through the dirt, the smoke swirling around them now, getting thicker with each step.

Harlan's world was spinning, nausea rolling through his stomach in waves. He wanted to fight back, but his strength had been drained by the blow, his muscles weak, his limbs refusing to cooperate.

Bickham kept dragging him, the dirt and rock cutting

into his back, and Harlan twisted slightly trying to see where they were headed, wondering where Callie was, worried that she might be hurt.

Or worse.

He caught a glimpse of the cabin, smoke billowing out of its windows, and something thudded in his stomach. He didn't know what had happened here, but the fact that Bickham was still alive and on the loose was not a good sign.

"You must be wondering what you got yourself into, Marshal. We're working on a little weeny roast, and you're the weeny. But don't worry, I'll tell 'em how you managed to save me right before the place went up."

They approached the open doorway and Harlan knew this was his chance to make a move.

But could he do it? Did he have the strength?

There was only one way to find out.

As they passed through the doorway, Harlan felt the heat of the flames and willed his muscles into motion. Throwing his arms out, he grabbed hold of the doorframe with both hands, bringing Bickham to an abrupt halt.

Bickham stumbled slightly and released Harlan's collar, and now Harlan twisted onto his stomach and lunged forward, grabbing Landry's leg.

Bickham cursed and tried to kick him loose, but Harlan hung on, pulling out and upward, sending Landry sprawling. He hit the floor with a thud, and it was only then that Harlan realized the entire interior of the cabin was ablaze, flames crawling up the walls toward the roof.

Harlan willed himself to his feet, the room spinning, the fire growing around him. But now Bickham was upright and fumbling for his gun, gripping it with both hands as he aimed it in Harlan's direction.

He fired and Harlan dropped to the ground again, narrowly avoiding the hit. Something cracked above him and a piece of the cabin wall came loose, splinters of fiery wood showering down toward him.

Harlan scrambled out of the way, and saw that Bickham was getting to his feet now, trying to clear smoke from his eyes as he pointed the barrel of the gun in Harlan's direction again.

The flames were growing in intensity and there was no place for Harlan to go. No way to avoid the shot.

But just as Landry was about to pull the trigger, there was another loud crack and a chunk of the roof caved in, a blackened, flaming beam of wood dropping down toward him. He snapped his head upward, saw what was coming and dove, but the edge of the beam caught his shoulder, knocking him forward.

He skidded across the floor, flames jutting up from the back of his jacket. He screamed in horror as he struggled to pull it off, then suddenly, another beam fell, the roof crashing down on him, the flames consuming him like a ravenous beast.

Harlan watched it all in a kind of stunned slow motion, but he didn't waste any time mourning the man's death. He knew that Callie and the others had to be in this cabin somewhere and he needed to get to them, fast.

Climbing to his feet again, he spun around and saw two doors, one of them already engulfed in flames. Fighting the smoke, he staggered to the door on his left, hoping and praying he had the right one. He pressed his hands against it, feeling for heat, then threw the door open.

He saw Callie cuffed to a bed post, her terrified face lit up by the flames. And to his surprise, Jonah Pritchard and his granddaughter Megan were sitting on the floor next to her, both bound with ropes. Pritchard was coughing violently, choking on the smoke.

As the flames started to eat up the doorway behind him, Harlan crossed to them, surprise and relief in Callie's eyes.

"Thank God," she said. "Thank God you're alive."

"Are you hurt?"

She shook her head. "Just the smoke. You need to get Jonah out of here."

"First things first," he said, then grabbed hold of the cuffs with one hand as he reached into the watch pocket of his jeans with the other, fumbling for the key.

It wasn't there.

"The key," he said. "I don't have the key."

"Landry. He must have taken it from you. That's how he got loose."

Harlan yanked at the cuffs, but they were securely fastened to the wooden bed post, impossible to break. Jonah started coughing again and Callie gestured. "I'll be all right for a few minutes. You really need to get Meg and Jonah out of here."

"I'm not leaving you."

"I'll be fine. Just hurry."

The smoke was growing thicker. Harlan swiveled around and found the window, then crossed to it and shoved it open, smoke immediately swirling toward it as cool air rushed in. Returning to Jonah, he quickly untied his bonds then pulled the old man to his feet.

There was no time to untie Meg.

"I'll get your granddaughter," he said. "Wait outside the window."

Jonah stifled a cough and nodded, then hurried across the room and climbed through the window, turning back to wait for Harlan. Harlan scooped Megan up in his arms and she groaned, but offered little resistance as he carried her through the smoke and handed her off to Jonah.

"Can you handle her alone?" he asked.

Jonah coughed, nodded. "I think so."

"Get as far away from this place as you can," Harlan said, then took a gulp of the fresh air and turned around, swaying slightly, the pain from his head injury weakening his knees.

Fighting his way through the smoke, he crossed back to Callie who was coughing violently now, struggling to free herself from the cuffs.

"I can't get them loose," she gasped. "There's no way to do it. Just go, get out of here before this place comes down."

"Forget it," Harlan told her.

Stepping back, he raised his right foot and slammed the sole of his boot into the bedpost.

It splintered slightly, but held fast.

The flames were getting closer now, crawling up the walls of the bedroom, eating their way toward the roof, the heat nearly as stifling as the smoke.

His head swimming, sweat pouring, Harlan stepped back and raised his foot again, slamming it into the post.

More splinters, but still no joy. He'd been running on pure adrenalin and he was losing strength fast.

"Go!" Callie shouted, her gaze on the flames. "Get out before it's too late!"

But Harlan refused, again stepping back and raising his foot a third time, mustering all the strength he could manage. Then he slammed it home and the bed post finally gave, coming apart from the frame. He kicked it again and again, breaking it loose, the flames crawling across the floor toward them as Callie finally pulled the cuffs free.

Relief charging through them, they both stumbled to the window and dove through the opening, rolling onto the dirt outside. Then they were on their feet and running, getting as far away from the cabin as they could.

And as they collapsed to the ground, the flames consumed the old structure as what remained of the roof finally gave way, fiery timbers cracking and tumbling until the walls started to cave in.

They stared at it in stunned silence for a moment, then Harlan touched the back of his head, feeling the wetness there. Callie moved over to him and checked it.

"He got you pretty good," she said. "You're gonna need stitches."

"Doesn't matter," Harlan told her. "All I care about is that you're alive. I don't know how I would have functioned without you. I tried that and it didn't work."

She smiled now, leaning her head on his shoulder, tears filling her eyes, glistening in the flickering firelight.

"I love you, Harlan. I've never stopped loving you. Even when I hated you."

"I know," he said. "I know."

Then he pulled her close and kissed her forehead. Her nose. Her lips.

And all the evils of the world went far, far away.

Chapter 23

It was up to Callie to go for help.

At daybreak she made her way up the trail and found Mercer's horses where they had left them, then rode for several hours until she was within cell phone range.

The rescue team came in helicopters, picking Callie up in a wide clearing, then following her directions until they found Robbers Canyon.

As Landry had warned, there was no real place to land, so the team was forced to hover above the canyon as rescuers made fast rope descends and hooked Megan, Jonah and Harlan into harnesses to pull them out of there.

Megan looked pale from the loss of blood, but Jonah's tourniquet had managed to stop the bleeding and the paramedics assured them that her prognosis was good.

"Until she comes to," Callie said to Harlan. "Then she'll probably wish she'd joined her boyfriend in the afterlife."

Harlan nodded. "I look at people like this and realize just how normal my life really is."

"You and me both," Callie said. "You and me both."

The wound in Harlan's head took twenty-three stitches. The doctor warned him of a possible concussion, but his pupils seemed fine, and his only real concern was a throbbing headache that was expected to last for several hours.

Callie herself had a body full of cuts and bruises, but nothing serious enough to warrant more than some healing salve and a bandage or two.

The same couldn't be said for Sheriff Mercer, however, who had nearly lost his leg to an infection over the past twenty-four hours. Fortunately the doctors had managed to fight it off, and Mercer was expected to make a full recovery.

It turned out that Rusty Wilcox's ankle had suffered a full-fledged fracture and he wound up in a cast.

"Looks like you're off the hook for a while," he told Callie. "Won't be stuck training me."

"You've pretty much proven yourself, Deputy. But don't think this gets you out of any work. Cast or no cast, there'll be plenty of paperwork to deal with."

"Not as fun as dodging bullets," he said, "but right now paperwork sounds pretty darn good."

Gloria Pritchard was missing in action.

Shortly after Rusty and Mercer had been picked up by the medevac team the night before, word of Landry Bickham's rogue behavior had been delivered to their colleagues, and a couple of homicide deputies had gone to the hospital to question her.

She had answered calmly and politely, claiming to

know nothing about what Landry might be up to. But within two hours of their departure, she had checked herself out of the hospital and left in a taxi.

She hadn't been seen since.

She wouldn't be getting any help from Jonah. Before Callie left Robbers Canyon to summon the rescue team, Pritchard had made it clear that he wanted nothing to do with his daughter, blaming her for everything, including all that was wrong with Megan.

"I don't understand that woman," he told them, his stoic pride still intact despite what had happened. "I've given her everything she ever wanted or needed. I can't believe she betrayed me like this."

There seemed, however, to be very little regret in his voice. Which, to Callie's mind, said a lot more about him than his words ever would. And blaming anyone but himself for the disaster his family had become was typical Jonah.

So now Gloria was on her own and would soon be struck from his will. She had once again failed to get what she had sought. She'd lost her youth, her looks and the Pritchard family fortune; all because of vanity and greed, and her stubborn refusal to allow time and fate to run their course.

She probably had a significant amount of cash stashed somewhere and had boarded a private plane shortly after she'd been questioned by the deputies. She must have assumed that Landry would be caught and would eventually give her up and was likely headed for Europe or South America.

Whether she had loved Landry or had merely used him as a means to an end was something only she knew. But Callie suspected that Gloria had no more conscience than her daughter did, and Callie was surprised it had taken Gloria so long to finally act on her hatred for her father.

As Callie and Harlan left the hospital, she caught a glimpse of Jonah in the waiting room holding vigil for his beloved granddaughter. He had to know that his money couldn't buy her out of a murder charge, and that Megan felt no more love for him than Gloria had. Yet there he was, still clinging to the pathetic hope that he might somehow turn it all around.

Were the rumors about him true? Had he done to Megan what Gloria had accused him of? Or had a mother indeed brainwashed her daughter into believing the unspeakable had happened?

There was no way to know, of course, and Callie decided to set aside her own prejudices and give Jonah the benefit of the doubt. Maybe because a very small part of her felt sorry for him.

Somewhere in there, beneath the stony exterior, was a man who was now very much alone.

And Callie wouldn't wish that on anyone.

Nana Jean's tests showed that she was anemic, which explained her occasional dizzy spells. Judith had been kind enough to take her home from the hospital the previous afternoon, and had spent the night making sure there were no more mishaps and that Nana took her prescribed medication.

Nana was ecstatic when she finally got Callie's call.

"I was worried sick about you. When are you coming home?"

"Just as soon as we wrap things up here."

"Are you bringing you-know-who with you?"

Callie knew she shouldn't be surprised by the question. She sometimes thought Nana knew her better than she knew herself. "I haven't asked him."

"Child, don't you dare blow this opportunity. You lost him once, don't lose him again. He's a keeper."

"You don't even know him," Callie said.

"Don't need to. I see it in your eyes every time you talk about him. Even when you're angry with him."

Callie thought about this and had to laugh. "You think you're pretty smart, don't you, Nana?"

"I just know what I know," she said.

When Harlan was done getting his head stitched up, Callie offered him another night's lodging.

She said, "I assume you don't have any objections."

"That sofa isn't the most comfortable thing I've ever slept on."

"Who says you'll be sleeping on the sofa? Someone has to keep an eye on you. Make sure you don't have a concussion."

He smiled. "In that case, how could I possibly refuse?"

It was well after sundown when they walked in the door to find Nana waiting for them in the parlor with a plate of sandwiches and a pitcher of iced tea.

After the hugs and kisses were over, she said to Harlan, "Glad to see you used your time wisely."

Harlan eyed her as if he'd just discovered that Nana was Wyoming's oldest and wisest sage. "You knew this would happen, didn't you?"

"I had a pretty good idea. I figured all you two had to do was stop bumping heads and sooner or later you'd start bumping—"

"Okay, Nana, we get the picture," Callie told her, her face turning red.

Then they all started laughing and Callie and Harlan pulled up chairs and ate their sandwiches and drank their tea.

When they were done clearing the dishes, Nana disappeared into her room to get some rest, giving Callie a squeeze of the hand and a wink as she left. "You be sure to take care of that plumbing now."

When she was gone, Callie and Harlan went into the living room and Callie gestured to the sofa. "So that dream you had?"

"What about it?"

"What exactly were we doing that got you so hot and bothered?"

"I think it would be much easier to show you than tell you."

Then he kissed her, and she slipped her tongue between his lips as she ran her hands along his lower back.

She said, "What about your head?"

"What about it?"

"I wouldn't want to jangle anything loose up there."

"Damage is already done," he said. "I'm crazy about you, Cal." Then he sighed. "I can't believe I let you go so easily. Instead of getting angry with you, I should have forced you to listen to me."

She kissed him again. "Let's forget about all that, okay?"

But he shook his head. "I don't want to spoil the mood, but we need to talk about it. The elephant in the room. If you want this to work, you need to hear my side of what happened to Treacher, once and for all."

Callie stiffened. "Can't it wait?"

"You know it can't."

He was right. But just the mere mention of that time made the walls go up.

She fought against those walls and nodded, then pulled away from him and sat on the sofa.

"All right," she said. "Tell me your story."

Chapter 24

Harlan sat next to her, trying to find a way to ease into this without getting Callie's back up. But then he decided to just get on with it. No hedging. No sugarcoating.

"Treacher was stir-crazy that night," he said. "We'd all been studying so hard for finals and he insisted I go with him to the party. Tried to get you to go, too, remember?"

She nodded. "I remember."

"So we get there and the first thing he does is hit the cooler. Passes me a beer and tells me he's gonna circulate. I wasn't really in the mood, so I found a chair and kicked back, drank my beer." He looked at her. "And that was all I had to drink."

She nodded.

"So I'm sitting there doing the slow sip when Nicole Bittenger perches herself on the arm of the chair and starts talking to me. She was already three sheets to the wind, and I was worried she'd wind up flat on her face."

He saw Callie stiffen slightly. She had always believed the story circulated around campus that he and Nicole had hooked up that night, and all he could do was tell her the truth and hope for the best.

He said, "But that's *all* we did. Talk. Mostly about Treacher. Nicole was interested in him and wanted to know if I knew what Treacher thought of her."

Callie didn't look convinced. "And what did you tell her?"

"I told her I didn't know, but that Treacher was a straightforward guy and if she wanted to find out, all she had to do was ask." He paused. "You knew Nicole, so you can imagine how that worked out."

"She threw herself at him."

"In all her drunken glory. But by that time Treacher was pretty drunk himself and when I finally climbed out of my chair, I found them out on the back patio in the middle of a clinch, and it didn't look like either of them was ready to come up for air. But just as I was about to leave, Treacher saw me standing there and gave the look."

"The look?"

"The *get me out of here* look. As drunk as he was, he still seemed to have the presence of mind to know that getting involved with Nicole was a huge mistake. Yet here he was, making out with her."

"That isn't the way *I* heard it," Callie said. "People told me that you and Treacher got in a fight over her. That you were angry because he'd lured her away."

Harlan shook his head. "Not true at all. I just told him I wanted to go home and I thought he should, too, and I asked him for his keys so I could drive. He agreed and got to his feet, but Nicole didn't want him to leave and started getting upset. I tried to calm her down, but she was a pretty nasty drunk and things got ugly. We were alone out there, so I have to assume that people heard the yelling and thought it was Treacher and me going at each other with Nicole in the middle."

He could see that Callie was still on the fence. The old wounds were opening again. "So they were lying when they said they saw you take Nicole upstairs?"

He shook his head. "No. That much is true. She was in the middle of her tirade when all of sudden she said she was gonna be sick, so I told Treacher to stay put and rushed her upstairs to the bathroom." He paused. "I spent the next twenty minutes holding her hair as she leaned over the toilet bowl."

And paid dearly for his chivalry.

"You expect me to believe this?"

"I expect you to trust me, Cal. Did I ever give you reason not to?"

She hesitated. "No. I guess you didn't."

"When Nicole was done being sick, I cleaned her up, then took her into one of the bedrooms and laid her across the bed. But by the time I got back downstairs, Treacher was nowhere to be found. I checked the patio and every room of that house, then finally went outside and saw his car was gone. He'd left without me." Harlan looked at her. "And I haven't lived a day without wishing I'd ignored Nicole and just taken him home."

He waited as Callie processed the story. It was the truth—the truth he'd never had a chance to tell her after she'd been corrupted by rumors and vicious backbiting lies. But he had no way of knowing if she believed him now.

All he could do was hope.

Then her eyes filled with tears and she brought her hands to her face.

"Oh, my God," she said. "Oh, my God. I feel so… ashamed."

He ran a hand over her shoulder. "No. This isn't your fault."

"I should have listened to you."

"And I should have *made* you hear me. But neither of us was thinking rationally at the time. We'd just lost our best friend. We were upset and angry and too caught up in our own pain to realize what we were doing to each other."

"I'm no better than Jonah Pritchard," she said.

"What do you mean?"

"I let pride control me. Every time I thought about you, every time I wondered where you were or what you were up to, I let it keep me from contacting you. Maybe I *am* part of that family after all."

"Don't even think that, Cal. You're the exact opposite of what those people are."

"It's in my blood."

"Blood has nothing to do with it," he said. "All that matters is what's in here." He touched his chest, then touched hers. "Maybe you jumped to conclusions, maybe you believed what people told you, but you were broken and grieving and that can cloud anyone's judgment. But your heart is pure, Cal. Gentle. Kind. You would never purposely hurt another human being unless you were forced to."

"I hurt *you*," she said.

Harlan shook his head. "You went with what felt right at the time. We both did. And it was mistake. A terrible mistake." He cupped her chin. Tilted her head toward him. "But now we're free. No more walls between us."

Then he kissed her.

They made love in the shower.

Both of them had been anxious to wash away the past couple days, and the decade preceding them.

They undressed together in her bathroom, Callie staring at his body, marveling at how age had made him even more attractive. The wide, hard shoulders. The strong, workingman's arms. The ripple of his abs. And below... already showing signs of awakening as he pulled off her shirt, her jeans, her bra, her panties.

She felt her excitement build as she stared at him, anticipating him inside her, remembering the exquisite pleasure they had shared so many times, so long ago.

Then they were beneath the water, its glorious warmth washing down over them as they lathered each other with soap. Harlan rubbed the bar between his palms, then ran his hands over her breasts, pausing to caress her hardened nipples, gently clipping them between his fingers, squeezing them.

Something loosened inside of Callie. Something wet and wonderful. And as the water washed away the suds, Harlan leaned forward and put his mouth where his hands had been, using his tongue and teeth to tease her.

All she could think about was feeling him inside her. Gently pushing him away, she turned her back to him and pressed up against him, feeling his hardness. The urgency of it.

Grabbing hold of him, she guided him forward and he brought his hands to her hips and thrust into her, grunting softly. He kissed her neck, her shoulders, and Callie felt heat rising inside her, tunneling its way toward her brain, causing tiny bursts of pleasure along the way.

Then his right hand moved forward, pressing against her pelvis as he thrust, and soon they were groaning in unison, working toward that place that seemed so hard to find with other men.

But Harlan wasn't just any man. He was her soul mate. Her true love. Her *only* love.

And as their duet of groans built to a crescendo, Callie felt her scalp start to prickle and thought for a moment that she might not survive the explosion inside her head. But then it came, wave after wave of intense pleasure causing her to cry out as Harlan went rigid against her.

But she suddenly realized that something was wrong. His reaction felt more like surprise than enjoyment. And as the last of the waves began to pass, he quickly pulled away from her, his hand gripping her arm.

Then a voice said, "Well, well, like mother like daughter. I guess skank runs in the family."

Dread sluiced through Callie's body as she whipped her head around to find the shower door hanging open.

Gloria Pritchard was pointing a gun at them.

Chapter 25

"Come on, now, don't be shy," she said, gesturing with the gun. Her wounded thigh was stained with blood, but she didn't seem to feel it. "Callie, I need you to step out of that shower and get yourself dried off. We're going for a ride."

Callie was trying to cover herself with her hands. "What are you doing here, Gloria? What do you want?"

"To finish what I started thirty-four years ago." She gestured again. "Now get out and towel off." She pointed the gun toward Harlan. "And you stay put, Marshal. I've got no argument with you." She ran her gaze over his nakedness. "No argument at all."

Harlan started forward. "Don't be stupid, Ms. Pritchard. Put that thing down before you—"

The gun went off, the sound of the shot reverberating against the walls as a hole opened up in the tile above Harlan's head.

Both Callie and Harlan flinched, ducking down involuntarily.

"You were saying, Marshal?"

Harlan didn't move.

Gloria pointed the gun at Callie. "You'd both better listen to me or the next one ends it right here and now."

"Ends what?" Callie asked. "Are you here because of Landry?"

Gloria laughed. "Oh, please, give me more credit than that. Now, hurry it up. I don't like to be kept waiting."

Callie's heart was pounding, but she did what she was told, grabbing a towel from the rack and quickly drying herself. Then she crossed to a hook on the wall next to the sink and took her robe down, slipping into it.

As she tied it at her waist, she said, "We thought you'd be long gone by now."

"So did I," Gloria said. "But when I started thinking about it, I knew I had some unfinished business before I left town. I was hoping Landry would take care of you out there in Robbers Canyon, but he blew it, as usual. I hope his last minutes were painful."

"You're sick," Callie said.

"Now you sound like my dear father. But you're right. I'm sick, he's sick, we're all sick. Every single one of us. Including you and your love toy here. All it takes are the right circumstances at the right time. But if you want to lay blame for this, point that finger at your little slut of a mother. She's the reason I'm here." She gestured with the gun again. "Now turn around and back toward me."

Again Callie did as she was told. "What does my mother have to do with any of this?"

"More than you could possibly know."

"I don't understand."

Gloria grabbed hold of Callie's waist tie and pulled her close, putting the gun to the side of Callie's head. "Marshal, I can see that look in your eyes, but if you try anything, the first bullet is for her, the second one for you. Then I'll go find her precious Nana Jean and put one in the old biddy while she sleeps."

"Ms. Pritchard," Harlan said. "Please. This isn't gonna get you anything. There's no upside here."

"I beg to differ, hot stuff. The upside is the satisfaction I'll feel when your little love muffin is finally dead."

Callie stiffened. "But why? What have I ever done to you?"

"What do you think, Callie? You were born, that's what."

Again Callie was at a loss.

"You don't get it, do you?" Gloria said, now backing her through the doorway into the bedroom. "The minute my father found out that my dear brother had gotten your mother pregnant, my entire world changed."

"But why? What did you have to with it?"

"Because it was *my fault*, don't you see? Your mother was my best friend, and I was the one who introduced her to Riley. If it hadn't been for me, they never would have done the dirty."

"That's ridiculous."

"Not according to Jonah," Gloria said. "And because I made that happen, it only followed that it was my fault that Riley was dead. After that Jonah fed and clothed me, and gave me a place to live, but I might as well have been one of the help."

"And you're blaming that on my *mother*?"

Gloria backed her slowly toward the bedroom doorway. "I told her not to have the baby, but she didn't listen to me. Said she was in love with Riley and wanted to bring his child into the world." She paused. "So I decided to spoil her fun."

Callie frowned. "What do you mean?"

"I started feeding her rat poison. Just little bits of it over the course of her pregnancy. I'd come over for sandwiches with her and your Nana Jean, and slip it into her iced tea."

Callie felt gut-punched.

Gloria had *murdered* her mother?

How was that possible?

She looked toward the bathroom and saw Harlan standing there now, wearing nothing but his jeans.

Gloria said, "No need to cover up on my account, Marshal. But I wouldn't advise you to go any farther."

Harlan didn't move.

"So where were we?" Gloria said to Callie. "Oh, right. Rat poison. Do you have any idea what it can do to a body?"

"I think I can figure it out."

"It has a little substance in it called warfarin. An anti-coagulant. And if you give little doses to someone over a long period of time, the symptoms are minimal, but the cumulative effect is devastating, especially for a pregnant woman."

Callie understood. "The hemorrhaging. That's why she bled to death."

"The thing is," Gloria said, "you were supposed to die, too. And if it hadn't been for your grandmother's fast thinking, you would have. Right here in this room." She paused in the doorway. "I can't tell you how many times I thought about coming over here and putting a pillow over your face. My brother was gone, my father barely spoke to me, and I had every reason in the world to see you dead. But I couldn't get up the courage. A pillow isn't rat poison, and I knew if I tried, I'd probably wind up getting caught. And I didn't want that."

Callie nodded. "But now you have nothing to lose."

"Nothing at all," Gloria said. "It's all been taken away, thanks to—"

Callie hadn't prepared for it. The move was more instinctive than planned. Swinging a fist back, she slammed it into Gloria's wounded thigh.

Gloria grunted in pain and stumbled back—

Now Harlan was flying across the room toward them, launching into a tackle—

But Gloria recovered quickly, then raised the gun and fired. The bullet hit Harlan in the shoulder and he went down hard onto the carpet as Callie turned and grabbed hold of Gloria's hand, trying to twist the gun away from her.

They struggled, stumbling sideways across the room, tumbling to the ground, Gloria grunting in pain again. But then she managed to break free from Callie's grip and swung the butt of the gun toward Callie's head, stunning her.

She scrambled away from Callie and got to her feet, holding her thigh with one hand as she turned the gun toward Callie.

"Nice try, but no cigar." Her finger brushed against the trigger. "Like I said, Cal, better late than nev—"

A gunshot rang out and Gloria froze in place, her eyes at first quizzical, then widening as she realized she'd been hit.

She looked down in surprise at the hole in her chest, then pitched forward, dead.

That was when Callie saw Nana Jean standing on the other side of the doorway, Grandpa's old World War Two revolver in her hand.

"That little witch killed my Mary."

Then she stared at the gun as if it were a foreign object, and dropped it to the floor.

Epilogue

No one mourned for Gloria. Jonah Pritchard refused to pay for her funeral, so she was buried in a pauper's plot at the city cemetery.

Megan Pritchard's trial was mercifully short, with minimal publicity—a near miracle in this day of electronic communications. She was found guilty of murder, kidnapping and conspiracy to commit murder and sentenced to life imprisonment at Wyoming State Penitentiary.

Sheriff's investigators took a closer look at the fire at Pritchard Ranch and came to the conclusion that Landry Bickham was the likely culprit, having set it to help make Gloria look like a victim. No one was ever sure who killed Billy Boy's partner, Brett, but at this point it didn't much matter.

Nobody saw much of Jonah Pritchard after that. He

lived in seclusion at the newly built Pritchard Ranch, surrounded by people who saw him as nothing more than a paycheck.

It was, Callie thought, a fitting punishment for man who had no soul.

Despite her initial shock, Nana Jean told Callie that she was sleeping better than ever at night, and would be around for a long time to come. And true enough, she seemed to have grown stronger over the months, her dizzy spells gone. And for reasons known only to Callie and Harlan, she stopped serving iced tea every afternoon.

Harlan recovered from his gunshot wound and he and Callie went down to Colorado Springs to pack up his apartment and move him to Williamson to live with her and Nana. Before leaving Colorado they stopped by the cemetery and laid flowers at Treacher's grave, quietly remembering his crooked smile, happy to have known him, if only for a short time.

At Sheriff Mercer's request, Harlan quit the Marshals Service and took a job with the Williamson County Sheriff's Office where an important vacancy had to be filled. A month later, Harlan got down on one knee and proposed to the only woman he had ever loved.

After nearly eight years on the job Callie took a leave of absence, planning to eat well and get plenty of exercise and sleep.

She was pregnant with their first child.

* * * * *

"You need a bodyguard."

Allie Burton's jaw dropped as soon as her dad's old friend Detective
Max Roles spoke the words.

It took a few beats for Allie to reply. "Oh, come on, Max. That's over-
the-top. I'm sure Mr. Ellis was talking about all his international businesses,
about protecting his companies. He said he'd put the auditing firm on it."

Max was getting up in years. His jowls made him look like a bloodhound
with a bald head. Allie had known him all her life, thanks to his friendship
with her father, who had died years ago. She trusted him, but this?

"What were his *exact* words, Allie?"

She pulled them up from recent memory. "He said, *exactly*, that I
shouldn't tell anyone anything about what I'd found in the books."

Max shook his head. "And the rest?"

She shrugged. "He said, and I quote, *Bad things can happen.* Well, of
course they could. He's a tycoon with companies all over the world. Any
irregularity in the books could cause big problems."

"Right," Max said. "I want you to think about that. Bad things can
happen."

Allie frowned. "I guess you're one of the people I shouldn't have told
about this. I thought you'd laugh and wouldn't tell anyone."

"I won't tell anyone except the bodyguard you're going to hire. You've been on the inside of Jasper Ellis's success."

"So what?"

Max leaned forward. "I have nothing against the man's success. We've been investigating him for years, and we've never found a thing we could hang on him. He's good at covering evidence."

"You've been investigating him for what?"

Max blew a cloud. "For the unexplained disappearances and supposed suicides of a number of his employees."

Allie felt a chill run down her spine. Her own dismissal of the situation began to feel naive. "You're kidding," she murmured.

"I wish I was. Here's the thing. At first it could be dismissed. But then the numbers really caught our attention and we started looking into it. Nothing traces directly back to Ellis except he's at the top of the pyramid. You may remember I fought against you going to work for him."

Allie did. Max had strenuously argued with her, something he never did. He was not a man given to conspiracy theories. A hard-nosed detective, he stuck to the facts. He seemed to have some facts right now.

"So I'm going to call that bodyguard. I've known him for years, since he was still in the Marines. I trust him with your life. And you're not leaving my house before he gets here."

"God, Max!"

"Just go make yourself a cup of whatever. But you are *not* going anywhere."

He punctuated those words like bullet shots. Truly shaken, Allie rose to get that drink. She trusted Max. Completely. He'd been like an uncle to her for most of her life. If Max said it, it was true.

As she passed through the short hallway, she saw her reflection in the full-length mirror. Allie paused, wondering who that woman in there was. She felt so changed that she shouldn't look the same. Neat dark blue business slack suit, a blue-striped button-down shirt, collar open. Her ash-blond hair in a fluffed, loose short cut because she didn't feel like fussing with it. A trim every couple of weeks solved that problem.

A bodyguard? The thought sent a tendril of ice creeping along her spine. Seriously?

Don't miss
Conard County: Christmas Bodyguard *by Rachel Lee,*
available December 2021 wherever
Harlequin Intrigue books and ebooks are sold.

Harlequin.com

HIEXP1121

Love Harlequin romance?

DISCOVER.

Be the first to find out about promotions, news and exclusive content!

f Facebook.com/HarlequinBooks

🐦 Twitter.com/HarlequinBooks

📷 Instagram.com/HarlequinBooks

📌 Pinterest.com/HarlequinBooks

You Tube YouTube.com/HarlequinBooks

ReaderService.com

EXPLORE.

Sign up for the Harlequin e-newsletter and download a free book from any series at **TryHarlequin.com**

CONNECT.

Join our Harlequin community to share your thoughts and connect with other romance readers!
Facebook.com/groups/HarlequinConnection

HARLEQUIN

Heartfelt or thrilling, passionate or uplifting—Harlequin is more than just happily-ever-after.

With twelve different series to choose from and new books available every month, you are sure to find stories that will move you, uplift you, inspire and delight you.

SIGN UP FOR THE HARLEQUIN NEWSLETTER

Be the first to hear about great new reads and exciting offers!

Harlequin.com/newsletters

Made in the USA
Middletown, DE
14 December 2021

BOX
INSPECTOR

and other important
JOBS FOR CATS

Swerling & Lazar

© 2017 Lisa Swerling & Ralph Lazar
Published by Last Lemon Productions
60 Woodside Dr. San Anselmo, CA 94960, USA

ISBN 978-0-9997316-0-4

First Printing, 2017

www.lastlemon.com

This book is
dedicated to

KIC

BELLA

&

CAPTAIN FLOOF

Table of Contents

IMPORTANT CAT JOBS

You humans are not quite sure what us cats do all day.

I tell you, there is a lot we do, a plethora of unspoken, critical jobs that go un-noticed. We're there, in the background, day in, day out, working, without complaint.

ICE CREAM
QUALITY ASSESSOR

LAP WARMER

ALARM CLOCK

MASSAGE
THERAPIST

MORALE BOOSTER

CHIEF PILLOW
APPRAISER

SLEEP STUDY
SPECIALIST

ASSISTANT SUITCASE PACKER

PAPER WEIGHT

CHIEF
TECHNOLOGY
OFFICER

LAUNDRY PRESS

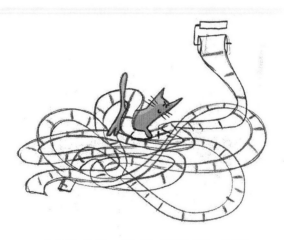

HEAD OF TOILET
PAPER OPERATIONS

9

STAIRCASE
SUPERVISOR

GIFTWRAP TECHNICIAN

LITERARY CRITIC

ASSISTANT BEDSHEET
CHANGER

PEST CONTROL

POLTERGEIST CHASER

STRESS
RELIEVER

CHIEF HOUSE PLANT
DECOMMISSIONER

FOOD CRITIC

BOX INSPECTOR

BED SUPERVISOR

FOOD SURVEYOR

HEAD COZY

DOCUMENT EDITOR

BATH TESTER

LAUNDRY STANDARDS DIRECTOR

SHOPPING BAG CHECKER

GHOST SPOTTER

PEN PUSHER

BATHROOM ATTENDANT

22

GRAVITY
APPRAISER

CHIEF PROCRASTINATOR

WATER INSPECTOR

CURTAIN PATROL

TV SUPERVISOR

NINJA

CHIEF SPIDER
SPOTTER

NIGHT WATCHMAN

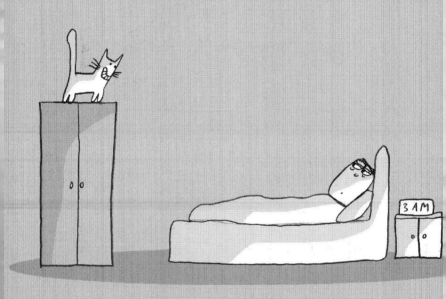

SOUS CHEF

LIBRARIAN

BOX SHREDDER

UNDERWEAR AUDITOR

BAG CHECKER

WALL
INSPECTOR

SHOELACE
MONITOR

QUILT TESTER

33

KEYBOARD
WARMER

MAIL INSPECTOR

NEIGHBORHOOD
WATCH

35

INTERIOR
DESIGNER

DISHWASHING
ASSISTANT

SUNBEAM
ANALYST

37

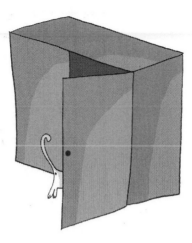

GLOBAL HEAD OF
CUPBOARD INSPECTION

SECURITY OFFICER

PASSAGE CHAPERONE

ROAST CHICKEN
FOCUS GROUP

SNUGGLE AGENT

COMMANDER OF THE
101ST AIRBORNE
PIZZA REGIMENT

TRAILBLAZER

FENG SHUI
CONSULTANT

WILDLIFE
EXPERT

MATTRESS TESTER

HUNTER

BOSS

Although us cats can do just about everything better than humans, there are still some

USES FOR HUMANS

SOFA
WARMER

LADDER

WAITER

DOORMAN

VANTAGE
POINT

WHOLE BODY PILLOW

LANDING PAD

OBSTACLE
COURSE
TRAINER

FRIEND WITH
BENEFITS

THE QUESTIONS CATS ASK

Who is feeding me?

How are you feeding me?
Which bowl are you using?
Why haven't you fed me yet?
When are you feeding me?
What are you feeding me?

What are you cooking?

What does this button do?

Why are you exactly 8 minutes later
than usual getting home from work?
No, seriously why? We almost starved
waiting for you!!

Do you love me
as much as
I love you?

59

What's in that bag?
And that bag?

What are you doing behind
that door?

will I fit in?

Where are you going?

Can I have some. Can I? Can I?
Pleaaaaase....

Can I sit with you while
you pee?

Can I go out? Can I go out? Can I go out? Can I go out?

So when is
the real food coming?

Snack? Snack?
Snack?

Why are you in my spot?

Your bed? No, this is
my bed. Actually, my room
and my house.

Shall we
have a staring
competition?

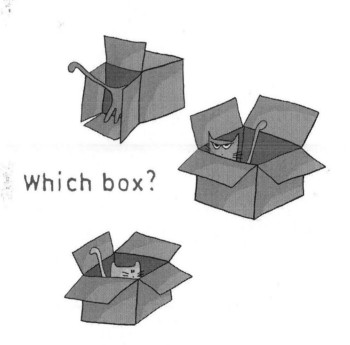

Which box?

Wanna play?

What's for
dinner?

Would you move your
hand over a bit?

What else can
I teach you?

SIGNS THAT YOU'RE A CRAZY CAT PARENT

Are YOU a crazy cat parent?

No, of course you're not.
Or maybe you are.

If one or more of these apply
to you, then by definition,
you are.

You watch a show
specifically for your
cat's enjoyment,
not your own.

You apologize when it's
time to leave for work.

...and you ask how their day
was when you get home.

You REALLY need to pee,
but you won't get up
because there's a cat
on your lap.

You get super-excited by home
deliveries because you know
your cat's about to get an
empty box to play in.

Cat gets
most of the bed.

You have framed photos
of your cats on your
desk at work.

You're secretly hoping someone
invents a way of messaging your
cat while you're at work, so you
can check in on it.

You spend more time in the supermarket's cat food aisle than all the other aisles combined.

If the sofa is occupied,
you're fine to take the
uncomfortable chair.

You refuse to stroke
other cats because it
feels like a betrayal.

You're sensitive to your cat's every mood

Angry   Annoyed   Happy   Tense   Welcoming

Sad   Contemplative   Coy   Bellicose   Enigmatic

Shy   Threatening   Bashful   Bitter   Calm

Here's your dinner!

SUSHI

The food you feed your cat costs more than your own.

You have more photos of cats on your phone than humans.

You lie awake all night
because your cat is
sleeping on your stomach,
so you can't move.

Do you ever notice your
cat behaving strangely?

Maybe something is
going on?

IS YOUR CAT
PERHAPS AN
ALIEN?

DOES YOUR CAT SPEND
A LOT OF TIME JUST
WATCHING YOU?

DOES IT SUDDENLY DASH
ACROSS THE ROOM?

RUSHING TO PICK UP
A MESSAGE FROM
THE MOTHERSHIP
PERCHANCE?

DESPITE FEARING
WATER, DOES IT
CONSTANTLY
ANALYZE IT?

WHAT'S ALL THIS
STUFF WITH BOXES?
TRAINING FOR
TELEPORTING?

WHAT *IS* PURRING?
DO WE ACTUALLY KNOW?
COMMUNICATING WITH
THE MOTHERSHIP?

DOES IT STUDY
WHAT YOU EAT?

DOES IT MONITOR
EVERYTHING
YOU DO ONLINE?

DOES IT SEE THINGS
THAT YOU DON'T?

DOES IT SEEM VERY
INTERESTED IN
TASTING YOU?

YES, YOUR CAT
IS AN ALIEN.

OUR SECOND CAT BOOK IS

"BE HUNGRY 24/7
AND OTHER SECRETS
TO BEING A CAT"

BE HUNGRY 24/7

and other secrets to
BEING A CAT

Swerling & Lazar

AVAILABLE FROM AMAZON

EXCERPTS FROM
BE HUNGRY 24/7

Get inside the
dishwasher
while it's being
loaded.

Put your butt in
the visitor's face.

Look cute enough
to attract cuddles.

Mold yourself to the shape of
the container.

MEET TWO-TAILED DEVIL-CAT,

THE LOVEABLE VILLAIN
FROM OUR NEW KIDS'
BOOK SERIES...

TOTAL MAYHEM

HILARIOUS, ACTION-FILLED, ILLUSTRATED MYSTERY STORIES, JAM-PACKED WITH CRAZY STUFF THAT MAKES KIDS LAUGH-OUT-LOUD. DASH'S ADVENTURES ARE WRITTEN FOR 5-9 YEAR-OLDS BUT APPEAL TO THE WHOLE FAMILY. THEY EXPLORE UNIVERSAL THEMES OF COURAGE, FRIENDSHIP AND TAKING THE INITIATIVE.

A NEW UNPUTDOWNABLE SERIES FROM NYT BESTSELLING RALPH LAZAR, STARRING DASH CANDOO, AN INGENIOUS PROBLEM-SOLVER WITH FANTASTIC FRIENDS AND A BOT-TOMLESS BACKPACK OF BRILLIANT GADGETS.

UNEXPECT THE EXPECTED.

ABOUT THE AUTHORS

Lisa Swerling & Ralph Lazar live in California.

They are the creators of the popular illustrated
project Happiness Is..., which has sold nearly
half a million books and has over three million
followers online.

They also wrote and illustrated the
New York Times bestseller Me Without You.

Ralph's art website: ralphlazar.com
Lisa's art website: glasscathedrals.com

VISIT US ONLINE

We have a huge library of funny and sweet
cat cartoons online at www.lastlemon.com/cats

And we have a quarter of a million followers
on Facebook here
www.facebook.com/itsthecatpage